序　言

　　剛升上高三的同學們，正踏入最混亂的時期。從此刻起，你們將面臨如影隨形的課後輔導，以及永遠考不完的考試。每天幾乎都有複習考，每天都不只考一科，一學期有三次段考，一邊學習全新的高三課程，一邊還要準備令人措手不及的模擬考試，有這麼多考試，根本沒有時間好好準備！

　　高三生活要分秒必爭，目標就是在「學科能力測驗」和「指定科目考試」中拿高分。如果分數夠高，你就能選擇自己想讀的學校和科系；如果分數不高，就只能聽天由命。在這麼重要的時刻，要用最有效率的方式來規劃時間。首先，要把高三新課程學好；第二，要把握每一次的模擬考試，模擬考試可以讓你知道自己目前的程度在哪裡，是很好的參考標準。

準備愈多，分數愈高

　　即使時間很緊迫，模擬考前也一定要有所準備，絕不能隨便應考。考前雖然沒有時間複習每一冊課本，但是至少要把「指考英文模擬試題」拿出來練習做，做題目能讓你馬上知道自己不會的地方。你一定要先做題目，再對答案，然後仔細研究詳解，把不會的地方確實弄懂。考試最忌諱兩件事，一是沒準備，二是一錯再錯。只要你能善用這本書，你就會成功。

　　「指考英文模擬試題」中所有的考題，都是萬中選一，都是最有練習價值的題目，而且出題方式完全仿照「大學入學指定科目考試」，讓同學們一邊練習，一邊複習，一邊習慣指考的題型，一舉三得。本書在編審及校對的每一階段，均力求完善，但恐有疏漏之處，誠盼各界先進不吝批評指正。

劉　毅

CONTENTS

大學入學指定科目考試英文模擬試題 ① ·········· 1

大學入學指定科目考試英文模擬試題 ① 詳解 ······· 13

大學入學指定科目考試英文模擬試題 ② ·········· 37

大學入學指定科目考試英文模擬試題 ② 詳解 ······· 50

大學入學指定科目考試英文模擬試題 ③ ·········· 73

大學入學指定科目考試英文模擬試題 ③ 詳解 ······· 86

大學入學指定科目考試英文模擬試題 ④ ·········· 111

大學入學指定科目考試英文模擬試題 ④ 詳解 ······· 122

大學入學指定科目考試英文模擬試題 ⑤ ·········· 145

大學入學指定科目考試英文模擬試題 ⑤ 詳解 ······· 158

大學入學指定科目考試英文模擬試題 ⑥ ·········· 183

大學入學指定科目考試英文模擬試題 ⑥ 詳解 ······· 195

★近年指考與學測英文科出題來源 ·········· 218

大學入學指定科目考試英文模擬試題 ①

第壹部份：選擇題（佔72分）

一、詞彙（10％）

說明： 第1至10題，每題選出一個最適當的選項，標示在答案卡之「選擇題答案區」。每題答對得1分，答錯或劃記多於一個選項者倒扣 1/3 分，倒扣到本大題之實得分數爲零爲止，未作答者，不給分亦不扣分。

1. The success of Jack Smith, a handicapped athlete who won an Olympic gold medal, has become an _____ to many young people.
   (A) introduction (B) immigration
   (C) inspiration (D) impression

2. It is not _____ for Chinese to attend a funeral wearing loud clothing.
   (A) permanent (B) consistent
   (C) appropriate (D) hospitable

3. "Please don't _____ to raise your hand and ask if you have any questions regarding this topic," said the lecturer.
   (A) challenge (B) hesitate
   (C) balance (D) perform

4. The two finalists are _____ to compete for the championship at 2:00 PM next Monday.
   (A) reserved (B) constructed
   (C) emphasized (D) scheduled

5. Do not give the boy any chocolate or cookies. If you do, it will spoil his _____ and he will not eat anything at lunchtime.
   (A) expression (B) appetite
   (C) privilege (D) research

6. One of the requirements of being either a good teacher or a good nurse is to be _____.
　(A) patient　　　(B) artificial　　(C) familiar　　(D) original

7. A passerby called the fire department _____ when he saw that the building was in flames.
　(A) magnificently　　　　　(B) ordinarily
　(C) gradually　　　　　　　(D) immediately

8. John did not know he had been entirely _____ by the salesman until he discovered the antique was a fake.
　(A) defeated　　(B) deceived　　(C) detected　　(D) disguised

9. In the past few years, juvenile crime has shown a _____ to increase. In other words, there are more and more teenagers violating laws.
　(A) tendency　　(B) commercial　(C) motive　　　(D) profession

10. The soccer game has been _____ postponed due to the coming typhoon. As soon as the weather improves, we will hold the game.
　(A) anxiously　　　　　　(B) mysteriously
　(C) extensively　　　　　(D) temporarily

二、綜合測驗（20％）

說明： 第 11 至 30 題，每題一個空格。請依文意選出一個最適當的選項，標示在答案卡之「選擇題答案區」。每題答對得 1 分，答錯或劃記多於一個選項者倒扣 1/3 分，倒扣到本大題之實得分數爲零爲止。未作答者，不給分亦不扣分。

第 11 至 20 題爲題組

　　According to a news report, drug abuse and trafficking have been spreading in our society like an epidemic. ___11___ is even more astonishing is that the police records show drug abuse has become the second most common type of crime among teenagers. Nowadays a great many people hardly raise an eyebrow ___12___ the sight of people selling drugs, especially amphetamines, in places where teenagers hang out. To make matters worse, drug dealers even invade ___13___. In 1990, 27% of all drug addicts were addicted to amphetamines, ___14___ the percentage in 1992 reached 74%. These statistics show the incredible increase in the number of amphetamine addicts, and unfortunately, more than 50% of them are ___15___ addicts.

　　As we know, drugs can, ___16___, give us sheer sensual pleasures but the sensation is momentary, whereas the severe pains they cause can ___17___ long enough to weaken our will, destroy our health, and worst of all, rot our soul. ___18___, drug addicts, to get the money needed for the purchase of drugs, ___19___ commit horrible crimes such as robbery, kidnapping, or blackmail. Drug addicts not only hurt themselves physically and ___20___ but also become a threat to society. Therefore, it is everybody's business to kick drugs out of school and out of society.

11. (A) It　　(B) What　　(C) There　　(D) Which
12. (A) to　　(B) on　　(C) from　　(D) at
13. (A) campuses　　(B) campgrounds
　　(C) chapels　　(D) chambers
14. (A) while　　(B) when　　(C) until　　(D) since
15. (A) infant　　(B) adult　　(C) teenage　　(D) senior
16. (A) in a pet　　(B) in a word　　(C) in a way　　(D) in a jam
17. (A) keep　　(B) last　　(C) extend　　(D) maintain
18. (A) Accordingly　　(B) Furthermore
　　(C) Consequently　　(D) Otherwise

19. (A) are supposed to   (B) get used to
    (C) look forward to   (D) are likely to
20. (A) movably   (B) minimally   (C) maturely   (D) mentally

第 21 至 30 題爲題組

From Taitung, the plane ride to Orchid Island takes only about 20 minutes. ___21___, however short the journey, it brings one to a place entirely different from modern Taiwan. The aborigines of Orchid Island refer to themselves as the "Tao," which ___22___ their term for the island: "Pongso No Tao." There are seven tribal villages on the island, ___23___ the population standing at over 4,000. Because they are isolated at sea, they have ___24___ their traditional culture better than any other group of Taiwanese aborigines.

The "flying fish season" of the spring and summer is the best-known Orchid Island tradition. The significance of these migrating fish has influenced the Tao's way of life, ___25___ their calendar of holidays and inspiring their unique aesthetic sensibility.

Every year from June to September, the island's ___26___ culture is fully revealed. As observed by some researchers, the Tao depend upon fish for a high percentage of their diet. They've divided fish into several categories, and each person, ___27___ age and gender, must eat only fish from a suitable category.

The Tao have also attached great social significance to their chief means of catching fish — their boats. Even ashore, Tao men are often grouped socially based on the boat crews ___28___ they belong. The boats themselves are works of ___29___, giving full expression to the Tao's talents for beauty. Furthermore, the fertility of their imaginations is matched by the fertility of Orchid Island's volcanic geology. ___30___, this is a place that enjoys the double good fortune of possessing equally rich natural and cultural heritages.

21. (A) Conversely   (B) Meanwhile   (C) Similarly   (D) Yet
22. (A) deals with   (B) consists of
    (C) originates from   (D) insists on
23. (A) as   (B) for   (C) with   (D) while
24. (A) abandoned   (B) remained   (C) retained   (D) attempted
25. (A) determined   (B) determining   (C) determine   (D) to determine
26. (A) farming   (B) hunting   (C) continental   (D) ocean
27. (A) according to   (B) in case of
    (C) with regard to   (D) by means of
28. (A) which   (B) whichever   (C) in which   (D) to which
29. (A) art   (B) religion   (C) science   (D) superstition
30. (A) Clearly   (B) Hopefully   (C) Instead   (D) Nevertheless

三、文意選填（10％）

說明： 第 31 至 40 題，每題一個空格。請依文意在文章後所提供的 (A) 到 (J) 選項中分別選出最適當者，並將其字母代號標示在答案卡之「選擇題答案區」。每題答對得 1 分，答錯或劃記多於一個選項者倒扣 1/9 分，倒扣到本大題之實得分數為零為止。未作答者，不給分亦不扣分。

第 31 至 40 題為題組

In many ways, talking is an art and we must not underestimate the effect of words. Well-used words become masterpieces, which can create and nourish. ___31___, words shaped without thoughtful consideration can hurt and destroy, causing unbearable pain and deep regret.

So before we speak, perhaps it would be wise to first give ___32___ thought to what we wish to say. Will it hurt anyone? Will it start an unnecessary dispute? Will it reopen old wounds? ___33___ a few jokes or frank remarks are OK, many of us can't tell ___34___ the thin line between acceptable and unacceptable is. What might seem a ___35___ joke to us may send someone else over the edge. ___36___, things of no real importance are often best left ___37___. Wise are those who heed this fine rule of life and who talk little and carefully, for while we are perfectly free to give ___38___ to our thoughts, we must not forget the rights of others—the right not to be made a laughing stock, to be ___39___, and to enjoy the music of our ___40___.

(A) conversation   (B) unsaid   (C) careful   (D) voice
(E) In fact   (F) harmless   (G) Though   (H) respected
(I) However   (J) where

四、篇章結構（10％）

說明：第 41 至 45 題，每題一個空格。請依文意在文章後所提供的 (A) 到 (E) 選項中分別選出最適當者，填入空格中，使篇章結構清晰有條理，並將其英文字母代號標示在答案卡之「選擇題答案區」。每題答對得 2 分，答錯或劃記多於一個選項者倒扣 1/2 分，倒扣到本大題之實得分數爲零爲止。未作答者，不給分亦不扣分。

第 41 至 45 題爲題組

World War II gave us a sad example of a translation problem. By July 1945, Germany and Italy had already surrendered to the Allies. ___41___ During the first weeks of July, Japan's premier thought over this demand. ___42___ At the conference, he said that his country would *mokusatsu* the demand. But the use of the word *mokusatsu* was a very unfortunate choice. ___43___ It can mean either "to consider" or "to take no notice of." The premier intended the first meaning, but the Allies understood the second. Thus the Allies believed that Japan had rejected their demand. ___44___ This mistranslation made the U.S. decide to send B-29s with atomic bombs to the cities of Hiroshima and Nagasaki. ___45___

(A) This word has two meanings.
(B) Finally, he called a press conference.
(C) But in fact the Japanese government was still considering it.
(D) Soon after this, the Allies demanded that Japan also surrender.
(E) If *mokusatsu* had been translated correctly, the atomic bombs might never have been dropped.

五、閱讀測驗（22％）

說明： 第 46 至 56 題，每題請分別根據各篇文章的文意選出一個最適當的選項，標示在答案卡之「選擇題答案區」。每題答對得 2 分，答錯或劃記多於一個選項者倒扣 2/3 分，倒扣到本大題之實得分數爲零爲止。未作答者，不給分亦不扣分。

第 46 至 48 題爲題組

Market prices may move up or down (or remain the same) due to a number of factors that cause changes in supply or demand.

Bad weather makes prices go up—not just the prices of farm products, but of many other goods ranging from steel to skirts—because of interruptions in production, breakdowns in transportation, power failures, etc.

Advances in technology help to lower prices. Increases in the scale of production resulting from new technology cause shifts in supply, which in turn lead to the lowering of product prices. For example, a more efficient way of making transistors enables the manufacturers to lower the prices of computers, radios, television sets, and tape recorders.

Also, when the market for handmade pocketbooks, grandfather clocks, custom-tailoring and handmade furniture contracts, it forces the prices of such products to go up relatively far above what they were in the old days, when skilled labor was cheaper and more abundant. These shrinking scales of production caused by the decline of market demands push prices up.

46. With which of the following topics is the author mainly concerned?
    (A) The increasing cost of skilled labor on the market.
    (B) The effects of shifts in supply and demand on market prices.
    (C) The relation between market prices and technological changes.
    (D) The effects of climate on the prices of agricultural products.

47. Which of the following is not mentioned as an effect of bad weather?
    (A) Problems with transportation.
    (B) Production delays.
    (C) Failures in the supply of electricity.
    (D) Illness among workers.

48. What does the author think causes the changes in the prices of goods such as handmade pocketbooks or chairs?
    (A) The fact that few are being made and so are more expensive to make.
    (B) The changes in technology that have made such goods cheaper to make.
    (C) The fact that they can not be made by machine.
    (D) The low pay of skilled labor in the old days.

第 49 至 52 題爲題組

Succession, or changes in habitats, occurs because plants and animals cause a change in the environment in which they live. The first weeds and grasses that appear on a bare field, for example, change the environment by shielding the soil from direct sunlight. As these plants spread, the ground surface becomes cooler and moister than it was originally. Thus, the environment at the ground surface has been changed. The new surface conditions favor the sprouting of shrubs. As shrubs grow, they kill the grasses by preventing sunlight from reaching them and also build up the soil in the area. In addition, they attract animals that also enhance the soil. Pine seedlings soon take hold and as they grow, they in turn shade out the shrubs. However, they are not able to shade out oak and hickory seedlings that have found the forest floor suitable. These seedlings grow into large trees that eventually shade out the pines.

49. What is the best title for this passage?
 (A) The Importance of Weeds and Grasses
 (B) The Succession of Oak and Hickory
 (C) How Habitats Change
 (D) Animal and Plant Habitats

50. It can be inferred from the passage that _____.
 (A) birds discourage the growth of shrubs
 (B) pines and grasses can exist together
 (C) weeds and grasses prefer cold climates
 (D) oak and hickory trees grow taller than pines

51. Which is the correct order of plant succession in the example in this passage?

(A) Weeds, shrubs, pines, oak.

(B) Weeds, pines, shrubs, oak.

(C) Oak, pines, shrubs, weeds.

(D) Shrubs, weeds, oak, pines.

52. Which of the following is a possible example of succession as described in this passage?

(A) A forest cut down to build an airport.

(B) A flood washing away a crop of wheat.

(C) Wildflowers growing in an unused parking lot.

(D) Animals being raised by children.

第 53 至 56 題為題組

Success means many wonderful, positive things. Success means personal prosperity: a big and beautiful home, luxurious vacations, and financial security. Success means winning admiration, leadership, and being respected by people in your business and social life. Success means freedom: freedom from worries, fears, frustrations and failure. Success means self-respect, continually finding more real happiness and satisfaction from life, and being able to do more for those who depend on you.

Success—achievement—is the goal of life for every human being. How can we achieve success? We can win success by believing we can succeed. Belief, the "I can" attitude, generates the power, skill, and energy needed to move toward success. When we believe we can do it, the "how to do it" develops.

Every day, all over the nation, young people start working in new jobs. Each of them "wishes" that someday he could enjoy the success that goes with reaching the top. But the majority of these young people simply do not have the belief that it takes to reach the top rungs. Believing it is impossible to climb high, they do not discover the steps that lead to great heights. Their behavior remains that of the "average" person. As a result, they do not reach the top.

But a small number of these young people really believe they will succeed. They approach their work with an "I'm going to the top" attitude. And with substantial belief they reach the top. Believing they will succeed—and that it is not impossible—these folks study and observe the behavior of senior executives. They learn how successful people approach problems and make decisions. They observe the attitudes of successful people. The "how to do it" always comes to the person who believes he can do it and such a person will eventually achieve success.

53. What is the main idea of this passage?
   (A) The definition of success.
   (B) The key to being successful.
   (C) The benefits of being successful.
   (D) The steps to reach the top in life successfully.

54. Which is not mentioned in this passage as part of being successful?
   (A) Having sufficient money.
   (B) Winning others' respect.
   (C) Feeling satisfied and happy.
   (D) Knowing someone important.

55. According to the passage, where do we get the strength and ability we need to obtain success?
(A) Confidence in ourselves.
(B) Strong wishes to succeed.
(C) The attitudes of successful people.
(D) Self-respect and people's admiration.

56. According to the passage, some people do not reach the top in life because they do not _____.
(A) have the power to climb high
(B) have the know-how to do it
(C) have the right attitude and belief
(D) know how to approach problems

第貳部份：非選擇題（佔 28 分）

一、英文翻譯（8％）

說明： 1. 將下列兩句中文翻譯成適當之英文，並將答案寫在「答案卷」上。
　　　 2. 未按題意翻譯者，不予計分。

1. 自助旅行是很值得的，因為它能帶給人們成就感和較大的自由。

2. 儘管如此，也是需要有相當多的準備來規劃自己的行程。

二、英文作文（20％）

說明： 1. 依提示在「答案卷」上寫一篇英文作文。
　　　 2. 文長至少 120 個單詞。

提示： 從小到大你和你的全家人，必定共同經歷許多事。請以 "The Most Unforgettable Experience I Have Shared with My Family" 為題寫一篇英文作文，敘述其中一件最令你難忘的共享經歷並說明這個經歷對你們全家的影響。

大學入學指定科目考試英文模擬試題①詳解

第壹部分：單一選擇題

一、詞彙：

1. (**C**) The success of Jack Smith, a handicapped athlete who won an Olympic gold medal, has become an <u>inspiration</u> to many young people.
   贏得奧運金牌的殘障運動員傑克‧史密斯，他的成功<u>激勵</u>了許多年輕人。
   (A) introduction (ˌɪntrəˈdʌkʃən) *n.* 介紹
   (B) immigration (ˌɪməˈgreʃən) *n.* 移入
   (C) ***inspiration*** (ˌɪnspəˈreʃən) *n.* 激勵
   (D) impression (ɪmˈprɛʃən) *n.* 印象

   handicapped (ˈhændɪˌkæpt) *adj.* 殘障的
   athlete (ˈæθlit) *n.* 運動員
   Olympic (oˈlɪmpɪk) *adj.* 奧林匹克運動會的
   medal (ˈmɛdl̩) *n.* 獎牌

2. (**C**) It is not <u>appropriate</u> for Chinese to attend a funeral wearing loud clothing.
   對中國人而言，穿著鮮豔的衣服參加葬禮，是不<u>適當的</u>。
   (A) permanent (ˈpɝmənənt) *adj.* 永久的
   (B) consistent (kənˈsɪstənt) *adj.* 一致的
   (C) ***appropriate*** (əˈproprɪɪt) *adj.* 適當的
   (D) hospitable (ˈhɑspɪtəbl̩) *adj.* 好客的

   attend (əˈtɛnd) *v.* 參加
   funeral (ˈfjunərəl) *n.* 葬禮　　loud (laud) *adj.* 鮮豔的
   clothing (ˈkloðɪŋ) *n.* 衣服

3. (**B**) "Please don't <u>hesitate</u> to raise your hand and ask if you have any
questions regarding this topic," said the lecturer.

「如果你有任何關於這個題目的問題，請不要<u>猶豫</u>，舉起你的手
發問，」那名演講者說。

(A) challenge（'tʃælɪndʒ）v. 挑戰

(B) *hesitate*（'hɛzə,tet）v. 猶豫

(C) balance（'bæləns）v. 使平衡

(D) perform（pəˈfɔrm）v. 執行；表演

raise（rez）v. 舉起　　regarding（rɪˈɡardɪŋ）prep. 關於
topic（'tɑpɪk）n. 題目；主題　　lecturer（'lɛktʃərə）n. 演講者

4. (**D**) The two finalists are <u>scheduled</u> to compete for the championship
at 2:00 PM next Monday.

那兩位決賽選手，被<u>安排</u>在下星期一的下午兩點，爭奪冠軍。

(A) reserve（rɪˈzɜv）v. 預訂

(B) construct（kənˈstrʌkt）v. 建造

(C) emphasize（'ɛmfə,saɪz）v. 強調

(D) *schedule*（'skɛdʒul）v. 安排；排定

finalist（'faɪnl̩ɪst）n. 決賽選手　　compete（kəmˈpit）v. 競爭 <*for*>
championship（'tʃæmpɪən,ʃɪp）n. 冠軍資格

PM 下午（↔ *AM* 上午）

5. (**B**) Do not give the boy any chocolate or cookies. If you do, it will
spoil his <u>appetite</u> and he will not eat anything at lunchtime.

不要給那個男孩任何巧克力或餅乾。如果你這麼做，會破壞他的
<u>食慾</u>，到了午餐時間，他就不會吃任何東西了。

(A) expression（ɪkˈsprɛʃən）n. 表達；表情；說法

(B) *appetite*（'æpə,taɪt）n. 食慾

(C) privilege（'prɪvl̩ɪdʒ）n. 特權

(D) research（'risɜtʃ, rɪˈsɜtʃ）n. 研究

chocolate（'tʃɔkəlɪt）n. 巧克力　　cookie（'kʊkɪ）n. 餅乾
spoil（spɔɪl）v. 破壞
lunchtime（'lʌntʃ,taɪm）n. 午餐時間

6. (**A**) One of the requirements of being either a good teacher or a good nurse is to be <u>patient</u>.

當一位好老師或是好護士，其中一個必備條件，就是要<u>有耐心</u>。

(A) **patient** ('peʃənt) *adj.* 有耐心的

(B) artificial (,ɑrtə'fɪʃəl) *adj.* 人造的；人工的

(C) familiar (fə'mɪljɚ) *adj.* 熟悉的

(D) original (ə'rɪdʒən!) *adj.* 最初的；原來的

requirement (rɪ'kwaɪrmənt) *n.* 必備條件

7. (**D**) A passerby called the fire department <u>immediately</u> when he saw that the building was in flames.

有個路人一看到建築物失火，就<u>立刻</u>打電話給消防隊。

(A) magnificently (mæg'nɪfəsn̩tlɪ) *adv.* 宏偉地；華麗地

(B) ordinarily ('ɔrdn̩,ɛrɪlɪ) *adv.* 一般地

(C) gradually ('grædʒʊəlɪ) *adv.* 逐漸地

(D) **immediately** (ɪ'midɪɪtlɪ) *adv.* 立刻

passerby ('pæsɚ'baɪ) *n.* 過路人　　**fire department** 消防隊

flame (flem) *n.* 火焰　　**in flames** 燃燒著；失火 (= *on fire*)

8. (**B**) John did not know he had been entirely <u>deceived</u> by the salesman until he discovered the antique was a fake.

約翰直到發現古董是贗品時，才知道他完全被推銷員<u>欺騙</u>了。

(A) defeat (dɪ'fit) *v.* 打敗

(B) **deceive** (dɪ'siv) *v.* 欺騙

(C) detect (dɪ'tɛkt) *v.* 查出

(D) disguise (dɪs'gaɪz) *v.* 偽裝

not…until~ 直到~才…　　entirely (ɪn'taɪrlɪ) *adv.* 完全地

salesman ('selzmən) *n.* 推銷員

discover (dɪ'skʌvɚ) *v.* 發現　　antique (æn'tik) *n.* 古董

fake (fek) *n.* 贗品；仿冒品

9. (**A**) In the past few years, juvenile crime has shown a <u>tendency</u> to increase. In other words, there are more and more teenagers violating laws. 在過去幾年，青少年犯罪顯然有增加的<u>趨勢</u>。換句話說，有越來越多的青少年違反法律。

    (A) ***tendency*** (ˈtɛndənsɪ) *n.* 趨勢

    (B) commercial (kəˈmɝʃəl) *n.* (電視、廣播的) 商業廣告

    (C) motive (ˈmotɪv) *n.* 動機

    (D) profession (prəˈfɛʃən) *n.* 職業

    juvenile (ˈdʒuvənḷ) *adj.* 青少年的   crime (kraɪm) *n.* 犯罪
    increase (ɪnˈkris) *v.* 增加   ***in other words*** 換句話說
    teenager (ˈtinˌedʒɚ) *n.* 青少年   violate (ˈvaɪəˌlet) *v.* 違反

10. (**D**) The soccer game has been <u>temporarily</u> postponed due to the coming typhoon. As soon as the weather improves, we will hold the game. 這場足球賽因為颱風即將來臨而<u>暫時延期</u>。一旦天氣有所改善，我們將會舉行比賽。

    (A) anxiously (ˈæŋkʃəslɪ) *adv.* 焦慮地

    (B) mysteriously (mɪsˈtɪrɪəslɪ) *adv.* 神秘地

    (C) extensively (ɪkˈstɛnsɪvlɪ) *adv.* 廣泛地

    (D) ***temporarily*** (ˈtɛmpəˌrɛrəlɪ) *adv.* 暫時地

    soccer (ˈsɑkɚ) *n.* 足球   postpone (postˈpon) *v.* 使延期
    due to 由於   coming (ˈkʌmɪŋ) *adj.* 即將來臨的
    improve (ɪmˈpruv) *v.* 改善   hold (hold) *v.* 舉行

二、綜合測驗：

第 11 至 20 題為題組

    According to a news report, drug abuse and trafficking have been spreading in our society like an epidemic. <u>What</u> is even more astonishing

11

is that the police records show drug abuse has become the second most common type of crime among teenagers. Nowadays a great many people hardly raise an eyebrow <u>at</u> the sight of people selling drugs, especially

12

amphetamines, in places where teenagers hang out.

　　根據新聞報導，吸毒和毒品交易，在我們的社會中，已經像傳染病一般蔓延開來了。更加令人驚訝的是，警方的記錄顯示，吸毒已經成為青少年之中，第二常見的犯罪類型。現在，有許多人在看到有人在青少年常去的地方販賣毒品，特別是安非他命，甚至都不會感到吃驚。

> abuse〔ə'bjus〕*n.* 濫用　　***drug abuse*** 吸毒
> trafficking〔'træfɪkɪŋ〕*n.* 非法交易　　spread〔sprɛd〕*v.* 散播
> epidemic〔͵ɛpə'dɛmɪk〕*n.* 傳染病
> astonishing〔ə'stɑnɪʃɪŋ〕*adj.* 令人驚訝的（= *shocking*）
> nowadays〔'naʊə͵dez〕*adv.* 現在　　***a great many*** 很多
> eyebrow〔'aɪ͵braʊ〕*n.* 眉毛　　***raise an eyebrow*** 揚起眉毛；吃驚
> amphetamine〔æm'fɛtə͵min〕*n.* 安非他命　　***hang out*** 常去

11.(**B**) 在此需要複合關代 ***What***，不但引導名詞子句，做整句話的主詞，而且在名詞子句中，也做主詞，選 (B)。

12.(**D**) ***at the sight of~*** 一看到~的時候

To make matters worse, drug dealers even invade <u>campuses</u>. In 1990, 27%
13
of all drug addicts were addicted to amphetamines, <u>while</u> the percentage
14
in 1992 reached 74%. These statistics show the incredible increase in the
number of amphetamine addicts, and unfortunately, more than 50% of them
are <u>student</u> addicts.
15
更糟的是，毒販甚至已侵入校園。在 1990 年，有 27%的吸毒者，是吸食安非他命上癮，而這個百分比在 1992 年，已達到 74%。這些統計數字顯示，安非他命吸食者有驚人的增加，而且，遺憾的是，其中超過 50%的上癮者都是學生。

> ***to make matters worse*** 更糟的是（= *what is worse*）
> dealer〔'dilə〕*n.* 商人　　invade〔ɪn'ved〕*v.* 入侵
> addict〔'ædɪkt〕*n.* 上癮者　〔ə'dɪkt〕*v.* 使上癮 < *to* >
> percentage〔pə'sɛntɪdʒ〕*n.* 百分比
> statistics〔stə'tɪstɪks〕*n. pl.* 統計數字
> incredible〔ɪn'krɛdəbḷ〕*adj.* 令人難以置信的
> unfortunately〔ʌn'fɔrtʃənɪtlɪ〕*adv.* 不幸地；遺憾地

13. (**A**) (A) ***campus*** 〔'kæmpəs 〕*n.* 校園

        (B) campground 〔'kæmp͵graʊnd 〕*n.* 露營地

        (C) chapel 〔'tʃæpḷ 〕*n.* 小禮拜堂

        (D) chamber 〔'tʃembɚ 〕*n.* 房間；議事廳

14. (**A**) 依句意，1990 年為 27%，「而」1992 年則達到 74%，選 (A) ***while***，用於表示前後對照、句意轉折。

15. (**C**) 依句意，很多上癮者都是「青少年」，選 (C) ***teenage*** 〔'tin͵edʒ 〕*adj.* 十幾歲的；青少年的。而 (A) infant「嬰兒的」, (B) adult「成年的」, (D) senior「年長的」, 則不合句意。

    As we know, drugs can, <u>in a way</u>, give us sheer sensual pleasures but
                             16
the sensation is momentary, whereas the severe pains they cause can <u>last</u>
                                                17
long enough to weaken our will, destroy our health, and worst of all, rot
our soul. <u>Furthermore</u>, drug addicts, to get the money needed for the
           18
purchase of drugs, <u>are likely to</u> commit horrible crimes such as robbery,
                    19
kidnapping, or blackmail. Drug addicts not only hurt themselves
physically and <u>mentally</u> but also become a threat to society. Therefore, it
                20
is everybody's business to kick drugs out of school and out of society.

    正如我們所知，毒品在某方面，可以給我們純粹的感官樂趣，但這種感覺只是短暫的，然而它們所帶來的劇烈痛苦，卻是會持續很久的，足以削弱我們的意志力、損害我們的健康，而且最糟糕的是，會使我們的靈魂墮落。此外，吸毒者為了得到購買毒品所需要的錢，可能會犯下可怕的罪行，例如搶劫、綁架，或恐嚇勒索。吸毒者不但在身心上殘害自己，同時也會成為社會的一大威脅。因此，把毒品趕出校園、趕出社會，是每個人的責任。

        sheer 〔 ʃɪr 〕*adj.* 完全的；全然的
        sensual 〔'sɛnʃʊəl 〕*adj.* 肉體的；感官的   pleasure 〔'plɛʒɚ 〕*n.* 樂趣
        sensation 〔 sɛn'seʃən 〕*n.* 感覺（= *feeling*）

momentary (ˈmomənˌtɛrɪ) *adj.* 短暫的

whereas (hwɛrˈæz) *conj.* 然而

severe (səˈvɪr) *adj.* 嚴重的；劇烈的　　pain (pen) *n.* 痛苦

weaken (ˈwikən) *v.* 使衰弱　　will (wɪl) *n.* 意志力

worst of all 最糟的是　　rot (rɑt) *v.* 使腐敗；使墮落

soul (sol) *n.* 靈魂　　purchase (ˈpɝtʃəs) *n.* 購買

commit (kəˈmɪt) *v.* 犯 (罪)　　horrible (ˈhɑrəbl̩) *adj.* 可怕的

robbery (ˈrɑbərɪ) *n.* 搶劫　　kidnap (ˈkɪdnæp) *v.* 綁架

blackmail (ˈblækˌmel) *n.* 勒索；恐嚇

physically (ˈfɪzɪkl̩ɪ) *adv.* 身體上　　threat (θrɛt) *n.* 威脅

business (ˈbɪznɪs) *n.* 職責；本分　　kick (kɪk) *v.* 踢

kick…out of 把…從～趕出去

16. (**C**) (A) in a pet 不開心；耍孩子脾氣　　pet (pɛt) *n.* 不開心；孩子脾氣
　　　(B) in a word 簡言之
　　　(C) ***in a way*** 就某方面而言；有點
　　　(D) in a jam 陷入困境　　jam (dʒæm) *n.* 困境；困難

17. (**B**) 依句意，痛苦會「持續」很久，選 (B) *last*。而 (A) keep「保持」，
　　　應用 keep *sth.* long，(C) extend (ɪkˈstɛnd) *v.* 延長，(D) maintain
　　　(menˈten) *v.* 維持，均爲及物動詞，在此用法不合。

18. (**B**) (A) accordingly (əˈkɔrdɪŋlɪ) *adv.* 因此
　　　(B) ***furthermore*** (ˈfɝðəˌmor) *adv.* 此外
　　　(C) consequently (ˈkɑnsəˌkwɛntlɪ) *adv.* 因此
　　　(D) otherwise (ˈʌðəˌwaɪz) *adv.* 否則

19. (**D**) (A) be supposed to + V. 應該…
　　　(B) get used to + N / V-ing 習慣於…
　　　(C) look forward to + N / V-ing 期待…
　　　(D) ***be likely to + V.*** 可能…

20. (**D**) (A) movably (ˈmuvəbl̩ɪ) *adv.* 可移動地
　　　(B) minimally (ˈmɪnɪml̩ɪ) *adv.* 最小地
　　　(C) maturely (məˈtjʊrlɪ) *adv.* 成熟地
　　　(D) ***mentally*** (ˈmɛntl̩ɪ) *adv.* 心理上

第 21 至 30 題爲題組

From Taitung, the plane ride to Orchid Island takes only about 20 minutes. <u>Yet</u>, however short the journey, it brings one to a place entirely
                    21
different from modern Taiwan. The aborigines of Orchid Island refer to themselves as the "Tao," which <u>originates from</u> their term for the island:
                                                          22
"Pongso No Tao." There are seven tribal villages on the island, <u>with</u> the
                                                                  23
population standing at over 4,000. Because they are isolated at sea, they have <u>retained</u> their traditional culture better than any other group of
        24
Taiwanese aborigines.

　　從台東出發，坐飛機到蘭嶼只需要二十分鐘。然而，無論這趟行程多麼短暫，卻將人帶到了一個與現代化的台灣完全不同的地方。蘭嶼的原住民稱自己爲「達悟人」，源於他們這個島的名字「蓬守諾達悟」。島上有七個部族村落，人口超過四千人。因爲他們在海上與世隔絕，所以他們保存的傳統文化，勝過台灣其他任何原住民部落。

> orchid (ˈɔrkɪd) *n.* 蘭花　　***Orchid Island*** 蘭嶼
> journey (ˈdʒɝnɪ) *n.* 旅程　　entirely (ɪnˈtaɪrlɪ) *adv.* 完全地
> aborigine (ˌæbəˈrɪdʒəni) *n.* 原住民　　***refer to A as B*** 稱呼 A 爲 B
> term (tɝm) *n.* 名詞　　tribal (ˈtraɪbḷ) *adj.* 部落的
> isolated (ˈaɪsḷˌetɪd) *adj.* 孤立的；隔離的

21. (**D**) 根據句意，前後語氣轉折，故選 (D) **Yet**「然而」。而 (A) conversely
    (kənˈvɝslɪ) *adv.* 相反地，(B) meanwhile (ˈminˌhwaɪl) *adv.* 同時，
    (C) similarly (ˈsɪmələˌlɪ) *adv.* 同樣地，則不合句意。

22. (**C**) (A) deal with 處理；應付
    (B) consist of 由～組成
    (C) ***originate*** (əˈrɪdʒəˌnet) *v.* 起源於 <*from* >
    (D) insist on 堅持

23. (**C**) 表附帶狀態，附帶說明島上人口「有」超過四千人，介系詞用 ***with*** ，
    選 (C)。

24. (**C**)　(A) abandon〔ə'bændən〕*v.* 放棄

(B) remain〔rɪ'men〕*v.* 保持；依然（為不及物動詞，不加受詞）

(C) ***retain***〔rɪ'ten〕*v.* 保留；保存

(D) attempt〔ə'tɛmpt〕*v.* 嘗試

The "flying fish season" of the spring and summer is the best-known Orchid Island tradition. The significance of these migrating fish has influenced the Tao's way of life, <u>determining</u> their calendar of holidays
　　　　　　　　　　　　　　　　　　　　25
and inspiring their unique aesthetic sensibility.

春夏時的「飛魚季」，是蘭嶼最著名的傳統。這些迴游魚類非常重要，影響到達悟人的生活方式，決定他們的假日，也激發了他們獨特的審美觀念。

significance〔sɪg'nɪfəkəns〕*n.* 重要性（= *importance*）

migrate〔'maɪgret〕*v.* 遷移；（魚類）迴游

way of life 生活方式　　　calendar〔'kæləndɚ〕*n.* 曆法；行事曆

inspire〔ɪn'spaɪr〕*v.* 激發　　　unique〔ju'nik〕*adj.* 獨特的

aesthetic〔ɛs'θɛtɪk〕*adj.* 美學的；審美的

sensibility〔͵sɛnsə'bɪlətɪ〕*n.* 感覺；感受

25. (**B**)　主要子句的動詞 has influenced 與空格中的動詞 determine 並無連接詞連接，可見在此應用分詞構句，故選 (B) ***determining***。

determine〔dɪ'tɝmɪn〕*v.* 決定

Every year from June to September, the island's <u>ocean</u> culture is fully
　　　　　　　　　　　　　　　　　　　　　　　26
revealed. As observed by some researchers, the Tao depend upon fish for a high percentage of their diet. They've divided fish into several categories,

and each person, <u>according to</u> age and gender, must eat only fish from a
　　　　　　　　　27
suitable category.

每年從六月到九月，島上的海洋文化便充分顯露出來。有些研究人員觀察到，達悟人的飲食中，魚類占有很大的比例。他們將魚分成數個部位，每個人依據年齡和性別，只能吃魚的某個適合的部位。

reveal〔rɪ'vil〕v. 顯露
observe〔əb'zɝv〕v. 觀察　　researcher〔rɪ'sɝtʃə〕n. 研究人員
percentage〔pə'sɛntɪdʒ〕n. 比例　　diet〔'daɪət〕n. 飲食
divide〔də'vaɪd〕v. 區分 < *into* >　　category〔'kætə,gorɪ〕n. 種類
gender〔'dʒɛndə〕n. 性別　　suitable〔'sutəbl̩〕adj. 適合的

26.(**D**) 依句意，生活以魚類為主，應屬於「海洋」文化，故選 (D) *ocean*。
　　　(A) farming「農耕」，(B) hunting「打獵」，(C) continental
　　　〔,kɑntə'nɛntl̩〕adj. 大陸的，均不合。

27.(**A**) (A) *according to* 根據　　　　(B) in case of 萬一發生
　　　(C) with regard to 關於　　　　(D) by means of 藉由

　　　The Tao have also attached great social significance to their chief
means of catching fish — their boats. Even ashore, Tao men are often
grouped socially based on the boat crews <u>to which</u> they belong. The boats
　　　　　　　　　　　　　　　　　　　　　　　　　　　　28
themselves are works of <u>art</u>, giving full expression to the Tao's talents for
　　　　　　　　　　　　29
beauty. Furthermore, the fertility of their imaginations is matched by the
fertility of Orchid Island's volcanic geology. <u>Clearly</u>, this is a place that
　　　　　　　　　　　　　　　　　　　　　　　　30
enjoys the double good fortune of possessing equally rich natural and
cultural heritages.

　　達悟人也認為，他們的主要捕魚工具——船，具有重要的社會意義。即使在
岸上社交時，達悟男人通常也會按照他們所屬的船，分散成組。船的本身即是
藝術作品，充分表現出達悟人在美這方面的天賦。此外，他們豐富的想像力，
與蘭嶼豐富的火山地質也互相配合。顯然，這是一個享有雙重財富的好地方，
擁有同樣豐富的自然及文化遺產。

attach〔ə'tætʃ〕v. 附加；貼上 < *into* >
attach significance / importance to 認為～很重要；重視
social〔'soʃəl〕adj. 社會的　　chief〔tʃif〕adj. 主要的
ashore〔ə'ʃor〕adv. 在岸上　　group〔grup〕v. 分組
based on 根據　　crew〔kru〕n. 船員

expression〔ɪkˋsprɛʃən〕*n.* 表達　　talent〔ˋtælənt〕*n.* 天賦；才能
fertility〔fɝˋtɪlətɪ〕*n.* 豐富　　match〔mætʃ〕*v.* 配合
volcanic〔vɑlˋkænɪk〕*adj.* 火山的　　geology〔dʒiˋɑlədʒɪ〕*n.* 地質
possess〔pəˋzɛs〕*v.* 擁有　　equally〔ˋikwəlɪ〕*adv.* 同樣地
heritage〔ˋhɛrətɪdʒ〕*n.* 遺產

28. (**D**) 此處需要關代，引導形容詞子句，修飾先行詞 crews，而在形容詞子
句中，關代亦做動詞 belong to 的受詞，介系詞可移至關代之前，故
選 (D) *to which*。

29. (**A**) 依句意，達悟人的船也是「藝術」品，選 (A) *art*。(B) 宗教，(C) 科學，
(D) superstition〔͵supɚˋstɪʃən〕*n.* 迷信，均不合。

30. (**A**) (A) *clearly*〔ˋklɪrlɪ〕*adv.* 顯然
(B) hopefully〔ˋhopfəlɪ〕*adv.* 順利的話
(C) instead〔ɪnˋstɛd〕*adv.* 相反地
(D) nevertheless〔͵nɛvɚðəˋlɛs〕*adv.* 然而（= *however*）

三、文意選填：

第 31 至 40 題為題組

　　In many ways, talking is an art and we must not underestimate the
effect of words. Well-used words become masterpieces, which can create
and nourish. [31](I) However, words shaped without thoughtful consideration
can hurt and destroy, causing unbearable pain and deep regret.

　　談話在很多方面，都是一門藝術，我們絕不能低估談話的影響力。使用得
當的話語會變成傑作，傑作能創造、能滋養。然而，不經仔細考慮就說出來的
話，會傷人、會毀滅，造成無法忍受的痛苦，和深深的悔恨。

way〔we〕*n.* 方面　　underestimate〔ˋʌndɚˋɛstə͵met〕*v.* 低估
masterpiece〔ˋmæstɚ͵pis〕*n.* 傑作　　nourish〔ˋnɝɪʃ〕*v.* 滋養
effect〔ɪˋfɛkt〕*n.* 影響　　shape〔ʃep〕*v.* 使成形
thoughtful〔ˋθɔtfəl〕*adj.* 體貼的
consideration〔kən͵sɪdəˋreʃən〕*n.* 考慮　　destroy〔dɪˋstrɔɪ〕*v.* 摧毀
unbearable〔ʌnˋbɛrəbl̩〕*adj.* 無法忍受的　　regret〔rɪˋgrɛt〕*n.* 後悔

So before we speak, perhaps it would be wise to first give ³²(C) careful thought to what we wish to say. Will it hurt anyone? Will it start an unnecessary dispute? Will it reopen old wounds? ³³(G) Though a few jokes or frank remarks are OK, many of us can't tell ³⁴(J) where the thin line between acceptable and unacceptable is. What might seem a ³⁵(F) harmless joke to us may send someone else over the edge.

所以在我們開口之前，或許比較明智的做法是，先仔細思考過想說的話。這些話會傷害任何人嗎？會引發無謂的爭端嗎？會再次撕開舊傷口嗎？雖然一些笑話或是坦白的意見，都還過得去，但我們當中仍有許多人無法分辨可接受和不可接受之間，細微的分界線在哪裏。對我們而言，好像是無傷大雅的笑話，卻可能使別人發狂。

> ***give thought to*** 思考　　***wish to*** 想要 (= *want to*)
> dispute〔 dɪ'spjut 〕*n.* 爭論　　reopen〔 ri'opən 〕*v.* 重新開啓
> wound〔 wund 〕*n.* 傷口　　frank〔 fræŋk 〕*adj.* 坦白的
> remark〔 rɪ'mɑrk 〕*n.* 評論；話　　tell〔 tɛl 〕*v.* 分辨；知道
> thin〔 θɪn 〕*adj.* 細微的　　***send sb. over the edge*** 使某人發狂

³⁶(E) In fact, things of no real importance are often best left ³⁷(B) unsaid. Wise are those who heed this fine rule of life and who talk little and carefully, for while we are perfectly free to give ³⁸(D) voice to our thoughts, we must not forget the rights of others—the right not to be made a laughing stock, to be ³⁹(H) respected, and to enjoy the music of our ⁴⁰(A) conversation.

事實上，無關緊要的事，最好別說出來。會注意生活上這項細則，話說得既少又謹慎的人，是最有智慧的，因為當我們非常自由地發表想法時，我們絕不能忘記，別人也有權利——有不被當成笑柄的權利、有被尊重的權利，以及享受美妙談話的權利。

> leave〔 liv 〕*v.* 使處於…狀態　　heed〔 hid 〕*v.* 注意
> fine〔 faɪn 〕*adj.* 細微的　　perfectly〔'pɜfɪktlɪ 〕*adv.* 完全地
> ***give voice to*** 發表　　right〔 raɪt 〕*n.* 權利
> ***a laughing stock*** 笑柄　　music〔'mjuzɪk 〕*n.* 美妙的聲音

四、篇章結構：

第 41 至 45 題為題組

World War II gave us a sad example of a translation problem. By July 1945, Germany and Italy had already surrendered to the Allies. ⁴¹(D) Soon after this, the Allies demanded that Japan also surrender. During the first weeks of July, Japan's premier thought over this demand. ⁴²(B) Finally, he called a press conference.

第二次世界大戰是一個翻譯出問題，而造成悲劇的例子。到了一九四五年七月時，德國和義大利已經向同盟國投降了。不久以後，同盟國要求日本也要投降。在七月前幾週，日本首相一直在考慮這項要求。最後，他召開了記者會。

translation〔træns'leʃən〕*n.* 翻譯　　surrender〔sə'rɛndɚ〕*v.* 投降
ally〔'ælaɪ〕*n.* 同盟　　***the Allies*** 同盟國
demand〔dɪ'mænd〕*v., n.* 要求　　premier〔'primɪɚ, prɪ'mɪr〕*n.* 首相
think over 考慮　　press〔prɛs〕*n.* 媒體；新聞界
conference〔'kɑnfərəns〕*n.* 會議　　***press conference*** 記者招待會

At the conference, he said that his country would *mokusatsu* the demand. But the use of the word *mokusatsu* was a very unfortunate choice. ⁴³(A) This word has two meanings. It can mean either "to consider" or "to take no notice of." The premier intended the first meaning, but the Allies understood the second. Thus the Allies believed that Japan had rejected their demand. ⁴⁴(C) But in fact the Japanese government was still considering it.

在記者會上，他說他的國家會 mokusatsu 這項要求。但是使用 mokusatsu 這個字，是個非常不幸的選擇。這個字有兩個意思，可以指「考慮」，或是「漠視」。首相指的是第一個意思，而同盟國卻以為是第二個意思。於是同盟國認為日本拒絕了這項要求。但事實上，日本政府還在考慮。

unfortunate〔ʌn'fɔrtʃənɪt〕*adj.* 不幸的　　***take notice of*** 注意
intend〔ɪn'tɛnd〕*v.* 意圖；意指
understand〔ˌʌndɚ'stænd〕*v.* 以為；認為；猜想
reject〔rɪ'dʒɛkt〕*v.* 拒絕

This mistranslation made the U.S. decide to send B-29s with atomic bombs to the cities of Hiroshima and Nagasaki. [45](E) If *mokusatsu* had been translated correctly, the atomic bombs might never have beendropped.

這個錯誤的翻譯使得美國決定派遣 B-29 轟炸機，帶著原子彈去轟炸廣島和長崎。如果 mokusatsu 被翻譯正確的話，原子彈可能就永遠不會被投擲下去了。

> mistranslation (ˌmɪstræns'leʃən) *n.* 翻譯錯誤
> atomic (ə'tɑmɪk) *adj.* 原子的　　bomb (bɑm) *n.* 炸彈
> *atomic bomb* 原子彈　　Hiroshima （日本的）廣島
> Nagasaki （日本的）長崎　　drop (drɑp) *v.* 投下

五、閱讀測驗：

第 46 至 48 題為題組

Market prices may move up or down (or remain the same) due to a number of factors that cause changes in supply or demand.

由於許多導致供需變動的因素，使得市場價格可能會上下波動（或保持不變）。

> market ('mɑrkɪt) *n.* 市場　　move (muv) *v.* 移動
> remain (rɪ'men) *v.* 保持　　*due to* 由於
> *a number of* 許多的；好幾個　　factor ('fæktə) *n.* 因素
> supply (sə'plaɪ) *n.* 供給　　demand (dɪ'mænd) *n.* 需求

Bad weather makes prices go up—not just the prices of farm products, but of many other goods ranging from steel to skirts—because of interruptions in production, breakdowns in transportation, power failures, etc.

壞天氣會使價格上漲——不只是農產品的價格，還有許多其他的商品，範圍從鋼鐵到裙子都有——因為有生產受阻、交通中斷、停電等情況。

> product ('prɑdʌkt) *n.* 產品　　*farm products* 農產品
> goods (gudz) *n.pl.* 商品　　range (rendʒ) *v.* （範圍）包括
> *range from* A *to* B 範圍從 A 到 B 都有　　steel (stil) *n.* 鋼鐵
> interruption (ˌɪntə'rʌpʃən) *n.* 打斷；阻礙

production〔prə'dʌkʃən〕*n.* 生產
breakdown〔'brek,daʊn〕*n.* 故障；崩潰
transportation〔,trænspə'teʃən〕*n.* 交通運輸
power failure 停電　　　*etc.* 等等（= *et cetera*〔ɛt'sɛtərə〕）

Advances in technology help to lower prices. Increases in the scale of production resulting from new technology cause shifts in supply, which in turn lead to the lowering of product prices. For example, a more efficient way of making transistors enables the manufacturers to lower the prices of computers, radios, television sets, and tape recorders.

科技的進步有助於降低價格。新的科技使生產規模增加，導致供給的變動，接著造成產品價格的下降。舉例來說，一種更有效率的電晶體製造法，使得製造商能夠降低電腦、收音機、電視機，和錄音機的價格。

advance〔əd'væns〕*n.* 進步　　　technology〔tɛk'nɑlədʒɪ〕*n.* 科技
lower〔'loɚ〕*v.* 降低　　　increase〔'ɪnkris〕*n.* 增加
scale〔skel〕*n.* 規模　　***result from*** 起因於；由於
cause〔kɔz〕*v.* 導致；造成　　shift〔ʃɪft〕*n.* 變動
in turn 必然也　　***lead to*** 導致；造成
efficient〔ə'fɪʃənt〕*adj.* 有效率的
transistor〔træn'zɪstɚ〕*n.* 電晶體　　enable〔ɪn'ebḷ〕*v.* 使能夠
manufacturer〔,mænjə'fæktʃərɚ〕*n.* 製造商
tape recorder 錄音機

Also, when the market for handmade pocketbooks, grandfather clocks, custom-tailoring and handmade furniture contracts, it forces the prices of such products to go up relatively far above what they were in the old days, when skilled labor was cheaper and more abundant. These shrinking scales of production caused by the decline of market demands push prices up.

此外，當手工製的小筆記本、老爺鐘、量身訂做，和手工家俱的市場萎縮時，就會迫使這些產品的價格上漲，比以前高出許多，因為從前技術熟練的勞工較便宜，而且較多。這些因為市場需求減少，而縮小的生產規模，就使得價格上漲。

also〔'ɔlso〕*adv.* 此外；而且

handmade〔'hænd'med〕*adj.* 手工製的

pocketbook〔'pakɪt,buk〕*n.* 小筆記本

grandfather clock 利用鐘擺計時的老式時鐘

custom-tailor〔,kʌstəm'telə〕*v.* 訂製（= *custom-made* = *tailor-made*）

furniture〔'fɜnɪtʃə〕*n.* 家具　　contract〔kən'trækt〕*v.* 縮小

force〔fors〕*v.* 強迫；迫使　　relatively〔'rɛlətɪvlɪ〕*adv.* 相對地

in the old days 以前　　skilled〔skɪld〕*adj.* 熟練的

labor〔'lebə〕*n.* 勞工　　abundant〔ə'bʌndənt〕*adj.* 豐富的

shrinking〔'ʃrɪŋkɪŋ〕*adj.* 逐漸縮小的

decline〔dɪ'klaɪn〕*n.* 下降；衰退　　***push…up*** 將…向上推

46.（**B**）以下何者是作者最關心的主題？

(A) 市場上技術熟練的勞工成本增加。

(B) 供需的改變對市場價格的影響。

(C) 市場價格和科技變化之間的關係。

(D) 氣候對農產品價格的影響。

topic〔'tapɪk〕*n.* 主題　　author〔'ɔθə〕*n.* 作者

mainly〔'menlɪ〕*adv.* 主要地　　***be concerned with*** 關心

relation〔rɪ'leʃən〕*n.* 關係

technological〔,tɛknə'ladʒɪkḷ〕*adj.* 科技的

agricultural〔,ægrɪ'kʌltʃərəl〕*adj.* 農業的

47.（**D**）以下何者並未被提到是壞天氣的影響？

(A) 交通問題。

(B) 生產延誤。

(C) 停電。

(D) 工人生病。

mention〔'mɛnʃən〕*v.* 提到　　delay〔dɪ'le〕*n.* 延誤

failure〔'feljə〕*n.* 停止　　electricity〔ɪ,lɛk'trɪsətɪ〕*n.* 電力

illness〔'ɪlnɪs〕*n.* 疾病

48. (**A**) 作者認為是什麼原因，造成像是手工製的小型筆記本或椅子這類商品的價格改變？
   (A) 生產量少，生產成本也就提高了。
   (B) 科技的改變，使得這類商品的製造成本變得較便宜。
   (C) 它們不能用機器製造。
   (D) 以前技術熟練的勞工工資較低。
   pay〔pe〕*n.* 薪水

第 49 至 52 題為題組

Succession, or changes in habitats, occurs because plants and animals cause a change in the environment in which they live. The first weeds and grasses that appear on a bare field, for example, change the environment by shielding the soil from direct sunlight. As these plants spread, the ground surface becomes cooler and moister than it was originally. Thus, the environment at the ground surface has been changed.

生物演替，也就是生物棲息地的改變，之所以會發生，都是由於植物或動物，造成其生存環境的改變。例如，在一片光禿的原野上，最先長出的雜草和青草，就會因為阻擋了直接照射在土壤上的陽光，而造成環境的改變。當這些植物蔓延生長時，地表就會變得比原先更濕冷。因此，地表的環境就被改變了。

succession〔sək'sɛʃən〕*n.*【生物】演替　　or〔ɔr〕*conj.* 也就是
habitat〔'hæbə,tæt〕*n.* (動植物的) 棲息地　　cause〔kɔz〕*v.* 造成
weed〔wid〕*n.* 雜草　　grass〔græs〕*n.* 草
bare〔bɛr〕*adj.* 赤裸的　　field〔fild〕*n.* 原野
shield〔ʃild〕*v.* 掩蓋；遮住 (免受…) < *from* >
soil〔sɔil〕*n.* 土壤　　spread〔sprɛd〕*v.* 蔓延
surface〔'sɝfɪs〕*n.* 表面　　moist〔mɔist〕*adj.* 潮濕的
originally〔ə'rɪdʒənḷɪ〕*adv.* 最初；原本

The new surface conditions favor the sprouting of shrubs. As shrubs grow, they kill the grasses by preventing sunlight from reaching them and also build up the soil in the area. In addition, they attract animals that also enhance the soil. Pine seedlings soon take hold and as they grow, they in turn shade out the shrubs. However, they are not able to shade out oak and hickory seedlings that have found the forest floor suitable. These seedlings grow into large trees that eventually shade out the pines.

這層新的地表，其環境有利於灌木的萌芽。當灌木生長時，會因為阻擋了陽光，而使得青草枯死，因而使該地區的土壤逐漸增加。此外，灌木會吸引動物，所以也會強化土壤。松樹樹苗很快地就會生根成長，繼而遮擋灌木叢原本的陽光。然而，它們卻遮蔽不到，適合在樹林底層生長的橡樹和山胡桃樹的樹苗。這些樹苗最後就長成大樹，遮蔽松樹的陽光。

> conditions〔kən'dıʃənz〕*n. pl.* 環境　　favor〔'fevə〕*v.* 對～有利
> sprouting〔'spraʊtɪŋ〕*n.* 發芽　　shrub〔ʃrʌb〕*n.* 灌木
> ***build up*** 逐漸積聚　　***in addition*** 此外
> enhance〔ɪn'hæns〕*v.* 增強　　pine〔paɪn〕*n.* 松樹
> seedling〔'sidlɪŋ〕*n.* 幼苗　　***take hold*** 生根
> ***shade out*** 為…遮陽；為…擋光　　hickory〔'hɪkərɪ〕*n.* 山胡桃樹
> suitable〔'sutəbl〕*adj.* 適合的　　eventually〔ɪ'vɛntʃʊəlɪ〕*adv.* 最後

49. (**C**) 最適合本文的標題是什麼？

　　(A) 雜草和青草的重要

　　(B) 橡樹和山胡桃樹的演替

　　(C) 植物的棲息地如何改變

　　(D) 動物和植物的棲息地

　　title〔'taɪtl〕*n.* 標題

50. (**D**) 從這篇文章中可推知 ＿＿＿＿＿＿ 。

　　(A) 鳥類會妨礙灌木的生長

　　(B) 松樹和青草可以共存

　　(C) 雜草和青草偏好寒冷的氣候

　　(D) 橡樹和山胡桃樹長得比松樹高

　　infer〔ɪn'fɝ〕*v.* 推論　　discourage〔dɪs'kɝɪdʒ〕*v.* 阻礙
　　exist〔ɪg'zɪst〕*v.* 生存

51. (**A**) 何者是本文範例中，正確的植物演替順序？

(A) 雜草，灌木，松樹，橡樹。

(B) 雜草，松樹，灌木，橡樹。

(C) 橡樹，松樹，灌木，雜草。

(D) 灌木，雜草，橡樹，松樹。

order〔'ɔdɚ〕*n.* 順序

52. (**C**) 依照本文的敘述，下列何者是可能的演替的例子？

(A) 砍伐森林來建造機場。

(B) 洪水沖走小麥的收成。

(C) 生長在廢棄停車場的野花。

(D) 小孩飼養的動物。

describe〔dɪ'skraɪb〕*v.* 描述　　***wash away*** 沖走

crop〔krɑp〕*n.* 一次收穫量；收成　　flood〔flʌd〕*n.* 水災；洪水

wheat〔hwit〕*n.* 小麥　　wildflower〔'waɪld,flauɚ〕*n.* 野花

grow〔gro〕*v.* 生長　　unused〔ʌn'juzd〕*adj.* 不用的

parking lot 停車場　　raise〔rez〕*v.* 飼養

第 53 至 56 題為題組

　　Success means many wonderful, positive things. Success means personal prosperity: a big and beautiful home, luxurious vacations, and financial security. Success means winning admiration, leadership, and being respected by people in your business and social life. Success means freedom: freedom from worries, fears, frustrations and failure. Success means self-respect, continually finding more real happiness and satisfaction from life, and being able to do more for those who depend on you.

　　成功意味著許多很棒而且正面的事物。成功代表個人的成就：一個寬敞漂亮的家、豪華的假期，以及財務穩定。成功表示能贏得讚賞、獲得領導地位，並在商場上及社交場合中，受人尊敬。成功代表自由：免於憂慮、恐懼、挫折及失敗的自由。成功表示有自尊心，能不斷地從生活中，找尋真正的快樂及滿足，並且能為依賴你的人做更多的事。

positive〔'pɑzətɪv〕*adj.* 正面的
prosperity（prɑs'pɛrətɪ）*n.* 成功
luxurious（lʌg'ʒʊrɪəs, lʌk'ʃʊrɪəs）*adj.* 豪華的；奢侈的
financial〔fə'nænʃəl〕*adj.* 財務的　　security〔sɪ'kjʊrətɪ〕*n.* 穩定
admiration〔, ædmə'reʃən〕*n.* 讚賞；欽佩
leadership〔'lidɚʃɪp〕*n.* 領導地位　　respect〔rɪ'spɛkt〕*v. n.* 尊敬
social〔'soʃəl〕*adj.* 社交的
freedom〔'fridəm〕*n.* 自由；（精神上）免除…的負擔 *<from>*
worry〔'wɝɪ〕*n.* 煩惱的事　　frustration〔frʌs'treʃən〕*n.* 挫折
self-respect〔, sɛlfrɪ'spɛkt〕*n.* 自尊心
continually（kən'tɪnjʊəlɪ）*adv.* 不斷地
satisfaction〔, sætɪs'fækʃən〕*n.* 滿足（感）　　***depend on*** 依賴

Success—achievement—is the goal of life for every human being.
How can we achieve success? We can win success by believing we can
succeed. Belief, the "I can" attitude, generates the power, skill, and energy
needed to move toward success. When we believe we can do it, the "how
to do it" develops.

　　成功，即成就，是每個人的生活目標。我們要如何才能成功呢？我們可以
藉由相信自己做得到而成功。這種信念，也就是「我可以」的態度，能產生邁
向成功所須具備的力量、技巧，和精力。當我們相信自己做得到時，「該如何做
到」的方法，就會隨之而來。

achievement〔ə'tʃivmənt〕*n.* 成就　　goal〔gol〕*n.* 目標
human being 人；人類　　achieve〔ə'tʃiv〕*v.*（經努力而）獲得
belief〔bɪ'lif〕*n.* 信念　　attitude〔'ætə,tjud〕*n.* 態度
generate〔'dʒɛnə,ret〕*v.* 產生　　***move toward*** 朝…前進；邁向
develop〔dɪ'vɛləp〕*v.* 逐漸產生

Every day, all over the nation, young people start working in new jobs.
Each of them "wishes" that someday he could enjoy the success that goes
with reaching the top. But the majority of these young people simply do
not have the belief that it takes to reach the top rungs. Believing it is

impossible to climb high, they do not discover the steps that lead to great heights. Their behavior remains that of the "average" person. As a result, they do not reach the top.

在全國各地，每天都有年輕人開始做新的工作。每個人都「希望」將來有一天，能夠達到社會地位最上層，享受成功的滋味。但是大部分的年輕人，實在沒有達到社會階層頂端所須具備的信念。因為他們認為，要達到社會階層的頂端，是不可能的事情，所以他們就沒有發現達到高階地位的方法。他們的所作所為仍然和「一般」人一樣。因此，他們就達不到社會階層的頂端。

all over 遍及　　**go with** 伴隨　　reach〔ritʃ〕*v.* 達到
top〔tɑp〕*n.*（階級、地位的）頂端　*adj.* 最高的
majority〔mə'dʒɔrətɪ〕*n.* 大多數　　take〔tek〕*v.* 需要
rung〔rʌŋ〕*n.*（社會的）階層
climb〔klaɪm〕*v.*（在社會地位等方面）往上爬
high〔haɪ〕*adv.* 高　　**climb high** 爬到高處
step〔stɛp〕*n.* 方法；步驟　　**lead to** 通往
heights〔haɪts〕*n.pl.* 高處　　remain〔rɪ'men〕*v.* 仍然是
average〔'ævərɪdʒ〕*adj.* 一般的；普通的　　**as a result** 因此

But a small number of these young people really believe they will succeed. They approach their work with an "I'm going to the top" attitude. And with substantial belief they reach the top. Believing they will succeed—and that it is not impossible—these folks study and observe the behavior of senior executives. They learn how successful people approach problems and make decisions. They observe the attitudes of successful people. The "how to do it" always comes to the person who believes he can do it and such a person will eventually achieve success.

但是這些年輕人當中，有少數人真的相信他們會成功。他們以「我要達到社會階層頂端」的態度面對工作。他們以這種堅定的信念達到頂端。相信自己會成功——而且這並非不可能的事情——這些人會研究並觀察上級主管的行為。他們學到成功的人是如何處理問題，以及做決定。他們觀察成功者的態度。相信自己能辦到的人，就知道「該如何做到」，而且這種人最後都會成功。

a small number of 少數的　　approach〔ə'protʃ〕*v.* 處理（問題）
substantial〔səb'stænʃəl〕*adj.* 堅固的
folks〔foks〕*n.pl.* 人們　　observe〔əb'zɝv〕*v.* 觀察
senior〔'sinjɚ〕*adj.* 資深的；上級的
executive〔ɪg'zɛkjutɪv〕*n.* 管理者；主管
achieve success 成功

53. (**B**) 本文的主旨爲何？
　　(A) 成功的定義。
　　(B) 成功的秘訣。
　　(C) 成功的好處。
　　(D) 在人生當中，要成功達到社會階層頂端的方法。
　　definition〔‚dɛfə'nɪʃən〕*n.* 定義
　　key〔ki〕*n.* 秘訣 *< to >*　　benefit〔'bɛnəfɪt〕*n.* 利益

54. (**D**) 在本文對於成功的定義中，並未提到哪個部份？
　　(A) 擁有足夠的金錢。
　　(B) 贏得他人的尊敬。
　　(C) 感到滿足與快樂。
　　(D) 認識重要人士。
　　sufficient〔sə'fɪʃənt〕*adj.* 足夠的

55. (**A**) 根據本文，我們會從何處獲得成功所需的力量及能力？
　　(A) 對自己有信心。
　　(B) 強烈希望自己能成功。
　　(C) 成功者的態度。
　　(D) 自尊心及別人的欽佩。
　　strength〔strɛŋθ〕*n.* 力量　　obtain〔əb'ten〕*v.* 獲得
　　confidence〔'kɑnfədəns〕*n.* 信心 *< in >*

56. (**C**) 根據本文，有些人在一生中都沒有達到社會階層頂端，是因為他們沒有 —————。

(A) 爬到高處的能力

(B) 具備做某事的實用知識

(C) <u>正確的態度和信念</u>

(D) 知道如何處理問題

know-how ('no,hau) *n.* 實用知識；要訣

第貳部分：非選擇題

一、英文翻譯：

1. 自助旅行是很值得的，因為它能帶給人們成就感和較大的自由。

Independent travel is rewarding as it gives people a sense of achievement and greater freedom.

2. 儘管如此，也是需要有相當多的準備來規劃自己的行程。

Nevertheless, it also takes lots of preparation to plan one's own trip.

二、英文作文：(作文範例)

The Most Unforgettable Experience I Have Shared with My Family

The most unforgettable experience I have shared with my family came during the massive flooding caused by Typhoon Nari a few years ago. Our family was living happily in Mucha just by the mountains. *However*, the typhoon changed everything for us.

On the night of the typhoon, we did not think that it would cause us any harm because we had never had any problems before. About four hours after we went to bed, our house started to flood. We all got up and tried to block the water, but the water level rose too quickly. Then some firemen came into our house and evacuated us all. As we pulled away in the life raft our eyes swelled with tears as we watch our home slowly disappearing into the muddy flood water. We returned home the next afternoon and there were no salvageable items left in the house. We had lost everything in a single night. Mom comforted us by telling us that we were getting a fresh start since we would have to repurchase everything. She promised us that it would be a fun experience.

This flood did indeed impact our lives greatly. *However*, we learned that no matter what happens in the future, our family will always support each other and we will always pick ourselves up and keep going.

unforgettable〔͵ʌnfɚˋgɛtəbḷ〕*adj.* 難忘的
share〔ʃɛr〕*v.* 分享；共同擁有　　massive〔ˋmæsɪv〕*adj.* 大規模的
flooding〔ˋflʌdɪŋ〕*n.* 水災　　*cause sb. harm* 對某人造成傷害
flood〔flʌd〕*v.* 氾濫；淹水　　block〔blɑk〕*v.* 阻擋
level〔ˋlɛvḷ〕*n.* 水平面　　rise〔raɪz〕*v.* 上升
fireman〔ˋfaɪrmən〕*n.* 消防隊員　　evacuate〔ɪˋvækjʊ͵et〕*v.* 疏散
pull away （船）駛離　　*life raft* 救生筏
swell〔swɛl〕*v.* 充滿<*with*>　　tear〔tɪr〕*n.* 眼淚
disappear〔͵dɪsəˋpɪr〕*v.* 消失　　muddy〔ˋmʌdɪ〕*adj.* 泥濘的
salvageable〔ˋsælvədʒəbḷ〕*adj.* 可搶救的
item〔ˋaɪtəm〕*n.* 物品　　single〔ˋsɪŋgḷ〕*adj.* 單一的
comfort〔ˋkʌmfɚt〕*v.* 安慰　　fresh〔frɛʃ〕*adj.* 新的
repurchase〔riˋpɝtʃəs〕*v.* 再購買　　promise〔ˋprɑmɪs〕*v.* 保證
impact〔ɪmˋpækt〕*v.* 影響　　fun〔fʌn〕*adj.* 有趣的
indeed〔ɪnˋdid〕*adv.* 的確　　*pick oneself up* 使自己振作

大學入學指定科目考試英文模擬試題 ②

第壹部份：選擇題（佔72分）

一、詞彙與慣用語（15％）

說明： 第1至15題，每題選出一個最適當的選項，標示在答案卡之「選擇題答案區」。每題答對得1分，答錯或劃記多於一個選項者倒扣1/3分，倒扣到本大題之實得分數為零為止，未作答者，不給分亦不扣分。

1. Inspired by the _____ sights of the Grand Canyon, people have sought to capture them in panoramic photographs.
   (A) delicate
   (B) turbulent
   (C) reliable
   (D) spectacular

2. Joseph's employees were _____ by the impolite manner in which he dealt with them.
   (A) irritated
   (B) weakened
   (C) pleased
   (D) encouraged

3. Ozone in the upper layers of Earth's _____ is beneficial, protecting animal and plant life from dangerous ultraviolet radiation.
   (A) atmosphere
   (B) extension
   (C) analysis
   (D) completion

4. So _____ was the saleswoman's pitch about the value of the used car that Helen nearly missed the error in its logic.
   (A) suspicious
   (B) convincing
   (C) sarcastic
   (D) relieving

5. Doing much more than was expected of her, Jenny _____ the responsibilities of a department supervisor's position before she finally received the title.
   (A) undertook
   (B) underestimated
   (C) participated
   (D) undermined

6. The two runners crossed the finish line _____; they got the same prize.
   (A) occasionally (B) frequently
   (C) temporarily (D) simultaneously

7. After inventing a sign language for the deaf in the mid-1700s, Giacobbo Pereira _____ his business activities in order to devote himself to social work.
   (A) abused (B) accelerated
   (C) abandoned (D) allocated

8. An animal center in New York studies highly _____ animal diseases like foot-and-mouth disease and African swine fever.
   (A) precious (B) cautious (C) absurd (D) infectious

9. College admissions officers use high school grades as one important _____ in predicting a student's success in college.
   (A) experiment (B) miracle (C) factor (D) subject

10. With constant changes in the government, it was only possible to _____ about what would happen in the future.
    (A) speculate (B) haunt (C) sustain (D) meditate

11. A brief outline of the course and bibliography were _____ to the students at the first meeting.
    (A) filled in (B) put out
    (C) handed out (D) knocked off

12. I am so excited about going out tonight. I hope you are not going to _____ my plans by saying you can't go.
    (A) do justice to (B) wear down
    (C) look forward to (D) throw cold water on

13. Although it's warm today, I think you should take a sweater, just to _____.
    (A) be on the safe side   (B) stay in touch
    (C) hit the roof   (D) break the news

14. Kevin is an excellent tour guide because he knows all the _____ of the itinerary.
    (A) odds and ends   (B) ins and outs
    (C) pins and needles   (D) p's and q's

15. A: What do you usually do on weekends, Fred?
    B: _____ I stay at home, but next weekend I'm going to Kaohsiung with a friend.
    (A) As a rule   (B) By all means
    (C) Once in a blue moon   (D) As a result

二、綜合測驗（15％）

說明： 第 16 至 30 題，每題一個空格。請依文意選出一個最適當的選項，標示在答案卡之「選擇題答案區」。每題答對得 1 分，答錯或劃記多於一個選項者倒扣 1/3 分，倒扣到本大題之實得分數為零為止。未作答者，不給分亦不扣分。

第 16 至 20 題為題組

From both a medical and a psychological standpoint, alcohol abuse is one of the greatest social problems in the United States. Between 30 and 40 percent of the homeless are people ___16___ alcohol problems. Drunkenness is the biggest law enforcement problem today, accounting for millions of arrests each year. The Department of Transportation has estimated that alcohol is involved in more than 39,000 automobile deaths each year. Although the number of deaths ___17___ by alcohol-related accidents has decreased in the last few years, the number in the next three years might still exceed the American death toll of the Vietnam War. ___18___, people who have committed violent crimes and suicide are often found to have been drinking.

Although alcoholism is seen as a social disease because of its devastating social consequences, it is also a medical problem. Biomedical researchers look for the effects of alcohol ___19___ the brain, as well as anything about the brains and basic genetics of alcoholics that may predispose them to alcoholism. Researchers know that chronic excessive drinking is ___20___ with loss of brain tissue, liver malfunction and impaired cognitive and motor abilities.

16. (A) who has   (B) have   (C) with   (D) had
17. (A) is caused   (B) caused   (C) cause   (D) causing
18. (A) Yet   (B) Therefore   (C) Despite   (D) In addition
19. (A) on   (B) of   (C) at   (D) in
20. (A) acquainted   (B) armed   (C) associated   (D) faced

第 21 至 25 題為題組

From the philosopher's point of view, wisdom and knowledge are two different things. One may know countless facts without being a lover of wisdom. The philosopher is not satisfied with a mere combination of facts. ___21___, he seeks to interrelate and interpret the facts in order to discern the subtle meaning and deeper sense that lie ___22___ the seemingly obvious facts. Philosophers assume that each person is born with an ___23___ love of wisdom. Deep inside his heart, each person seeks to penetrate the mysteries of life, thereby ___24___ the potential to become a philosopher. Hence, every human being, ___25___ the extent that he is a lover of wisdom, possesses a philosophy of life.

21. (A) Nevertheless   (B) Rather   (C) Still   (D) Likewise
22. (A) against   (B) ahead   (C) before   (D) beyond
23. (A) inherent   (B) anonymous   (C) ethnic   (D) outrageous
24. (A) has   (B) which has   (C) have   (D) having
25. (A) in   (B) with   (C) to   (D) for

第 26 至 30 題為題組

The 50-million-year-old fossils of an ancient whale ___26___ in the Himalayan foothills give strong evidence that modern whales are descended ___27___ a four-legged, land-dwelling animal. The fossils consist of part of the skull, some teeth and the well-preserved middle ear of an animal that was 6 to 8 feet long, and ___28___ a wolflike snout and jaws with sharp, triangular teeth. Analysis indicated that the animal had eardrums, ___29___ do not work in water. Moreover, the right and left ears were not isolated from each other. The separation of these bones in modern marine whales ___30___ them to detect the direction of underwater sounds.

26. (A) was found   (B) finding
     (C) which were found   (D) that found
27. (A) in   (B) from   (C) after   (D) over
28. (A) was   (B) were   (C) had   (D) have
29. (A) what   (B) which   (C) with that   (D) where it
30. (A) makes   (B) enables   (C) prohibits   (D) prevents

三、文意選填（10％）

說明： 第 31 至 40 題，每題一個空格。請依文意在文章後所提供的 (A) 到 (J)
選項中分別選出最適當者，並將其字母代號標示在答案卡之「選擇題
答案區」。每題答對得 1 分，答錯或劃記多於一個選項者倒扣 1/9 分，
倒扣到本大題之實得分數爲零爲止。未作答者，不給分亦不扣分。

第 31 至 40 題爲題組

Sun City, South Africa, Disney World and Sentosa Island are
examples of artificial, all-purpose holiday resorts. These "tourism
ghettoes," ___31___ they are referred to by some travelers, separate
tourists from the real world and ___32___ provide a carefully-planned
package of pleasures. However much they are ridiculed and avoided
by those ___33___ for a cultural experience, they have proved their
worth to those who are concerned with the environmental ___34___ of
the planet.

Sun City, for example, was built on ___35___ had been useless
scrubland, but now provides a place for endangered or elusive wildlife.
Unlike some other resorts, such as beach resorts which have destroyed
the beauty of the area and coastal villages not ___36___ for a large influx
of people, Sun City is carefully planned to accommodate large ___37___
of tourists. An artificial resort can gather into one compact area the
best that the host country ___38___ to offer. Artificial lakes can ___39___
birds which would not normally be seen. Trees can be planted to provide
homes for animals and insects and even species which have been
___40___ in the wild can be reintroduced.

(A) wiped out	(B) has	(C) what	(D) numbers
(E) designed	(F) attract	(G) instead	(H) looking
(I) as	(J) well-being		

四、篇章結構（10%）

說明： 第 41 至 45 題，每題一個空格。請依文意在文章後所提供的 (A) 到 (E)
選項中分別選出最適當者，填入空格中，使篇章結構清晰有條理，並將
其英文字母代號標示在答案卡之「選擇題答案區」。每題答對得 2 分，
答錯或劃記多於一個選項者倒扣 1/2 分，倒扣到本大題之實得分數為零
為止。未作答者，不給分亦不扣分。

第 41 至 45 題為題組

There is no doubt that the phenomenon of road rage exists. ___41___
Road rage seems to be on the increase and this may be due to the
following factors. First, there are more cars competing for road space.
___42___ A person who must meet a deadline, but is caught in a tangle
of traffic, may feel increasingly frustrated. ___43___ Nowadays a
person may be bombarded with more concerns and worries than before
and forget how to be polite. Since cars are becoming a necessity,
drivers should consider a plan of action against road rage. ___44___
The drivers must know an attack of road rage will not get them any
farther but could result in a serious health problem. ___45___ This
could give drivers twenty or thirty minutes leeway.

(A) Another factor may be that people are not as courteous as they
used to be.

(B) A change in mental attitude is the first step.

(C) People also are far more subject to time constraints.

(D) In a recent survey, nine out of ten drivers admit to having felt intense
anger toward other drivers at some time.

(E) One could leave home earlier or make arrangements with the boss
to arrive between two fixed times.

五、閱讀測驗（22 %）

說明： 第 46 至 56 題，每題請分別根據各篇文章的文意選出一個最適當的選
項，標示在答案卡之「選擇題答案區」。每題答對得 2 分，答錯或劃
記多於一個選項者倒扣 2/3 分，倒扣到本大題之實得分數爲零爲止。
未作答者，不給分亦不扣分。

第 46 至 48 題爲題組

In September 1797, three hunters captured a boy about twelve years
of age in the Caune Woods in France. The people in Paris were greatly
interested in this boy, who had apparently lived most of his life without
human companionship. Some people imagined they would see man in his
most natural and noble state. Others expected to hear the boy speak the
original "unlearned" language of man, which they supposed would most
likely be Hebrew. What they saw, however, was a dirty creature who
scratched and bit, jumped about, and made noises like an animal. Dr.
Pinel, who specialized in treating mental disorders examined the boy and
announced that he was an idiot and would not likely be helped by any
kind of training.

Jean-Marc-Gaspard Itard, a young doctor, was convinced, however,
that the boy could be helped, since he believed that his low intelligence
was caused by his solitary life in the woods from about the age of seven
and by his ignorance of language. Itard took the boy and worked with him
for five years. Victor, as Itard called him, did not learn to speak French,
but he was able to understand a large number of written words and phrases.
He would obey simple written commands and could use word cards to
show his desires. He also acquired the manners and appearance of a
civilized young man. Victor had obviously been helped by education, but
Itard finally concluded that Victor could not be further improved because
his intelligence was subnormal.

46. Itard apparently believed at first that Victor had not learned a language because he _____.
    (A) had grown up away from human society
    (B) preferred to make human noises
    (C) disliked human companionship
    (D) possessed a low degree of intelligence

47. After seeing the boy, Pinel thought that education would _____.
    (A) raise Victor's intellectual capacity
    (B) ruin Victor's primitive character
    (C) help Victor adjust to human society
    (D) improve Victor very little

48. Itard was finally convinced that Victor _____.
    (A) could be taught to speak in time
    (B) was below average in intelligence
    (C) could never adjust to human companionship
    (D) was really a primitive man

第 49 至 52 題爲題組

　　Deep inside a mountain near Sweetwater in eastern Tennessee is a body of water known as the Lost Sea. It is listed by the Guinness Book of World Records as the world's largest underground lake. The Lost Sea is part of an extensive and historical cave system called Craighead Caverns.

　　The caverns have been known and used since the days of the Cherokee Indian nation. The cave expands into a series of huge rooms from a small opening on the side of the mountain. Approximately one mile from the entrance, in a room called "The Council Room," many Indian artifacts have been found. Some of the items discovered include pottery, arrowheads, weapons, and jewelry.

For many years there were persistent rumors of a large underground lake somewhere in the cave, but it was not discovered until 1905. In that year, a thirteen-year-old boy named Ben Sands crawled through a small opening three hundred feet underground. He found himself in a large cave half filled with water.

Today tourists visit the Lost Sea and ride far out onto it in glass-bottomed boats powered by electric motors. More than thirteen acres of water have been mapped out so far and still no end to the lake has been found. Even though teams of divers have tried to explore the Lost Sea, the full extent of it is still unknown.

49. According to the passage, the Lost Sea is unique because it is _____.
    (A) part of a historical cave system
    (B) listed in the Guinness Book of World Records
    (C) the biggest underground lake in the world
    (D) the largest body of water in Tennessee

50. How can the caverns be entered, based on the passage?
    (A) Through an opening in a mountainside.
    (B) By diving into the water.
    (C) By riding far out onto the lake.
    (D) From "The Council Room."

51. What was found in "The Council Room?"
    (A) A small natural opening.   (B) A large cave.
    (C) Another series of rooms.   (D) Many old Indian objects.

52. According to the passage, the area of the Lost Sea that has been explored is approximately _____.
    (A) 300 feet   (B) 1,900 feet
    (C) 1 mile   (D) 13 acres

第 53 至 56 題為題組

Geologists have long known about Japan's vulnerability to the rumbling earth. Back in 1978 the Japanese government enacted a law to ensure that the nation took steps to watch for impending earthquakes; by the end of 1994, it had spent more than $1.3 billion on monitoring programs. Yet in the early morning hours of Jan. 17, 1995, when the Great Hanshin-Awaji Earthquake came rumbling along at 7.2 on the Richter scale, it thoroughly surprised the port town of Kobe. The quake flipped the elevated Hanshin Expressway onto its side like a child's discarded slot-car track, and caused skyscrapers to collapse and gas fires to break out among the city's wooden houses. More than 6,400 people were killed and 43,000 injured. "Earthquake prediction research betrayed the public," snapped an editorial in Asahi Shimbun.

The Kobe earthquake forced both the Japanese government and researchers to take stock. In the past few years, Japanese scientists have been trying to find out why they failed in predicting the Kobe and other earthquakes that have hit Japan over the years. Now that effort is paying off. In a recent issue of the journal Science, Jin-Oh Park and his colleagues at the Japan Marine Science and Technology Center in Yokosuka, near Tokyo, uncovered a major cause of the most unpredictable earthquakes. It was a "splay" fault, a secondary fault that branches off a main one and can cause damage hundreds of kilometers from obvious trouble spots. This was the first time scientists had confirmed the existence of a splay fault. By shedding light on the vexing phenomenon, experts think they may be able eventually to predict many types of earthquakes that have tricked geologists in the past. "This brings us a step closer to knowing about earthquake mechanism, and could lead to a better chance of prediction," says Shozo Harada, a Diet member, who has helped draft anti-quake laws.

53. According to the passage, which of the following is not mentioned?
    (A) Gas fires broke out in Kobe.
    (B) The Japanese government was forced to shut down the stock market.
    (C) Skyscrapers collapsed.
    (D) More than 6,400 people were killed.

54. Which of the following statements is TRUE according to this passage?
    (A) The Kobe earthquake caused children to discard their slot-car tracks.
    (B) The Kobe earthquake took Japanese geologists by surprise.
    (C) After the Kobe earthquake, the Japanese government enacted a law to ensure that the nation took steps to watch for quakes.
    (D) By Jan. 17,1995, the Japanese government had spent more than $1.3 billion on monitoring programs.

55. Who helped draft anti-quake laws based on this passage?
    (A) An editorial in Asahi Shimbun.
    (B) Japanese geologists.
    (C) Shozo Harada.
    (D) Jin-Oh Park.

56. Which of the following is NOT true according to the passage?
    (A) Japanese scientists think it impossible to eventually predict many types of quakes.
    (B) Japanese scientists admit that they failed in predicting the Kobe earthquake.
    (C) Japanese scientists have uncovered a major cause of the most unpredictable quakes.
    (D) Japanese scientists have confirmed the existence of a splay fault.

第貳部份：非選擇題（佔 28 分）

一、英文翻譯（8%）

說明： 1. 將下列兩句中文翻譯成適當之英文，並將答案寫在「答案卷」上。

　　　 2. 未按題意翻譯者，不予計分。

1. 他的朋友一看到他贏得樂透彩，就開始嫉妒他。

2. 直到發生了致命的車禍，人們才會去注意交通規則。

二、英文作文（20%）

說明： 1. 依提示在「答案卷」上寫一篇英文道歉信。

　　　 2. 文長至少 120 個單詞。

提示： 文章請以 Dear Mom,（或 Dear Dad,）

　　　　I am sorry that I……開始，敘述你過去所犯的一個嚴重錯誤並詳述其原因。同時告訴你父母親你要如何彌補這個過錯。信末請署名 Wendy Wang（或 David Wang）。

【劉毅老師的話】

　　無論是「學測」或「指考」，英文作文都是必考題型，所以平時有機會，就要多練習寫，最好養成寫英文日記的習慣，寫完之後，請外籍老師校稿，更正錯誤，才能進步。

❄ 大學入學指定科目考試英文模擬試題②詳解 ❄

第壹部分：單一選擇題

一、詞彙及慣用語：

1. (**D**) Inspired by the <u>spectacular</u> sights of the Grand Canyon, people have sought to capture them in panoramic photographs.
   人們受到大峽谷<u>壯麗</u>景觀的啟發，一直試圖以全景照片把它們保存下來。
   (A) delicate（ˈdɛləkət, -kɪt）*adj.* 精巧的
   (B) turbulent（ˈtɝbjələnt）*adj.*（風、波浪等）狂烈的
   (C) reliable（rɪˈlaɪəbl̩）*adj.* 可靠的
   (D) ***spectacular***（spɛkˈtækjələ）*adj.* 壯麗的
   inspire（ɪnˈspaɪr）*v.* 激勵；給予靈感　　***Grand Canyon*** 大峽谷
   seek（sik）*v.* 試圖　　　capture（ˈkæptʃə）*v.*（用照片等）保存
   panoramic（ˌpænəˈræmɪk）*adj.* 全景的
   photograph（ˈfotəˌgræf）*n.* 照片

2. (**A**) Joseph's employees were <u>irritated</u> by the impolite manner in which he dealt with them.
   約瑟夫的員工<u>很生氣</u>，因為他用無禮的態度對待他們。
   (A) ***irritate***（ˈɪrəˌtet）*v.* 激怒；使生氣
   (B) weaken（ˈwikən）*v.* 使虛弱
   (C) please（pliz）*v.* 取悅
   (D) encourage（ɪnˈkɝɪdʒ）*v.* 鼓勵
   employee（ˌɛmplɔɪˈi）*n.* 員工　　impolite（ˌɪmpəˈlaɪt）*adj.* 無禮的
   manner（ˈmænə）*n.* 態度　　***deal with*** 對待

3. (**A**) Ozone in the upper layers of Earth's <u>atmosphere</u> is beneficial, protecting animal and plant life from dangerous ultraviolet radiation. 地球<u>大氣層</u>上層的臭氧是有益的，能夠保護動植物，免於遭受危險的紫外線輻射的傷害。

(A) *atmosphere* (ˈætməsˌfɪr) *n.* 大氣層

(B) extension (ɪkˈstɛnʃən) *n.* 延伸；(電話) 分機

(C) analysis (əˈnæləsɪs) *n.* 分析

(D) completion (kəmˈpliʃən) *n.* 完成

ozone (ˈozon) *n.* 臭氧　　upper (ˈʌpɚ) *adj.* 上面的

layer (ˈleɚ) *n.* 層　　beneficial (ˌbɛnəˈfɪʃəl) *adj.* 有益的

ultraviolet (ˌʌltrəˈvaɪəlɪt) *adj.* 紫外線的

radiation (ˌredɪˈeʃən) *n.* 輻射

4. (**B**) So <u>convincing</u> was the saleswoman's pitch about the value of the used car that Helen nearly missed the error in its logic.

這位女售貨員推銷那部二手車有多好的說辭太<u>有說服力</u>了，讓海倫幾乎沒聽出其邏輯上的錯誤。

(A) suspicious (səˈspɪʃəs) *adj.* 可疑的

(B) *convincing* (kənˈvɪnsɪŋ) *adj.* 有說服力的

(C) sarcastic (sɑrˈkæstɪk) *adj.* 諷刺的

(D) relieving (rɪˈlivɪŋ) *adj.* 令人放心的

pitch (pɪtʃ) *n.* 推銷商品的言辭　　value (ˈvælju) *n.* 價值

used car 二手車　　miss (mɪs) *v.* 沒聽到；沒看到

error (ˈɛrɚ) *n.* 錯誤　　logic (ˈlɑdʒɪk) *n.* 邏輯

5. (**A**) Doing much more than was expected of her, Jenny <u>undertook</u> the responsibilities of a department supervisor's position before she finally received the title.

珍妮做的事情比別人要求她的還要更多，在她最後終於擁有部門主管的頭銜之前，她就<u>承擔</u>部門主管的責任。

(A) *undertake* (ˌʌndɚˈtek) *v.* 承擔

(B) underestimate (ˈʌndɚˈɛstəˌmet) *v.* 低估

(C) participate (pɑrˈtɪsəˌpet) *v.* 參加 < *in* >

(D) undermine (ˌʌndɚˈmaɪn) *v.* 損害

expect (ɪkˈspɛkt) *v.* 指望；要求

responsibility (rɪˌspɑnsəˈbɪlətɪ) *n.* 責任

department (dɪˈpɑrtmənt) *n.* 部門

supervisor (ˌsjupɚˈvaɪzɚ) *n.* 主管　　position (pəˈzɪʃən) *n.* 職位

receive (rɪˈsiv) *v.* 得到　　title (ˈtaɪtḷ) *n.* 頭銜

6. (**D**) The two runners crossed the finish line <u>simultaneously</u>; they got
　　　 the same prize.
　　　 這兩位跑者同時越過終點線；他們獲得同一個獎項。

　　　 (A) occasionally〔əˈkeʒənlɪ〕*adv.* 偶爾

　　　 (B) frequently〔ˈfrikwəntlɪ〕*adv.* 經常

　　　 (C) temporarily〔ˈtɛmpə͵rɛrəlɪ〕*adv.* 暫時地

　　　 (D) *simultaneously*〔͵saɪml̩ˈtenɪəslɪ〕*adv.* 同時地

　　　 finish line （賽跑等的）終點線　　 prize〔praɪz〕*n.* 獎

7. (**C**) After inventing a sign language for the deaf in the mid-1700s,
　　　 Giacobbo Pereira <u>abandoned</u> his business activities in order to
　　　 devote himself to social work.
　　　 賈可伯・裴瑞拉在十八世紀中期爲聾人發明手語後，爲了致力於
　　　 社會福利的工作，而放棄生意。

　　　 (A) abuse〔əˈbjuz〕*v.* 濫用

　　　 (B) accelerate〔ækˈsɛlə͵ret〕*v.* 加速

　　　 (C) *abandon*〔əˈbændən〕*v.* 放棄

　　　 (D) allocate〔ˈælə͵ket〕*v.* 分配

　　　 invent〔ɪnˈvɛnt〕*v.* 發明　　 *sign language* 手語
　　　 the deaf 聾人　　 *in the mid-1700s* 在十八世紀中期
　　　 devote oneself *to* 致力於　　 *social work* 社會福利工作

8. (**D**) An animal center in New York studies highly <u>infectious</u> animal
　　　 diseases like foot-and-mouth disease and African swine fever.
　　　 位於紐約的一家動物中心，研究具高度傳染性的動物疾病，像是
　　　 口蹄疫和非洲豬瘟。

　　　 (A) precious〔ˈprɛʃəs〕*adj.* 珍貴的

　　　 (B) cautious〔ˈkɔʃəs〕*adj.* 小心謹愼的

　　　 (C) absurd〔əbˈsɝd〕*adj.* 荒謬的

　　　 (D) *infectious*〔ɪnˈfɛkʃəs〕*adj.* 傳染性的

　　　 highly〔ˈhaɪlɪ〕*adv.* 高度地；非常
　　　 foot-and-mouth disease 口蹄疫　　 swine〔swaɪn〕*n.* 豬
　　　 fever〔ˈfivɚ〕*n.* 熱病　　 *swine fever* 豬瘟

9. (**C**) College admissions officers use high school grades as one
important <u>factor</u> in predicting a student's success in college.
負責大學入學的招生人員，把高中成績當作是預測學生未來大
學成就的一個重要<u>因素</u>。

(A) experiment (ɪkˋspɛrəmənt) *n.* 實驗
(B) miracle (ˋmɪrəkḷ) *n.* 奇蹟
(C) *factor* (ˋfæktɚ) *n.* 因素　　(D) subject (ˋsʌbdʒɪkt) *n.* 科目
admissions (ədˋmɪʃənz) *adj.* 招生的；入學的
officer (ˋɔfəsɚ) *n.* 高級職員　　grade (gred) *n.* 成績
predict (prɪˋdɪkt) *v.* 預測

10. (**A**) With constant changes in the government, it was only possible
to <u>speculate</u> about what would happen in the future.
由於政府經常有變動，所以只能<u>推測</u>未來會有什麼變化。

(A) *speculate* (ˋspɛkjəˌlet) *v.* 推測
(B) haunt (hɔnt) *v.* 經常去（某地）；（鬼魂等）常出沒於
(C) sustain (səˋsten) *v.* 維持　　(D) meditate (ˋmɛdəˌtet) *v.* 沉思
constant (ˋkɑnstənt) *adj.* 不斷的；經常的
government (ˋgʌvɚnmənt) *n.* 政府

11. (**C**) A brief outline of the course and bibliography were <u>handed out</u>
to the students at the first meeting.
第一次見面，就<u>發給</u>學生課程及參考書目的簡短概要。

(A) fill in　填寫　　　　　　(B) put out　熄滅
(C) *hand out*　發放　　　　 (D) knock off　撞倒
brief (brif) *adj.* 簡短的　　outline (ˋautˌlaɪn) *n.* 概要；要點
course (kors) *n.* 課程　　bibliography (ˌbɪblɪˋɑgrəfɪ) *n.* 參考書目
meeting (ˋmitɪŋ) *n.* 會面

12. (**D**) I am so excited about going out tonight. I hope you are not going
to <u>throw cold water on</u> my plans by saying you can't go.
今晚要出去我很興奮。我希望你不要<u>潑我冷水</u>，說你不能去。

(A) do justice to　公平對待　　(B) wear down　削弱
(C) look forward to　期待　　　(D) *throw cold water on*　潑…冷水

13. (**A**) Although it's warm today, I think you should take a sweater, just to be on the safe side.

今天天氣雖然很暖和，我想你還是應該帶件毛衣，以防萬一。

　　(A) *be on the safe side* 為保險起見；以防萬一
　　(B) stay in touch 保持聯絡 (= *keep in touch*)
　　(C) hit the roof 勃然大怒 (= *hit the ceiling*)
　　(D) break the news to *sb.* 把壞消息告訴某人

14. (**B**) Kevin is an excellent tour guide because he knows all the ins and outs of the itinerary.

凱文是一位很棒的導遊，因為他知道行程所有的細節。

　　(A) odds and ends 零星物品
　　(B) *ins and outs* 詳情；細節
　　(C) on pins and needles 如坐針氈般地；焦躁不安地
　　(D) mind *one's* p's and q's 謹慎行事

excellent〔'ɛkslənt〕*adj.* 優秀的
tour guide 導遊　　itinerary〔aɪ'tɪnə,rɛrɪ〕*n.* 行程

15. (**A**) A : What do you usually do on weekends, Fred?
　　　 B : As a rule I stay at home, but next weekend I'm going to Kaohsiung with a friend.

　　　 A：佛瑞德，你在週末通常都做些什麼？
　　　 B：我通常會待在家裡，但下個週末我要和朋友去高雄。

　　(A) *as a rule* 通常　　　　(B) by all means 當然 (= *of course*)
　　(C) once in a blue moon 極少；極罕有地
　　(D) as a result 因此

二、綜合測驗：

第 16 至 20 題為題組

　　From both a medical and a psychological standpoint, alcohol abuse is one of the greatest social problems in the United States. Between 30 and 40 percent of the homeless are people with alcohol problems. Drunkenness

16

is the biggest law enforcement problem today, accounting for millions of arrests each year.

　　從醫療和心理的觀點來看，酗酒都是美國最嚴重的社會問題之一。有百分之三十到四十的遊民，都是有酗酒問題的人。酒醉是現今執法上最大的問題，每年有數百萬人因此被逮捕。

> medical〔'mɛdɪkḷ〕*adj.* 醫療的
> psychological〔,saɪkə'lɑdʒɪkḷ〕*adj.* 心理的
> standpoint〔'stænd,pɔɪnt〕*n.* 立場；觀點
> alcohol〔'ælkə,hɔl〕*n.* 酒　　abuse〔ə'bjus〕*n.* 濫用
> ***alcohol abuse*** 酗酒　　homeless〔'homlɪs〕*adj.* 無家可歸的
> ***the homeless*** 流浪漢；遊民
> drunkenness〔'drʌŋkənnɪs〕*n.* 酒醉
> enforcement〔ɪn'forsmənt〕*n.* （法律等的）執行
> ***account for*** 說明；成為～的原因　　arrest〔ə'rɛst〕*n.* 逮捕

16. (**C**) 表示「有～」，可用 ***with***、who have 或 having，故選 (C)。

The Department of Transportation has estimated that alcohol is involved in more than 39,000 automobile deaths each year. Although the number of deaths <u>caused</u> by alcohol-related accidents has decreased in the last few
　　　　　17
years, the number in the next three years might still exceed the American death toll of the Vietnam War. <u>In addition</u>, people who have committed
　　　　　　　　　　　　　　　　　18
violent crimes and suicide are often found to have been drinking.

交通部估計，每年有超過三萬九千人在車禍中死亡，都與喝酒有關。雖然在最近幾年來，與喝酒有關的車禍死亡人數已經減少，但未來三年中的人數，可能仍然會超過美國在越戰中的死亡人數。此外，暴力犯罪和自殺的人，也常被發現有喝酒的情況。

> department〔dɪ'pɑrtmənt〕*n.* 部門
> transportation〔,trænspɚ'teʃən〕*n.* 交通；運輸
> estimate〔'ɛstə,met〕*v.* 估計　　involve〔ɪn'vɑlv〕*v.* 包含；牽涉在內
> alcohol-related〔'ælkə,hɔl rɪ'letɪd〕*adj.* 與喝酒有關的
> exceed〔ɪk'sid〕*v.* 超過　　toll〔tol〕*n.* 死傷人數
> ***the Vietnam War*** 越戰　　commit〔kə'mɪt〕*v.* 犯（罪）
> violent〔'vaɪələnt〕*adj.* 暴力的　　suicide〔'suə,saɪd〕*n.* 自殺
> drink〔drɪŋk〕*v.* 喝酒

17. (**B**) 空格中原為 which are caused by…，省略 which are 而成分詞片語，
　　　選 (B) *caused*。

18. (**D**) 依句意，選 (D) *In addition*「此外」。(A) 然而，(B) 因此，(C) 儘管，
　　　均不合句意。

　　　Although alcoholism is seen as a social disease because of its
devastating social consequences, it is also a medical problem.　Biomedical
researchers look for the effects of alcohol <u>on</u> the brain, as well as anything
　　　　　　　　　　　　　　　　　　　　　　19
about the brains and basic genetics of alcoholics that may predispose them
to alcoholism.　Researchers know that chronic excessive drinking is
<u>associated</u> with loss of brain tissue, liver malfunction and impaired
　20
cognitive and motor abilities.

　　　雖然酗酒被視為是一種社會疾病，因為它對整個社會有毀滅性的影響，但
它也是一個醫療上的問題。生物醫療的研究人員，正在研究酒精對大腦、以及
任何與大腦相關部位的影響，還有酗酒者是否有一些基本的遺傳因子，可能使
他們有酗酒的傾向。研究人員現在已經知道，長期、過量地飲酒，與腦部組織
流失、肝功能失常、認知及運動能力受損，都有關係。

　　　　alcoholism〔'ælkəhɔl,ɪzəm〕*n.* 酗酒；酒精中毒
　　　　be seen as 被視為　　devastating〔'dɛvəs,tetɪŋ〕*adj.* 毀滅性的
　　　　consequence〔'kɑnsə,kwɛns〕*n.* 後果；影響
　　　　biomedical〔,baɪə'mɛdɪkḷ〕*adj.* 生物醫療的
　　　　researcher〔rɪ'sɝtʃɚ〕*n.* 研究人員　　effect〔ɪ'fɛkt〕*n.* 影響
　　　　as well as 以及　　genetics〔dʒə'nɛtɪks〕*n.* 遺傳性；遺傳現象
　　　　alcoholic〔,ælkə'hɔlɪk〕*n.* 酗酒者
　　　　predispose〔,prɪdɪs'poz〕*v.* 使~傾向於 < *to* >
　　　　chronic〔'krɑnɪk〕*adj.* 慢性的；長期的
　　　　excessive〔ɪk'sɛsɪv〕*adj.* 過度的
　　　　tissue〔'tɪʃu〕*n.* 組織　　liver〔'lɪvɚ〕*n.* 肝臟
　　　　malfunction〔mæl'fʌŋkʃən〕*n.* 故障；機能失常
　　　　impair〔ɪm'pɛr〕*v.* 損害　　cognitive〔'kɑgnətɪv〕*adj.* 認知的
　　　　motor〔'motɚ〕*adj.* 運動的

19. (**A**) 表示「對~的影響」，介系詞要用 *on*，故選 (A)。

20. (**C**)　(A) be acquainted with　認識；熟悉
　　　　　　(B) be armed with　有～武器；有～裝備
　　　　　　(C) *be associated with*　與～有關　　(D) be faced with　面對

第 21 至 25 題為題組

　　From the philosopher's point of view, wisdom and knowledge are two different things.　One may know countless facts without being a lover of wisdom.　The philosopher is not satisfied with a mere combination of facts. <u>Rather</u>, he seeks to interrelate and interpret the facts in order to discern the
　　　21
subtle meaning and deeper sense that lie <u>beyond</u> the seemingly obvious facts.
　　　　　　　　　　　　　　　　　　　　22

　　從哲學家的觀點來看，智慧和知識是兩種不同的東西。有人可能會知道無數的事實，但並不熱愛智慧。哲學家並不會滿足於只將各種事實結合在一起。更確切地說，哲學家會試圖使事實相互關聯，並加以詮釋，以看出表面上似乎很明顯的事實之外，所隱藏的微妙意義，以及更深刻的涵義。

philosopher (fəˋlasəfɚ) *n.* 哲學家　　　*point of view*　觀點
wisdom (ˋwɪzdəm) *n.* 智慧　　　knowledge (ˋnɑlɪdʒ) *n.* 知識
countless (ˋkauntlɪs) *adj.* 無數的　　　fact (fækt) *n.* 事實
lover (ˋlʌvɚ) *n.* 愛好者；熱愛者
satisfied (ˋsætɪs͵faɪd) *adj.* 滿意的　　　*be satisfied with*　對…感到滿意
mere (mɪr) *adj.* 僅僅；只是　　　combination (͵kɑmbəˋneʃən) *n.* 結合
seek (sik) *v.* 試圖；企圖　　　interrelate (͵ɪntɚrɪˋlet) *v.* 使相互關聯
interpret (ɪnˋtɝprɪt) *v.* 詮釋；解釋　　　*in order to V.*　以便於
discern (dɪˋsɝn) *v.* 分辨；看出　　　subtle (ˋsʌtḷ) *adj.* 微妙的
meaning (ˋminɪŋ) *n.* 意義　　　sense (sɛns) *n.* 意義
lie (laɪ) *v.* 位於　　　seemingly (ˋsimɪŋlɪ) *adv.* 表面上；似乎
obvious (ˋɑbvɪəs) *adj.* 明顯的

21. (**B**)　依句意，選 (B) *Rather* (ˋræðɚ) *adv.* 更確切地說。而 (A) nevertheless
　　　(͵nɛvɚðəˋlɛs) *adv.* 然而，(C) still (stɪl) *adv.* 儘管如此；仍然，(D)
　　　likewise (ˋlaɪk͵waɪz) *adv.* 同樣地，均不合句意。

22. (**D**)　依句意，選 (D) *beyond* (bɪˋjɑnd) *prep.* 超出；在…之外。
　　　lie beyond　在…之外

Philosophers assume that each person is born with an <u>inherent</u> love of
                                                      23
wisdom. Deep inside his heart, each person seeks to penetrate the
mysteries of life, thereby <u>having</u> the potential to become a philosopher.
                            24
Hence, every human being, <u>to</u> the extent that he is a lover of wisdom,
                           25
possesses a philosophy of life.

哲學家認為，每個人都天生熱愛智慧。在人們的內心深處，都會試圖想要了
解人生的奧秘，因此都具有成為哲學家的潛力。所以，凡是能達到熱愛智慧
的程度，就是個擁有人生哲學的人。

> assume〔ə'sjum〕v. 假定；認為　　 ***be born with*** 生來就有
> heart〔hɑrt〕n. 心　　 penetrate〔'pɛnə,tret〕v. 洞察；了解
> mystery〔'mɪstrɪ〕n. 奧秘；謎　　 thereby〔ðɛr'baɪ〕adv. 因此
> potential〔pə'tɛnʃəl〕n. 潛力　　 hence〔hɛns〕adv. 因此
> ***human being*** 人；人類　　 extent〔ɪk'stɛnt〕n. 程度
> possess〔pə'zɛs〕v. 擁有　　 ***philosophy of life*** 人生哲學；人生觀

23. (**A**) (A) ***inherent***〔ɪn'hɪrənt〕adj. 固有的；天生的
    (B) anonymous〔ə'nɑnəməs〕adj. 匿名的
    (C) ethnic〔'ɛθnɪk〕adj. 種族的
    (D) outrageous〔aʊt'redʒəs〕adj. 殘暴的；駭人聽聞的

24. (**D**) 兩個動詞之間沒有連接詞，第二個動詞須改為現在分詞，故選 (D)
    having。

25. (**C**) ***to the extent that***… 到…程度（ = ***to the degree that***… ）

第 26 至 30 題為題組

The 50-million-year-old fossils of an ancient whale <u>which were found</u>
                                                     26
in the Himalayan foothills give strong evidence that modern whales are
descended <u>from</u> a four-legged, land-dwelling animal. The fossils consist of
           27
part of the skull, some teeth and the well-preserved middle ear of an animal

that was 6 to 8 feet long, and <u>had</u> a wolflike snout and jaws with sharp,
28
triangular teeth.　Analysis indicated that the animal had eardrums, <u>which</u> do
29
not work in water.　Moreover, the right and left ears were not isolated from
each other.　The separation of these bones in modern marine whales <u>enables</u>
30
them to detect the direction of underwater sounds.

　　在喜馬拉雅山山麓小丘發現的古鯨魚化石，是五千萬年前的生物，這些古
化石的出土，提供了強有力的證據，證實現代的鯨魚，是由四隻腳的陸居動物
演化而來。這些動物化石，是由部分頭蓋骨、一些牙齒，和保存良好的中耳所
構成，這隻動物應有六到八呎長，牠的鼻子很像狼的鼻子，嘴巴裡也有尖銳的
三角形牙齒。分析研究顯示，這隻動物有耳膜，不過牠的耳膜在水裡並沒有用。
此外，牠的左耳和右耳並不是分開的。現代海洋中的鯨魚，其耳朵的骨頭是分
開的，這讓牠們可以察覺水底聲音的方向。

> fossil ('fɑsḷ) *n.* 化石　　ancient ('enʃənt) *adj.* 古代的
> whale (hwel) *n.* 鯨魚　　Himalayan (hɪ'mɑljən) *adj.* 喜馬拉雅山的
> foothill ('fʊt,hɪl) *n.* 山麓小丘　　evidence ('ɛvədəns) *n.* 證據
> descend (dɪ'sɛnd) *v.* 下降；使～系出
> **be descended from** 是～的後裔；由～演化而來
> dwell (dwɛl) *v.* 居住　　*consist of* 由～組成
> skull (skʌl) *n.* 頭蓋骨　　preserve (prɪ'zɝv) *v.* 保存
> **middle ear** 中耳　　wolflike ('wʊlf,laɪk) *adj.* 像狼的
> snout (snaʊt) *n.* 鼻子　　jaws (dʒɔz) *n. pl.* 嘴巴
> sharp (ʃɑrp) *adj.* 銳利的　　triangular (traɪ'æŋgjələ) *adj.* 三角形的
> analysis (ə'næləsɪs) *n.* 分析研究　　indicate ('ɪndə,ket) *v.* 顯示
> eardrum ('ɪr,drʌm) *n.* 耳膜　　isolate ('aɪsḷ,et) *v.* 使分離
> **be isolated from** 和～分離　　separation (,sɛpə'reʃən) *n.* 分離；獨立
> marine (mə'rin) *adj.* 海洋的　　detect (dɪ'tɛkt) *v.* 發現；察覺
> underwater ('ʌndə,wɔtə) *adj.* 水底的

26. (**C**) 依句意，這些古化石是在喜馬拉雅山下「被」發現的，為被動語態。
　　　關代 which 引導形容詞子句，修飾先行詞 the 50-million-year-old
　　　fossils，故選 (C)。

27. (**B**) 依句意，這些古化石是「從」四隻腳的陸居動物演化而來，故選
　　　(B) *from*。

28. (**C**) 對等連接詞 and 連接文法作用相同的單字、片語或子句。前面動詞為
was，故此處也用過去式動詞，選 (C) *had*。

29. (**B**) 關代代替先行詞 eardrums，在形容詞子句中做主詞，故選 (B) *which*。

30. (**B**) 依句意，由於現代鯨魚的耳朵的骨頭是分開的，這讓牠們「能夠」察
覺水底聲音的方向，故選 (B)。　*enable ~ to V.* 使 ~ 能夠

三、文意選填：

第 31 至 40 題為題組

　　Sun City, South Africa, Disney World and Sentosa Island are examples
of artificial, all-purpose holiday resorts. These "tourism ghettoes," 31(**I**) as
they are referred to by some travelers, separate tourists from the real world
and 32(**G**) instead provide a carefully-planned package of pleasures.
However much they are ridiculed and avoided by those 33(**H**) looking for
a cultural experience, they have proved their worth to those who are
concerned with the environmental 34(**J**) well-being of the planet.

　　南非的太陽城、迪士尼樂園和聖淘沙島，都是人造全功能渡假勝地的範例。
這些被某些遊客稱作「觀光貧民區」的地方，將遊客與現實世界分離，反而提
供精心規劃的娛樂套裝行程。不論它們遭到尋求文化體驗的人們如何地恥笑和
避開，它們已經向那些關心地球環境福祉的人們，證明了它們的價值。

> ***Sentosa Island*** 聖淘沙島（位於新加坡的渡假勝地）
> artificial (ˌɑrtəˈfɪʃəl) *adj.* 人造的；人工的
> all-purpose (ˈɔlˌpɝpəs) *adj.* 適用於多種目的的；多用途的
> resort (rɪˈzɔrt) *n.* 渡假勝地　　tourism (ˈtʊrɪzm) *n.* 觀光
> ghetto (ˈgɛto) *n.* 貧民區　　*be referred to as* 被稱為
> separate (ˈsɛpəˌret) *v.* 使分離　　instead (ɪnˈstɛd) *adv.* 作為替代
> package (ˈpækɪdʒ) *n.* 套裝（行程）　　ridicule (ˈrɪdɪkjul) *v.* 嘲笑
> avoid (əˈvɔɪd) *v.* 避開　　worth (wɝθ) *n.* 價值
> ***be concerned with*** 關心
> environmental (ɪnˌvaɪrənˈmɛntl̩) *adj.* 環境的
> well-being (ˈwɛlˈbiɪŋ) *n.* 幸福；健康；福利
> planet (ˈplænɪt) *n.* 行星（在此指「地球」）

Sun City, for example, was built on ³⁵(C) what had been useless scrubland, but now provides a place for endangered or elusive wildlife. Unlike some other resorts, such as beach resorts which have destroyed the beauty of the area and coastal villages not ³⁶(E) designed for a large influx of people, Sun City is carefully planned to accommodate large ³⁷(D) numbers of tourists. An artificial resort can gather into one compact area the best that the host country ³⁸(B) has to offer. Artificial lakes can ³⁹(F) attract birds which would not normally be seen. Trees can be planted to provide homes for animals and insects and even species which have been ⁴⁰(A) wiped out in the wild can be reintroduced.

　　舉例來說，太陽城建造於一片曾經無用的灌木叢林地，如今卻為瀕臨絕種或行跡難覓的野生動物，提供了一個棲息地。太陽城和某些破壞當地美景的海邊勝地，以及沒有為了負荷大量人潮而設計的沿海村落不同，它經過精心規劃以容納大量的遊客。人造渡假區可以把該國所能提供的最好事物，聚集在一個緊密的區域內。人造湖可以吸引罕見的鳥類。可以種植樹木，為動物和昆蟲提供棲息地，甚至一些已經絕跡的野生動物，也可以再次和世人見面。

scrubland (ˈskrʌbˌlænd) *n.* 灌木叢林地
endangered (ɪnˈdendʒəd) *adj.* 瀕臨絕種的
elusive (ɪˈlusɪv) *adj.* (巧妙地) 躲藏的
wildlife (ˈwaɪldˌlaɪf) *n.* 野生動物　　destroy (dɪˈstrɔɪ) *v.* 破壞
coastal (ˈkostḷ) *adj.* 沿海的　　village (ˈvɪlɪdʒ) *n.* 村落
be designed for 預定要　　influx (ˈɪnˌflʌks) *n.* 湧進；匯集
a large influx of people 大量的人潮
accommodate (əˈkɑməˌdet) *v.* 容納
gather (ˈɡæðə) *v.* 集結　　compact (kəmˈpækt) *adj.* 緊密的
host (host) *adj.* 主辦的　　attract (əˈtrækt) *v.* 吸引
normally (ˈnɔrmḷɪ) *adv.* 通常　　plant (plænt) *v.* 種植
home (hom) *n.* (動物的) 棲息地　　insect (ˈɪnsɛkt) *n.* 昆蟲
species (ˈspiʃɪz) *n. pl.* 種　　***wipe out*** 摧毀；殲滅
wild (waɪld) *n.* 荒野　　reintroduce (ˌriɪntrəˈdjus) *v.* 再引入

四、篇章結構：

第 41 至 45 題爲題組

There is no doubt that the phenomenon of road rage exits. **<u>41(D) In a
recent survey, nine out of ten drivers admit to having felt intense anger
toward other drivers at some time.</u>** Road rage seems to be on the increase
and this may be due to the following factors. First, there are more cars
competing for road space. **<u>42(C) People also are far more subject to time
constraints.</u>** A person who must meet a deadline, but is caught in a tangle
of traffic, may feel increasingly frustrated.

無疑地，「路怒」的現象確實存在。最近有個調查指出，有十分之九的駕駛
人，承認他們有時對其他駕駛人會有強烈憤怒的感覺。路怒的現象似乎持續增
加中，這可能是由於以下的原因。第一，因爲有更多的車輛在爭奪道路空間。
人們也更常有時間上的限制。有人必須趕上截止期限，但卻被困在紊亂的交通
中，就會覺得越來越沮喪。

phenomenon (fə'namə,nan) *n.* 現象　　rage (redʒ) *n.* 憤怒
road rage 路怒 (指因開車所引起的憤怒)　　exist (ɪg'zɪst) *v.* 存在
survey (sə've) *n.* 調查　　intense (ɪn'tɛns) *adj.* 強烈的
on the increase 增加中　　***due to*** 由於
factor ('fæktə) *n.* 因素；原因　　compete (kəm'pit) *v.* 爭奪 < *for* >
be subject to 易受～的　　constraint (kən'strent) *n.* 束縛
deadline ('dɛd,laɪn) *n.* 截止期限　　***meet a deadline*** 趕上截止期限
tangle ('tæŋgl̩) *n.* 紊亂　　increasingly (ɪn'krisɪŋlɪ) *adv.* 越來越
frustrated ('frʌstretɪd) *adj.* 沮喪的

**<u>43(A) Another factor may be that people are not as courteous as they used
to be.</u>** Nowadays a person may be bombarded with more concerns and
worries than before and forget how to be polite. Since cars are becoming
a necessity, drivers should consider a plan of action against road rage.

另一個原因可能是人們不再像以前那樣有禮貌了。現代人比以前受更多事情和
憂慮的轟炸，所以忘了如何有禮貌了。既然車子已經變成一種必需品，駕駛人
應該想一想對付路怒的行動方案。

courteous ('kɝtɪəs) *adj.* 有禮貌的　　***used to*** 以前
bombard (bam'bard) *v.* 轟炸　　concerns (kən'sɝnz) *n. pl.* 事物
necessity (nə'sɛsətɪ) *n.* 必需品

[44](B) A change in mental attitude is the first step. The drivers must know an attack of road rage will not get them any farther but could result in a serious health problem. [45](E) One could leave home earlier or make arrangements with the boss to arrive between two fixed times. This could give drivers twenty or thirty minutes leeway.

第一步就是要改變心態。駕駛人必須要明白路怒的發作，不但不會讓他們往前進，反而會導致嚴重的健康問題。我們可以早點從家裡出發，或是跟老闆約好在某一段約定好的時間內到達。這樣可以多給駕駛人二三十分鐘的充裕時間。

mental (ˈmɛntḷ) adj. 心理的　　attitude (ˈætə,tjud) n. 態度
attack (əˈtæk) n. 發作　　farther (ˈfɑrðɚ) adv. 向前地
result in 導致　　arrangement (əˈrendʒmənt) n. 約定
fixed (fɪkst) adj. 定好的　　leeway (ˈli,we) n. 充裕的時間

五、閱讀測驗：
第 46 至 48 題為題組

In September 1797, three hunters captured a boy about twelve years of age in the Caune Woods in France. The people in Paris were greatly interested in this boy, who had apparently lived most of his life without human companionship. Some people imagined they would see man in his most natural and noble state. Others expected to hear the boy speak the original "unlearned" language of man, which they supposed would most likely be Hebrew. What they saw, however, was a dirty creature who scratched and bit, jumped about, and made noises like an animal. Dr. Pinel, who specialized in treating mental disorders examined the boy and announced that he was an idiot and would not likely be helped by any kind of training.

在一七九七年九月，有三個獵人在法國的貢恩森林，抓到了一個大約十二歲的男孩。巴黎人對這個男孩非常有興趣，他顯然大部份的時間都不曾和人類相處過。有些人幻想，他們會見到一個處於最自然且高貴狀態的人。有些人則希望聽到這個男孩說出原始的、「未受教育的」人類語言，人們認為這種語言最有可能是希伯來文。然而，他們看到的卻是一個像動物般骯髒的生物，搔身體、咬東西、跳來跳去，並且發出難聽的聲音。皮內爾醫生專精於心理疾病的治療，他檢查過這個男孩後，宣稱他是個白痴，不可能透過任何形式的訓練來幫助他。

capture〔'kæptʃɚ〕*v.* 捕捉　　woods〔wʊdz〕*n. pl.* 森林

apparently〔ə'pærəntlɪ〕*adv.* 明顯地（= *obviously*）

human〔'hjumən〕*adj.* 人類的

companionship〔kəm'pænjənʃɪp〕*n.* 友誼；交往

imagine〔ɪ'mædʒɪn〕*v.* 想像；幻想　　noble〔'nobḷ〕*adj.* 高貴的

state〔stet〕*n.* 狀態　　expect〔ɪk'spɛkt〕*v.* 期望

original〔ə'rɪdʒənḷ〕*adj.* 原始的（= *primitive*〔'prɪmətɪv〕）

unlearned〔ʌn'lɝnɪd〕*adj.* 未受教育的

suppose〔sə'poz〕*v.* 推測；以爲　　likely〔'laɪklɪ〕*adv.* 可能

Hebrew〔'hibru〕*n.* 希伯來文　　creature〔'kritʃɚ〕*n.* 生物

scratch〔skrætʃ〕*v.* 搔癢　　bite〔baɪt〕*v.* 咬

about〔ə'baʊt〕*adv.* 到處（= *around*）

specialize〔'spɛʃəl,aɪz〕*v.* 專攻 < *in* >　　treat〔trit〕*v.* 治療

mental〔'mɛntḷ〕*adj.* 心理的；精神上的

disorder〔dɪs'ɔrdɚ〕*n.* 疾病　　examine〔ɪg'zæmɪn〕*v.* 檢查

announce〔ə'naʊns〕*v.* 宣布　　idiot〔'ɪdɪət〕*n.* 白痴

training〔'trenɪŋ〕*n.* 訓練

Jean-Marc-Gaspard Itard, a young doctor, was convinced, however, that the boy could be helped, since he believed that his low intelligence was caused by his solitary life in the woods from about the age of seven and by his ignorance of language. Itard took the boy and worked with him for five years. Victor, as Itard called him, did not learn to speak French, but he was able to understand a large number of written words and phrases. He would obey simple written commands and could use word cards to show his desires. He also acquired the manners and appearance of a civilized young man. Victor had obviously been helped by education, but Itard finally concluded that Victor could not be further improved because his intelligence was subnormal.

　　然而，一位年輕的醫生，尙馬克嘉斯帕·伊塔，相信他能幫助這個男孩，因爲他認爲，男孩的智能很低，是由於他從大約七歲開始，就獨自在森林裡生活，加上他不懂語言所導致的。伊塔醫生把這個男孩帶走，並且教育他有五年

之久。伊塔醫生叫這個男孩維多，而維多並沒有學會說法文，但能了解許多寫下來的單字和片語。他可以遵守簡單的書寫命令，並能用字卡表達他的願望。他也學到了禮貌，外表就像個文明的年輕人。很明顯地，教育幫助了維多，但是伊塔最後下結論說，因為維多的智力低於一般人，所以無法有更進一步的改善了。

convince (kən'vɪns) v. 使確信　　intelligence (ɪn'tɛlədʒəns) n. 智力
solitary ('sɑlə,tɛrɪ) adj. 孤獨的　　ignorance ('ɪgnərəns) n. 無知
a large number of 許多的　　phrase (frez) n. 片語
obey (ə'be) v. 服從　　command (kə'mænd) n. 命令
desire (dɪ'zaɪr) n. 慾望；願望　　acquire (ə'kwaɪr) v. 學得
manners ('mænəz) n. pl. 禮貌；規矩
appearance (ə'pɪrəns) n. 外表　　civilized ('sɪvḷ,aɪzd) adj. 文明的
education (,ɛdʒə'keʃən) n. 教育　　conclude (kən'klud) v. 下結論
further ('fɝðə) adv. 更進一步地　　improve (ɪm'pruv) v. 改善
subnormal (sʌb'nɔrmḷ) adj. 智力低於一般的

46. (**A**) 一開始，伊塔顯然認為維多沒有學語言，因為他 _____。
　　(A) 是在遠離人類社會的環境下長大的
　　(B) 比較喜歡製造人類的噪音
　　(C) 不喜歡和人類在一起
　　(D) 具有非常低的智力

47. (**D**) 皮內爾見過那個男孩後，認為教育會 _____。
　　(A) 提升維多的智力　　(B) 破壞維多原始的性格
　　(C) 幫助維多適應人類社會　　(D) 對維多只有極少的助益
raise (rez) v. 提升　　intellectual (,ɪntḷ'ɛktʃʊəl) adj. 智力的
capacity (kə'pæsətɪ) n. 能力　　ruin ('rʊɪn) v. 破壞；毀滅
adjust (ə'dʒʌst) v. 適應 <to>

48. (**B**) 伊塔最後終於相信維多 _____。
　　(A) 遲早可以被教到會說話　　(B) 的智力低於一般的平均標準
　　(C) 永遠無法適應和人類在一起　　(D) 真的是個原始人

第 49 至 52 題為題組

Deep inside a mountain near Sweetwater in eastern Tennessee is a body of water known as the Lost Sea. It is listed by the Guinness Book of World Records as the world's largest underground lake. The Lost Sea is part of an extensive and historical cave system called Craighead Caverns.

靠近田納西州東部的甜水鎮，在一座山的深處，有一片水域，那就是眾所皆知的失落之海。它被金氏世界紀錄列為世界上最大的地下湖。失落之海是廣大且存在已久的洞穴系統的一部份，這個洞穴系統被稱為葛來特海德洞穴。

eastern (ˈistən) adj. 東方的　　Tennessee (ˈtɛnəˌsi) n. 田納西州
body of water 水域　　**be known as** 被稱為
list (lɪst) v. 列入　　**Guinness Book of World Records** 金氏世界紀錄
underground (ˈʌndəˈgraʊnd) adj. 地下的　(ˈʌndəˈgraʊnd) adv. 在地下
cave (kev) n. 洞穴　　cavern (ˈkævən) n. 洞穴

The caverns have been known and used since the days of the Cherokee Indian nation. The cave expands into a series of huge rooms from a small opening on the side of the mountain. Approximately one mile from the entrance, in a room called "The Council Room," many Indian artifacts have been found. Some of the items discovered include pottery, arrowheads, weapons, and jewelry.

自從柴拉基印地安部落時期以來，這個洞穴就一直為人所知，且被人使用。這個洞穴從山腰上的小開口，一路發展為成群的洞窟。離入口約一哩處，有個洞窟叫做「會議窟」，裡面發現了很多印地安人的藝術品。一些出土的物品中，包括了有陶器、箭頭、武器，以及珠寶。

Cherokee (ˈtʃɛrəˌki) n. 柴拉基族 (北美印地安人的一部落)
nation (ˈneʃən) n. 部族　　expand (ɪkˈspænd) v. 擴大 < *into* >
a series of 一連串的　　opening (ˈopənɪŋ) n. 開口；穴
approximately (əˈprɑksəmɪtlɪ) adv. 大約
entrance (ˈɛntrəns) n. 入口　　council (ˈkaʊnsḷ) n. 會議
artifact (ˈɑrtɪˌfækt) n. 工藝品；藝術品　　item (ˈaɪtəm) n. 項目
pottery (ˈpɑtərɪ) n. 陶器　　arrowhead (ˈæroˌhɛd) n. 箭頭
weapon (ˈwɛpən) n. 武器　　jewelry (ˈdʒuəlrɪ) n. 珠寶

　　For many years there were persistent rumors of a large underground lake somewhere in a cave, but it was not discovered until 1905. In that year, a thirteen-year-old boy named Ben Sands crawled through a small opening three hundred feet underground. He found himself in a large cave half filled with water.

　　多年來，一直都有謠傳指出，有個大型的地下湖，就在洞穴的某處，但是直到一九〇五年才被發現。當年一個名叫班‧山德斯的十三歲男孩，從一個小洞穴，一路爬到地下三百呎處。他發現自己在一個大型洞穴裡，而且這個洞穴有一半都是水。

> persistent〔pə'zɪstənt〕adj. 持續的
> rumor〔'rumɚ〕n. 傳聞　　crawl〔krɔl〕v. 爬行

　　Today tourists visit the Lost Sea and ride far out onto it in glass-bottomed boats powered by electric motors. More than thirteen acres of water have been mapped out so far and still no end to the lake has been found. Even though teams of divers have tried to explore the Lost Sea, the full extent of it is still unknown.

　　現在，遊客們會去遊覽失落之海，他們會乘船遠行直到湖面，這些船的底部是由玻璃做成的，並由電動馬達來推動。目前有超過十三英畝的水域，已在地圖上標示出來了，不過這個湖的邊界尚未被找到。即使有好多隊潛水夫試著去探測這個失落之海，可是它的大小目前仍是個謎。

> out〔aʊt〕adv. 離開陸地　　bottom〔'bɑtəm〕n. 底部
> power〔'paʊɚ〕v. 供以…動力；以動力驅動
> electric〔ɪ'lɛktrɪk〕adj. 電力的　　motor〔'motɚ〕n. 馬達
> acre〔'ekɚ〕n. 英畝　　map〔mæp〕v. 在（地圖上）標示出
> **so far** 到目前為止　　diver〔'daɪvɚ〕n. 潛水人員
> explore〔ɪk'splor〕v. 探測　　extent〔ɪk'stɛnt〕n. 範圍

49.（**C**）根據本文，失落之海很獨特，因為它 ＿＿＿＿＿＿＿＿。

　　(A) 是歷史上有名洞穴系統的一部份
　　(B) 名列金氏世界紀錄中
　　(C) 世界上最大的地下湖
　　(D) 田納西州最大的湖

> unique〔ju'nik〕adj. 獨特的

50. (**A**) 根據本文，要如何才能進入洞穴？
    (A) <u>從山腰的入口處。</u>　　　　　(B) 潛入水中。
    (C) 乘船遠行直到湖上。　　　　　(D) 從「會議洞窟」。

    mountainside〔'mauntn̩,saɪd〕*n.* 山腰　　dive〔daɪv〕*v.* 潛水

51. (**D**) 在「會議洞窟」找到了什麼？
    (A) 小型天然洞口。　　　　　　　(B) 大型洞穴。
    (C) 另一系列的洞窟。　　　　　　(D) <u>許多古老的印地安人的物品。</u>

    object〔'abdʒɪkt〕*n.* 物品

52. (**D**) 根據本文，失落之海附近地區已經被探索到的面積大約是 _____。
    (A) 三百呎　　　　　　　　　　　(B) 一千九百呎
    (C) 一哩　　　　　　　　　　　　(D) <u>十三英畝</u>

第 53 至 56 題為題組

　　Geologists have long known about Japan's vulnerability to the rumbling earth. Back in 1978 the Japanese government enacted a law to ensure that the nation took steps to watch for impending earthquakes; by the end of 1994, it had spent more than $ 1.3 billion on monitoring programs.

　　長久以來，地質學家都知道，日本容易受到地震的侵害。早在一九七八年，日本政府就制定一條法律，確保國內已經採取行動，注意觀察隨時可能發生的地震；到了一九九四年年底，政府已經花了超過十三億的金錢，在監控計劃上。

　　　　geologist〔dʒi'alədʒɪst〕*n.* 地質學家
　　　　vulnerability〔,vʌlnərə'bɪlətɪ〕*n.* 易受傷害 *< to >*
　　　　rumbling〔'rʌmblɪŋ〕*adj.* 發出隆隆聲的　　earth〔ɝθ〕*n.* 陸地
　　　　government〔'gʌvənmənt〕*n.* 政府　　enact〔ɪn'ækt〕*v.* 制定
　　　　ensure〔ɪn'ʃur〕*v.* 保證；確保　　step〔stɛp〕*n.* 步驟；措施
　　　　take steps 採取措施　　　***watch for*** 注意觀察
　　　　impending〔ɪm'pɛndɪŋ〕*adj.* 迫近的；隨時可能發生的
　　　　earthquake〔'ɝθ,kwek〕*n.* 地震　　monitor〔'manətɚ〕*v.* 監控
　　　　program〔'progræm〕*n.* 計劃

Yet in the early morning hours of Jan. 17, 1995, when the Great Hanshin-Awaji Earthquake came rumbling along at 7.2 on the Richter scale, it thoroughly surprised the port town of Kobe. The quake flipped the elevated Hanshin Expressway onto its side like a child's discarded slot-car track, and caused skyscrapers to collapse and gas fires to break out among the city's wooden houses. More than 6,400 people were killed and 43,000 injured. "Earthquake prediction research betrayed the public," snapped an editorial in Asahi Shimbun.

但是在一九九五年一月十七日的一大清早，大阪神淡陸島地區發生了芮氏規模 7.2 級的地震，這場地震徹底震驚了神戶港都。地震將高架的阪神快速道路翻轉側倒，就像被小朋友丟棄的軌道車軌道一樣，導致摩天大樓倒塌，城市中的木造房屋，爆發了瓦斯火災。超過六千四百人喪生，四萬三千人受傷。「地震預測研究有負大眾所託，」朝日新聞的社論痛批。

hours〔 aʊrz 〕*n. pl.* 時刻　　***the Richter scale*** 芮氏地震儀
thoroughly〔 ˈθɝolɪ 〕*adv.* 十分地；徹底地　　flip〔 flɪp 〕*v.* **翻轉**
elevated〔 ˈɛləˌvetɪd 〕*adj.* 高架的；抬高的
expressway〔 ɪkˈsprɛsˌwe 〕*n.* 快速道路
discard〔 dɪsˈkɑrd 〕*v.* 拋棄　　***slot-car*** 軌道車　　track〔 træk 〕*n.* 軌道
cause〔 kɔz 〕*v.* 導致　　skyscraper〔 ˈskaɪˌskrepɚ 〕*n.* 摩天大樓
collapse〔 kəˈlæps 〕*v.* 倒塌　　***gas fire*** 瓦斯火災
break out 爆發　　wooden〔 ˈwʊdn̩ 〕*adj.* 木造的　　***be killed*** 喪生
injured〔 ˈɪndʒɚd 〕*adj.* 受傷的　　prediction〔 prɪˈdɪkʃən 〕*n.* 預測
betray〔 bɪˈtre 〕*v.* 背叛；負（某人）所託　　***the public*** 大眾
snap〔 snæp 〕*v.* 痛批　　editorial〔 ˌɛdəˈtorɪəl 〕*n.* 社論

The Kobe earthquake forced both the Japanese government and researchers to take stock. In the past few years, Japanese scientists have been trying to find out why they failed in predicting Kobe and other earthquakes that have hit Japan over the years. Now that effort is paying off. In a recent issue of the journal Science, Jin-Oh Park and his colleagues at the Japan Marine Science and Technology Center in Yokosuka, near Tokyo, uncovered a major cause of the most unpredictable earthquakes. It was a "splay" fault, a secondary fault that branches off a main one and can cause damage hundreds of kilometers from obvious trouble spots.

　　神戶大地震迫使日本政府和研究人員去評估。在過去的幾年當中，日本科學家一直努力想了解，為什麼他們會預測不出神戶地震，以及在過去幾年當中，曾經侵襲過日本的地震。現在努力得到了結果。在最近一期的「科學」期刊中，任職於靠近東京，位在橫阪的「日本海洋科學及科技中心」的朴仁和及他的同事，揭露了一個大部分不可預測地震的主因。那就是「向外擴張的」斷層，一個由主斷層分岔出來的次斷層，可以造成明顯問題區之外數百公里的損害。

Kobe〔'kobɪ〕*n.* 神戶　　　***take stock*** 評估
fail〔fel〕*v.* 失敗；無法　　predict〔prɪ'dɪkt〕*v.* 預測
hit〔hɪt〕*v.* 侵襲　　***pay off*** 得到結果　　recent〔'risn̩t〕*adj.* 最近的
issue〔'ɪʃu〕*n.* 發行（一期）　　journal〔'dʒɝn̩l〕*n.* 期刊
colleague〔'kɑlig〕*n.* 同事　　marine〔mə'rin〕*adj.* 海洋的
technology〔tɛk'nɑlədʒɪ〕*n.* 科技　　uncover〔ʌn'kʌvɚ〕*v.* 揭露
major〔'medʒɚ〕*adj.* 主要的　　cause〔kɔz〕*n.* 原因
unpredictable〔ˌʌnprɪ'dɪktəbl̩〕*adj.* 不可預測的
splay〔sple〕*adj.* 向外擴張的　　fault〔fɔlt〕*n.* 斷層
secondary〔'sɛkənˌdɛrɪ〕*adj.* 次要的　　***branch off*** 分岔；岔開
main〔men〕*adj.* 主要的　　damage〔'dæmɪdʒ〕*n.* 損害
spot〔spɑt〕*n.* 地點　　***trouble spot*** 問題區

This was the first time scientists had confirmed the existence of a splay fault. By shedding light on the vexing phenomenon, experts think they may be able eventually to predict many types of earthquakes that have tricked geologists in the past. "This brings us a step closer to knowing about earthquake mechanism, and could lead to a better chance of prediction," says Shozo Harada, a Diet member, who has helped draft anti-quake laws.
這是第一次科學家證實向外擴張斷層的存在。藉由闡明這個令人困擾的現象，專家們認為，他們最後也許可以預測出，許多過去曾經欺騙過地質學家的地震類型。「這使我們更進一步知道地震形成的過程，也可以導致更精準的預測，」國會議員省三原田如此說，他還幫忙起草防禦地震的條款。

confirm〔kən'fɝm〕*v.* 確認　　existence〔ɪg'zɪstəns〕*n.* 存在
shed light on 闡明　　vexing〔'vɛksɪŋ〕*adj.* 令人困擾的
phenomenon〔fə'nɑməˌnɑn〕*n.* 現象
expert〔'ɛkspɝt〕*n.* 專家　　eventually〔ɪ'vɛntʃuəlɪ〕*adv.* 最後
trick〔trɪk〕*v.* 欺騙　　mechanism〔'mɛkəˌnɪzəm〕*n.* 形成的過程
lead to 導致　　Diet〔'daɪət〕*n.* 國會　　draft〔dræft〕*v.* 起草
anti-quake〔'æntɪ'kwek〕*adj.* 防禦地震的

53. (B) 根據本文，下列哪一項未被提及？
　　(A) 神戶市爆發瓦斯火災。　　　(B) 日本政府被迫關閉股市。
　　(C) 摩天大樓倒塌。　　　　　　(D) 超過六千四百人喪生。
　　mention (ˈmɛnʃən) v. 提到　　*shut down* 關閉；停工
　　stock market 股市

54. (B) 根據本文，下列哪一個敘述是正確的？
　　(A) 神戶地震導致小朋友丟棄他們的軌道車軌道。
　　(B) 神戶地震讓日本地質學家大感意外。
　　(C) 神戶地震之後，日本政府才制定一條法律，以確保國家已經採取
　　　　行動，來注意觀察地震。
　　(D) 到了一九九五年一月十七日時，日本政府已經花了超過十三億元
　　　　在監控計劃上。
　　statement (ˈstetmənt) n. 敘述　　*take ~ by surprise* 使 ~ 驚訝

55. (C) 根據本文，誰幫忙起草防禦地震的條款？
　　(A) 朝日新聞的社論。　　　　　(B) 日本的地質學家。
　　(C) 省三原田。　　　　　　　　(D) 朴仁和。

56. (A) 根據本文，下列哪一個敘述是不正確的？
　　(A) 日本科學家認爲最後有可能，可以預測出很多類型的地震。
　　(B) 日本科學家承認他們不能預測神戶地震。
　　(C) 日本科學家已經揭露一個大部分不可預測地震的主因。
　　(D) 日本科學家已經確認向外擴張的斷層的存在。
　　admit (ədˈmɪt) v. 承認

第貳部分：非選擇題

一、英文翻譯：

1. 他的朋友一看到他贏得樂透彩，就開始嫉妒他。
　　On seeing that he had won the lottery, his friends began to be jealous
　　of him.

2. 直到發生了致命的車禍，人們才會去注意交通規則。

Not until a fatal accident happened did people pay attention to traffic rules.

二、英文作文：(作文範例)

Dear Dad,

I am writing you in regards to a terrible thing I did last week. Last Monday, when I was home all alone, I had a wild idea. I had always wanted to drive a car and I was going to do it that night. Then, without your permission, I took your car key and got into the car and went for a ride. Even though I do not know how to drive a car, I still did it anyway. In the process, I damaged the car severely.

I know that you always thought the car was damaged by a drunk driver but the truth is that it was me who committed this irresponsible act. I am very sorry for what I have done. I promise that I will never do anything irresponsible or lie to you ever again. I will take a job this summer after the college entrance exam to pay for the repairs. Once again, I am very sorry for lying to you and I hope you will forgive me.

Your loving son,

David Wang

write〔raɪt〕v. 寫信給　　***in regards to*** 關於

alone〔əˈlon〕adv. 獨自地　　wild〔waɪld〕adj. 瘋狂的

permission〔pəˈmɪʃən〕n. 允許　　***go for a ride*** 去兜風

even though 即使　　anyway〔ˈɛnɪˌwe〕adv. 不管怎樣；反正

process〔ˈprɑsɛs〕n. 過程　　severely〔səˈvɪrlɪ〕adv. 嚴重地

drunk〔drʌŋk〕adj. 喝醉的　　commit〔kəˈmɪt〕v. 做(錯事)

irresponsible〔ˌɪrɪˈspɑnsəbḷ〕adj. 不負責任的

act〔ækt〕n. 行為　　lie〔laɪ〕v. 說謊

take〔tek〕v. 接受　　***college entrance exam*** 大學入學考試

repairs〔rɪˈpɛrz〕n. pl. 修理

loving〔ˈlʌvɪŋ〕adj. 親愛的；充滿深情的

大學入學指定科目考試英文模擬試題 ③

第壹部份：選擇題（佔72分）

一、詞彙及慣用語（15％）

說明：　第1至10題，每題選出一個最適當的選項，標示在答案卡之「選擇題答案區」。每題答對得1分，答錯或劃記多於一個選項者倒扣1/3分，倒扣到本大題之實得分數為零為止，未作答者，不給分亦不扣分。

1. The bad weather discouraged Jack and his friends from climbing the mountain last weekend. Therefore, Jack _____ an alternative plan to have fun.
   (A) proposed　　　　　　　(B) concluded
   (C) expressed　　　　　　　(D) extended

2. We had better make a reservation in advance in case there are no _____ at the hotel during the holiday season.
   (A) vacancies　　　　　　　(B) facilities
   (C) possibilities　　　　　　(D) varieties

3. We saw some roads in the earthquake-hit areas were _____. Some of them were even higher than the houses.
   (A) alleviated　　(B) eliminated　　(C) elevated　　(D) associated

4. His new book greatly _____ the intelligence of a monkey, claiming that it can talk and deal with human difficulties.
   (A) invades　　(B) measures　　(C) overcomes　　(D) exaggerates

5. Young people _____ their health for wealth; old people offer wealth for health.
   (A) devote　　(B) contribute　　(C) sacrifice　　(D) appreciate

6. It never disappoints you to fish in a river _____ in salmon.
   (A) occupied　　(B) acceptable　　(C) abundant　　(D) confident

7. With two equally qualified candidates, you can be sure that the mayoral election in Taipei at the end of this year will be very _____.
   (A) competitive   (B) accurate
   (C) sincere   (D) separate

8. She became _____ when her best friend stole her boyfriend away from her.
   (A) awake   (B) furious   (C) direct   (D) repetitive

9. My pen pal was _____ wrong about Taiwan, saying it was in the southern hemisphere next to Australia.
   (A) extensively (B) continually (C) graciously (D) definitely

10. A man with a _____ negative attitude is miserable and stupid. Life is too precious to be wasted on endless complaints and sighs.
    (A) temporarily   (B) professionally
    (C) wonderfully   (D) consistently

11. Deep inside the human heart is the _____ about what other people do in private. That's why the media pursue and people peep.
    (A) attraction   (B) curiosity
    (C) dependence   (D) experiment

12. Soccer is popular in Europe but it never really _____ in Taiwan.
    (A) set up   (B) got fired   (C) stopped off   (D) caught on

13. I bought her a delicate bracelet _____ her hospitality during my stay.
    (A) out of   (B) in return for (C) for sure   (D) in use

14. The violent typhoon had _____ the electricity in this small town. As a result, the residents here were not able to use any electrical appliances.
    (A) cut back   (B) cut off   (C) cut out   (D) cut down

15. To keep in shape, you have to _____ to squeeze some exercise into your busy schedule.

    (A) make it a rule   (B) make out   (C) turn out   (D) live it up

二、綜合測驗（15％）

說明：　第 16 至 30 題，每題一個空格。請依文意選出一個最適當的選項，標示
　　　　在答案卡之「選擇題答案區」。每題答對得 1 分，答錯或劃記多於一
　　　　個選項者倒扣 1/3 分，倒扣到本大題之實得分數爲零爲止。未作答者，
　　　　不給分亦不扣分。

第 16 至 20 題爲題組

Aston began playing soccer when he was a young boy in England. In 1936, when he was 19 years old, he hurt his ankle and ___16___ soccer. He decided to become a referee.

Aston made an important ___17___ to the sport. He invented the card system. Referees give cards to players ___18___. A yellow card is a warning. A red card means you are out of the game. According to Aston, the card system prevents language problems. The cards are an international language. Every player understands ___19___ the yellow and red cards mean.

Aston said he got the idea from a traffic signal. He was driving home from a 1966 World Cup match. In that game a German-speaking referee didn't make his calls ___20___. Some of the players could not understand him. Today all soccer players understand the meanings of the cards.

16. (A) tried playing   (B) stopped playing
    (C) intended to play   (D) continued playing

17. (A) tribulation   (B) attribution
    (C) contribution   (D) distribution

18. (A) break rules   (B) violated rules
    (C) to break rules   (D) who violate rules

19. (A) that   (B) which   (C) what   (D) how
20. (A) clean   (B) cleanly   (C) clear   (D) clearly

第 21 至 25 題為題組

In the lecture hall, the speaker says, "I'm going to give this US$100 bill to one of you. Who wants it?" A sea of hands go up immediately. "But first let me do this." He then crumples the bill up. "Who still wants it?" the speaker asks. Again the hands go up ____21____. "Well, it seems that you all learned a valuable lesson today." Some students frown. "I don't ____22____ it," a student whispers. "Wasn't he supposed to give a lecture on suicide?"

"No matter what I did to the money, you still wanted it," the speaker says. "Why? ____23____ I crumpled it, it still had the same value. It was still worth US$100. ____24____ this US$100 bill, we are often scarred in life. We are dropped, crumpled and stepped on. We all feel worthless at one time or another, but like the bill, ____25____ happens to us, we will never lose our value. We learn valuable lessons from our disappointments."

21. (A) reluctantly   (B) permanently   (C) artificially   (D) eagerly
22. (A) have   (B) make   (C) take   (D) get
23. (A) Even though   (B) Instead of   (C) Because of   (D) Despite
24. (A) Like   (B) Likely   (C) Unlike   (D) Dislike
25. (A) no matter why   (B) whatever   (C) however   (D) what

第 26 至 30 題為題組

The sites people spend the most time on each month are known as "sticky" sites. The hard part for sticky sites is making money. Ironically, the stickier a site is, ____26____ it is to advertisers. If a site is sticky, that means people are not clicking on ads. __27__, stickiness is a meaningless measure for sites that sell products. __28__ advantage of such loyalty, the sites have supplemented traditional banner ads at the top of each Web page with sponsorship within the site itself. The secret to their success is that they're not trying to create the latest, greatest, coolest thing. __29__, they've just paid attention to what people do — 100 million Americans play cards every day; 50 million play bingo. So go ahead. Squander your time on that PC playing games until 3:00 in the morning. After all, you're hardly the only one __30__ on silly sites.

26. (A) the less appealing   (B) the most profitable
    (C) the least rich   (D) the more attractive
27. (A) What's better   (B) In addition to
    (C) What's more   (D) In case
28. (A) Take   (B) To take   (C) Taken   (D) Been taken
29. (A) Besides   (B) Therefore   (C) Nevertheless   (D) Instead
30. (A) absorbed (B) hooked   (C) involved   (D) dedicated

三、文意選填（10％）

說明： 第31至40題，每題一個空格。請依文意在文章後所提供的 (A) 到 (J)
選項中分別選出最適當者，並將其字母代號標示在答案卡之「選擇題
答案區」。每題答對得1分，答錯或劃記多於一個選項者倒扣 1/9 分，
倒扣到本大題之實得分數爲零爲止。未作答者，不給分亦不扣分。

第31至40題爲題組

Relationships among brothers and sisters are of main concern. Positive sibling relationships can be a __31__ of strength, whereas unresolved early conflicts can create lasting wounds. In order not to be __32__ in a spiral of sibling fighting or conflict, parents should know what to do when their kids are fighting.

Parents shouldn't compare a kid with a sibling—even ___33___. (Most parents know better than to ask, "Why can't you be more like your brother?") Comparison sets one child against another, and it subtly ___34___ their relationships when a parent says, "You're much better organized than your sister." Each child should be appreciated individually—though not ___35___ equally.

Parents can't step in in every kid's quarrel, but neither can they just let things be. They should ___36___ a "no-hitting, no-hurting" rule, so kids will know they are expected to work out their problems peacefully, sometimes with assistance. A parent can be helpful by listening to each side and then framing the problems aloud: "So, I see that you're really mad because…" Depending on the severity of the problem, a parent might then express ___37___ that the kids can solve it and leave the room.

Parents should step in directly, however, whenever an argument turns ___38___. Most kids hate fighting. They do it because they don't have other tools for dealing with their frustrations. Fighters should be ___39___ to cool off, and a parent should later listen to both parties, asking the kids to help come up with a solution. The parents shouldn't ___40___ one child as a bully and the other as the victim; fights among siblings are seldom this simple.

By dealing with sibling fighting in a proper way, parents can help develop good sibling relationships, which are a powerful source of support in life.

(A) separated	(B) undermines	(C) caught	(D) confidence
(E) violent	(F) favorably	(G) source	(H) cast
(I) establish	(J) necessarily		

四、篇章結構（10％）

說明： 第 41 至 45 題，每題一個空格。請依文意在文章後所提供的 (A) 到 (E)
選項中分別選出最適當者，填入空格中，使篇章結構清晰有條理，並將
其英文字母代號標示在答案卡之「選擇題答案區」。每題答對得 2 分，
答錯或劃記多於一個選項者倒扣 1/2 分，倒扣到本大題之實得分數爲零
爲止。未作答者，不給分亦不扣分。

第 41 至 45 題爲題組

News is everywhere and serves many different functions. ___41___
News also provides facts and information. ___42___: a way to make
money by selling advertising and/or newspapers and magazines.
Sometimes news is propaganda or disinformation: a way to control a
population. ___43___ We can't escape it. Every day we are bombarded
by information: newspapers, magazines, television and the Internet.

"News" does not always mean something that is unquestionably
true. Although the news seems to be based on facts, these facts are
usually reported the way the media chooses to report them. ___44___
Furthermore, many journalists and reporters sensationalize or dramatize
a news event in order to make a story more interesting. ___45___
Therefore, as consumers of news we must learn to think critically
about the news, the media, and what the truth is.

(A) In addition, news is business

(B) But whatever news is, it is all around us.

(C) News gives instant coverage of important events.

(D) Unfortunately, sensationalism often prevents us from learning the
truth and causes great pain to the people it victimizes.

(E) For example, some information that appears as news is really only
speculation or theories formed by the reporters.

五、閱讀測驗（22％）

說明： 第 46 至 56 題，每題請分別根據各篇文章的文意選出一個最適當的選項，標示在答案卡之「選擇題答案區」。每題答對得 2 分，答錯或劃記多於一個選項者倒扣 2/3 分，倒扣到本大題之實得分數為零為止。未作答者，不給分亦不扣分。

第 46 至 48 題為題組

There are many cats in China. Chinese people are very fond of cats. Chen Lee was a schoolteacher in Honan, China. Chen had a beautiful white cat, and he loved her very much. But a very sad thing happened one day. A rich man's car ran over the cat, and that was the end of her. Chen ran out onto the road.

"Oh, you poor thing!" he cried. "What shall I do without you? You were the light of my life."

People stopped and cried with Chen. The rich man stopped his car and came back. He put his arms around Chen and said, "I am very, very sorry about this accident. Please let me——"

"You don't understand!" Chen cried. "She was a wonderful pupil!"

"A pupil?" the man asked. "This cat? What do you mean?"

"You couldn't buy that cat for all the money in China!" Chen said. "I taught her every day. That cat could talk, sir!"

"Then I must help you," the man said. He took a handful of notes from his pocket. "Here, have this. Three hundred pounds. Is it enough? Will you forgive me? Can we be friends now?"

Chen took the money. "Thank you," he said. "I'll get another cat. Then I must begin all the work again."

The rich man went away in his car. A woman said to Chen, "Was it true? Could your cat talk? What could it say?"

"It was true, madam," Chen answered. "My cat had many difficult lessons. At last she could say the word CAT."

Everybody laughed. What is the Chinese word for cat? It is MIAW.

46. What was 'the end' of Chen's cat?
    (A) Her lessons stopped.
    (B) Chen sold her to a rich man.
    (C) She began to learn.
    (D) She died in an accident.

47. Why did the people stop and cry with Chen? Because _____.
    (A) they didn't like the rich man   (B) they were poor
    (C) Chen's cat was dead   (D) the cat was something

48. How many lessons did the cat really have? The answer is _____.
    (A) three hundred   (B) one lesson every day
    (C) many difficult lessons   (D) no lessons at all

第 49 至 52 題爲題組

International Office

The University offers students an opportunity to live, study, and travel abroad in semester or year-long programs, as well as summer programs. Semester or year-long programs are maintained in Paris, Madrid, Copenhagen, Japan, Britain, Russia, and Australia. Programs in other countries may be added from time to time. Instruction in all programs is offered in English, except for courses in foreign languages and literature. Students in good standing at Southern Methodist University(SMU) and other universities may participate in SMU's International Programs.

Semester Programs

SMU-in-Paris and SMU-in-Spain. The University has well-established programs in both Paris and Madrid. Participants in SMU-in-Spain should have completed their first year of college-level Spanish. A minimum G.P.A of 2.70 normally is required. Students can take a variety of courses such as communications, history, language and literature, political science, and studio art. Students are housed with local families. Orientation trips and cultural events are an integral part of both programs. Participation in either program for a full academic year is recommended, but students may attend either the fall or spring semester.

SMU-in-Japan. SMU students have an unusual and challenging opportunity to live and study for the fall or the full academic year through a well-established exchange program with Kwansei Gakuin University, which is located near Osaka, Japan. Students enroll for specially designed courses taught in English. Field trips and cultural events are an integral part of the Japan experience. Students should have completed one year of college Japanese.

SMU-in-Britain. For students desiring a year of study in England, the University offers counseling and assistance in gaining admission to a British university. For all work successfully completed under this arrangement, appropriate academic credit will be recorded at SMU. Over the years, students have studied arts, science, engineering, economics, history, and English at various British institutions.

49. Where could the above description be found?
    (A) A college catalogue.   (B) A tourist itinerary.
    (C) A government report.   (D) A WTO statement.

50. What is the above description about?
    (A) The instruction in SMU's international programs.
    (B) A summer preview for an international concert season.
    (C) An acceptable score for getting into a college.
    (D) Information on B&Bs for accommodation.

51. Which course is NOT included in SMU's well-established semester programs?
    (A) Political science.　　　　(B) Language and literature.
    (C) Studio classroom.　　　　(D) History.

52. What language is used to teach students who enroll for specially designed courses in the exchange program provided in Osaka, Japan?
    (A) French.　(B) Japanese.　(C) English.　(D) Spanish.

第 53 至 56 題為題組

　　In the 1980s, overnight delivery services such as FedEx knew when they received a package and when it was delivered. Facing stiff competition, FedEx re-evaluated its business processes and determined that most customers eagerly wanted to know where in the delivery process a package was, especially when it was not delivered as expected. FedEx reached its first stage in the use of computers by making such information available to its customers via the Web.

　　To do this, the company first sought to automate the extensive information by including truck loading, driver delivery, and customer signature on a hand-held computer. The hand-held computers were plugged into a dashboard radio device that transmitted the signature and delivery information within seven seconds to the centralized FedEx database in Memphis, Tennessee. Customers could access this information by calling a toll-free number and speaking to a customer service representative to learn, to the minute, where their packages were in transit.

FedEx moved to the second stage when it made its package delivery database available on the Web to its customers. This allowed users to determine the status of any of their packages. The move was taken to reduce demands on the customer service department, but it had the added effect of increasing business by 15% almost immediately, while at the same time reducing the cost of customer service dramatically. This shift had several other subtle effects. FedEx was now viewed as being the innovator in the package delivery industry. Even though its shipment process was unchanged, the Web-based information process enhanced the company's image. A secondary effect was to reduce the threat from all competitors simply because they initially could not offer the same service and, if they did, they would clearly be doing so in response to FedEx's innovation.

53. According to this article, what concerns customers most when they send their packages?
　　(A) How much the delivery of their packages costs.
　　(B) Who FedEx's other competitors are.
　　(C) How skillful the FedEx staff are in using computers.
　　(D) Where in the delivery process their package is.

54. How did FedEx automate the way business information was processed and transmitted to the centralized FedEx database?
　　(A) It demanded all customers have computers.
　　(B) It demanded customers dial a toll-free number.
　　(C) It placed all the related information on a hand-held computer.
　　(D) It demanded all truck drivers turn on a dashboard radio device when driving.

55. In the first stage, how could customers access the information to learn where their packages were in transit?
   (A) By checking the BBS.
   (B) By calling a toll-free number to the customer service department.
   (C) By playing with a keyboard.
   (D) By traveling to Memphis.

56. Which is NOT an advantage of FedEx's second move, which made its package delivery database available on the Web to its customers?
   (A) It increased demands on the customer service department.
   (B) It increased business by 15%.
   (C) It reduced the cost of customer service.
   (D) It enhanced the company's image and reduced the threat from competitors.

第貳部份：非選擇題（佔 28 分）

一、英文翻譯（8 %）

說明：　1. 將下列兩句中文翻譯成適當之英文，並將答案寫在「答案卷」上。
　　　　2. 未按題意翻譯者，不予計分。

1. 我們真的很擔心傑夫，因為他期末考考不及格。

2. 如果他不能克服這次失敗所引起的挫折，他很可能會再次失敗。

二、英文作文（20 %）

說明：　1. 依提示在「答案卷」上寫一篇英文作文。
　　　　2. 文長至少 120 個單詞。

提示：　文章第一段請以 "I shall never forget what happened between ＿＿＿ and me when I was ＿＿＿＿＿." 開始，敘述從小到大你父母親與你（或長輩與你）之間所發生過最難忘的一件事。第二段請描述該件事對你的影響或啟發。

大學入學指定科目考試英文模擬試題③詳解

第壹部分：單一選擇題

一、詞彙及慣用語：

1. (**A**) The bad weather discouraged Jack and his friends from climbing the mountain last weekend. Therefore, Jack <u>proposed</u> an alternative plan to have fun.
   上週末天氣不好，使得傑克和他的朋友不敢去爬山。因此，傑克<u>提出</u>了另一個計劃去玩。

   (A) *propose* (prə'poz) *v.* 提議　(B) conclude (kən'klud) *v.* 下結論
   (C) express (ɪk'sprɛs) *v.* 表達　(D) extend (ɪk'stɛnd) *v.* 延伸

   discourage (dɪs'kɝɪdʒ) *v.* 勸阻；使不敢做 < *from* >
   alternative (ɔl'tɝnətɪv) *adj.* 另一可供選擇的；代替的
   have fun 玩得愉快

2. (**A**) We had better make a reservation in advance in case there are no <u>vacancies</u> at the hotel during the holiday season.
   我們最好事先預訂，以防萬一在假期間，旅館沒有<u>空房間</u>。

   (A) *vacancy* ('vekənsɪ) *n.* 空房間
   (B) facility (fə'sɪlətɪ) *n.* 設備
   (C) possibility (,pasə'bɪlətɪ) *n.* 可能性
   (D) variety (və'raɪətɪ) *n.* 多樣性

   reservation (,rɛzɚ'veʃən) *n.* 預訂　　*in advance* 事先
   in case 以防萬一　　*the holiday season* 假期

3. (**C**) We saw some roads in the earthquake-hit areas were <u>elevated</u>. Some of them were even higher than the houses.
   我們看見發生地震的地區，有些道路<u>隆起</u>。其中有些甚至比房子還高。

   (A) alleviate (ə'livɪ,et) *v.* 減輕
   (B) eliminate (ɪ'lɪmə,net) *v.* 消除
   (C) *elevate* ('ɛlə,vet) *v.* 提高
   (D) associate (ə'soʃɪ,et) *v.* 聯想

   hit (hɪt) *v.* 襲擊

4. (**D**) His new book greatly <u>exaggerates</u> the intelligence of a monkey, claiming that it can talk and deal with human difficulties.
他的新書<u>誇大</u>猴子的智力，說牠可以說話，並應付人類所遭遇的困難。
(A) invade (ɪn'ved) v. 入侵　　　　(B) measure ('mɛʒə) v. 測量
(C) overcome (,ovə'kʌm) v. 克服
(D) *exaggerate* (ɪg'zædʒə,ret) v. 誇大

intelligence (ɪn'tɛlədʒəns) n. 智力　　claim (klem) v. 宣稱
deal with 應付；處理

5. (**C**) Young people <u>sacrifice</u> their health for wealth; old people offer wealth for health.
年輕人爲了財富<u>犧牲</u>健康；老年人則爲了健康願意獻出財富。
(A) devote (dɪ'vot) v. 奉獻 < *to* >
(B) contribute (kən'trɪbjut) v. 貢獻 < *to* >
(C) *sacrifice* ('sækrə,faɪs) v. 犧牲
(D) appreciate (ə'priʃɪ,et) v. 欣賞；感激

wealth (wɛlθ) n. 財富　　　offer ('ɔfə) v. 提供；奉獻

6. (**C**) It never disappoints you to fish in a river <u>abundant</u> in salmon.
在<u>盛產</u>鮭魚的河裡釣魚，你絕不會失望。
(A) occupied ('akjə,paɪd) adj. 被佔據的
(B) acceptable (ək'sɛptəbl̩) adj. 可接受的
(C) *abundant* (ə'bʌndənt) adj. 豐富的 < *in* >
(D) confident ('kanfədənt) adj. 有信心的

disappoint (,dɪsə'pɔɪnt) v. 使失望　　salmon ('sæmən) n. 鮭魚

7. (**A**) With two equally qualified candidates, you can be sure that the mayoral election in Taipei at the end of this year will be very <u>competitive</u>. 由於兩位候選人實力相當，所以今年年底台北市的市長選舉，競爭一定非常<u>激烈</u>。
(A) *competitive* (kəm'pɛtətɪv) adj. 競爭激烈的
(B) accurate ('ækjərɪt) adj. 準確的
(C) sincere (sɪn'sɪr) adj. 眞誠的　　(D) separate ('sɛpərɪt) adj. 分開的
qualified ('kwɑlə,faɪd) adj. 有資格的；有能力的
mayoral ('meərəl) adj. 市長的

8. (**B**) She became <u>furious</u> when her best friend stole her boyfriend away from her.

當她最好的朋友，搶走她的男朋友時，她<u>非常生氣</u>。

(A) awake〔ə'wek〕*adj.* 醒著的

(B) *furious*〔'fjʊrɪəs〕*adj.* 狂怒的

(C) direct〔də'rɛkt〕*adj.* 直接的

(D) repetitive〔rɪ'pɛtɪtɪv〕*adj.* 重覆的

steal〔stil〕*v.* 用不正當手段取得

9. (**D**) My pen pal was <u>definitely</u> wrong about Taiwan, saying it was in the southern hemisphere next to Australia.

我的筆友對台灣<u>一定</u>有誤解，他說台灣位於南半球，就在澳洲的旁邊。

(A) extensively〔ɪk'stɛnsɪvlɪ〕*adv.* 廣泛地

(B) continually〔kən'tɪnjʊəlɪ〕*adv.* 持續地

(C) graciously〔'greʃəslɪ〕*adv.* 優雅地

(D) *definitely*〔'dɛfənɪtlɪ〕*adv.* 必定

pen pal 筆友　　hemisphere〔'hɛməsˌfɪr〕*n.*（地球）半球

next to 在～旁邊　　Australia〔ɔ'streljə〕*n.* 澳洲

10. (**D**) A man with a <u>consistently</u> negative attitude is miserable and stupid. Life is too precious to be wasted on endless complaints and sighs.

<u>老是</u>抱持著否定態度的人，是很可悲而愚蠢的。生命非常珍貴，不該浪費在無止盡的抱怨及嘆息上。

(A) temporarily〔'tɛmpəˌrɛrəlɪ〕*adv.* 暫時地

(B) professionally〔prə'fɛʃənəlɪ〕*adv.* 專業地

(C) wonderfully〔'wʌndəfəlɪ〕*adv.* 很棒地

(D) *consistently*〔kən'sɪstəntlɪ〕*adv.* 一直；老是

negative〔'nɛgətɪv〕*adj.* 負面的；否定的

miserable〔'mɪzərəbl̩〕*adj.* 可悲的

precious〔'prɛʃəs〕*adj.* 珍貴的

endless〔'ɛndlɪs〕*adj.* 無止盡的

complaint〔kəm'plent〕*n.* 抱怨

sigh〔saɪ〕*n.* 嘆息

11. (**B**) Deep inside the human heart is the <u>curiosity</u> about what other people do in private. That's why the media pursue and people peep. 人們的內心深處，都很<u>好奇</u>別人私底下在做什麼。那就是為什麼媒體會不斷追逐，以及人們會偷窺的原因。

    (A) attraction (ə'trækʃən) *n.* 吸引力
    (B) *curiosity* (ˌkjʊrɪ'ɑsətɪ) *n.* 好奇心
    (C) dependence (dɪ'pɛndəns) *n.* 依賴
    (D) experiment (ɪk'spɛrəmənt) *n.* 實驗

    in private 私底下　　media ('midɪə) *n. pl.* 媒體
    pursue (pə'su) *v.* 追逐　　peep (pip) *v.* 偷窺

12. (**D**) Soccer is popular in Europe but it never really <u>caught on</u> in Taiwan. 足球在歐洲很流行，但是在台灣卻從未真正<u>流行</u>過。

    (A) set up 設立　　　　　　(B) get fired 被解僱
    (C) stop off 中途停留片刻　　(D) *catch on* 流行

    soccer ('sɑkə) *n.* 足球

13. (**B**) I bought her a delicate bracelet <u>in return for</u> her hospitality during my stay.
為了<u>報答</u>她在我停留期間殷勤的招待，我買了一個精緻的手鐲給她。

    (A) out of 出於　　　　　　(B) *in return for* 作為報答
    (C) for sure 確定的　　　　　(D) in use 被使用中

    delicate ('dɛləkət) *adj.* 精緻的　　bracelet ('breslɪt) *n.* 手鐲
    hospitality (ˌhɑspɪ'tælətɪ) *n.* 殷勤招待　　stay (ste) *n.* 停留期間

14. (**B**) The violent typhoon had <u>cut off</u> the electricity in this small town. As a result, the residents here were not able to use any electrical appliances.
強烈颱風<u>切斷</u>了小鎮的電力。因此，這裡的居民們無法使用任何電器用品。

    (A) cut back 縮減；削減　　(B) *cut off* 切斷
    (C) cut out 刪除；剪下　　　(D) cut down 砍伐；縮減

    violent ('vaɪələnt) *adj.* 強烈的　　electricity (ɪˌlɛk'trɪsətɪ) *n.* 電
    resident ('rɛzədənt) *n.* 居民　　*electrical appliances* 電器用品

15. (**A**) To keep in shape, you have to <u>make it a rule</u> to squeeze some exercise into your busy schedule.

　　為了保持健康，你<u>務必要</u>將一些運動擠入你緊湊的時間表中。

　　(A) *make it a rule* 務必要　　　(B) make out 理解
　　(C) turn out 結果　　　　　　　　(D) live it up 享受人生

　　keep in shape 保持健康　　squeeze〔skwiz〕*v.* 硬擠；硬塞

二、綜合測驗：

<u>第 16 至 20 題為題組</u>

Aston began playing soccer when he was a young boy in England. In 1936, when he was 19 years old, he hurt his ankle and <u>stopped playing</u>
　　　　　　　　　　　　　　　　　　　　　　　　　　　　　16
soccer. He decided to become a referee.

　　當艾斯頓是個小男孩的時候，他開始在英國踢足球。1936 年，當他 19 歲時，他的腳踝受傷，因而停止踢足球。他決定要成為一位裁判。

　　　　ankle〔'æŋkḷ〕*n.* 腳踝　　referee〔,rɛfə'ri〕*n.* 裁判

16. (**B**) 依句意，選 (B) *stopped playing soccer*「停止踢足球」。

Aston made an important <u>contribution</u> to the sport. He invented the card
　　　　　　　　　　　　　　17
system. Referees give cards to players <u>who violate rules</u>. A yellow card is
　　　　　　　　　　　　　　　　　　　18
a warning. A red card means you are out of the game. According to Aston, the card system prevents language problems. The cards are an international language. Every player understands <u>what</u> the yellow and red cards mean.
　　　　　　　　　　　　　　　　　19

　　艾斯頓為這項運動提供了一個重要的貢獻。他發明了舉牌制度。裁判把牌判給違反規定的球員。黃牌是警告，紅牌表示你出局了。根據艾斯頓的看法，舉牌制度可防止語言方面的問題。牌子是一種國際性的語言，每個球員都了解黃牌和紅牌的意義。

　　　　invent〔ɪn'vɛnt〕*v.* 發明　　card〔kɑrd〕*n.* 卡片；牌
　　　　system〔'sɪstəm〕*n.* 系統；制度　　player〔'pleɚ〕*n.* 球員
　　　　warning〔'wɔrnɪŋ〕*n.* 警告　　*be out of the game* 在球賽中出局
　　　　prevent〔prɪ'vɛnt〕*v.* 防止　　international〔,ɪntɚ'næʃənḷ〕*adj.* 國際的

17. (**C**) (A) tribulation〔͵trɪbjə'leʃən〕 *n.* 苦難
　　　　　(B) attribution〔͵ætrə'bjuʃən〕 *n.* 歸因
　　　　　(C) *contribution*〔͵kɑntrə'bjuʃən〕 *n.* 貢獻
　　　　　(D) distribution〔͵dɪstrə'bjuʃən〕 *n.* 分配

18. (**D**) 依句意，要選形容詞子句修飾 players，所以 (A) break rules、(B) violated rules、(C) to break rules 用法皆不合，故選 (D) *who violate rules*。　break〔brek〕 *v.* 違背　violate〔'vaɪə͵let〕 *v.* 違反

19. (**C**) 依句意，選 (C) *what* the yellow and red cards mean「黃牌與紅牌代表什麼意義」。

Aston said he got the idea from a traffic signal. He was driving home from a 1966 World Cup match. In that game a German-speaking referee didn't make his calls <u>clear</u>. Some of the players could not understand him.
　　　　　　　　　　　20
Today all soccer players understand the meanings of the cards.
　　艾斯頓說他是從交通號誌得到這個靈感。他當時看完 1966 年的一場世界盃比賽，正要開車回家。在那場比賽中，一個說德文的裁判沒有把指示說清楚。一些球員不了解他的意思。現在，所有的足球員都了解卡片的意義。

　　　　idea〔aɪ'diə〕 *n.* 想法；靈感
　　　　traffic signal 交通號誌；紅綠燈
　　　　World Cup 世界盃（足球賽）
　　　　match〔mætʃ〕 *n.* 比賽
　　　　German〔'dʒɝmən〕 *n.* 德文
　　　　call〔kɔl〕 *n.* 指示；裁定

20. (**C**) make 接受詞後，須接形容詞當受詞補語，且依句意，選 (C) *clear*「清楚的」。而 (A) clean「乾淨的」，則不合句意。

第 21 至 25 題爲題組

In the lecture hall, the speaker says, "I'm going to give this US$100 bill to one of you. Who wants it?" A sea of hands go up immediately. "But first let me do this." He then crumples the bill up. "Who still wants it?" the speaker asks. Again the hands go up <u>eagerly</u>. "Well, it seems
21
that you all learned a valuable lesson today." Some students frown. "I don't <u>get</u> it," a student whispers. "Wasn't he supposed to give a lecture
22
on suicide?"

在演講廳裡，演說者說：「我要把這張一百元美金的鈔票，送給你們其中一人。有誰想要？」很多人的手立刻舉起。「不過，讓我先這麼做。」他接著把鈔票揉得皺皺的。演說者問道：「還有誰要呢？」再一次，大家熱烈地舉手。「嗯，今天，你們似乎都學到寶貴的教訓了。」有些學生在皺眉頭。一個學生低聲說：「我不懂。他不是應該發表有關自殺的演講嗎？」

> lecture ('lɛktʃɚ) *n.* 演講　　hall (hɔl) *n.* 大廳
> *a sea of* 很多；大量　　crumple ('krʌmpl) *v.* 使變皺 (= *wrinkle*)
> frown (fraʊn) *v.* 皺眉　　*be supposed to* 應該 (= *should*)
> suicide ('suə,saɪd) *n.* 自殺

21. (**D**) (A) reluctantly (rɪ'lʌktəntlɪ) *adv.* 不願意地
  (B) permanently ('pɝmənəntlɪ) *adv.* 永遠地
  (C) artificially (,ɑrtə'fɪʃəlɪ) *adv.* 人造地；人工地
  (D) *eagerly* ('igɚlɪ) *adv.* 熱烈地

22. (**D**) 依句意，選 (D) *get it*，表「了解」之意。(A) have it「擁有；挨罵」，(B) make it「成功；做到」，(C) take it「相信；認為」，句意均不合。

　　"No matter what I did to the money, you still wanted it," the speaker says. "Why? <u>Even though</u> I crumpled it, it still had the same
23
value. It was still worth US$100. <u>Like</u> this US$100 bill, we are often
24
scarred in life. We are dropped, crumpled and stepped on. We all feel

worthless at one time or another, but like the bill, <u>whatever</u> happens to
                                                         25
us, we will never lose our value. We learn valuable lessons from our
disappointments."

　　「無論我把這張鈔票怎麼樣，你們還是要它，」演說者說：「為什麼呢？
即使我把它揉皺了，它還是擁有同樣的價值，它仍然值美金一百元。我們就像
這張一百元的鈔票，在生命中常常傷痕累累。我們受挫敗、被蹂躪、被踐踏。
我們大家偶爾都會覺得自己沒價值，但就像這張鈔票一樣，無論發生任何事，
我們決不會失去自己的價值。我們從失望中學習到寶貴的教訓。」

> scar〔skɑr〕*v.* 留下傷痕　　drop〔drɑp〕*v.* 挫敗
> ***step on*** 踐踏　　worthless〔'wɝθlɪs〕*adj.* 沒有價值的
> ***at one time or another*** 有時；偶爾（= *sometimes*）
> disappointment〔͵dɪsə'pɔɪntmənt〕*n.* 失望

23. (**A**) 前後二子句之間，需要連接詞，故本題選 (A) ***Even though*** 「即使」。
　　　 (D) despite「儘管」，為介系詞，不能接子句，用法錯誤。
　　　 (B) instead of「而非」，(C) because of「因為」，文法、句意均不合。

24. (**A**) 依句意，我們「就像」這張鈔票一樣，選 (A) ***Like***。(B) likely「可能
　　　 的」，為形容詞，(C) unlike「不像」，(D) dislike「不喜歡」，均不合。

25. (**B**) 按照句意，「無論發生任何事」，選 (B) ***whatever***，相當於 no matter
　　　 what。

第 26 至 30 題為題組

　　The sites people spend the most time on each month are known as
"sticky" sites. The hard part for sticky sites is making money. Ironically,
the stickier a site is, <u>the less appealing</u> it is to advertisers. If a site is
                              26
sticky, that means people are not clicking on ads. <u>What's more</u>, stickiness
                                                        27
is a meaningless measure for sites that sell products.

　　人們每個月花最多時間上的網站，被稱為「閒掛的」網站。閒掛網站的難
處就是賺錢。很諷刺的是，人們越喜歡上的閒掛網站，對廣告商而言，越沒有
吸引力。如果人們喜歡上某一個閒掛網站，那就表示，他們不會點選廣告。此
外，對販賣商品的網站而言，黏著率是個無意義的標準。

site〔saɪt〕*n.* 網站（*＝website*）　*be known as* 被稱爲～
sticky〔'stɪkɪ〕*adj.* 黏的；閒掛的
ironically〔aɪ'rɑnɪklɪ〕*adv.* 諷刺地
advertiser〔'ædvə,taɪzə〕*n.* 廣告商
click〔klɪk〕*v.* 按滑鼠的聲音；引申爲「點選」之意
stickiness〔'stɪkɪnɪs〕*n.* 黏著率【即統計網頁使用者在單一網頁上停留
的時間長短】　measure〔'mɛʒə〕*n.* 標準

26. (**A**)　"*the*＋比較級～, *the*＋比較級…"，表示「越～，越…」之意，在
　　 此依句意應是，對廣告商而言，「越沒有吸引力」，故選 (A) *the less*
　　 appealing，appealing〔ə'pilɪŋ〕*adj.* 吸引人的，相當於 attractive。
　　 (B)、(C) 均爲最高級，文法不合。
　　 profitable〔'prɑfɪtəbḷ〕*adj.* 賺錢的；有利可圖的

27. (**C**)　(A) what's better　更好的是
　　　　　 (B) in addition to　除了～之外（*＝besides*）
　　　　　 (C) *what's more*　此外（*＝besides*；*in addition*）
　　　　　 (D) in case　以免

To take advantage of such loyalty, the sites have supplemented traditional
　　28
banner ads at the top of each Web page with sponsorship within the site
itself.　The secret to their success is that they're not trying to create the
latest, greatest, coolest thing.　Instead, they've just paid attention to what
　　　　　　　　　　　　　　　　　　　29
people do—100 million Americans play cards every day; 50 million play
bingo.　So go ahead.　Squander your time on that PC playing games until
3:00 in the morning.　After all, you're hardly the only one hooked on
　　　　　　　　　　　　　　　　　　　　　　　　30
silly sites.

爲了利用網友的這種忠誠度，網站會在每個網頁上方的傳統標語廣告中，添加
網站內部的廣告贊助。這些網站成功的秘訣在於，他們並非試圖創造出最新、
最棒、最酷的東西。相反地，他們只是注意到人們所做的事——有一億個美國人
每天都會玩撲克牌；五千萬人玩賓果遊戲。所以，請便，把你的時間浪費在個
人電腦上，玩遊戲玩到凌晨三點吧。畢竟，你並不是唯一一個迷上那些愚蠢網
站的人。

loyalty〔ˈlɔɪəltɪ〕*n.* 忠誠　　supplement〔ˈsʌpləˌmɛnt〕*v.* 補充；附加
banner〔ˈbænɚ〕*n.* 標語；旗幟
sponsórship〔ˈspɑnsɚˌʃɪp〕*n.* 贊助　　secret〔ˈsikrɪt〕*n.* 秘訣 < *to* >
create〔krɪˈet〕*v.* 創造　　squander〔ˈskwɑndɚ〕*v.* 浪費
after all 畢竟　　silly〔ˈsɪlɪ〕*adj.* 愚蠢的

28.(**B**) 依句意，「爲了要」利用…，用不定詞，選 (B) *To take*。
　　　 take advantage of 利用

29.(**D**) 前後句意爲相反之意，故選 (D) ***Instead***「相反地」。而 (A) besides「此
　　　 外」，(B) therefore「因此」，(C) nevertheless「然而」，均不合句意。

30.(**B**) (A) absorbed〔əbˈsɔrbd〕*adj.* 專心的 < *in* >
　　　 (B) ***hooked***〔hʊkt〕*adj.* 入迷的；上癮的 < *on* >
　　　 (C) involved〔ɪnˈvɑlvd〕*adj.* 牽涉在內的；專心的 < *in* >
　　　 (D) dedicated〔ˈdɛdəˌketɪd〕*adj.* 致力於；專心的 < *to* >

三、文意選填：

第 31 至 40 題爲題組

　　Relationships among brothers and sisters are of main concern. Positive
sibling relationships can be a <u>source</u> of strength, whereas unresolved early
　　　　　　　　　　　　　　　　　　31
conflicts can create lasting wounds. In order not to be <u>caught</u> in a spiral
　　　　　　　　　　　　　　　　　　　　　　　　　　　　32
of sibling fighting or conflict, parents should know what to do when their
kids are fighting.

　　手足之間的關係非常重要。良好的手足關係，是力量的來源，然而幼時的
衝突，若是懸而未解，則會造成永久的傷害。要避免被困在手足間惡鬥或衝突
的惡性循環裡的話，當孩子打架時，父母就應該知道要怎麼做。

relationship〔rɪˈleʃənˌʃɪp〕*n.* 關係　　***of main concern*** 非常重要
positive〔ˈpɑzətɪv〕*adj.* 良好的；正面的
sibling〔ˈsɪblɪŋ〕*n.* 兄弟姊妹　　strength〔strɛŋθ〕*n.* 力量
whereas〔hwɛrˈæz〕*conj.* 然而
unresolved〔ˌʌnrɪˈzɑlvd〕*adj.* 未解決的　　conflict〔ˈkɑnflɪkt〕*n.* 衝突
lasting〔ˈlæstɪŋ〕*adj.* 永久的　　wound〔wund〕*n.* 傷害
in order not to V. 爲了不要～　　spiral〔ˈspaɪrəl〕*n.* 惡性循環

31. (**G**) 依句意，良好的手足關係，是力量的「來源」，選 (G) *source*。

32. (**C**) 依句意，要避免「被困在」這種惡性循環中，選 (C) *caught*。

Parents shouldn't compare a kid with a sibling—even <u>favorably</u>. (Most
                        33

parents know better than to ask, "Why can't you be more like your brother?")

Comparison sets one child against another, and it subtly <u>undermines</u> their
                                        34

relationships when a parent says, "You're much better organized than

your sister." Each child should be appreciated individually—though not

<u>necessarily</u> equally.
35

　　父母不該拿孩子和其他的兄弟姊妹們相比——甚至是讚美的比較。(大部
分的父母，應該都知道要避免問孩子：「爲什麼你不能多學學你哥哥？」) 這種
比較，會讓小孩彼此對立，而且當父母親說：「你比妹妹有條理多了。」的時候，
也會逐漸損害手足關係。每個孩子都該分別受到重視——儘管受到重視的程度不
一定相同。

　　　　compare A *with* B　拿 A 和 B 相比
　　　　know better (*than to V.*)　不會笨到做～；應該不會～
　　　　comparison〔kəmˋpærəsn̩〕*n.* 比較
　　　　set against　使和…對立
　　　　subtly〔ˋsʌtlɪ〕*adv.* 細微地
　　　　organized〔ˋɔrgənˏaɪzd〕*adj.* 有條理的
　　　　appreciate〔əˋpriʃɪˏet〕*v.* 重視
　　　　individually〔ˏɪndɪˋvɪdʒʊəlɪ〕*adv.* 分別地
　　　　equally〔ˋikwəlɪ〕*adv.* 相等地

33. (**F**) 由下文 it subtly undermines their…sister 可知，甚至連「讚美」的比
　　　　較，也會對小孩造成影響，選 (F) *favorably*〔ˋfevərəblɪ〕*adv.* 讚許地。

34. (**B**) 依句意，父母親這麼說，會「逐漸損害」手足關係，選 (B) *undermines*。
　　　　undermine〔ˏʌndəˋmaɪn〕*v.* 逐漸損害

35. (**J**) *not necessarily*　不一定

　　Parents can't step in in every kid's quarrel, but neither can they just let things be. They should <u>establish</u> a "no-hitting, no-hurting" rule, so kids
36
will know they are expected to work out their problems peacefully, sometimes with assistance. A parent can be helpful by listening to each side and then framing the problems aloud: "So, I see that you're really mad because…" Depending on the severity of the problem, a parent might then express <u>confidence</u> that the kids can solve it and leave the room.
37

　　父母親不該每次孩子爭吵就介入，可是他們也不能放手不管。他們應該制定「不出手，不傷害」的規則，那麼孩子們就會明瞭他們必須和平解決問題，有時甚至要尋求協助。父母親必須聆聽雙方的說法，然後大聲說出問題所在，例如像是：「好，我知道你們很生氣，是因為…」，才有助於解決爭端。視問題的嚴重性而定，父母也許可以向子女說明他們有信心，相信孩子可以自己解決問題，然後就離開房間。

> ***step in*** 干涉；介入　　quarrel〔ˈkwɔrəl〕*n.* 爭吵
> expect〔ɪkˈspɛkt〕*v.* 認為…必要　　***work out*** 解決
> peacefully〔ˈpisfəlɪ〕*adv.* 和平地
> assistance〔əˈsɪstəns〕*n.* 幫助　　frame〔frem〕*v.* 擬出；說出
> aloud〔əˈlaʊd〕*adv.* 大聲地　　mad〔mæd〕*adj.* 生氣的
> ***depend on*** 視～而定　　severity〔səˈvɛrətɪ〕*n.* 嚴重

36. (**I**) 依句意，父母應該「制定」規則，故選 (I) ***establish***〔əˈstæblɪʃ〕*v.* 制定。

37. (**D**) 依句意，父母可以向子女說明他們有「信心」，相信他們可以自己解決問題，故選 (D) ***confidence***〔ˈkɑnfədəns〕*n.* 信心。

　　Parents should step in directly, however, whenever an argument turns <u>violent</u>. Most kids hate fighting. They do it because they don't have other
38
tools for dealing with their frustrations. Fighters should be <u>separated</u> to cool
39
off, and a parent should later listen to both parties, asking the kids to help come up with a solution. The parents shouldn't <u>cast</u> one child as a bully and
40
the other as the victim; fights among siblings are seldom this simple.

　　然而，當爭吵轉向暴力時，父母就該立刻插手。大部分的孩子並不喜歡打架。他們之所以會打起來，是因為他們沒有其他方法來應付挫折。父母應該把打架的人隔開，讓他們冷靜下來，然後聆聽雙方說詞，並要求他們幫忙想出解決之道。父母不該認定某一方就是欺負別人的人，另一方就是受害者；手足間打架，通常都不是這麼單純的。

> directly〔də'rɛktlɪ〕*adv.* 立刻
> argument〔'ɑrgjəmənt〕*n.* 爭論　　　***deal with*** 處理
> frustration〔frʌs'treʃən〕*n.* 挫折　　***cool off*** 冷卻；平息
> party〔'pɑrtɪ〕*n.* 一方　　***come up with*** 想出（主意、方法等）
> bully〔'bʊlɪ〕*n.* 欺負他人者　　　victim〔'vɪktɪm〕*n.* 受害者

38.（**E**）依句意，當爭吵轉向「暴力」時，父母就該立刻插手，故選 (E) ***violent***。

39.（**A**）依句意，打架的人應該「被隔開」，故選 (A) ***separated***。

40.（**H**）依句意，父母不該「認定」某一方就是欺負別人的人，另一方就是受害者，故選 (H) ***cast***。

　　By dealing with sibling fighting in a proper way, parents can help develop good sibling relationships, which are a powerful source of support in life.

　　父母若能妥善調解手足間的紛爭，就能幫助建立良好的手足關係，這種關係在人的一生中，是強而有力的支柱來源。

> fighting〔'faɪtɪŋ〕*n.* 爭論　　proper〔'prɑpɚ〕*adj.* 適當的
> powerful〔'paʊɚfəl〕*adj.* 強有力的　　support〔sə'port〕*n.* 支持

四、篇章結構：

第 41 至 45 題為題組

　　News is everywhere and serves many different functions. ⁴¹(C) News gives instant coverage of important events. News also provides facts and information. ⁴²(A) In addition, news is business: a way to make money by selling advertising and/or newspapers and magazines. Sometimes news is propaganda or disinformation: a way to control a population. ⁴³**(B) But whatever news is, it is all around us.** We can't escape it. Every day we are bombarded by information: newspapers, magazines, television and the Internet.

　　新聞到處都有，並提供許多不同的功能。新聞提供重要事件的即時報導。新聞同時也提供事實及資訊。此外，新聞是一種商業：一種藉由販賣廣告、報紙及雜誌，來賺錢的方式。有時候，新聞是一種宣傳，或是一種不正確的報導：一種控制群眾的方式。但是無論新聞到底是什麼，它總是充斥在我們身邊。我們不能避免它。我們每天被資訊所轟炸：報紙、雜誌以及網際網路。

serve〔sɝv〕v. 提供　　function〔'fʌŋkʃən〕n. 功能
give〔gɪv〕v. 提供　　instant〔'ɪnstənt〕adj. 立即的
coverage〔'kʌvərɪdʒ〕n. 報導　　event〔ɪ'vɛnt〕n. 事件
provide〔prə'vaɪd〕v. 提供　　fact〔fækt〕n. 事實
information〔,ɪnfə'meʃən〕n. 資訊　　*in addition* 此外
make money 賺錢　　advertising〔'ædvɚ,taɪzɪŋ〕n. 廣告
propaganda〔,prapə'gændə〕n. 宣傳
disinformation〔dɪs,ɪnfə'meʃən〕n. 不正確的報導
control〔kən'trol〕v. 控制
population〔,papjə'leʃen〕n.（具有共同特點的）一群人
escape〔ə'skep〕v. 避免　　bombard〔bam'bard〕v. 轟炸
Internet〔'ɪntɚ,nɛt〕n. 網際網路

"News" does not always mean something that is unquestionably true. Although the news seems to be based on facts, these facts are usually reported the way the media chooses to report them. ⁴⁴**(E) For example, some information that appears as news is really only speculation or theories formed by the reporters.** Furthermore, many journalists and reporters sensationalize or dramatize a news event in order to make a story more interesting. ⁴⁵**(D) Unfortunately, sensationalism often prevents us from learning the truth and causes great pain to the people it victimizes.** Therefore, as consumers of news we must learn to think critically about the news, the media, and what the truth is.

「新聞」並不代表百分之百是真實的。雖然新聞似乎以事實爲基礎,但這些事實通常是被以媒體選擇的方式來報導。舉例來說,有些看起來像新聞的資訊,實際上只是推測,或是記者自己形成的理論。此外,許多新聞從業人員及記者,都譁衆取寵,或將一個新聞事件戲劇化,只是爲了讓故事更有趣。很不幸地,譁衆取寵往往使我們無法得知事實,甚至造成受害者重大的傷痛。因此,身爲新聞的消費者,對於新聞、媒體及事實,我們必須學習批判性的思考。

unquestionably (ʌnˈkwɛstʃənəblɪ) *adv.* 無疑地

be based on 以~爲基礎　　media (ˈmidɪə) *n.* 媒體

appear (əˈpɪr) *v.* 看起來像　　speculation (ˌspɛkjəˈleʃən) *n.* 推測

theory (ˈθiərɪ) *n.* 理論　　form (fɔrm) *v.* 形成

reporter (rɪˈportɚ) *n.* 記者　　furthermore (ˈfɝðɚˌmor) *adv.* 此外

journalist (ˈdʒɝnḷɪst) *n.* 新聞工作者

sensationalize (sɛnˈseʃənḷˌaɪz) *v.* 追求轟動效應;譁衆取寵

dramatize (ˈdræməˌtaɪz) *v.* 使戲劇化;改編　　***in order to*** 爲了

unfortunately (ʌnˈfɔrtʃənɪtlɪ) *adv.* 不幸地

sensationalism (sɛnˈseʃənḷˌɪzəm) *n.* (新聞報導、文藝作品中) 追求
　轟動效應　　prevent (prɪˈvɛnt) *v.* 阻止 < *from* >

cause (kɔz) *v.* 導致　　pain (pen) *n.* 痛苦

victimize (ˈvɪktɪmˌaɪz) *v.* 使受害　　consumer (kənˈsumɚ) *n.* 消費者

critically (ˈkrɪtɪkḷɪ) *adv.* 批評性地

五、閱讀測驗:

第 46 至 48 題爲題組

　　There are many cats in China. Chinese people are very fond of cats. Chen Lee was a schoolteacher in Honan, China. Chen had a beautiful white cat, and he loved her very much. But a very sad thing happened one day. A rich man's car ran over the cat, and that was the end of her. Chen ran out onto the road.

　　中國境內有很多貓。中國人非常喜歡貓。陳黎是中國河南的一位學校老師。他養了一隻非常漂亮的白貓,也非常地疼愛牠。可是有一天,卻發生了一件悲慘的事情。一輛有錢人的車,輾過了這隻貓,結束了牠的生命。陳先生立刻飛奔到路上。

be fond of 喜歡　　***run over*** 輾過;壓過

"Oh, you poor thing!" he cried. "What shall I do without you? You were the light of my life."

People stopped and cried with Chen. The rich man stopped his car and came back. He put his arms around Chen and said, "I am very, very sorry about this accident. Please let me——"

"You don't understand!" Chen cried. "She was a wonderful pupil!"

"A pupil?" the man asked. "This cat? What do you mean?"

"You couldn't buy that cat for all the money in China!" Chen said. "I taught her every day. That cat could talk, sir!"

「喔，可憐的小東西！」他哭著。「沒有了你我該怎麼辦？你是我的生命之光。」

路人都停下來和陳先生一起哭了。那個有錢人把車停下，繞了回來。他把手搭在陳先生的肩上，說道：「發生這場意外我真的非常非常抱歉，請你讓我…」

「你不懂！」陳先生哭著說：「牠是一個很出色的學生！」

「學生？」這個人問道：「這隻貓？你的意思是？」

「就算用盡全中國的錢，你也買不到牠！」陳先生繼續說著：「我每天都在教牠。這隻貓是會說話的，先生！」

shall〔ʃel , ʃæl〕*aux.* 將會
accident〔'æksədənt〕*n.* 意外　　pupil〔'pjupl〕*n.* 學生

"Then I must help you," the man said. He took a handful of notes from his pocket. "Here, have this. Three hundred pounds. Is it enough? Will you forgive me? Can we be friends now?"

Chen took the money. "Thank you," he said. "I'll get another cat. Then I must begin all the work again."

The rich man went away in his car. A woman said to Chen, "Was it true? Could your cat talk? What could it say?"

"It was true, madam," Chen answered. "My cat had many difficult lessons. At last she could say the word CAT."

Everybody laughed. What is the Chinese word for cat? It is MIAW.

　　「那我非得幫你不可，」這個人回答。他從口袋裡拿出一把鈔票。「這些都拿去。三百英鎊。這樣夠嗎？你可以原諒我嗎？現在我們可以當朋友了嗎？」

　　陳先生收下了錢。「謝謝您，」他說：「我會再去買一隻貓。然後一切得重新來過。」

　　這個有錢人開著車離去後。有一個婦人問陳先生：「是真的嗎？你的貓真的會說話嗎？牠會說什麼？」

　　「當然是真的，夫人，」陳先生這麼回答。「我的貓上過很多很難的課。最後牠學會說『貓』這個字。」

　　每個人都笑出來了。因為中文字裡的貓怎麼叫呢？就是「貓」。

> handful〔ˈhænd͵fʊl〕n. 一把　　note〔not〕n. 紙鈔
> pocket〔ˈpɑkɪt〕n. 口袋　　forgive〔fəˈgɪv〕v. 原諒

46. (**D**) 陳先生的貓最後怎麼了？
　　　(A) 牠的課停了。　　　　　　　(B) 陳先生把牠賣給一個有錢人。
　　　(C) 牠開始學習。　　　　　　　(D) 牠在意外中死亡。

47. (**C**) 為什麼有人停下來和陳先生一起哭？因為 ＿＿＿＿＿＿＿。
　　　(A) 他們不喜歡那個有錢人。　　(B) 他們很窮
　　　(C) 陳先生的貓死了　　　　　　(D) 這隻貓很了不起
　　　something〔ˈsʌmθɪŋ〕n. 有價值或重要的人或物

48. (**D**) 這隻貓真的上過幾堂課？答案是 ＿＿＿＿＿＿＿。
　　　(A) 三百堂　　　　　　　　　　(B) 每天一堂課
　　　(C) 很多很難的課　　　　　　　(D) 一堂都沒有

第 49 至 52 題為題組

International Office

　　The University offers students an opportunity to live, study, and travel abroad in semester or year-long programs, as well as summer programs. Semester or year-long programs are maintained in Paris, Madrid, Copenhagen, Japan, Britain, Russia, and Australia. Programs in other countries may be added from time to time. Instruction in all programs is offered in English, except for courses in foreign languages and literature. Students in good standing at Southern Methodist University(SMU) and other universities may participate in SMU's International Programs.

國際事務處

　　本大學提供學生到國外生活、唸書及旅遊的機會，除了暑期課程之外，還有一學期或一學年的課程。學期或學年的課程，是在巴黎、馬德里、哥本哈根、日本、英國、俄國，以及澳洲進行。偶而會增加在其他國家的課程。除了外語及文學的課程之外，所有課程皆以英語教學。在南部衛理公會大學(SMU)以及其他大學表現優異的學生，可以參與南衛大的國際課程。

abroad〔ə'brɔd〕*adv.* 在國外　　year-long〔'jɪr'lɔŋ〕*adj.* 持續一年的
as well as 以及　　maintain〔men'ten〕*v.* 維持
Madrid〔mə'drɪd〕*n.* 馬德里（西班牙首都）
Copenhagen〔,kopən'hegən〕*n.* 哥本哈根（丹麥首都）
add〔æd〕*v.* 增加　　**from time to time** 偶而
instruction〔ɪn'strʌkʃən〕*n.* 教授；講課　　**except for** 除…之外
literature〔'lɪtərətʃə〕*n.* 文學　　standing〔'stændɪŋ〕*n.* 名次；等級
southern〔'sʌðən〕*adj.* 南部的
Methodist〔'mɛθədɪst〕*adj.* 衛理公會教徒或教派的
participate in 參與（ = *take part in* ）

Semester Programs

SMU-in-Paris and SMU-in-Spain. The University has well-established programs in both Paris and Madrid. Participants in SMU-in-Spain should have completed their first year of college-level Spanish. A minimum G.P.A. of 2.70 normally is required. Students can take a variety of courses such as communications, history, language and literature, political science, and studio art. Students are housed with local families. Orientation trips and cultural events are an integral part of both programs. Participation in either program for a full academic year is recommended, but students may attend either the fall or spring semester.

學期計劃

　　南衛大–在–巴黎及南衛大–在–西班牙。本大學在巴黎和馬德里都有聲望卓越的課程計劃。欲參加南衛大–在–西班牙者，應該完成大一西班牙語的課程。按照規定，學業成績總平均至少要 2.70 分以上。學生可選修各種不同的課程，像是傳播學、歷史、語言與文學、政治學，以及美術。學生會被安排和當地的家庭住在一起。新生訓練之旅和文化活動，皆是這兩個課程的重要部分。我們推薦欲參加這兩個課程中任一個的學生，參加一整個學年的課程，但是也可以只參加秋季班或春季班。

well-established (ˈwɛləˈstæblɪʃt) *adj.* 已建立良好聲譽的

participant (pəˈtɪsəpənt) *n.* 參與者　　complete (kəmˈplit) *v.* 完成

level (ˈlɛvḷ) *n.* 程度　　Spanish (ˈspænɪʃ) *n.* 西班牙語

minimum (ˈmɪnəməm) *n.* 最低限度

G.P.A. 學業成績總平均 (*Grade Point Average* 的略稱)

normally (ˈnɔrmḷɪ) *adv.* 標準地

a variety of 各式各樣的 (= various (ˈvɛrɪəs))

communications (kəˌmjunəˈkeʃənz) *n. pl.* 傳播學；通訊理論

political science 政治學　　*studio art* 在畫室上的美術課

house (haʊz) *v.* 使住宿　　local (ˈlokḷ) *adj.* 當地的

orientation (ˌorɪɛnˈteʃən) *n.* 新生訓練

integral (ˈɪntəgrəl) *adj.* 構成整體所必須的

participation (pɚˌtɪsəˈpeʃən) *n.* 參與

academic (ˌækəˈdɛmɪk) *adj.* 大學的

academic year 學年 (= *school year*)

recommend (ˌrɛkəˈmɛnd) *v.* 推薦

SMU-in-Japan. SMU students have an unusual and challenging opportunity to live and study for the fall or the full academic year through a well-established exchange program with Kwansei Gakuin University, which is located near Osaka, Japan. Students enroll for specially designed courses taught in English. Field trips and cultural events are an integral part of the Japan experience. Students should have completed one year of college Japanese.

南衛大-在-日本。參加秋季班或整學年課程的南衛大學生，有個特殊且具有挑戰性的機會，透過和 Kwansei Gakuin 大學的交換學生計劃，他們可以到日本居住及唸書，該大學位於日本大阪附近，而且這個計畫的聲譽良好。學生可上以英語教授的特別設計課程。校外教學和文化活動是體驗日本不可或缺的一部份。學生應該修完一年的大學日語。

challenging (ˈtʃælɪndʒɪŋ) *adj.* 具有挑戰性的

exchange (ɪksˈtʃendʒ) *n.* 交換 (這裡指交換學生)

be located 位於　　enroll (ɪnˈrol) *v.* 註冊

specially (ˈspɛʃəlɪ) *adv.* 特別地　　designed (dɪˈzaɪnd) *adj.* 設計好的

field trip 校外教學；實地參觀

SMU-in-Britain. For students desiring a year of study in England, the University offers counseling and assistance in gaining admission to a British university. For all work successfully completed under this arrangement, appropriate academic credit will be recorded at SMU. Over the years, students have studied arts, science, engineering, economics, history, and English at various British institutions.

南衛大-在-英國。對於渴望到英國唸一年書的學生而言，本大學提供諮詢及協助，幫助學生進入英國大學就讀。參與此計畫而且順利完成的部分，會在南衛大保有適當的學分記錄。好幾年來，學生已經在英國各個不同的機構，研讀藝術、科學、工程學、經濟學、歷史，以及英文。

counseling (ˈkaʊnslɪŋ) *n.* 指導　assistance (əˈsɪstəns) *n.* 協助
admission (ədˈmɪʃən) *n.* 入學許可 *< to >*
successfully (səkˈsɛsfəlɪ) *adv.* 成功地；順利地
arrangement (əˈrendʒmənt) *n.* 安排
appropriate (əˈproprɪɪt) *adj.* 適當的　credit (ˈkrɛdɪt) *n.* 學分
record (rɪˈkɔrd) *v.* 記錄　engineering (ˌɛndʒəˈnɪrɪŋ) *n.* 工程學
institution (ˌɪnstəˈtjuʃən) *n.* 機構

49. (**A**) 在哪裡可以找到上面這段敘述？
   (A) 一本大學的概況手冊。　　(B) 一張旅行行程表。
   (C) 一份官方報告。　　　　　(D) 一份世界貿易組織的聲明。
   description (dɪˈskrɪpʃən) *n.* 敘述
   catalogue (ˈkætḷˌɔg) *n.* 大學的概況手冊
   tourist (ˈtʊrɪst) *adj.* 觀光的
   itinerary (aɪˈtɪnəˌrɛrɪ) *n.* 旅行行程表
   statement (ˈstetmənt) *n.* 聲明

50. (**A**) 上列敘述是關於什麼？
   (A) 南衛大的國際課程教學。
   (B) 國際音樂季的夏季預告。
   (C) 可以就讀大學的分數。
   (D) 關於膳宿的資訊。
   preview (ˈpriˌvju) *n.* 預告　acceptable (əkˈsɛptəbḷ) *adj.* 可接受的
   B&B 床鋪 & 伙食；膳宿 (= *bed and breakfast*)
   get into 入學　accommodation (əˌkaməˈdeʃən) *n.* 住宿

51.(**C**) 哪一項課程並未包含在南衛大聲譽良好的學期課程中？
    (A) 政治學。   (B) 語言與文學。
    (C) 視聽教室。   (D) 歷史。
    studio classroom 視聽教室

52.(**C**) 在日本大阪的交換學生計劃的特別設計課程，是以何種語言教授
    學生？
    (A) 法文。   (B) 日文。
    (C) 英文。   (D) 西班牙文。

第 53 至 56 題爲題組

    In the 1980s, overnight delivery services such as FedEx knew when they received a package and when it was delivered. Facing stiff competition, FedEx re-evaluated its business processes and determined that most customers eagerly wanted to know where in the delivery process a package was, especially when it was not delivered as expected. FedEx reached its first stage in the use of computers by making such information available to its customers via the Web.

    在 1980 年代，限時快遞服務，如聯邦快遞，知道他們何時收到包裹，以及何時遞送包裹。面對激烈的競爭，聯邦快遞重新評估其企業運作，並確定大部份顧客最渴望知道的，是在運送過程中，他們的包裹在哪裡，尤其當包裹沒有如預期地送達時。聯邦快遞達到電腦化的第一個階段，就是使顧客可經由網際網路，得到這類的訊息。

> overnight〔ˋovɚˋnaɪt〕*adj.* 隔夜的   delivery〔dɪˋlɪvərɪ〕*n.* 遞送
> ***overnight delivery service*** 限時快遞服務   ***FedEx*** 聯邦快遞
> package〔ˋpækɪdʒ〕*n.* 包裹   stiff〔stɪf〕*adj.* 僵硬的；強烈的
> competition〔͵kɑmpəˋtɪʃən〕*n.* 競爭
> re-evaluate〔͵riɪˋvæljuͺet〕*v.* 重新評估
> process〔ˋprɑsɛs〕*n.* 過程；運作
> determine〔dɪˋtɝmɪn〕*v.* 確定
> eagerly〔ˋigɚlɪ〕*adv.* 渴望地；極想地   stage〔stedʒ〕*n.* 階段
> available〔əˋveləbl〕*adj.* 可獲得的
> via〔ˋvaɪə〕*prep.* 經由   ***the Web*** 網際網路

　　To do this, the company first sought to automate the extensive information by including truck loading, driver delivery, and customer signature on a hand-held computer.　The hand-held computers were plugged into a dashboard radio device that transmitted the signature and delivery information within seven seconds to the centralized FedEx database in Memphis, Tennessee.　Customers could access this information by calling a toll-free number and speaking to a customer service representative to learn, to the minute, where their packages were in transit.

　　為了達到這個目的，該公司最先以包括了卡車裝載、司機送貨、和使用掌上型電腦供顧客簽名的方式，設法使大量資訊自動化。這個掌上型電腦可以插在儀表板的無線電裝置，七秒內就將簽名及遞送資訊，傳到位於田納西州孟斐斯市的中央資料庫裡。顧客可以打免付費電話，詢問客服人員，以得知他們的包裹正在運輸途中的何處。

> sought〔sɔt〕*v.* 尋找（seek 的過去式）
> automate〔'ɔtə,met〕*v.* 使自動化
> extensive〔ɪk'stɛnsɪv〕*adj.* 大量的；廣泛的
> signature〔'sɪɡnətʃɚ〕*n.* 簽名　　hand-held〔'hænd'hɛld〕*adj.* 掌上的
> plug〔plʌɡ〕*v.* 使…接上插頭 *< into >*
> dashboard〔'dæʃ,bɔrd〕*n.*（汽車等的）儀表板
> device〔dɪ'vaɪs〕*n.* 裝置　　transmit〔træns'mɪt〕*v.* 傳送
> within〔wɪð'ɪn〕*prep.* 在～之內　　centralize〔'sɛntrəl,aɪz〕*v.* 集中
> database〔'detə,bes〕*n.* 資料庫　　Memphis〔'mɛmfɪs〕*n.* 孟斐斯市
> Tennessee〔,tɛnə'si〕*n.* 田納西州（美國東南部）
> access〔'æksɛs〕*v.* 取得　　toll-free〔'tol,fri〕*adj.* 免費的
> representative〔,rɛprɪ'zɛntətɪv〕*n.* 代表　　*to the minute* 正好；恰巧
> *in transit* 運輸途中

　　FedEx moved to the second stage when it made its package delivery database available on the Web to its customers.　This allowed users to determine the status of any of their packages.　The move was taken to reduce demands on the customer service department, but it had the added effect of increasing business by 15% almost immediately, while at the same time reducing the cost of customer service dramatically.　This shift had several other subtle effects.　FedEx was now viewed as being the innovator in the package delivery industry. Even though its shipment process was unchanged, the Web-based information process enhanced the company's image. A secondary effect was to reduce the threat from all competitors simply because they initially could not offer the same service and, if they did, they would clearly be doing so in response to FedEx's innovation.

當聯邦快遞使顧客能在網路上，獲得包裹遞送的資料時，便進入了第二個階段。這使得使用者能確定他們任何一件包裹的狀況。採行這個步驟，是爲了減少顧客對客服部門的需求，但其附加的效果，是馬上提升將近 15 % 的業績，同時也大大地減少了客服的成本。這個轉變產生了幾個細微的影響。聯邦快遞現在被視爲是快遞業的創新者。即使它的運送過程並沒有改變，但以網路爲基礎的資訊處理，卻提昇了公司的形象。第二個影響，就是減少所有競爭者的威脅，因爲它們一開始就無法提供同樣的服務，而且如果他們眞的做到了，很明顯的，就是在回應聯邦快遞的創新。

status〔'stetəs〕*n.* 情形　　move〔muv〕*n.* 步驟
demand〔dɪ'mænd〕*n.* 需求　　department〔dɪ'pɑrtmənt〕*n.* 部門
added〔'ædɪd〕*adj.* 增加的
dramatically〔drə'mætɪklɪ〕*adv.* 戲劇性地　　shift〔ʃɪft〕*n.* 改變
subtle〔'sʌtl̩〕*adj.* 細微的　　**be viewed as** 被視爲
innovator〔'ɪnə,vetɚ〕*n.* 創新者
shipment〔'ʃɪpmənt〕*n.* 運送
unchanged〔ʌn'tʃendʒd〕*adj.* 未改變的
enhance〔ɪn'hæns〕*v.* 提高　　image〔'ɪmɪdʒ〕*n.* 形象
secondary〔'sɛkən,dɛrɪ〕*adj.* 第二位的；從屬的
threat〔θrɛt〕*n.* 威脅　　competitor〔kəm'pɛtətɚ〕*n.* 競爭者
initially〔ɪ'nɪʃəlɪ〕*adv.* 起先；最初　　**in response to** 回應
innovation〔,ɪnə'veʃən〕*n.* 改革；革新

53.（**D**）根據本文，顧客在寄送包裹時，最關心什麼？
　　(A) 包裹運送的價格是多少。
　　(B) 聯邦快遞的其他競爭對手是誰。
　　(C) 聯邦快遞的員工有多擅長使用電腦。
　　(D) <u>運送過程中包裹在哪裡。</u>

concern〔kən'sɝn〕*v.* 使關心
skillful〔'skɪlfəl〕*adj.* 擅長的；熟練的

54. (**C**) 聯邦快遞如何使商業資訊的處理方式自動化，並傳送到聯邦快
遞的中央資料庫？

(A) 聯邦快遞要求所有的顧客要有電腦。

(B) 聯邦快遞要求顧客撥免付費電話。

(C) 聯邦快遞將所有的相關資訊放在掌上型電腦中。

(D) 聯邦快遞要求所有的卡車司機在駕駛的時候，打開儀表板上的
無線電裝置。

dial〔ˊdaɪəl〕*v.* 撥（電話）　　place〔ples〕*v.* 放置

related〔rɪˊletɪd〕*adj.* 相關的　　*turn on* 打開

55. (**B**) 在第一階段中，顧客如果想知道他們的包裹在運輸途中的何處，
要如何取得資訊？

(A) 查看 BBS。　　　　　　(B) 撥免付費電話到客服部門。

(C) 用鍵盤來玩。　　　　　　(D) 到孟斐斯旅行。

transit〔ˊtrænsɪt〕*n.* 運輸　　keyboard〔ˊki,bord〕*n.* 鍵盤

56. (**A**) 聯邦快遞為了方便顧客，在網路上取得包裹運送資料，所採取的第二
個步驟，並沒有以下哪一種好處？

(A) 增加對客服部門的需求。

(B) 增加 15% 的業績。

(C) 減少客戶服務的成本。

(D) 加強公司的形象，並減少競爭者的威脅。

advantage〔ədˊvæntɪdʒ〕*n.* 有利條件

第貳部分：非選擇題

一、英文翻譯：

1. 我們真的很擔心傑夫，因為他期末考考不及格。

We're really worried about Jeff, because he failed in the final exam.

2. 如果他不能克服這次失敗所引起的挫折，他很可能會再次失敗。

If he can't get over the frustration brought about by the failure, he
might fail again.

二、英文作文：（作文範例）

A Memorable Experience

I shall never forget what happened between my sister and me when I was in elementary school. My sister is two years older than me. We did everything together; she was my best friend. But one day we had a serious argument. A classmate of mine found out one of my secrets. I was sure that my sister had betrayed me and I swore I would never speak to her again. To my surprise, she did not even try to apologize. We did not talk to each other for a long time. Then one day I learned that I had dropped a note to my sister in the classroom and that someone else had read it. That was how my secret had got out. I apologized to my sister and she forgave me. I promised never to forget the lesson I had learned.

The lesson I learned from this experience was valuable. It is to never jump to conclusions. There are two sides to every story, and now I realize that I should make sure that I know both of them. *In other words*, I should have all the facts. Now when I feel that one of my friends has done something wrong, I listen to the explanation first. *Furthermore*, I keep this lesson in mind whenever I have to make an important decision. I carefully consider all the possibilities before I make up my mind. The lesson I learned has made me more thoughtful and less impulsive in everything I do. *As a result*, I make fewer mistakes. It is true that things are not always what they appear to be. I will always bear that in mind and try never to jump to conclusions again.

memorable〔'mɛmərəbḷ〕*adj.* 難忘的

betray〔bɪ'tre〕*v.* 出賣；背叛　　swear〔swɛr〕*v.* 發誓

to one's surprise 令某人驚訝的是　　*drop a note* 寫一封短信

lesson〔'lɛsṇ〕*n.* 教訓　　valuable〔'væljuəbl〕*adj.* 珍貴的

jump to a conclusion 遽下結論

There are two sides to every story. 凡事都有正反兩面。

keep sth. in mind 將某事牢記在心（= *bear sth. in mind*）

make up one's mind 下定決心

thoughtful〔'θɔtfəl〕*adj.* 小心謹慎的

impulsive〔'ɪmpʌlsɪv〕*adj.* 衝動的　　appear〔ə'pɪr〕*v.* 看起來

大學入學指定科目考試英文模擬試題④

第壹部份：選擇題（佔72分）

一、詞彙與慣用語（15％）

說明： 第1至15題，每題選出一個最適當的選項，標示在答案卡之「選擇題答案區」。每題答對得1分，答錯或劃記多於一個選項者倒扣1/3分，倒扣到本大題之實得分數為零為止，未作答者，不給分亦不扣分。

1. Could you give me the _____ for that wonderful dessert? I'd like to try making it myself.
   (A) receipt   (B) recipe   (C) recipient   (D) reflection

2. He found the smell of the lotus blossom _____, and asked for a different type of flower.
   (A) disgusting   (B) enjoyable   (C) delightful   (D) gloomy

3. As more and more factories went bankrupt, unemployment rose _____ in Taiwan.
   (A) deliberately   (B) intentionally
   (C) accidentally   (D) dramatically

4. Mozart's _____ for chocolate from Salzburg resulted in today's famous Mozart Kugeln chocolate.
   (A) merit   (B) connection   (C) preference   (D) benefit

5. When you put in for a job, you are a(n) _____ for it.
   (A) client   (B) applicant   (C) accountant   (D) customer

6. Some of the canned foods have been found to be _____ with bacteria. Let's avoid buying them.
   (A) sanitary   (B) nutritious   (C) contaminated (D) contagious

7. Thousands of soldiers are working to _____ food and blankets to the refugees.
   (A) distribute   (B) attribute   (C) propagate   (D) promote

8. When George came home at two in the morning, his wife said
_____, "I'm glad you came back home so early!"
   (A) sarcastically   (B) undoubtedly
   (C) exclusively   (D) triumphantly

9. According to the news report, a judge has had his license _____
for driving under the influence of alcohol repeatedly.
   (A) provoked   (B) revoked   (C) evoked   (D) invoked

10. Rumors that the Prince has got engaged have been neither _____
nor denied.
   (A) appreciated   (B) disputed
   (C) identified   (D) confirmed

11. To my surprise, I _____ an old friend at the railway station
yesterday.
   (A) jumped into   (B) came up against
   (C) came across   (D) ran over

12. The students all _____ to the teacher when she told them to
work harder. They didn't care a bit about what she said.
   (A) looked forward   (B) gave rise
   (C) turned off   (D) paid lip service

13. To excuse his absence, he _____ that he had the flu; actually,
he was quite well.
   (A) put up   (B) let on   (C) poured out (D) set out

14. His success is _____ because he fools around every day.
   (A) out of the question   (B) beyond doubt
   (C) on the contrary   (D) on the scene

15. Pollution is getting worse in many countries, industrialized countries
_____.
   (A) after all   (B) on purpose
   (C) by chance   (D) in particular

二、綜合測驗（15%）

說明：　第 16 至 30 題，每題一個空格。請依文意選出一個最適當的選項，標示
　　　　在答案卡之「選擇題答案區」。每題答對得 1 分，答錯或劃記多於一
　　　　個選項者倒扣 1/3 分，倒扣到本大題之實得分數爲零爲止。未作答者，
　　　　不給分亦不扣分。

第 16 至 20 題爲題組

　　When we read books in our own language, we frequently have a
good idea of the content before we actually read. A book cover gives
us a hint of what is in the book, and photographs and the title hint at
___16___ the book is about. The moment we get this hint, our brain
can help ___17___ what we are going to read. Expectations ___18___
and the active process of reading is ready to begin. Thus, in teaching
students to read articles, teachers should give them hints ___19___ they
can predict what's coming, too. It will ___20___ them better and more
engaged readers.

16. (A) which　　　 (B) what　　　　(C) that　　　　(D) whose
17. (A) being predicted　　　　　　 (B) predicted
　　(C) predict　　　　　　　　　　(D) to be predicted
18. (A) are set up　 (B) to set up　　(C) set up　　　 (D) are setting up
19. (A) as if　　　　(B) even though　(C) so as　　　　(D) so that
20. (A) require　　　(B) get　　　　 (C) transform　　 (D) make

第 21 至 25 題爲題組

　　Most Japanese eat three meals a day. Rice, the mainstay of the
Japanese diet ___21___ centuries, is eaten at almost every meal. At
breakfast it is usually supplemented by misoshiru (a bean-paste soup)
and tsukemono (pickled vegetables). In the cities, some Japanese have
___22___ these dishes ___22___ bread, butter and eggs. Lunch is a light
meal and may ___23___ salted fish, tsukemono, and tsukudani (seafood or

vegetables cooked and preserved in soy sauce), __24__ rice or noodles. Supper is the most important meal of the day, and it includes fish, beef, pork, or chicken with vegetables and rice. Meat is not as important in the Japanese diet as in __25__ of Western nations.

21. (A) for   (B) about   (C) in   (D) to
22. (A) turned…..into   (B) replaced…..with
    (C) applied…..for   (D) named…..as
23. (A) be included in   (B) mix with   (C) be made of   (D) consist of
24. (A) as for   (B) at least   (C) in addition to   (D) except for
25. (A) one   (B) that   (C) this   (D) others

第 26 至 30 題爲題組

Although science is still a long way from having any comprehensive understanding of dreams, one finding is __26__ most dreams seem to reflect things that have preoccupied our minds during the previous day or two. This is easy to see in ordinary dreams, but it is also __27__ those fantastic dreams far away from our everyday life, like __28__ down the street by a tiger or conversing with a dead person. Dreams express themselves in a special kind of picture language. __29__ this language is understood, we can see that the tiger symbolized something we found frightening the day or so before. The dead person, on the other hand, appeared to remind us of an idea he or she gave us many years ago, which has immediate __30__ to our present life.

26. (A) what   (B) which   (C) that   (D) when
27. (A) unique to   (B) true of   (C) owing to   (D) suggestive of
28. (A) chasing   (B) chased
    (C) being chased   (D) to be chased
29. (A) Unless   (B) Once   (C) Although   (D) Therefore
30. (A) relevance   (B) access   (C) exposure   (D) damage

三、文意選填（10%）

說明：　第 31 至 40 題，每題一個空格。請依文意在文章後所提供的 (A) 到 (J)
　　　　選項中分別選出最適當者，並將其字母代號標示在答案卡之「選擇題
　　　　答案區」。每題答對得 1 分，答錯或劃記多於一個選項者倒扣 1/9 分，
　　　　倒扣到本大題之實得分數為零為止。未作答者，不給分亦不扣分。

<u>第 31 至 40 題為題組</u>

　　For people who like to keep poultry, ducks offer certain advantages
___31___ hens. Ducks are ___32___ to some common diseases found in
hens and are less vulnerable to others. Some breeds of duck produce
bigger eggs than hens. In addition, ducks lay eggs over a longer season
than ___33___ hens.

　　Poultry keepers ___34___ gardens have less to worry about if they
keep ducks rather than hens because ___35___ are less apt to dig up
plants and roots. While both hens and ducks benefit the garden by eating
pests, hens are known to damage herb and grass beds. Ducks, ___36___,
will search for insects and snails more carefully.

　　When keeping ducks, one has to consider just how many the land
will ___37___. Generally the rule is 100 ducks per half hectare. If more
than this ___38___ is introduced, there is a risk of compacting the soil,
___39___ can lead to muddy conditions for long periods as the rain is
not easily ___40___ into the ground.

(A) absorbed	(B) support	(C) which	(D) do
(E) over	(F) on the other hand	(G) proportion	(H) with
(I) the former	(J) immune		

四、篇章結構（10%）

說明：　第 41 至 45 題，每題一個空格。請依文意在文章後所提供的 (A) 到 (E)
　　　　選項中分別選出最適當者，填入空格中，使篇章結構清晰有條理，並將
　　　　其英文字母代號標示在答案卡之「選擇題答案區」。每題答對得 2 分，
　　　　答錯或劃記多於一個選項者倒扣 1/2 分，倒扣到本大題之實得分數為零
　　　　為止。未作答者，不給分亦不扣分。

第 41 至 45 題為題組

One of the most important advances in medicine is the ability to transfuse blood. ___41___ It is because transfusions make certain surgical procedures possible.

When a transfusion is needed and a life is saved, the doctors are not the only heroes. ___42___ They have donated some of their own blood. ___43___ And they do not know the person who has received it. They know only that they helped another human being.

The Red Cross runs a widely known blood program. A person who wishes to donate blood can do so at a Red Cross center. ___44___ They screen out those whose blood may not be safe for the recipient, and then a pint of blood is taken from each donor's arm. ___45___ But a doughnut and a cup of coffee are just what the doctor ordered to put them quickly on their feet again.

(A) Countless lives are saved each year.
(B) The donor may feel a little weak afterwards.
(C) Women and men in all occupations have made this event possible.
(D) Trained staff interview each potential donor about his or her health.
(E) That is, they have donated blood to a "blood bank."

五、閱讀測驗（22％）

說明： 第 46 至 56 題，每題請分別根據各篇文章的文意選出一個最適當的選項，標示在答案卡之「選擇題答案區」。每題答對得 2 分，答錯或劃記多於一個選項者倒扣 2/3 分，倒扣到本大題之實得分數為零為止。未作答者，不給分亦不扣分。

第 46 至 48 題為題組

People express their personalities in their clothes, their cars, and their homes. Because we might choose certain foods to "tell" people something about us, our diets can also be an expression of our personalities. For example, some people eat mainly <u>gourmet</u> foods, such as caviar and lobster, and they eat only in expensive restaurants (never in cafeterias or snack bars). They might want to "tell" the world that they know about the "better things in life."

Human beings can eat many different kinds of food, but some people choose not to eat meat. Vegetarians often have more in common than just their diet. Their personalities might be similar, too. For example, vegetarians in the United States may be creative people, and they might not enjoy competitive sports or jobs. They worry about the health of the world, and they probably don't believe in war.

Some people eat mostly "fast food." One study shows that many fast-food eaters have a lot in common with one another, but they are very different from vegetarians. They are competitive and good at business. They are also usually in a hurry. Many fast-food eaters might not agree with this description of their personalities, but it is a common picture of them.

Some people also believe that people of the same astrological sign have similar food personalities. Arians usually like spicy food, with a lot of onions and pepper. People with the sign of Taurus prefer healthful fruits and vegetables, but they often eat too much. Sagittarians like ethnic foods from many different countries. Aquarians can eat as much meat and fish as they want, but sugar and cholesterol are sometimes problems for them.

46. What is the main idea of the article?
   (A) We can judge people's personalities from the expressions on their faces.
   (B) Different foods have different personalities.
   (C) The food people choose can reveal their personalities.
   (D) Men cannot be judged by their looks.

47. The word <u>gourmet</u> in the first paragraph refers to _____.
    (A) a food expert
    (B) healthy food
    (C) spicy tastes
    (D) exotic food

48. According to this article, which of the following statements is correct?
    (A) Vegetarians' personalities are vastly different.
    (B) Vegetarians are patriotic enough to fight for their country in any war.
    (C) Vegetarians are not concerned about environmental problems.
    (D) Competitive sports and jobs may be the last thing vegetarians enjoy.

第 49 至 52 題爲題組

Each year more than 500,000 Americans are diagnosed with congestive heart failure—a condition in which a weakened heart can't pump as much blood as the body needs. Drugs like beta-blockers help stabilize many patients in the earliest stages of the disease. But there aren't a lot of options for patients in the later stages. Heart transplants are one solution, but they're in short supply. The new AbioCor artificial heart shows promise, but it's still experimental; recently doctors reported that Robert Tools, the first recipient, had suffered a stroke.

That's why it's such good news to hear that another type of mechanical pump, called a left ventricular assist device (LVAD), may be an alternative. Instead of replacing the heart entirely, the LVAD is attached to the heart, boosting its output. The pump is twice as likely as drugs to keep patients alive for at least one year, according to a study that was published in the *New England Journal of Medicine*.

Although some patients still suffered from strokes and the LVADs sometimes failed, the quality of life for the majority of the patients in the study was significantly improved. At present, LVADs are used primarily to buy time for patients who are waiting for a heart transplant. But the pumps have developed such a good track record over the years that doctors have started to wonder if the devices could provide a more long-term solution.

49. The new AbioCor artificial heart _____.
    (A) helps patients in the earliest stages of heart disease
    (B) is an option for patients who need heart transplants
    (C) is used instead of the human heart and is flawless
    (D) is sure to help the heart pump as much blood as needed

50. Which of the following is **NOT** true?
    (A) The LVAD does not replace the heart entirely.
    (B) The LVAD may increase the blood flow.
    (C) The LVAD is likely to extend a patient's life.
    (D) The LVAD is put inside the patient's heart.

51. According to the passage, the LVAD _____.
    (A) , unlike the AbioCor, is not a mechanical pump
    (B) has been functioning in all patients perfectly
    (C) has bettered the quality of life for most patients
    (D) is definitely the solution to all heart problems

52. The passage would most likely be found in _____.
    (A) an autobiography   (B) a chemistry book
    (C) a science fiction book   (D) a news magazine

第 53 至 56 題爲題組

　　Sylvia Earle, a marine botanist and one of the foremost deep-sea explorers, has spent over 6,000 hours, more than seven months, underwater. From her earliest years, Earle had a fascination with marine life, and she took her first plunge into the open sea as a teenager. In the years since then she has taken part in a number of landmark underwater projects, from exploratory expeditions around the world to her well-known "Jim dive" in 1978, which was the deepest solo dive ever made without a cable connecting the diver to a support ship at the surface of the sea.

　　Clothed in a Jim suit, a futuristic suit of plastic and metal armor, which was secured to a manned submarine, Sylvia Earle plunged vertically into the Pacific Ocean, at times at a speed of 100 feet per minute. On reaching the ocean floor, she was released from the submarine and from that point her only connection to the sub was an 18-foot rope. For the next two and a half hours, Earle roamed the seabed taking notes, collecting specimens, and planting a U.S. flag. Having an irresistible desire to descend deeper still, in 1981 she became involved in the design and manufacture of deep-sea submersibles, one of which took her to a depth of 3,000 feet. This, however, did not end Sylvia Earle's accomplishments.

53. It can be inferred from the passage that Sylvia Earle _____.
    (A) has received a very good education
    (B) is uncomfortable in the submarine
    (C) does not have technical expertise
    (D) has devoted her life to ocean exploration

54. The main purpose of this passage is _____.
    (A) to explore the botany of the ocean floor
    (B) to present an account of what Sylvia Earle did
    (C) to provide an introduction to oceanography
    (D) to show the historical importance of the Jim dive

55. Which of the following is **NOT** true about the Jim dive?
(A) Sylvia Earle successfully made it in 1981.
(B) It was performed in the Pacific Ocean.
(C) Earle took notes while on the ocean floor.
(D) The submarine Earle was connected to was manned.

56. What will the paragraph following this passage probably be about?
(A) Sylvia Earle's early childhood.
(B) More information on the Jim suit.
(C) Earle's achievements after 1981.
(D) How deep-sea submersibles are made.

第貳部份：非選擇題（佔28分）

一、英文翻譯（8％）

說明： 1. 將下列兩句中文翻譯成適當之英文，並將答案寫在「答案卷」上。
　　　 2. 未按題意翻譯者，不予計分。

1. 人們常因「語言障礙」，嚇得不敢出國。
2. 不過，就算沒有任何外語技巧，你在歐洲仍然可以玩得很愉快。

二、英文作文（20％）

說明： 1. 依提示在「答案卷」上寫一篇英文作文。
　　　 2. 文長至少120個單詞。

提示： 即將畢業的你，回想高中三年來的生活點滴，是否有什麼遺憾的事呢？
　　　 請描述高中歲月裡一件令你遺憾的事，並說明你的感想及可能的彌補
　　　 方式。

大學入學指定科目考試英文模擬試題④詳解

第壹部分：單一選擇題

一、詞彙與慣用語：

1. (**B**) Could you give me the <u>recipe</u> for that wonderful dessert? I'd like to try making it myself.
   你可以給我那美味甜點的<u>食譜</u>嗎？我想要自己試做看看。
   (A) receipt〔rɪˈsit〕 *n.* 收據
   (B) *recipe*〔ˈrɛsəpɪ〕 *n.* 食譜
   (C) recipient〔rɪˈsɪpɪənt〕 *n.* 接受者；收受人
   (D) reflection〔rɪˈflɛkʃən〕 *n.* 反射
   dessert〔dɪˈzɝt〕 *n.* 餐後甜點

2. (**A**) He found the smell of the lotus blossom <u>disgusting</u>, and asked for a different type of flower.
   他覺得蓮花的味道<u>令人作嘔</u>，所以要求要不同種類的花。
   (A) *disgusting*〔dɪsˈgʌstɪŋ〕 *adj.* 令人作嘔的；噁心的
   (B) enjoyable〔ɪnˈdʒɔɪəbḷ〕 *adj.* 令人愉快的
   (C) delightful〔dɪˈlaɪtfəl〕 *adj.* 令人愉快的
   (D) gloomy〔ˈglumɪ〕 *adj.* 令人憂鬱的
   smell〔smɛl〕 *n.* 味道　　*lotus blossom* 蓮花

3. (**D**) As more and more factories went bankrupt, unemployment rose <u>dramatically</u> in Taiwan.
   因為有越來越多的工廠破產，所以台灣的失業率<u>大幅地</u>升高。
   (A) deliberately〔dɪˈlɪbərɪtlɪ〕 *adv.* 故意地
   (B) intentionally〔ɪnˈtɛnʃənḷɪ〕 *adv.* 有意地
   (C) accidentally〔͵æksəˈdɛntḷɪ〕 *adv.* 偶然地
   (D) *dramatically*〔drəˈmætɪkəlɪ〕 *adv.* 戲劇性地；大幅地
   go bankrupt 破產　　unemployment〔͵ʌnɪmˈplɔɪmənt〕 *n.* 失業率

4. (**C**) Mozart's <u>preference</u> for chocolate from Salzburg resulted in today's famous Mozart Kugeln chocolate. 莫札特<u>偏好</u>薩爾斯堡的巧克力，因而創造出現在很有名的莫札特・古傑林巧克力。

　　(A) merit〔'mɛrɪt〕*n.* 優點　　(B) connection〔kə'nɛkʃən〕*n.* 連結
　　(C) *preference*〔'prɛfərəns〕*n.* 偏好
　　(D) benefit〔'bɛnəfɪt〕*n.* 利益
　　Mozart〔'mozɑrt〕*n.* 莫札特（奧地利作曲家）
　　Salzburg〔'sɔlzbɝg〕*n.* 薩爾斯堡（奧地利的都市，爲莫札特的誕生地）
　　result in 造成

5. (**B**) When you put in for a job, you are an <u>applicant</u> for it. 當你在申請一份工作時，你就是個<u>應徵者</u>。

　　(A) client〔'klaɪənt〕*n.* 客戶　　(B) *applicant*〔'æpləkənt〕*n.* 應徵者
　　(C) accountant〔ə'kaʊntənt〕*n.* 會計
　　(D) customer〔'kʌstəmɚ〕*n.* 顧客
　　put in for 申請

6. (**C**) Some of the canned foods have been found to be <u>contaminated</u> with bacteria. Let's avoid buying them. 有些罐頭食品已被發現受到細菌<u>污染</u>。我們要避免購買這些罐頭食品。

　　(A) sanitary〔'sænə,tɛrɪ〕*adj.* 衛生的
　　(B) nutritious〔nju'trɪʃəs〕*adj.* 營養的
　　(C) *contaminated*〔kən'tæmə,netɪd〕*adj.* 受到污染的
　　(D) contagious〔kən'tedʒəs〕*adj.* 接觸傳染的
　　canned food 罐頭食品　　bacteria〔bæk'tɪrɪə〕*n.pl.* 細菌

7. (**A**) Thousands of soldiers are working to <u>distribute</u> food and blankets to the refugees. 數千名士兵正在<u>分發</u>食物和毛毯給難民。

　　(A) *distribute*〔dɪ'strɪbjut〕*v.* 分發
　　(B) attribute〔ə'trɪbjut〕*v.* 歸因於 < *to* >
　　(C) propagate〔'prɑpə,get〕*v.* 宣傳；傳播
　　(D) promote〔prə'mot〕*v.* 提倡；升遷
　　blanket〔'blæŋkɪt〕*n.* 毛毯　　refugee〔,rɛfju'dʒi〕*n.* 難民

8. (**A**) When George came home at two in the morning, his wife said
<u>sarcastically</u>, "I'm glad you came back home so early!"
喬治凌晨兩點才回家，他老婆諷刺地說：「真高興你這麼早回家！」
(A) **sarcastically**〔sɑr'kæstɪkḷɪ〕*adv.* 諷刺地
(B) undoubtedly〔ʌn'daʊtɪdlɪ〕*adv.* 無疑地
(C) exclusively〔ɪk'sklusɪvlɪ〕*adv.* 只有；獨家地
(D) triumphantly〔traɪ'ʌmfəntlɪ〕*adv.* 得意洋洋地

9. (**B**) According to the news report, a judge has had his license <u>revoked</u>
for driving under the influence of alcohol repeatedly.
根據新聞報導，有位法官因為一再地酒後駕車，所以被吊銷了駕照。
(A) provoke〔prə'vok〕*v.* 激怒
(B) **revoke**〔rɪ'vok〕*v.* 吊銷（執照）
(C) evoke〔ɪ'vok〕*v.* 喚起（感情、記憶）
(D) invoke〔ɪn'vok〕*v.* 祈求；求助於

judge〔dʒʌdʒ〕*n.* 法官　　license〔'laɪsn̩s〕*n.* 駕照
alcohol〔'ælkə,hɔl〕*n.* 酒
drive under the influence of alcohol 酒後駕車
repeatedly〔rɪ'pitɪdlɪ〕*adv.* 重複地

10. (**D**) Rumors that the Prince has got engaged have been neither
<u>confirmed</u> nor denied.
謠傳王子已經訂婚了，不過這個謠言尚未被證實或否認。
(A) appreciate〔ə'priʃɪ,et〕*v.* 欣賞；感激
(B) dispute〔dɪ'spjut〕*v.* 爭論
(C) identify〔aɪ'dɛntə,faɪ〕*v.* 確認（身分）；識別
(D) **confirm**〔kən'fɝm〕*v.* 證實；確認

rumor〔'rumɚ〕*n.* 謠言　　prince〔prɪns〕*n.* 王子
engaged〔ɪn'gedʒd〕*adj.* 訂婚的　　deny〔dɪ'naɪ〕*v.* 否認

11. (**C**) To my surprise, I <u>came across</u> an old friend at the railway station
yesterday. 我昨天在火車站偶然遇見一位老朋友，令我十分驚訝。
(A) jump into 跳入　　　　(B) come up against 碰到；面臨（困難）
(C) **come across** 偶然遇見（ = *run into* = *bump into*）
(D) run over 輾過
to *one's* **surprise** 令某人驚訝的是　　*railway station* 火車站

12. (**D**) The students all <u>paid lip service</u> to the teacher when she told them to work harder. They didn't care a bit about what she said.
老師叫學生要努力用功，但這些學生卻只是<u>敷衍</u>她。他們根本就不理會老師所說的話。

    (A) look forward to　期待
    (B) give rise to　導致
    (C) turn off　關掉（電源）
    (D) *pay lip service to sb.* 敷衍某人

    not…a bit 一點也不

13. (**B**) To excuse his absence, he <u>let on</u> that he had the flu; actually, he was quite well. 他為了替自己的缺席辯解，就<u>假裝</u>得了流行性感冒；事實上，他好端端的。

    (A) put up　張貼   (B) *let on* 假裝
    (C) pour out　倒出來   (D) set out　出發

    excuse〔ɪkˋskjuz〕*v.* 為～辯解   absence〔ˋæbsn̩s〕*n.* 缺席
    flu〔flu〕*n.* 流行性感冒   actually〔ˋæktʃʊəlɪ〕*adv.* 事實上
    well〔wɛl〕*adj.* 健康的

14. (**A**) His success is <u>out of the question</u> because he fools around every day.
因為他每天都游手好閒，所以要成功是<u>不可能的</u>。

    (A) *out of the question* 不可能的
    (B) beyond doubt　毫無疑問的
    (C) on the contrary　相反地
    (D) on the scene　當場

    fool around 游手好閒；鬼混

15. (**D**) Pollution is getting worse in many countries, industrialized countries <u>in particular</u>.
在許多國家，污染愈來愈嚴重，<u>尤其是</u>工業國家。

    (A) after all　畢竟   (B) on purpose　故意地
    (C) by chance　偶然地   (D) *in particular* 尤其是

    pollution〔pəˋluʃən〕*n.* 污染
    industrialized〔ɪnˋdʌstrɪəl͵aɪzd〕*adj.* 工業化的

二、綜合測驗：

第 16 至 20 題為題組

　　When we read books in our own language, we frequently have a good idea of the content before we actually read. A book cover gives us a hint of what is in the book, and photographs and the title hint at <u>what</u> the book

16

is about. The moment we get this hint, our brain can help <u>predict</u> what we

17

are going to read. Expectations <u>are set up</u> and the active process of reading is

18

ready to begin. Thus, in teaching students to read articles, teachers should give them hints <u>so that</u> they can predict what's coming, too. It will <u>make</u>

19　　　　　　　　　　　　　　　　　　　20

them better and more engaged readers.

　　當我們在閱讀以我們自己的語言寫成的書時，經常在眞正開始閱讀之前，就對內容有了相當的了解。書的封面可以暗示我們內容，照片和書名也暗示著，這本書與什麼有關。一得到這些暗示，大腦就可以幫助我們預測將會讀到些什麼。期望被設定好之後，主動閱讀的過程也即將開始。因此，在敎導學生閱讀文章時，老師也應該給予學生暗示，如此他們也能預測會讀到什麼，這將會使他們成爲更優秀、更專注的讀者。

> frequently〔ˈfrikwəntlɪ〕*adv.* 經常地
> content〔ˈkɑntɛnt〕*n.* 內容
> cover〔ˈkʌvɚ〕*n.* 封面　　hint〔hɪnt〕*n., v.* 暗示
> photograph〔ˈfotəˌgræf〕*n.* 照片 (= *photo*)
> title〔ˈtaɪtl〕*n.* 書名；標題
> ***the moment*** 一～就 (= *as soon as*)
> expectation〔ˌɛkspɛkˈteʃən〕*n.* 期望
> active〔ˈæktɪv〕*adj.* 主動的
> process〔ˈprɑsɛs〕*n.* 過程　　predict〔prɪˈdɪkt〕*v.* 預測
> engaged〔ɪnˈgedʒd〕*adj.* 忙於～的；專注的

16. (**B**) 依句意，照片和書名可以暗示我們，書中文章與「什麼」有關，選 (B) ***what***。

17. (**C**) help 之後，可接不定詞或原形動詞，故選 (C) *predict*。而 (D) 為被動，用法不合。

18. (**A**) Expectations 為本句的主詞，其後應接動詞，且依句意為被動，故選 (A) *are set up*「被設定」。

19. (**D**) (A) as if　就好像 (= *as though*)
　　　　(B) even though　即使 (= *even if*)
　　　　(C) so as to + V.　以便於 (用法不合)
　　　　(D) *so that* + 子句　所以；如此一來

20. (**D**) 依句意，「使」他們「成為」更優秀、更專注的讀者，選 (D) *make*「使成為」，make 加受詞後，直接接受詞補語。
　　　　(A) require ﹝rɪ'kwaɪr﹞ v. 需要 (句意不合)
　　　　(B) 原句須改為：It will *get* them *to become* better and more…。
　　　　(C) transform ﹝træns'fɔrm﹞ v. 轉變，原句須改為：It will *transform* them *into* better and more…。

<u>第 21 至 25 題為題組</u>

　　Most Japanese eat three meals a day.　Rice, the mainstay of the Japanese diet <u>for</u> centuries, is eaten at almost every meal.　At breakfast it is usually
21
supplemented by misoshiru (a bean-paste soup) and tsukemono (pickled vegetables).　In the cities, some Japanese have <u>replaced</u> these dishes <u>with</u>
22　　　　　　　　22
bread, butter and eggs.　Lunch is a light meal and may <u>consist of</u> salted fish,
23
tsukemono, and tsukudani (seafood or vegetables cooked and preserved in soy sauce), <u>in addition to</u> rice or noodles.　Supper is the most important
24
meal of the day, and it includes fish, beef, pork, or chicken with vegetables and rice.　Meat is not as important in the Japanese diet as in <u>that</u> of Western
25
nations.

大部分的日本人一天吃三餐。好幾世紀以來，米飯一直都是日本人飲食的主食，他們幾乎每餐都吃。早餐通常是白飯，再配上味噌湯和醃漬的蔬菜。在都市裡，有些日本人已經用麵包、奶油和蛋，來取代這些菜餚。午餐則吃得很簡單，大概就是鹹魚、用醬油醃製的蔬菜，或海鮮類，再配上白飯或麵。晚餐是一天中最重要的一餐，包括魚、牛肉、豬肉或雞肉，配蔬菜和白飯。肉類在日本人的飲食中，並不像在西方國家那麼重要。

> meal〔mil〕 n. 一餐
>
> mainstay〔'men,ste〕 n. 主要的依靠
>
> diet〔'daɪət〕 n. 飲食
>
> supplement〔'sʌplə,mɛnt〕 v. 補充
>
> misoshiru （日語）味噌湯　　bean〔bin〕 n. 豆子
>
> paste〔pest〕 n. 糊狀物　　tsukemono （日語）漬物
>
> pickled〔'pɪkl̩d〕 adj. 醃漬的　　dish〔dɪʃ〕 n. 菜餚
>
> light〔laɪt〕 adj. 清淡的；份量少的
>
> salted〔'sɔltɪd〕 adj. 醃製的
>
> tsukudani （日語）佃煮（用醬油醃製的貝類、魚等）
>
> preserve〔prɪ'zɝv〕 v. 保存　　*soy sauce* 醬油
>
> noodles〔'nudl̩z〕 n. pl. 麵　　supper〔'sʌpɚ〕 n. 晚餐
>
> beef〔bif〕 n. 牛肉　　pork〔pɔrk〕 n. 豬肉
>
> meat〔mit〕 n. 肉類

21.(**A**) 表持續多久時間，介系詞用 *for*，選 (A)。

22.(**B**) (A) turn A into B　把 A 變成 B
　　　　(B) *replace* A *with* B　用 B 取代 A
　　　　(C) apply for　申請
　　　　(D) name A B　把 A 命名為 B（不加 *as*）

23.(**D**) (A) be included in　被包括在內
　　　　(B) mix A with B　把 A 和 B 混合在一起
　　　　(C) be made of　由～（材料）製成
　　　　(D) *consist of*　由～組成（= *be composed of* = *be made up of*）

24. (**C**) (A) as for 至於
   (B) at least 至少
   (C) ***in addition to*** 除了～之外還有 (= *besides*)
   (D) except for 除了～不算

25. (**B**) 本句原為 Meat is not as important in the Japanese diet as in ***the diet*** of Western nations. 為了避免重複，故用單數代名詞 ***that*** 代替 the diet，選 (B)。

第 26 至 30 題為題組

 Although science is still a long way from having any comprehensive understanding of dreams, one finding is <u>that</u> most dreams seem to reflect
26
things that have preoccupied our minds during the previous day or two. This is easy to see in ordinary dreams, but it is also <u>true of</u> those fantastic
27
dreams far away from our everyday life, like <u>being chased</u> down the street
28
by a tiger or conversing with a dead person.

　雖然科學還未能廣泛地理解夢境，但有一項發現指出，大部分的夢似乎都反映出一兩天前盤據在我們心中的事。從普通的夢境中很容易看出這一點，但離日常生活很遙遠的奇特夢境，也同樣適用，例如夢到在街上被老虎追，或是和已過世的人談話等。

　　　　a long way from 離～很遠
　　　　comprehensive〔ˌkɑmprɪˋhɛnsɪv〕*adj.* 廣泛的
　　　　finding〔ˋfaɪndɪŋ〕*n.* 發現　　reflect〔rɪˋflɛkt〕*v.* 反射；反映
　　　　preoccupy〔priˋɑkjəˌpaɪ〕*v.* 盤據；使專注
　　　　previous〔ˋpriviəs〕*adj.* 先前的
　　　　fantastic〔fænˋtæstɪk〕*adj.* 奇特的；怪異的
　　　　converse〔kənˋvɝs〕*v.* 談話 < *with* >

26. (**C**) 連接詞 ***that*** 引導名詞子句，做主詞補語，選 (C)。

27. (**B**) (A) be unique to 是～所特有的
    (B) *be true of* 適用於
    (C) owing to 由於
    (D) be suggestive of 暗示；使人聯想起

28. (**C**) 依句意，「被老虎追」為被動用法，且根據後句 conversing 可知，
    此處亦須用動名詞，選 (C) *being chased*。
    chase〔tʃes〕*v.* 追逐

Dreams express themselves in a special kind of picture language. <u>Once</u> this
                                                                  29
language is understood, we can see that the tiger symbolized something we
found frightening the day or so before. The dead person, on the other hand,
appeared to remind us of an idea he or she gave us many years ago, which
has immediate <u>relevance</u> to our present life.
                30
夢境會以一種特別的圖畫式語言來呈現。一旦這種語言被了解，我們就知道，
老虎象徵大約在當天之前，我們覺得很嚇人的東西；而另一方面，已過世的人
出現，是為了使我們想起，他或她多年前提供給我們的意見，而那些意見與我
們現在的生活有直接關聯。

> symbolize〔'sɪmbl̩,aɪz〕*v.* 象徵
> frightening〔'fraɪtn̩ɪŋ〕*adj.* 嚇人的
> *or so* 大約（= *around*） appear〔ə'pɪr〕*v.* 出現
> remind〔rɪ'maɪnd〕*v.* 提醒；使想起 < *of* >
> immediate〔ɪ'midɪɪt〕*adj.* 立即的；直接的
> present〔'prɛznt〕*adj.* 現在的

29. (**B**) 依句意，「一旦」這種語言被了解，我們就知道…，選 (B) *Once*。
    而 (A) 除非，(C) 雖然，(D) 因此，均不合句意。

30. (**A**) (A) *relevance*〔'rɛləvəns〕*n.* 關聯
    (B) access〔'æksɛs〕*n.* 接近；使用權
    (C) exposure〔ɪk'spoʒɚ〕*n.* 暴露
    (D) damage〔'dæmɪdʒ〕*n.* 損害

三、文意選填：

<u>第 31 至 40 題爲題組</u>

For people who like to keep poultry, ducks offer certain advantages
[31](E) over hens.　Ducks are [32](J) immune to some common diseases
found in hens and are less vulnerable to others.　Some breeds of duck
produce bigger eggs than hens.　In addition, ducks lay eggs over a longer
season than [33](D) do hens.

　　對喜歡養家禽的人而言，鴨子在某些地方是優於母雞的。鴨子對某些母雞
常患的疾病，具有免疫力，而且也比較不容易感染其他疾病。有些品種的鴨子
所下的蛋，比雞蛋還大。此外，鴨子的下蛋期，也比母雞長。

> poultry ('poltrɪ) *n.* 家禽　　　duck (dʌk) *n.* 鴨子
> advantage (əd'væntɪdʒ) *n.* 優勢 < *over* >
> hen (hɛn) *n.* 母雞
> ***be immune to~*** 對~免疫
> common ('kɑmən) *adj.* 常見的
> vulnerable ('vʌlnərəb!) *adj.* 易受傷害的 < *to* >
> breed (brid) *n.* 品種　　　***in addition*** 此外
> lay (le) *v.* 下 (蛋)　　　season ('sizn̩) *n.* 時期

Poultry keepers [34](H) with gardens have less to worry about if they
keep ducks rather than hens because [35](I) the former are less apt to dig up
plants and roots.　While both hens and ducks benefit the garden by eating
pests, hens are known to damage herb and grass beds.　Ducks, [36](F) on the
other hand, will search for insects and snails more carefully.

　　有花園的家禽飼主，如果飼養的是鴨子，而不是母雞，就比較不必擔心，
因爲前者比較不會挖掘植物和根部。雖然母雞和鴨子會吃害蟲，對花園助益不
少，但是母雞也會破壞藥草和青草的苗床。另一方面，鴨子則會比較小心地尋
找昆蟲和蝸牛。

keeper〔ˈkipɚ〕*n.* 飼養者　　***worry about*** 擔心

rather than 而不是　　 former〔ˈfɔrmɚ〕*n.* 前者（此處指鴨子）

be apt to 易於；傾向於　　 dig〔dɪg〕*v.* 挖掘

root〔rut〕*n.*（植物的）根部　　 benefit〔ˈbɛnəfɪt〕*v.* 使獲益

pest〔pɛst〕*n.* 害蟲　　 herb〔ɝb, hɝb〕*n.* 藥草；香料

bed〔bɛd〕*n.*（花、草的）苗床

on the other hand 另一方面　　 ***search for*** 尋找

insect〔ˈɪnsɛkt〕*n.* 昆蟲　　 snail〔snel〕*n.* 蝸牛

When keeping ducks, one has to consider just how many the land will [37](B) support. Generally the rule is 100 ducks per half hectare. If more than this [38](G) proportion is introduced, there is a risk of compacting the soil, [39](C) which can lead to muddy conditions for long periods as the rain is not easily [40](A) absorbed into the ground.

飼養鴨子時，我們必須考慮土地所能負荷的數量。一般說來，規則是每半公頃養一百隻。如果所採用的比例，大過這個數目的話，土壤就有被擠壓的危險，如此一來，會使土地長時間泥濘不堪，因爲雨水不易被地面吸收。

support〔səˈport〕*v.* 負荷

generally〔ˈdʒɛnərəlɪ〕*adv.* 一般說來

per〔pɚ〕*prep.* 每一　　 hectare〔ˈhɛktɛr〕*n.* 公頃

proportion〔prəˈporʃən〕*n.* 比例

introduce〔ˌɪntrəˈdjus〕*v.* 引進；採用

compact〔kəmˈpækt〕*v.* 壓緊

soil〔sɔɪl〕*n.* 土壤　　 ***lead to*** 導致

muddy〔ˈmʌdɪ〕*adj.* 泥濘的　　 absorb〔əbˈsɔrb〕*v.* 吸收

四、篇章結構：

第 41 至 45 題爲題組

One of the most important advances in medicine is the ability to transfuse blood. [41](A) Countless lives are saved each year. It is because transfusions make certain surgical procedures possible.

輸血是醫學方面最重要的進步之一。每年有無數的生命得救。因爲輸血讓某些外科手術得以進行。

> advance〔əd'væns〕*n.* 進步
> transfuse〔træns'fjuz〕*v.* 輸血
> countless〔'kauntlıs〕*adj.* 無數的
> transfusion〔træns'fjuʒən〕*n.* 輸血
> certain〔'sɝtn̩〕*adj.* 某些　　surgical〔'sɝdʒıkl̩〕*adj.* 手術的
> procedure〔prə'sidʒɚ〕*n.* 程序

When a transfusion is needed and a life is saved, the doctors are not the only heroes. <u>⁴²(C) Women and men in all occupations have made this event possible.</u> They have donated some of their own blood. <u>⁴³(E) That is, they have donated blood to a "blood bank."</u> And they do not know the person who has received it. They know only that they helped another human being.

當需要輸血，並因此有一條人命獲救時，醫生並不是唯一的英雄。各行各業的男男女女都讓救人成爲可能的事。他們捐出自己部分的血液。也就是說，他們捐血給「血庫」。此外，他們不知道是誰用了他們的血。他們只知道自己幫了另一個人。

> hero〔'hıro〕*n.* 英雄　　occupation〔ˌɑkjə'peʃən〕*n.* 職業
> donate〔'donet〕*v.* 捐贈 *< to >*　　*that is* 也就是說
> bank〔bæŋk〕*n.* 儲存所；庫　　*blood bank* 血庫

The Red Cross runs a widely known blood program. A person who wishes to donate blood can do so at a Red Cross center. <u>⁴⁴(D) Trained staff interview each potential donor about his or her health.</u> They screen out those whose blood may not be safe for the recipient, and then a pint of blood is taken from each donor's arm. <u>⁴⁵(B) The donor may feel a little weak afterwards.</u> But a doughnut and a cup of coffee are just what the doctor ordered to put them quickly on their feet again.

紅十字會實施了一個廣為人知的捐血計劃。想捐血的人，可以到紅十字會中心。受過訓練的工作人員，會與即將捐血的人面談，得知其健康情況。他們必須過濾掉，可能對接受捐贈血液的人有害的人選，然後再從每一位捐血者的手臂上，抽取一品脫的血。事後，捐血者可能會覺得有點虛弱。但是醫生囑咐，只要給他們吃一個甜甜圈及喝一杯咖啡，就能使他們很快地復原。

the Red Cross 紅十字會（慈善團體）		run〔rʌn〕v. 進行；實施	
program〔'progræm〕n. 計劃		staff〔stæf〕n. 工作人員	
interview〔'ɪntə,vju〕v. 面談		potential〔pə'tɛnʃəl〕adj. 可能的	
screen out （經篩選）去除		recipient〔rɪ'sɪpɪənt〕n. 接受者	
pint〔paɪnt〕n. 品脫（容量單位）			
afterwards〔'æftəwədz〕adv. 之後		doughnut〔'donət〕n. 甜甜圈	
order〔'ɔrdə〕v.（醫生）囑咐；處方			
put sb. on sb.'s feet 使某人復原			

五、閱讀測驗：

第 46 至 48 題為題組

People express their personalities in their clothes, their cars, and their homes. Because we might choose certain foods to "tell" people something about us, our diets can also be an expression of our personalities. For example, some people eat mainly <u>gourmet</u> foods, such as caviar and lobster, and they eat only in expensive restaurants (never in cafeterias or snack bars). They might want to "tell" the world that they know about the "better things in life."

人們會用服裝、汽車，以及房子，來表現自己的個性。因為我們可能會選擇某些食物來「告訴」別人自己的一些特性，所以飲食也就成為一種表現個性的方式。例如，有些人大多只吃美食，像是魚子醬及龍蝦，而且只去昂貴的餐廳吃飯（絕不會去自助餐廳或小吃店）。他們可能是想要告訴大家，他們懂得享受人生中較高級的事物。

personality〔,pɜsn'ælətɪ〕n. 個性		expression〔ɪk'sprɛʃən〕n. 表達	
mainly〔'menlɪ〕adv. 主要地		gourmet〔'gurme〕adj. 精美的	
caviar〔,kævɪ'ar〕n. 魚子醬		lobster〔'labstə〕n. 龍蝦	
cafeteria〔,kæfə'tɪrɪə〕n. 自助餐廳		*snack bar* 小吃店	
the world 全世界的人			

Human beings can eat many different kinds of food, but some people choose not to eat meat. Vegetarians often have more in common than just their diet. Their personalities might be similar, too. For example, vegetarians in the United States may be creative people, and they might not enjoy competitive sports or jobs. They worry about the health of the world, and they probably don't believe in war.

人類可以吃許多不同種類的食物，但是有些人選擇不吃肉。素食者常常除了飲食習慣相似之外，還有其他的共同點，他們的個性可能也很相似。例如，美國的素食者，可能會是很有創造力的人，而且可能不喜歡競爭激烈的運動或工作。他們擔心世人的健康，而且可能不認為戰爭是好的。

> vegetarian〔ˌvɛdʒə'tɛrɪən〕 *n.* 素食者
> ***have~in common*** 有~共同點
> creative〔krɪ'etɪv〕 *adj.* 有創造力的
> competitive〔kəm'pɛtətɪv〕 *adj.* 競爭激烈的
> ***believe in*** 相信~是好的

Some people eat mostly "fast food." One study shows that many fast-food eaters have a lot in common with one another, but they are very different from vegetarians. They are competitive and good at business. They are also usually in a hurry. Many fast-food eaters might not agree with this description of their personalities, but it is a common picture of them.

有些人大多是吃「速食」。有一項研究顯示，很多吃速食的人，彼此有許多的共同點，但是卻和素食者大不相同。吃速食的人喜歡和人競爭，而且擅長做生意。他們也總是匆匆忙忙的。許多愛吃速食的人，可能不同意別人這樣描述他們的個性，但他們卻通常都是如此。

> mostly〔'mostlɪ〕 *adv.* 大多　　study〔'stʌdɪ〕 *n.* 研究
> ***be good at*** 擅長　　***be in a hurry*** 很匆忙
> description〔dɪ'skrɪpʃən〕 *n.* 描述
> picture〔'pɪktʃɚ〕 *n.* 描寫；情況

Some people also believe that people of the same astrological sign have similar food personalities. Arians usually like spicy food, with a lot of onions and pepper. People with the sign of Taurus prefer healthful fruits and vegetables, but they often eat too much. Sagittarians like ethnic foods from many different countries. Aquarians can eat as much meat and fish as they want, but sugar and cholesterol are sometimes problems for them.

有些人也認為,相同星座的人,在飲食方面的性格也會很相似。牡羊座的人,通常喜歡吃辣的食物,並且加上很多洋蔥及胡椒。金牛座的人比較喜歡有益健康的蔬果,但常常吃太多。射手座的人喜歡吃來自許多不同國家,具有民族風味的食物。水瓶座的人可以盡情地吃大魚大肉,但是有時候會有糖分及膽固醇方面的問題。

astrological〔͵æstrə'lɑdʒɪkḷ〕*adj.* 占星的
sign〔saɪn〕*n.*【天文】(黃道十二宮的) 宮;星座
astrological sign 星座 (= *sign*)
Arian〔'ɛrɪən〕*n.* 牡羊座的人 (*cf.* Aries〔'ɛriz〕*n.* 牡羊座)
spicy〔'spaɪsɪ〕*adj.* 辣的　　onion〔'ʌnjən〕*n.* 洋蔥
pepper〔'pɛpɚ〕*n.* 胡椒　　Taurus〔'tɔrəs〕*n.* 金牛座
Sagittarian〔͵sædʒɪ'tɛrɪən〕*n.* 射手座的人
　(*cf.* Sagittarius〔͵sædʒɪ'tɛrɪəs〕*n.* 射手座)
ethnic〔'ɛθnɪk〕*adj.* 民族的;種族的
Aquarian〔ə'kwɛrɪən〕*n.* 水瓶座的人
　(*cf.* Aquarius〔ə'kwɛrɪəs〕*n.* 水瓶座)
sugar〔'ʃugɚ〕*n.* 糖　　cholesterol〔kə'lɛstə͵rol〕*n.* 膽固醇

46. (**C**) 本文的主旨為何?
　　(A) 我們可以從人們的臉部表情來判斷其個性。
　　(B) 不同的食物具有不同的個性。
　　(C) 人們所選擇的食物,可以透露其個性。
　　(D) 我們不能以貌取人。

main idea 主旨　　article〔'ɑrtɪkḷ〕*n.* 文章
judge〔dʒʌdʒ〕*v.* 判斷　　reveal〔rɪ'vil〕*v.* 透露
looks〔luks〕*n.pl.* 外表

47.(**D**) 第一段的 gourmet 是指 _____。

(A) 食物專家　　　　(B) 健康食物

(C) 辣味　　　　　　(D) 奇特的食物

refer to 是指　　expert ('ɛkspɝt) *n.* 專家

taste (test) *n.* 味道

exotic (ɪg'zɑtɪk) *adj.* 奇特的

48.(**D**) 根據本文,下列敘述何者正確?

(A) 素食者的個性大不相同。

(B) 素食者非常愛國,在任何戰爭中,都會為自己的國家而戰。

(C) 素食者不關心環境問題。

(D) 素食者可能最不喜歡競爭激烈的運動和工作。

vastly ('væstlɪ) *adv.* 非常地

patriotic (ˌpetrɪ'ɑtɪk) *adj.* 愛國的

be concerned about 關心　　**the last~** 最不可能的~

第 49 至 52 題為題組

Each year more than 500,000 Americans are diagnosed with
congestive heart failure—a condition in which a weakened heart can't
pump as much blood as the body needs. Drugs like beta-blockers help
stabilize many patients in the earliest stages of the disease. But there
aren't a lot of options for patients in the later stages. Heart transplants are
one solution, but they're in short supply. The new AbioCor artificial heart
shows promise, but it's still experimental; recently doctors reported that
Robert Tools, the first recipient, had suffered a stroke.

每年有超過五十萬名美國人,被診斷出患有充血性心臟衰竭 —— 這是一種
心臟衰弱,因此無法打出身體所需要的血液的疾病。像 β 受體阻滯藥這種藥物,
在疾病的最初期,有助於穩定許多病人的病情。但是在之後的階段,病人就沒
有太多選擇。心臟移植是一種解決之道,但是卻供不應求。新式的 AbioCor 人
工心臟顯示出希望,但是它還在實驗階段;最近,醫生指出,羅勃特·圖爾斯,
這位第一位接受人工心臟移植的病人,已經罹患中風了。

diagnose (ˌdaɪəgˈnoz) v. 診斷

congestive (kənˈdʒɛstɪv) adj. 充血的　　failure (ˈfeljɚ) n. 衰竭

heart failure 心臟衰竭　　condition (kənˈdɪʃən) n. 疾病

weaken (ˈwikən) v. 使變弱　　pump (pʌmp) v. 打出

beta-blocker (ˈbetəˌblɑkɚ) n. (防止心臟病突發的) β受體阻滯藥品

stabilize (ˈstebḷˌaɪz) v. 使穩定　　patient (ˈpeʃənt) n. 病人

stage (stedʒ) n. 階段　　option (ˈɑpʃən) n. 選擇

transplant (ˈtrænsˌplænt) n. 移植　　short (ʃɔrt) adj. (數量) 不足的

supply (səˈplaɪ) n. 供應　　artificial (ˌɑrtəˈfɪʃəl) adj. 人工的

show (ʃo) v. 顯示　　promise (ˈprɑmɪs) n. 希望

experimental (ɪkˌspɛrəˈmɛntḷ) adj. 實驗的

recently (ˈrisṇtlɪ) adv. 最近　　suffer (ˈsʌfɚ) v. 罹患

stroke (strok) n. 中風

That's why it's such good news to hear that another type of mechanical pump, called a left ventricular assist device (LVAD), may be an alternative. Instead of replacing the heart entirely, the LVAD is attached to the heart, boosting its output. The pump is twice as likely as drugs to keep patients alive for at least one year, according to a study that was published in the *New England Journal of Medicine*.

那就是為什麼聽到另一種機械式唧筒，又稱為左心室輔助器 (LVAD) 可能是另一種選擇時，會覺得是大好消息的原因。左心室輔助器 (LVAD) 被連在心臟上面，增加其血液輸出量，而不是完全取代心臟。根據在新英格蘭醫學期刊中刊登的一項研究指出，唧筒讓病人至少存活一年的可能性，是藥物的兩倍。

type (taɪp) n. 型式　　mechanical (məˈkænɪkḷ) adj. 機械的

pump (pʌmp) n. 唧筒；幫浦

ventricular (vɛnˈtrɪkjəlɚ) adj. 心室的

assist (əˈsɪst) n. 幫助；輔助　　device (dɪˈvaɪs) n. 裝置；儀器

alternative (ɔlˈtɜnətɪv) n. 另一個選擇　　***instead of*** 而不是

replace (rɪˈples) v. 取代　　entirely (ɪnˈtaɪrlɪ) adv. 完全地

attach (əˈtætʃ) v. 連接 <*to*>　　boost (bust) v. 提高；增加

output (ˈaʊtˌpʊt) n. 輸出　　likely (ˈlaɪklɪ) adj. 可能的

alive (əˈlaɪv) adj. 活著的　　publish (ˈpʌblɪʃ) v. 刊登

journal (ˈdʒɜnḷ) n. 期刊

Although some patients still suffered from strokes and the LVADs sometimes failed, the quality of life for the majority of the patients in the study was significantly improved. At present, LVADs are used primarily to buy time for patients who are waiting for a heart transplant. But the pumps have developed such a good track record over the years that doctors have started to wonder if the devices could provide a more long-term solution.

雖然有些病人仍然罹患中風，且左心室輔助器（LVAD）有時候會失去作用，但是在這項研究中，大多數病人的生活品質，卻大大地改善了。目前，左心室輔助器主要被用來替那些等候心臟移植的人爭取時間。但是這些年來，唧筒的記錄十分良好，以致於醫生們開始思考，這種儀器是否可以提供一個較長期的解決之道。

> fail〔fel〕*v.* 失敗；失去作用　　quality〔'kwɑlətɪ〕*n.* 品質
> majority〔mə'dʒɔrətɪ〕*n.* 大多數
> significantly〔sɪg'nɪfəkəntlɪ〕*adv.* 大大地；值得注目地
> improve〔ɪm'pruv〕*v.* 改善　　***at present*** 目前
> primarily〔'praɪ,mɛrəlɪ〕*adv.* 主要地（= *chiefly* = *mainly*）
> buy〔baɪ〕*v.* 換取　　develop〔dɪ'vɛləp〕*v.* 發展
> track〔træk〕*n.* 蹤跡；路程　　***a good track record*** 記錄良好
> wonder〔'wʌndɚ〕*v.* 想知道　　long-term〔'lɔŋ,tɝm〕*adj.* 長期的

49. (**B**) 新的 AbioCor 人工心臟 ＿＿＿＿＿＿＿。
  (A) 在心臟病初期對病人有幫助
  (B) 是那些需要心臟移植的病人的另一個選擇
  (C) 被用來代替人類的心臟，並且它是毫無瑕疵的
  (D) 一定可以幫助心臟打出和人體所需要一樣多的血液
  instead of 代替　　flawless〔'flɔlɪs〕*adj.* 無瑕疵的

50. (**D**) 下列何者不正確？
  (A) 左心室輔助器（LVAD）並未完全取代心臟。
  (B) 左心室輔助器（LVAD）可能會增進血液流動。
  (C) 左心室輔助器（LVAD）可能可以延長病人的壽命。
  (D) 左心室輔助器（LVAD）被放在病人的心臟裡面。
  flow〔flo〕*n.* 流動　　extend〔ɪk'stɛnd〕*v.* 延長

51.(**C**) 根據本文，左心室輔助器（LVAD）_____。

    (A) 不像 AbioCor，並不是個機械式唧筒

    (B) 已經在所有病人的身上都完全發揮功能

    (C) <u>已經改善大部分病人的生活品質</u>

    (D) 的確是所有心臟問題的解決之道

    function〔ˋfʌŋkʃən〕*v.* 起作用；產生功能

    perfectly〔ˋpɝfɪktlɪ〕*adv.* 完全地

    better〔ˋbɛtɚ〕*v.* 改善

    definitely〔ˋdɛfənɪtlɪ〕*adv.* 的確

52.(**D**) 這篇文章最有可能出現在_____中。

    (A) 自傳   (B) 化學書籍

    (C) 科幻小說   (D) <u>新聞雜誌</u>

    autobiography〔͵ɔtəbaɪˋɑgrəfɪ〕*n.* 自傳

    chemistry〔ˋkɛmɪstrɪ〕*n.* 化學   ***science fiction*** 科幻小說

<u>第 53 至 56 題為題組</u>

    Sylvia Earle, a marine botanist and one of the foremost deep-sea explorers, has spent over 6,000 hours, more than seven months, underwater. From her earliest years, Earle had a fascination with marine life, and she took her first plunge into the open sea as a teenager. In the years since then she has taken part in a number of landmark underwater projects, from exploratory expeditions around the world to her well-known "Jim dive" in 1978, which was the deepest solo dive ever made without a cable connecting the diver to a support ship at the surface of the sea.

    席維亞‧艾兒是一位海洋植物學家，也是最早期的深海探險家之一，她在海裏的時間超過六千個小時，也就是七個多月。艾兒早年就對海洋世界十分著迷，十幾歲就初次跳入海中。此後她參加許多重要的海底計畫，從環球的探險之旅，到一九七八年著名的「吉姆潛水」，即有史以來最深的單人潛水，那次潛水者的身上並沒有用纜線與海面上的支援船隻相連接。

marine〔məˈrin〕*adj.* 海洋的
botanist〔ˈbɑtn̩ɪst〕*n.* 植物學家
foremost〔ˈforˌmost〕*adj.* 最早的
explorer〔ɪkˈsplorɚ〕*n.* 探險者
underwater〔ˈʌndɚˌwɔtɚ〕*adv.* 在水中　*adj.* 水中的
fascination〔ˌfæsn̩ˈeʃən〕*n.* 著迷　　plunge〔plʌndʒ〕*n.* 跳入
the open sea 外海；公海　　***take part in*** 參加
a number of 許多的　　landmark〔ˈlændˌmɑrk〕*n.* 重要事件；地標
project〔ˈprɑdʒɛkt〕*n.* 計畫
exploratory〔ɪkˈsplorəˌtori〕*adj.* 探險的
expedition〔ˌɛkspɪˈdɪʃən〕*n.* 探險　　dive〔daɪv〕*n. v.* 潛水
solo〔ˈsolo〕*adj.* 單獨的　　cable〔ˈkebl̩〕*n.* 大的纜線
diver〔ˈdaɪvɚ〕*n.* 潛水者

Clothed in a Jim suit, a futuristic suit of plastic and metal armor, which was secured to a manned submarine, Sylvia Earle plunged vertically into the Pacific Ocean, at times at a speed of 100 feet per minute. On reaching the ocean floor, she was released from the submarine and from that point her only connection to the sub was an 18-foot rope. For the next two and a half hours, Earle roamed the seabed taking notes, collecting specimens, and planting a U.S. flag. Having an irresistible desire to descend deeper still, in 1981 she became involved in the design and manufacture of deep-sea submersibles, one of which took her to a depth of 3,000 feet. This, however, did not end Sylvia Earle's accomplishments.

　　席維亞‧艾兒穿著吉姆裝，那是一種非常先進的潛水衣，用塑膠和金屬製成，且牢牢綁在有人操控的潛水艇上，然後她縱身跳入太平洋中，速度有時高達每分鐘一百英呎。潛水艇一觸及海底，她就離開潛水艇，從此以後，她與潛水艇唯一的聯繫，是一條十八英呎長的繩子。之後的二個半小時裏，艾兒在海底漫遊，記筆記，收集樣本，並插上一支美國國旗。她心中有一種無法抗拒的慾望，想潛得更深，所以在一九八一年，她加入深海潛水艇的設計與製造計畫，其中一艘潛水艇載她深入三千英呎深的海底。然而，席維亞‧艾兒的成就，並非到此爲止。

futuristic〔ˌfjutʃə'rɪstɪk〕*adj.* 未來的；非常先進的

metal〔'mɛtḷ〕*n.* 金屬　　armor〔'armɚ〕*n.* 潛水衣

secure〔sɪ'kjʊr〕*v.* 縛牢

manned〔mænd〕*adj.* 有人駕駛的

submarine〔'sʌbmə,rin〕*n.* 潛水艇（＝*sub*）

vertically〔'vɝtɪkḷɪ〕*adv.* 垂直地

release〔rɪ'lis〕*v.* 放鬆；鬆開

connection〔kə'nɛkʃən〕*n.* 連接

roam〔rom〕*v.* 漫遊　　seabed〔'si,bɛd〕*n.* 海底

specimen〔'spɛsəmən〕*n.* 樣本

plant〔plænt〕*v.* 插；種

irresistible〔ˌɪrɪ'zɪstəbḷ〕*adj.* 無法抗拒的

descend〔dɪ'sɛnd〕*v.* 下降　　involve〔ɪn'valv〕*v.* 捲入；加入

submersible〔səb'mɝsəbḷ〕*n.* 潛水艇　　depth〔dɛpθ〕*n.* 深度

accomplishment〔ə'kamplɪʃmənt〕*n.* 成就

53.（**D**）由本文可推論出，席維亞・艾兒 ＿＿＿＿＿＿＿。

(A) 受非常好的教育

(B) 在潛水艇裏不太自在

(C) 沒有科技上的專業技術

(D) <u>一生都貢獻給海洋探險</u>

expertise〔ˌɛkspɚ'tiz〕*n.* 專業技術

devote〔dɪ'vot〕*v.* 奉獻

54.（**B**）本文主旨是 ＿＿＿＿＿＿＿。

(A) 探索海底的植物

(B) <u>描述席維亞・艾兒的所作所爲</u>

(C) 介紹海洋學

(D) 顯示吉姆潛水在歷史上的重要性

botany〔'batṇɪ〕*n.* 植物（集合名詞）

account〔ə'kaʊnt〕*n.* 描述

oceanography〔ˌoʃɪən'agrəfɪ〕*n.* 海洋學

55. (**A**) 有關吉姆潛水，以下何者錯誤？

  (A) 席維亞·艾兒在一九八一年成功地做到了。

  (B) 是在太平洋裏進行。

  (C) 艾兒在海底記筆記。

  (D) 與艾兒相連接的潛水艇是有人駕駛的。

56. (**C**) 文章的下一段可能談論什麼？

  (A) 席維亞·艾兒的早期童年。

  (B) 提供更多吉姆潛水裝的訊息。

  (C) 艾兒在一九八一年之後的成就。

  (D) 深海潛水艇的製作。

第貳部分：非選擇題

一、英文翻譯：

1. 人們常因「語言障礙」，嚇得不敢出國。

   People are often scared of going abroad because of the "language barrier."

2. 不過，就算沒有任何外語技巧，你在歐洲仍然可以玩得很愉快。

   However, you can still have a great time in Europe without any foreign language skills.

二、英文作文：(作文範例)

  It is impossible to live life without some regrets, for we are faced with decisions every day and do not always make the best ones. Although I am only eighteen years old, I already have a few regrets, and one of these is something I did not do in high school.

  Like most high school students in Taiwan, I am very concerned about getting into a good college after I graduate. *As a result*, I studied very hard for three years in order to be well prepared for the college entrance exam. I do feel ready for the exam but, now that I am about to graduate, I also feel that I missed out on some of the other things that high school has to offer, especially the opportunity to join clubs and other activities. Because I was so focused on my studies, I did not want to waste any time on things not related to schoolwork. But now I realize that these activities are not just a way to kill time, but also a way to explore interests and make lasting friendships.

Unfortunately, I cannot change the past. It is too late for me to join a club now. *However*, I can change what I will do in the future. When I begin my college life, I will make a point of participating in a wide variety of activities. Perhaps some of them will be a waste of time, but I think they will all help me to discover what I like and don't like. *More importantly*, joining some clubs will give me the opportunity to meet many people and to have more fun. There is so much more to life than what is in our textbooks. While it is impossible to live without regrets, we can learn from our mistakes and use them to make a better future for ourselves.

regret〔rɪ'grɛt〕*n.* 令人後悔、遺憾的事
be faced with 面對　　*as a result* 因此
be about to + *V.* 即將　　*miss out on* 錯過良機
be focused on 專注於
related〔rɪ'letɪd〕*adj.* 有關聯的 < *to* >
explore〔ɪk'splor〕*v.* 探索　　lasting〔'læstɪŋ〕*adj.* 持續的
unfortunately〔ʌn'fɔrtʃənɪtlɪ〕*adv.* 不幸的是
make a point of 一定
participate〔par'tɪsə,pet〕*v.* 參加 < *in* >
a wide variety of 各式各樣的
textbook〔'tɛkst,bʊk〕*n.* 教科書

大學入學指定科目考試英文模擬試題 ⑤

第壹部份：選擇題（佔72分）

一、詞彙與慣用語（15％）

說明： 第1至15題，每題選出一個最適當的選項，標示在答案卡之「選擇題
答案區」。每題答對得1分，答錯或劃記多於一個選項者倒扣 1/3 分，
倒扣到本大題之實得分數爲零爲止，未作答者，不給分亦不扣分。

1. Please keep a safe distance. When startled, the tamed animal can become very _____.
   (A) aggressive
   (B) protective
   (C) attentive
   (D) permissive

2. I spent my holiday afternoons _____ in the countryside, enjoying the peaceful atmosphere.
   (A) scrambling (B) hurrying (C) strolling (D) stumbling

3. Yellow Stone National Park is _____ beautiful; it attracts numerous visitors each year.
   (A) ambiguously
   (B) notoriously
   (C) inevitably
   (D) overwhelmingly

4. All the guests at the party were embarrassed when the hostess got terribly drunk and made a(n) _____.
   (A) experiment (B) scene (C) deal (D) example

5. As a father, my top _____ is to take care of my family. My family always comes first.
   (A) priority (B) privacy (C) possession (D) privilege

6. The discussion _____ around the terrible conditions in the community but no solutions came up.
   (A) dissolved (B) evolved (C) resolved (D) revolved

7. Some men are too _____ to ask for directions when they can't find their way; they consider it beneath their dignity.
   (A) arrogant
   (B) courteous
   (C) eloquent
   (D) willing

8. One of the _____ of dining here is that it is difficult to find a parking space.
   (A) interruptions
   (B) delights
   (C) annoyances
   (D) attractions

9. He was _____ of robbing the bank, but actually he had nothing to do with the robbery.
   (A) deprived   (B) accused   (C) warned   (D) informed

10. As the singer appeared in the spotlight, her fans screamed and shouted _____.
    (A) timidly   (B) ironically   (C) critically   (D) hysterically

11. Stop _____ and tell us straight the outcome of the speech contest.
    (A) idling around
    (B) messing up
    (C) beating about the bush
    (D) speaking of the devil

12. Some citizens do not follow the rules of traffic because they think they can _____ it.
    (A) take charge of
    (B) make up for
    (C) live up to
    (D) get away with

13. I am going on a self-guided tour to England, so I should _____ my English.
    (A) brush up   (B) put down   (C) back up   (D) pin down

14. The discovery was significant _____ its influence on later development of technology.
    (A) in memory of
    (B) in view of
    (C) in pursuit of
    (D) in care of

15. Despite seven years' stay in England, I still find it hard to speak
    English well, _____ perfectly.
    (A) at most   (B) all but
    (C) let alone   (D) beyond question

二、綜合測驗（15 %）

說明： 第 16 至 30 題，每題一個空格。請依文意選出一個最適當的選項，標示
在答案卡之「選擇題答案區」。每題答對得 1 分，答錯或劃記多於一
個選項者倒扣 1/3 分，倒扣到本大題之實得分數為零為止。未作答者，
不給分亦不扣分。

第 16 至 25 題為題組

Forget the south of France, forget Bali. Forget run-of-the-mill
earthbound ___16___. Instead, get ready for something else: a holiday in
a futuristic space hotel, or a journey into orbit to see all the spectacular
___17___ of our planet in a single trip. For more than 30 years there
have been promises that space travel for all is just ___18___. Now, at
the end of the millennium, that dream is starting to become reality.

The space market used to be driven by government. ___19___ big
business has woken up to the fact that there's money in the stars. Firms
such as Interglobal Space Lines are offering "weightless" training for
amateur astronauts, and for about $5,000 you can ___20___ yourself to
zero gravity in a private jet. It sounds like something out of science
fiction, but tour operators are taking ___21___ for the first commercial
passenger flights into space, ___22___ to take place in a few years.
Lucky passengers will travel to about 100 kilometers above Earth.
The price? At least $90,000 a ticket. It's not cheap but thousands of
wealthy travelers will be ___23___ to go.

While the first tourists will spend only a few minutes in space,
companies are already thinking ahead to those ___24___ a room.

Astronauts will soon ___25___ the $92 billion International Space Station. It is obvious that the final frontier is opening up. So, you'd better book your tickets now.

16. (A) resorts   (B) depths   (C) responses   (D) resources

17. (A) disasters   (B) sights   (C) indicators   (D) factors

18. (A) around the corner   (B) on the spot
    (C) at the sight   (D) beyond comparison

19. (A) Even   (B) Only   (C) Now   (D) Such

20. (A) adapt   (B) accomplish
    (C) transfer   (D) transform

21. (A) conservation   (B) reservations
    (C) precaution   (D) advantages

22. (A) estimated   (B) recommended
    (C) displayed   (D) stimulated

23. (A) keen   (B) reluctant   (C) devoted   (D) involved

24. (A) wanting   (B) wanted   (C) who wants   (D) what want

25. (A) provide for   (B) be heading for
    (C) compete with   (D) catch up with

第 26 至 30 題為題組

Concerned about the growing number of people who smoke on this island, the government recently put into effect a tough anti-smoking law. The action is praiseworthy, considering the harm tobacco can ___26___ to one's health.

Currently, the law forbids the use of tobacco in public places and the sale of cigarettes at convenience stores to people under the age of 18. Strict enforcement of the law is difficult, ___27___ not impossible. As the health officials have admitted, the government does not have enough resources to monitor compliance. Furthermore, the violations are nearly unavoidable ___28___ businesses such as restaurants, bars and KTVs probably will not risk losing customers ___29___ reporting those who violate the law.

　　In our opinion, therefore, an anti-smoking law alone can hardly reduce the number of smokers. Some other measures have to be adopted ___30___ if we are to see a significant drop in the consumption of tobacco products in our society.

26. (A) do　　　　(B) get　　　　(C) make　　　　(D) take
27. (A) then　　　(B) if　　　　　(C) since　　　　(D) as
28. (A) thus　　　(B) while　　　　(C) that　　　　(D) because
29. (A) with　　　(B) for　　　　　(C) on　　　　　(D) by
30. (A) for the most part　　　　　(B) at the same time
　　 (C) in the long run　　　　　　(D) for the time being

三、文意選填（10％）

說明：　第 31 至 40 題，每題一個空格。請依文意在文章後所提供的 (A) 到 (J) 選項中分別選出最適當者，並將其字母代號標示在答案卡之「選擇題答案區」。每題答對得 1 分，答錯或劃記多於一個選項者倒扣 1/9 分，倒扣到本大題之實得分數爲零爲止。未作答者，不給分亦不扣分。

第 31 至 40 題爲題組

　　One of the saddest observations I have made is this: many of us are ___31___ to learn from the people closest to us — our parents, spouses, children, and friends. Rather than being ___32___ to learning, we close ourselves off out of fear, stubbornness or pride. It's almost as if we say to ___33___, "I have already learned all that I can learn. There is nothing ___34___ I need to learn."

　　It's sad, because often the people closest to us know us the best and can offer very simple ___35___. If we are too proud or stubborn to learn, we lose out on some wonderful, simple ways to ___36___ our lives.

I have tried to remain open to suggestions from my friends and family. In fact, I have gone so ___37___ as to ask my family and friends, "What are some of my blind spots?" Not only ___38___ this make the person you are asking feel wanted and special, but you end up getting some terrific advice. It's such a simple shortcut for growth, ___39___ few people use it. All it takes is a little ___40___ and humility, and the ability to let go of your ego.

(A) does   (B) far   (C) else   (D) solutions
(E) courage   (F) reluctant   (G) ourselves   (H) yet
(I) improve   (J) open

四、篇章結構（10％）

說明： 第 41 至 45 題，每題一個空格。請依文意在文章後所提供的 (A) 到 (E) 選項中分別選出最適當者，填入空格中，使篇章結構清晰有條理，並將其英文字母代號標示在答案卡之「選擇題答案區」。每題答對得 2 分，答錯或劃記多於一個選項者倒扣 1/2 分，倒扣到本大題之實得分數為零為止。未作答者，不給分亦不扣分。

第 41 至 45 題為題組

A legend is a popular type of folk tale. ___41___ But myths describe events from antiquity and usually deal with religious subjects, such as the birth of a god. Legends tell of recognizable people and places and often take place in comparatively recent times. ___42___ Legends of superhuman accomplishments are often imaginary. ___43___ All societies have legends. ___44___ For example, John Henry was a legendary hero of black Americans, and Casey Jones of railroads workers. ___45___ They are no longer well known only to certain groups of people.

(A) Over time, however, these figures have become national heroes.

(B) Some legends are based on real persons or events but many are entirely fictional.

(C) By contrast, legends about Washington and Lincoln are mostly exaggerations of their real qualities.

(D) In some ways, legends resemble myths, another type of folk tale.

(E) Most legends began as stories about heroes of a particular group of people.

五、閱讀測驗（22％）

說明： 第 46 至 56 題，每題請分別根據各篇文章的文意選出一個最適當的選項，標示在答案卡之「選擇題答案區」。每題答對得 2 分，答錯或劃記多於一個選項者倒扣 2/3 分，倒扣到本大題之實得分數為零為止。未作答者，不給分亦不扣分。

第 46 至 48 題為題組

Sleep is a basic human need, as basic as the need for oxygen. Getting a good night's sleep is not only directly related to how we feel the next day, but to our long-term health as well. Still, many of us suffer from at least occasional insomnia. Even more of us report at least one night of restless sleep per week that leaves us feeling ill and irritable. This is a serious problem. If you think otherwise, consider this. People who sleep four hours or less per night are twice as likely not to survive in six years as those who sleep the normal eight hours or so.

Given the seriousness of sleep, how can we make sure that we rest well and stay healthy? While there are no foolproof methods, here are some suggestions from sleep experts. If you do have trouble sleeping and these methods don't help, it's important that you see a doctor before insomnia causes your health to suffer. Start with these suggestions, though.

First, if you can't sleep in the middle of the night, don't get up. Exposing yourself to bright light will affect your body clock and worsen your insomnia. Stay in bed.

Second, get regular exercise each day, but finish at least six hours before bedtime. Exercising in the evening can help keep you awake.

Third, take a bath for thirty minutes within two hours of bedtime. The bath will warm you, relax you, and make you feel sleepy.

Finally, don't drink alcohol. Although having a drink before bed makes you sleepy, alcohol changes its effects after a bit of time. These secondary effects of alcohol can wake you up during the second half of your night's sleep.

46. What is the main idea of the first two paragraphs of this article?
    (A) Sleep can influence how we feel the next day.
    (B) We should take sleep seriously because it's related to our health.
    (C) People who sleep less than four hours live less than six years.
    (D) Always consult a doctor first if you have insomnia.

47. What does the word "insomnia" mean?
    (A) A status that makes one drowsy.
    (B) A sickness that takes away one's life.
    (C) The inability to fall asleep.
    (D) A disease that hurts one while in sleep.

48. According to the author, which of the following statements is FALSE?
    (A) Many of us suffer from insomnia.
    (B) Not enough sleep may cost one one's life.
    (C) If you want the hot bath to help you sleep, you must take it more than two hours before you go to bed.
    (D) Alcohol can help you feel sleepy.

第 49 至 52 題為題組

Around the end of the eighteenth century, some families trooped north from Mexico to California. On a stream along the desert's edge, they built a settlement called Los Angeles. For many years it was a market town, where nearby farmers and ranchers met to trade.

From 1876 to 1885, many railroads were built. Los Angeles was linked to San Francisco and, through San Francisco to the rest of the country. Eventually, the railroad provided a direct route between Los Angeles and Chicago.

Then in the 1890's, oil was discovered in the city. As derricks went up, workers built many highways and pipelines. Digging began on a harbor that would make Los Angeles not only an ocean port but also a fishing center. In 1914, the harbor was completed and the Panama Canal opened. Suddenly Los Angeles became the busiest port on the Pacific Coast.

Today, Los Angeles is the main industrial center in the West. It produces goods not only for other West Coast communities but also for those in other parts of the country. It leads the nation in making airplanes and equipment for exploring outer space. Many motion pictures and television programs are filmed in Los Angeles. The city is also the business center for states in the West. Improvements in transportation are the main reason for Los Angeles' growth.

49. When did Los Angeles start to become the busiest port on the Pacific Coast?
    (A) In the 1890's.　　　　　　(B) In 1914.
    (C) In 1885.　　　　　　　　(D) In 1920.

50. Choose an appropriate title for this passage.
    (A) The Past of Los Angeles
    (B) The Future of Los Angeles
    (C) The Growth of Los Angeles
    (D) The Industries in Los Angeles

51. During the years directly following its settlement, the main commercial activity of Los Angeles was _____.
    (A) fishing   (B) trading
    (C) filming   (D) oil drilling

52. San Francisco is mentioned in the passage for which of the following reasons?
    (A) San Francisco was very near Los Angeles.
    (B) San Francisco was linked to Chicago.
    (C) Oil was discovered in San Francisco in the 1890's.
    (D) San Francisco linked Los Angeles to the rest of the country.

第 53 至 56 題為題組

Until I met Mrs. Bench, nursing wasn't quite what I had expected. Mrs. Bench, a tiny, ancient lady, was my first patient. That morning, I bustled in with my equipment and said cheerily, "Good morning, Mrs. Bench. I'm your nurse today. I'm here to give you a bath, and make your bed."

"March yourself right out of here. I don't intend to have a bath today."

Squaring my shoulders, I looked her right in the eye. "Mrs. Bench, my job is to give you a bath. Now, let's get started." To my alarm, big tears formed in her eyes.

"I'm dying, and nobody cares, just as long as I'm clean."

"Don't be silly," I said briskly. "Nobody is going to die." I ignored her protests and bulldozed ahead with the bath.

The next day, <u>Mrs. Bench anticipated my coming and had her **ammunition** ready.</u> "Before you do anything," she said, "define 'nursing.'"

I eyed her doubtfully. "Well, nursing is hard to define," I hedged. "It has to do with taking care of sick people."

At that Mrs. Bench whisked out a dictionary. "Just as I suspected. You don't even know what you're supposed to do." She flipped to a page and read slowly: "'To nurse: to tend the sick or aged; to take care of, nourish, foster, develop or cherish.'" She closed the book with a bang. "I'm ready to be cherished."

"Good heavens, Mrs. Bench," I said, "what are you talking about?"

Grinning broadly, she patted a chair next to the bed. "Just sit down. Cherishing is easy to learn. You start by listening."

Listen I did. She told me about Mr. Bench. "He was a tall, raw-boned farmer. When he came courting, he tracked mud into the parlor. Of course, I thought I was meant for finer things, but I married him anyway.

"For our first anniversary, I wanted a love token, coins of silver or gold hung on a fine chain." She smiled and fingered the silver chain she always wore. "The anniversary day came, and Ben hitched the wagon to drive into town. In a fever of anticipation, I waited on a slope, looking for the dust in the distance that would mark his coming." Her eyes clouded. "He never came. Riders found the wagon the next morning. They came out with the news, and this." Reverently, she drew it out. It was faded now from rubbing against her skin, but one side was wreathed with tiny hearts and the reverse said simply, "Ben and Alma. Love eternal."

"But it's a penny," I said. "Didn't you say they were silver or gold?"

Tears rimmed her eyes. "It's sad to admit, but if he'd come home that day, I'd have seen only the penny. As it was, I saw only the love."

Mrs. Bench died that night. I could never forget how she faced me with a piercing look and said, "Young lady, as a nurse, you only see the penny. Don't be fooled by the penny. Look for the love."

53. In the story, Mrs. Bench _____.

   (A) refused to bathe because she thought she was clean enough

   (B) was satisfied with what the nurse had done for her

   (C) thought she married the wrong man and she didn't love him

   (D) gave the nurse a good lesson of what nursing really meant

54. In the sentence "Mrs. Bench anticipated my coming and had her *ammunition* ready," "*ammunition*" refers to _____.

   (A) the act of cherishing

   (B) an emphasis on listening

   (C) bullets or shells

   (D) a test for the nurse

55. From the story it can be inferred that Mr. Bench _____.

　(A) was socially skilled and knew what to do when courting

　(B) gave Mrs. Bench a chain with silver coins hung on it

　(C) left Mrs. Bench a penny with their names on it

　(D) deserted Mrs. Bench on their first anniversary

56. What is the best title for this story?

　(A) Consulting a dictionary.

　(B) A Penny.

　(C) Mrs. Bench's Love Story.

　(D) My Experience as a Nurse.

第貳部份：非選擇題（佔 28 分）

一、英文翻譯（8%）

說明： 1. 將下列兩句中文翻譯成適當之英文，並將答案寫在「答案卷」上。

　　　 2. 未按題意翻譯者，不予計分。

1. 擁有手機的優點之一，就是無論你去哪裡，都很容易聯絡得上。

2. 此外，如果有緊急的情況，你可以立刻打電話。

二、英文作文（20%）

說明： 1. 依提示在「答案卷」上寫一篇英文作文。

　　　 2. 文長至少 120 個單詞。

提示： 每個人在初到一個新環境時，往往會有興奮、期待、憧憬、或是焦慮、恐懼等情緒。請根據個人經驗，描述你乍到某個新環境時的感受、調適的過程以及你從中學到的心得或教訓。

大學入學指定科目考試英文模擬試題⑤詳解

第壹部分：單一選擇題

一、詞彙及慣用語：

1. (**A**) Please keep a safe distance. When startled, the tamed animal can become very aggressive.

   請保持安全距離。當這隻被馴服的動物受到驚嚇時，可能會變得非常具有攻擊性。
   (A) *aggressive* ﹝ ə'grɛsɪv ﹞ *adj.* 有攻擊性的
   (B) protective ﹝ prə'tɛktɪv ﹞ *adj.* 保護的
   (C) attentive ﹝ ə'tɛntɪv ﹞ *adj.* 專心的
   (D) permissive ﹝ pə'mɪsɪv ﹞ *adj.* 允許的
   startle ﹝'startḷ﹞ *v.* 驚嚇　　tamed ﹝ temd ﹞ *adj.* 被馴服的

2. (**C**) I spent my holiday afternoons strolling in the countryside, enjoying the peaceful atmosphere.

   我假日的午后會去鄉間散步，享受寧靜的氣氛。
   (A) scramble ﹝'skræmbḷ﹞ *v.* 攀登；炒（蛋）
   (B) hurry ﹝'hɝɪ﹞ *v.* 匆忙
   (C) *stroll* ﹝ strol ﹞ *v.* 漫步
   (D) stumble ﹝'stʌmbḷ﹞ *v.* 絆倒
   countryside ﹝'kʌntrɪ,saɪd ﹞ *n.* 鄉村地區
   peaceful ﹝'pisfəl ﹞ *adj.* 寧靜的　　atmosphere ﹝'ætməs,fɪr ﹞ *n.* 氣氛

3. (**D**) Yellow Stone National Park is overwhelmingly beautiful; it attracts numerous visitors each year.

   黃石國家公園的風景非常漂亮；每年都會吸引許多遊客前來。
   (A) ambiguously ﹝ æm'bɪgjuəslɪ ﹞ *adv.* 含糊地；模稜兩可地
   (B) notoriously ﹝ no'torɪəslɪ ﹞ *adv.* 惡名昭彰地
   (C) inevitably ﹝ ɪn'ɛvətəbḷɪ ﹞ *adv.* 不可避免地
   (D) *overwhelmingly* ﹝,ovə'hwɛlmɪŋlɪ ﹞ *adv.* 壓倒性地；極度地
   numerous ﹝'njumərəs ﹞ *adj.* 非常多的

4. (**B**) All the guests at the party were embarrassed when the hostess got
terribly drunk and made a <u>scene</u>.
當女主人喝得爛醉，在宴會上<u>大吵大鬧</u>時，所有的客人都覺得很
尷尬。
(A) experiment〔ɪkˈspɛrəmənt〕*n.* 實驗
(B) *scene*〔sin〕*n.* 吵鬧的場面；大鬧　　*make a scene* 大吵大鬧
(C) deal〔dil〕*n.* 交易
(D) example〔ɪgˈzæmpḷ〕*n.* 例子
guest〔gɛst〕*n.* 客人　　embarrassed〔ɪmˈbærəst〕*adj.* 尷尬的
hostess〔ˈhostɪs〕*n.* 女主人　　terribly〔ˈtɛrəblɪ〕*adv.* 非常地
drunk〔drʌŋk〕*adj.* 喝醉的

5. (**A**) As a father, my top <u>priority</u> is to take care of my family.　My
family always comes first.
身為父親，我的<u>首要之務</u>就是照顧我的家人。我總是將家人擺在
第一位。
(A) *priority*〔praɪˈɔrətɪ〕*n.* 優先的事物
　　a top priority 最優先的事物
(B) privacy〔ˈpraɪvəsɪ〕*n.* 隱私權
(C) possession〔pəˈzɛʃən〕*n.* 擁有
(D) privilege〔ˈprɪvḷɪdʒ〕*n.* 特權
take care of 照顧　　*come first* 是最優先的

6. (**D**) The discussion <u>revolved</u> around the terrible conditions in the
community but no solutions came up.
這次的討論，是<u>以社區的惡劣環境為主題</u>，但是並沒有提出任何
解決之道。
(A) dissolve〔dɪˈzalv〕*v.* 溶解
(B) evolve〔ɪˈvalv〕*v.* 進化
(C) resolve〔rɪˈzalv〕*v.* 解決；決心
(D) *revolve*〔rɪˈvalv〕*v.* 環繞　　*revolve around* 以～為中心
conditions〔kənˈdɪʃənz〕*n. pl.* 環境
solution〔səˈluʃən〕*n.* 解決之道　　*come up* 被提出

7. (**A**) Some men are too <u>arrogant</u> to ask for directions when they can't find their way; they consider it beneath their dignity.

有些人找不到路時，會因爲太<u>自大</u>，而不肯問路；他們認爲這樣做有損他們的尊嚴。

(A) ***arrogant***〔ˈærəgənt〕*adj.* 自大的；傲慢的

(B) courteous〔ˈkɜtɪəs〕*adj.* 有禮貌的

(C) eloquent〔ˈɛləkwənt〕*adj.* 口才好的

(D) willing〔ˈwɪlɪŋ〕*adj.* 願意的

ask for directions 問路

beneath〔bɪˈniθ〕*prep.* 有損…的尊嚴；有失…的身份

dignity〔ˈdɪgnətɪ〕*n.* 尊嚴

8. (**C**) One of the <u>annoyances</u> of dining here is that it is difficult to find a parking space.

在這裏吃飯，<u>令人討厭的事</u>之一，就是很難找到停車位。

(A) interruption〔ˌɪntəˈrʌpʃən〕*n.* 打斷

(B) delight〔dɪˈlaɪt〕*n.* 高興；樂趣

(C) ***annoyance***〔əˈnɔɪəns〕*n.* 討厭的事物

(D) attraction〔əˈtrækʃən〕*n.* 吸引人的事物

dine〔daɪn〕*v.* 用餐　　***parking space*** 停車位

9. (**B**) He was <u>accused</u> of robbing the bank, but actually he had nothing to do with the robbery.

他被<u>指控</u>搶銀行，但實際上，他和這宗搶案毫無關係。

(A) deprive〔dɪˈpraɪv〕*v.* 剝奪 < *of* >

(B) ***accuse***〔əˈkjuz〕*v.* 指控　　***be accused of*** 被指控~

(C) warn〔wɔrn〕*v.* 警告 < *of* >

(D) inform〔ɪnˈfɔrm〕*v.* 通知 < *of* >

rob〔rɑb〕*v.* 搶劫　　actually〔ˈæktʃʊəlɪ〕*adv.* 實際上

have nothing to do with 與~無關

robbery〔ˈrɑbərɪ〕*n.* 搶案

10. (**D**) As the singer appeared in the spotlight, her fans screamed and shouted <u>hysterically</u>.
當那位歌手出現在聚光燈下時，她的歌迷就開始<u>歇斯底里地</u>尖叫。

(A) timidly (ˈtɪmɪdlɪ) *adv.* 膽小地
(B) ironically (aɪˈrɑnɪklɪ) *adv.* 諷刺地
(C) critically (ˈkrɪtɪklɪ) *adv.* 批評地
(D) ***hysterically*** (hɪsˈtɛrɪklɪ) *adv.* 歇斯底里地

spotlight (ˈspɑt,laɪt) *n.* 聚光燈　　fan (fæn) *n.* 迷
scream (skrim) *v.* 尖叫

11. (**C**) Stop <u>beating about the bush</u> and tell us straight the outcome of the speech contest. 別再<u>拐彎抹角</u>了，你就直接告訴我們演講比賽的結果。

(A) idle around 鬼混；無所事事 (= *fool around*)
(B) mess up 弄糟；搞砸
(C) ***beat about the bush*** 拐彎抹角 (= *beat around the bush*)
(D) speak of the devil 說曹操，曹操就到

straight (stret) *adv.* 直接地　　outcome (ˈaʊt,kʌm) *n.* 結果
speech (spitʃ) *n.* 演講　　contest (ˈkɑntɛst) *n.* 比賽

12. (**D**) Some citizens do not follow the rules of traffic because they think they can <u>get away with</u> it.
有些市民不遵守交通規則，因爲他們認爲自己可以<u>逃避懲罰</u>。

(A) take charge of 負責管理
(B) make up for 彌補 (= *compensate for*)
(C) live up to 遵守、實踐 (諾言、原則)；不辜負 (期望)
(D) ***get away with*** 逃避懲罰

citizen (ˈsɪtəzn̩) *n.* 市民；公民　　follow (ˈfɑlo) *v.* 遵守

13. (**A**) I am going on a self-guided tour to England, so I should <u>brush up</u> my English. 我即將去英國自助旅行，所以應該要<u>複習</u>一下英文。

(A) ***brush up*** 複習 (= *brush up on*)
(B) put down 放下；寫下　　(C) back up 支持
(D) pin down 用釘子釘住；確定

self-guided (ˈsɛlfˈgaɪdɪd) *adj.* 自己引導自己的
go on a self-guided tour 去自助旅行

14. (**B**) The discovery was significant <u>in view of</u> its influence on later development of technology.

<u>由於</u>這項發現影響了後來的科技發展，所以它是非常重要的。

(A) in memory of 紀念 (= *in honor of* = *in remembrance of*)

(B) *in view of* 由於；有鑑於

(C) in pursuit of 追求　　　(D) in care of 由～轉交

significant〔 sɪgˋnɪfəkənt 〕*adj.* 非常重要的

influence〔ˋɪnfluəns〕*n.* 影響＜ *on* ＞

later〔ˋletɚ〕*adj.* 以後的　　technology〔 tɛkˋnɑlədʒɪ 〕*n.* 科技

15. (**C**) Despite seven years' stay in England, I still find it hard to speak English well, <u>let alone</u> perfectly.

儘管我在英國待了七年，但仍然覺得要把英文說好很難，<u>更不用說</u>要說得完美了。

(A) at most 最多　　　　　(B) all but 幾乎 (= *almost*)

(C) *let alone* 更不用說　　(D) beyond question 毫無疑問

despite〔 dɪˋspaɪt 〕*prep.* 儘管　　stay〔 ste 〕*n.* 停留（時間）

perfectly〔ˋpɝfɪktlɪ〕*adv.* 完美地

二、綜合測驗：

Forget the south of France, forget Bali. Forget run-of-the-mill earthbound <u>resorts</u>. Instead, get ready for something else: a holiday in a
16
futuristic space hotel, or a journey into orbit to see all the spectacular <u>sights</u>
17
of our planet in a single trip. For more than 30 years there have been promises that space travel for all is just <u>around the corner</u>. Now, at the end
18
of the millennium, that dream is starting to become reality.

忘了法國南部，忘了峇里島。忘了那些地球上普通的渡假勝地。相反地，要準備嘗試一些其他的：在前衛的太空旅館渡個假，或者進入天體的運行軌道旅行，這一趟旅程能讓你飽覽地球上的所有壯觀景色。三十多年來，一直有人保證，不久就可讓大家上太空去旅行。現在，就在公元二千年即將結束時，那樣的夢想就快實現了。

Bali〔'bɑlɪ〕*n.* 峇里島
run-of-the-mill〔'rʌnəvðə'mɪl〕*adj.* 普通的；平凡的
earthbound〔'ɝθ,baʊnd〕*adj.* 不能離開地球的；陸地上的
futuristic〔,fjutʃə'ɪstɪk〕*adj.* 前衛的；未來（風格）的
orbit〔'ɔrbɪt〕*n.* 天體或人造衛星繞行的軌道
spectacular〔spɛk'tækjələ〕*adj.* 壯觀的
planet〔'plænɪt〕*n.* 行星　　single〔'sɪŋl̩〕*adj.* 單一的
millennium〔mə'lɛnɪəm〕*n.* 一千年；千禧年

16.(**A**)　(A) ***resort***〔rɪ'zɔrt〕*n.* 渡假勝地
　　　　(B) depths〔dɛpθs〕*n. pl.* 深處
　　　　(C) response〔rɪ'spɑns〕*n.* 回答；反應
　　　　(D) resource〔rɪ'sors〕*n.* 資源

17.(**B**)　(A) disaster〔dɪz'æstɚ〕*n.* 災難
　　　　(B) ***sights***〔saɪts〕*n. pl.* 風景
　　　　(C) indicator〔'ɪndə,ketɚ〕*n.* 指示物；標誌
　　　　(D) factor〔'fæktɚ〕*n.* 因素

18.(**A**)　依句意，選 (A) ***around the corner***「即將發生的；即將來臨的」。而
　　　　(B) on the spot「當場」，(C) at the sight of「一看見～」，(D) beyond
　　　　comparison「無與倫比地」，均不合句意。

The space market used to be driven by government. <u>Now</u> big business
　　　　　　　　　　　　　　　　　　　　　　　　　19
has woken up to the fact that there's money in the stars. Firms such as
Interglobal Space Lines are offering "weightless" training for amateur
astronauts, and for about $5,000 you can <u>adapt</u> yourself to zero gravity in a
　　　　　　　　　　　　　　　　　　　　　　　20
private jet. It sounds like something out of science fiction, but tour operators
are taking <u>reservations</u> for the first commercial passenger flights into
　　　　　　21
space, <u>estimated</u> to take place in a few years. Lucky passengers will travel
　　　　22
to about 100 kilometers above Earth. The price? At least $90,000 a ticket.
It's not cheap but thousands of wealthy travelers will be <u>keen</u> to go.
　　　　　　　　　　　　　　　　　　　　　　　　　　　　　23

　　太空市場以前是由政府在推動。現在，大型公司已經察覺到，可以靠星星來賺錢的這個事實。像是「星際太空運輸公司」這類的公司，現在正提供「無重力」訓練給業餘的太空人，而且只要付大約五千美元，你就可以在私人的噴射機上，讓自己適應無重力的狀態。這聽起來像是科幻小說的情節，但是已經有旅行業者，正在接受第一批商用客機的預訂，據估計再過幾年就可成行。幸運的旅客，將能夠在地球上空約一百公里處旅行。價格呢？每張票至少要九萬美元。票價並不便宜，但有數以千計的有錢旅客，非常渴望能成行。

> *used to V*. 以前　　drive〔draɪv〕*v.* 推動
> business〔'bɪznɪs〕*n.* 公司
> *wake up to the fact that* 意識到～的事實
> firm〔fɝm〕*n.* 公司　　line〔laɪn〕*n.* 運輸公司
> weightless〔'wetlɪs〕*adj.* 無重力的；無重量的
> amateur〔'æmə,tʃʊr〕*adj.* 業餘的
> astronaut〔'æstrə,nɔt〕*n.* 太空人；太空旅行者
> zero〔'zɪro〕*adj.* 零的；全無的　　gravity〔'grævətɪ〕*n.* 重力
> jet〔dʒɛt〕*n.* 噴射機　　*science fiction* 科幻小說
> operator〔'ɑpə,retɚ〕*n.* 經營者
> commercial〔kə'mɝʃəl〕*adj.* 商業的
> passenger〔'pæsn̩dʒɚ〕*adj.* 客運的　　*n.* 乘客
> *take place* 發生　　wealthy〔'wɛlθɪ〕*adj.* 有錢的

19. (**C**) 依句意，以前是由政府推動，「現在」已有許多大公司察覺星星能賺錢的事實，故選 (C) *Now*。

20. (**A**) (A) *adapt oneself to* 使自己適應 (= *be adapted to*)
　　　　 (B) accomplish〔ə'kɑmplɪʃ〕*v.* 完成
　　　　 (C) transfer〔træns'fɝ〕*v.* 轉移
　　　　 (D) transform〔træns'fɔrm〕*v.* 轉變

21. (**B**) 依句意，選 (B) *take reservations for*「接受～的預訂」。
　　　　 而 (A) conservation〔,kɑnsɚ'veʃən〕*n.* 保存，(C) precaution〔prɪ'kɔʃən〕*n.* 預防措施，(D) advantage〔əd'væntɪdʒ〕*n.* 優點，均不合句意。

22. (**A**) (A) ***estimate*** ('ɛstə,met) *v.* 估計
 (B) recommend (,rɛkə'mɛnd) *v.* 推薦
 (C) display (dɪ'sple) *v.* 陳列；展示
 (D) stimulate ('stɪmjə,let) *v.* 刺激

23. (**A**) (A) ***keen*** (kin) *adj.* 渴望的 < *to* >
 (B) reluctant (rɪ'lʌktənt) *adj.* 不情願的 < *to* >
 (C) devoted (dɪ'votɪd) *adj.* 致力於 < *to* >
 (D) involved (ɪn'vɑlvd) *adj.* 牽涉在內的 < *in* >

　　While the first tourists will spend only a few minutes in space, companies are already thinking ahead to those <u>wanting</u> a room. Astronauts
24

will soon <u>be heading for</u> the $92 billion International Space Station. It is
25

obvious that the final frontier is opening up. So, you'd better book your tickets now.

　　雖然首批旅客只能在太空中停留幾分鐘，但是這些公司已有先見之明，考慮到那些想在太空中過夜的旅客。上太空旅行的人，很快就會前往造價高達九百二十億美元的國際太空站。顯然這最後的新領域即將被開啓。所以，你最好現在就去預訂太空旅行的票。

　　ahead (ə'hɛd) *adv.* 預先；較早
　　billion ('bɪljən) *n.* 十億
　　International Space Station 國際太空站
　　obvious ('ɑbvɪəs) *adj.* 明顯的
　　frontier (frʌn'tɪr) *n.* 新領域　　book (bʊk) *v.* 預訂

24. (**A**) 原句是由 ⋯to those ***who want*** a room. 省略關代 who，並將動詞改爲現在分詞轉化而來。

25. (**B**) 依句意，選 (B) ***be heading for*** 「前往」。而 (A) provide *sth.* for *sb.* 「提供某人某物」，(C) compete with 「與～競爭」，(D) catch up with 「趕上」，則不合句意。

第 26 至 30 題為題組

Concerned about the growing number of people who smoke on this island, the government recently put into effect a tough anti-smoking law. The action is praiseworthy, considering the harm tobacco can <u>do</u> to one's
26
health.

擔心本島抽煙的人數越來越多，政府最近實施了一項強硬的禁煙法令。就香煙對人體健康所造成的傷害而言，這項行動是值得稱讚的。

> ***be concerned about*** 擔心　　growing (ˋgroɪŋ) *adj.* 越來越多的
> ***put into effect*** 實施 (= *bring into effect*)
> tough (tʌf) *adj.* 強硬的
> praiseworthy (ˋprez͵wɝðɪ) *adj.* 值得稱讚的
> considering (kənˋsɪdərɪŋ) *prep.* 就～而論
> tobacco (təˋbæko) *n.* 香煙

26. (**A**) ***do harm to*** 對～造成傷害

Currently, the law forbids the use of tobacco in public places and the sale of cigarettes at convenience stores to people under the age of 18. Strict enforcement of the law is difficult, <u>if</u> not impossible. As the health
27
officials have admitted, the government does not have enough resources to monitor compliance.

目前，這項法令禁止在公共場所吸煙，以及便利商店不准販售香煙給十八歲以下的青少年。嚴格執法縱然不是不可能，但非常困難。正如衛生官員所承認那樣，政府沒有足夠的人力資源，來監督大家是否守法。

> currently (ˋkɝəntlɪ) *adv.* 目前　　forbid (fɚˋbɪd) *v.* 禁止
> ***convenience store*** 便利商店　　strict (strɪkt) *adj.* 嚴格的
> enforcement (ɪnˋforsmənt) *n.* 實施；執行
> official (əˋfɪʃəl) *n.* 官員　　admit (ədˋmɪt) *v.* 承認
> resource (rɪˋsors) *n.* 資源
> monitor (ˋmɑnətɚ) *v.* 監視；監督
> compliance (kəmˋplaɪəns) *n.* 服從；遵守

27. (**B**) 依句意，嚴格執法「縱然」不是不可能，但非常困難，選 (B) *if*，在此
　　　為表讓步的用法。而 (A) 然後，(C) 既然，(D) 如同，均不合句意。

Furthermore, the violations are nearly unavoidable <u>because</u> businesses
　　　　　　　　　　　　　　　　　　　　　　　　　 28
such as restaurants, bars and KTVs probably will not risk losing
customers <u>by</u> reporting those who violate the law.
　　　　　 29

此外，違法事件幾乎無法避免，因為商家們，例如餐廳、酒吧和 KTV 等，大
概不會冒著失去顧客的危險，而舉發那些違法的客人。

　　　　　violation 〔͵vaɪə'leʃən 〕 *n.* 違反　　　nearly 〔'nɪrlɪ 〕 *adv.* 幾乎
　　　　　unavoidable 〔͵ʌnə'vɔɪdəbl̩ 〕 *adj.* 無法避免的
　　　　　risk 〔 rɪsk 〕 *v.* 冒險　　　violate 〔'vaɪə͵let 〕 *v.* 違反

28. (**D**) 依句意，選 (D) *because*，在此解釋原因。

29. (**D**) *by* + *V-ing* 表示「藉由」某種方法，而其他介系詞無此用法。

In our opinion, therefore, an anti-smoking law alone can hardly
reduce the number of smokers.　Some other measures have to be adopted
<u>at the same time</u> if we are to see a significant drop in the consumption of
　　　　　　　30
tobacco products in our society.

　　因此，依我們之見，單單只有禁煙令，幾乎無法減少吸煙者的人數。如果
我們想要看到我們的社會上，香煙製品的消耗量大幅減少，必須同時再採取一
些其他的措施。

　　　　　in one's opinion 依某人之見　　　measure 〔'mɛʒɚ 〕 *n.* 措施
　　　　　adopt 〔 ə'dɑpt 〕 *v.* 採用　　　significant 〔 sɪg'nɪfəkənt 〕 *adj.* 大幅的
　　　　　drop 〔 drɑp 〕 *n.* 下降　　　consumption 〔 kən'sʌmpʃən 〕 *n.* 消耗量

30. (**B**) (A) for the most part　大部分；多半
　　　　　(B) *at the same time* 同時
　　　　　(C) in the long run　終究；到最後
　　　　　(D) for the time being　暫時

三、文意選填：

第 31 至 40 題為題組

One of the saddest observations I have made is this: many of us are
<u>reluctant</u> to learn from the people closest to us—our parents, spouses,
　31
children, and friends. Rather than being <u>open</u> to learning, we close ourselves
　　　　　　　　　　　32
off out of fear, stubbornness or pride. It's almost as if we say to <u>ourselves</u>,
　　　　　　　　　　　　　　　　　　　　　　　　　　　33
"I have already learned all that I can learn. There is nothing <u>else</u> I need
　　　　　　　　　　　　　　　　　　　　　　　34
to learn."

　　我所觀察到的最悲哀的事情之一就是，我們當中有許多人，不願意向我們
最親近的人學習——我們的父母、配偶、子女和朋友。我們由於恐懼、固執或自
尊，將自己封閉起來，而不願敞開心胸學習。這就好像我們對自己說：「我已經
學完所有我能學的東西了。沒有其他我需要學習的東西了。」

　　　observation〔͵ɑbzɚˈveʃən〕*n.* 觀察
　　　close〔klos〕*adj.* 親近的〈*to*〉
　　　spouse〔spaʊs〕*n.* 配偶　　　***rather than*** 而非
　　　out of 出於（動機）
　　　stubbornness〔ˈstʌbɚnnɪs〕*n.* 固執；頑固
　　　pride〔praɪd〕*n.* 驕傲；自尊

31. (**F**) 依句意，許多人「不願意」學習，選 (F)。
　　　reluctant〔rɪˈlʌktənt〕*adj.* 不願意的

32. (**J**) ***be open to learning*** 敞開心胸學習

33. (**G**) 依句意，我們對「自己」說，用反身代名詞 ***ourselves***，選 (G)。

34. (**C**) 沒有「其他」需要學習的東西，用 ***else***，選 (C)。

　　It's sad, because often the people closest to us know us the best and
can offer very simple <u>solutions</u>. If we are too proud or stubborn to learn,
　　　　　　　　　　　　35
we lose out on some wonderful, simple ways to <u>improve</u> our lives.
　　　　　　　　　　　　　　　　　　　　　　　　36

　　這是很悲哀的,因為通常,和我們最親近的人也最了解我們,能提供我們非常簡單的解決方法。如果我們太驕傲、太固執,而不願學習,我們就失去了一些又好、又簡單的方法來改善生活。

　　　　too ~ to + V 太~而不…　　　***lose out*** 失敗;虧損 *< on >*

35. (**D**) solution〔 sə'luʃən 〕*n.* 解決方法

36. (**I**) improve〔 ɪm'pruv 〕*v.* 改善

I have tried to remain open to suggestions from my friends and family. In fact, I have gone so <u>far</u> as to ask my family and friends, "What
　　　　　　　　　　　　　　　　　37
are some of my blind spots?" Not only <u>does</u> this make the person you are
　　　　　　　　　　　　　　　　　　　38
asking feel wanted and special, but you end up getting some terrific advice.
It's such a simple shortcut for growth, <u>yet</u> few people use it. All it takes
　　　　　　　　　　　　　　　　　39
is a little <u>courage</u> and humility, and the ability to let go of your ego.
　　　　40

　　我對於朋友和家人的建議,一直努力保持開放的態度。事實上,我甚至會問我的家人和朋友,「我的盲點在哪裡?」這不只會使你所詢問的對象,覺得被需要、很特別,而你最後也可以得到一些很棒的忠告。如此簡單的成長捷徑,卻很少有人使用。唯一所需要的,是一點點勇氣和謙虛,以及能夠放開自我的能力。

　　　　　　remain〔 rɪ'men 〕*v.* 保持　　　spot〔 spɑt 〕*n.* 點
　　　　　　blind spot 盲點　　　***end up*** 最後
　　　　　　terrific〔 tə'rɪfɪk 〕*adj.* 很棒的　　　advice〔 əd'vaɪs 〕*n.* 勸告
　　　　　　shortcut〔'ʃɔrt͵kʌt 〕*n.* 捷徑　　　humility〔 hju'mɪlətɪ 〕*n.* 謙虛
　　　　　　let go of 放開　　　ego〔'igo 〕*n.* 自我;自尊

37. (**B**) ***go so far as to + V*** 甚至;竟然

38. (**A**) not only 引導子句置於句首時,其後助動詞和主詞需倒裝,故此處選 (A) *does*。

39.(**H**) 此處需要語氣轉折的連接詞，故選 (H) *yet*。

40.(**E**) courage〔'kɝɪdʒ〕*n.* 勇氣

四、篇章結構：

第 41 至 45 題為題組

A legend is a popular type of folk tale. <u>**41**(**D**) In some ways, legends resemble myths, another type of folk tale.</u> But myths describe events from antiquity and usually deal with religious subjects, such as the birth of a god. Legends tell of recognizable people and places and often take place in comparatively recent times. <u>**42**(**B**) Some legends are based on real persons or events but many are entirely fictional.</u> Legends of superhuman accomplishments are often imaginary.

傳說是一種十分受歡迎的民間故事。在某些方面，傳說很像神話，而神話則是另一種民間故事。但是，神話描述的都是古代的事件，而且通常是有關宗教方面的主題，像是神的誕生。傳說都敘述一些一般人認得的人物和地點，而且經常是發生在近代。有些傳說是根據真實的人物或事件，但是，有許多則完全都是虛構的。與超乎常人的成就有關的傳說，經常都是想像的。

legend〔'lɛdʒənd〕*n.* 傳說　　　*folk tale* 民間故事
resemble〔rɪ'zɛmbl̩〕*v.* 相像　　　myth〔mɪθ〕*n.* 神話
antiquity〔æn'tɪkwətɪ〕*n.* 古代　　*deal with* 討論；與～有關
religious〔rɪ'lɪdʒəs〕*adj.* 宗教的
subject〔'sʌbdʒɪkt〕*n.* 主題　　*tell of* 談到
recognizable〔'rɛkəg͵naɪzəbl̩〕*n.* 可被認出的
comparatively〔kəm'pærətɪvlɪ〕*adv.* 相當地
be based on 根據　　entirely〔ɪn'taɪrlɪ〕*adv.* 完全地
fictional〔'fɪkʃənl̩〕*adj.* 虛構的
superhuman〔͵supɚ'hjumən〕*adj.* 超乎常人的
accomplishment〔ə'kɑmplɪʃmənt〕*n.* 成就
imaginary〔ɪ'mædʒə͵nɛrɪ〕*adj.* 想像的

[43](C) By contrast, legends about Washington and Lincoln are mostly exaggerations of their real qualities. All societies have legends. [44](E) Most legends began as stories about heroes of a particular group of people. For example, John Henry was a legendary hero of black Americans, and Casey Jones of railroads workers. [45](A) Over time, however, these figures have become national heroes. They are no longer well known only to certain groups of people.

對比之下，與華盛頓和林肯有關的傳說，大多是他們真實品德的誇大版本。所有的社會都會有傳說。大部份的傳說一開始都是某一群人中的英雄的故事。例如，約翰・亨利是美國黑人傳說中的英雄人物，而凱薩・瓊斯則是鐵路工人的英雄。然而，隨著時間的過去，這些人物都變成了國家英雄。他們的名聲不再僅限於某些群體。

> *by contrast* 對比之下
> exaggeration (ɪgˌzædʒəˈreʃən) *n.* 誇張；誇大
> quality (ˈkwɑlətɪ) *n.* 品德；特性
> particular (pɚˈtɪkjəlɚ) *adj.* 特定的
> legendary (ˈlɛdʒəndˌɛrɪ) *adj.* 傳說中的
> *over time* 隨著時間的過去　　figure (ˈfɪgjɚ) *n.* 人物
> *no longer* 不再　　*well known* 有名的　　certain (ˈsɝtn̩) *adj.* 某些

五、閱讀測驗：

第 46 至 48 題為題組

Sleep is a basic human need, as basic as the need for oxygen. Getting a good night's sleep is not only directly related to how we feel the next day, but to our long-term health as well. Still, many of us suffer from at least occasional insomnia. Even more of us report at least one night of restless sleep per week that leaves us feeling ill and irritable. This is a serious problem. If you think otherwise, consider this. People who sleep four hours or less per night are twice as likely not to survive in six years as those who sleep the normal eight hours or so.

睡眠是人類的基本需求，就像人類需要氧氣一樣。一夜好眠不僅直接影響我們隔天的心情，也會影響我們長期的健康。但是，至少有很多人爲偶發性的失眠所苦。甚至有很多人說每個禮拜至少有一晚睡不著，並因此覺得不舒服和脾氣暴躁。這是一個嚴重的問題。如果你不這麼認爲，請考慮以下這一點。每晚睡四個小時或更少的人，活不過六年的可能性大約是睡正常時間八小時左右的人的兩倍。

oxygen ('aksədʒən) *n.* 氧氣　　***be related to*** 與～有關

directly (də'rɛktlɪ) *adv.* 直接地

long-term ('lɔŋ,tɝm) *adj.* 長期的

suffer ('sʌfə) *v.* 苦於… *< from >*

occasional (ə'keʒənḷ) *adj.* 偶爾的

insomnia (ɪn'samnɪə) *n.* 失眠

restless ('rɛstlɪs) *adj.* 無法入眠的　　irritable ('ɪrətəbḷ) *adj.* 易怒的

otherwise ('ʌðə,waɪz) *adv.* 不那樣　　***be likely to*** 有可能

survive (sə'vaɪv) *v.* 存活

normal ('nɔrmḷ) *adj.* 正常的　　***or so*** 大約

Given the seriousness of sleep, how can we make sure that we rest well and stay healthy? While there are no foolproof methods, here are some suggestions from sleep experts. If you do have trouble sleeping and these methods don't help, it's important that you see a doctor before insomnia causes your health to suffer. Start with these suggestions, though.

有鑑於睡眠的重要性，我們怎麼能確定得到充份的休息，保持身體健康呢？雖然沒有百分之百正確的方法，但這裡有一些睡眠專家提供的建議。如果你在睡眠方面有困擾，而且這些方法都不管用，那麼你一定要在失眠對你的健康造成傷害之前，去看醫生。不過，提供的建議如下。

given ('gɪvən) *prep.* 有鑑於　　***make sure*** 確定

while (hwaɪl) *conj.* 雖然

foolproof ('ful'pruf) *adj.* 錯不了的

suggestion (sə'dʒɛstʃən) *n.* 建議

expert ('ɛkspɝt) *n.* 專家　　though (ðo) *adv.* 然而；不過

First, if you can't sleep in the middle of the night, don't get up. Exposing yourself to bright light will affect your body clock and worsen your insomnia. Stay in bed.

第一，如果你半夜睡不著，不要起床。處於光亮的環境之下會影響你的生理時鐘，讓失眠的情況更嚴重。待在床上。

expose〔ɪk'spoz〕v. 暴露＜to＞　　**body clock** 生理時鐘
worsen〔'wɜsn̩〕v. 惡化

Second, get regular exercise each day, but finish at least six hours before bedtime. Exercising in the evening can help keep you awake.

第二，每天要規律地運動，但至少要在就寢前六小時做完。晚上運動有助於讓你保持清醒。

regular〔'rɛgjələ〕adj. 定期的；規律的
awake〔ə'wek〕adj. 清醒的

Third, take a bath for thirty minutes within two hours of bedtime. The bath will warm you, relax you, and make you feel sleepy.

第三，在上床前兩個小時內泡澡三十分鐘。泡澡會使你的身體暖和，放鬆身心，讓你覺得想睡覺。

Finally, don't drink alcohol. Although having a drink before bed makes you sleepy, alcohol changes its effects after a bit of time. These secondary effects of alcohol can wake you up during the second half of your night's sleep.

最後，不要喝酒。雖然睡前喝杯酒會讓你想睡覺，但是過一段時間後，酒的作用就會改變。這些喝酒所引發的作用，可能會讓你睡到一半以後醒過來。

alcohol〔'ælkə,hɔl〕n. 酒
secondary〔'sɛkən,dɛrɪ〕adj. 續發性的

46. (**B**) 本文前兩段的主旨爲何？

    (A) 睡眠會影響我們隔天的心情。

    (B) <u>我們應該認真看待睡眠，因爲那和我們的健康有關。</u>

    (C) 睡眠少於四小時的人壽命少於六年。

    (D) 如果你有失眠的情況，一定要先請教醫生。

    consult〔kən'sʌlt〕v. 請教

47. (**C**) "insomnia" 這個字的意思爲何？

    (A) 一種讓人想睡覺的狀態。   (B) 一種奪人性命的疾病。

    (C) <u>無法入睡。</u>   (D) 一種讓人在睡夢中痛苦的疾病。

    status〔'stetəs〕n. 狀態   drowsy〔'drauzɪ〕adj. 昏昏欲睡的

    inability〔,ɪnə'bɪlətɪ〕n. 無能力

48. (**C**) 根據作者，下列敘述何者爲非？

    (A) 我們當中，有很多人爲失眠所苦。

    (B) 睡眠不足有可能讓人死亡。

    (C) <u>如果你想泡澡幫助入睡，你必須在上床前泡澡超過兩個小時。</u>

    (D) 酒會讓你覺得想睡覺。

<u>第 49 至 52 題爲題組</u>

    Around the end of the eighteenth century, some families trooped north from Mexico to California. On a stream along the desert's edge, they built a settlement called Los Angeles. For many years it was a market town, where nearby farmers and ranchers met to trade.

    大約在十八世紀末，有些家庭成群結隊地往北方走，從墨西哥走到加州。在沙漠邊緣的一條溪流旁，他們建立了一個殖民地，名爲洛杉磯。多年來，它一直是個市集城鎮，附近的農夫和牧場主人都會到這裏進行交易。

      around〔ə'raund〕prep. 大約

      troop〔trup〕v. 成群結隊地走   stream〔strim〕n. 小溪

      desert〔'dɛzət〕n. 沙漠   edge〔ɛdʒ〕n. 邊緣

      settlement〔'sɛtḷmənt〕n. 殖民地

      market town 市集城鎮   nearby〔'nɪr,baɪ〕adj. 附近的

      rancher〔'ræntʃə〕n. 牧場主人   trade〔tred〕v. 從事交易

From 1876 to 1885, many railroads were built. Los Angeles was linked to San Francisco and, through San Francisco to the rest of the country. Eventually, the railroad provided a direct route between Los Angeles and Chicago.

從一八七六年到一八八五年，興建了許多條鐵路。洛杉磯連接舊金山，並可經由舊金山到全國的其他地方。最後，鐵路提供了一條從洛杉磯直接到芝加哥的路線。

> link (lɪŋk) v. 連接　　route (rut) n. 路線
> direct (dəˈrɛkt) adj. 直接的　　eventually (ɪˈvɛntʃuəlɪ) adv. 最後

Then in the 1890's, oil was discovered in the city. As derricks went up, workers built many highways and pipelines. Digging began on a harbor that would make Los Angeles not only an ocean port but also a fishing center. In 1914, the harbor was completed and the Panama Canal opened. Suddenly Los Angeles became the busiest port on the Pacific Coast.

後來在一八九〇年代，該市發現了石油。探油井建好之後，工人還建造了很多公路和管線。開挖的工程始於一個港口，這讓洛杉磯不僅成為一個海港，也是個漁業中心。在一九一四年，港口興建完成，而且巴拿馬運河也開始通航。突然間，洛杉磯成為太平洋沿岸最繁忙的港口。

> derrick (ˈdɛrɪk) n. 探油井　　*go up* 被興建
> pipeline (ˈpaɪpˌlaɪn) n. (長距離輸送油、氣、水等的地下) 管線
> dig (dɪg) v. 挖掘　　harbor (ˈharbɚ) n. 港口
> port (port) n. 港口　　fishing (ˈfɪʃɪŋ) adj. 漁業的
> complete (kəmˈplit) v. 完成　　open (ˈopən) v. 開放

Today, Los Angeles is the main industrial center in the West. It produces goods not only for other West Coast communities but also for those in other parts of the country. It leads the nation in making airplanes and equipment for exploring outer space. Many motion pictures and television programs are filmed in Los Angeles. The city is also the business center for states in the West. Improvements in transportation are the main reason for Los Angeles' growth.

現在洛杉磯是美國西部地區的主要工業中心。它生產的商品，不僅可供給美國西岸的其他社區，而且也提供給美國其他地方的社區。它在製造飛機和探測外太空的設備方面，居全國的領導地位。很多電影和電視節目都在洛杉磯拍攝。該市也是美國西部各州的商業中心。交通運輸的改善是洛杉磯能夠發展的主要原因。

the West 美國西部地區　　*West Coast* 美國西海岸
community〔kə'mjunətɪ〕*n.* 社區
equipment〔ɪ'kwɪpmənt〕*n.* 設備
explore〔ɪk'splor〕*v.* 探測　　*outer space* 外太空
motion picture 電影　　film〔fɪlm〕*v.* 拍攝
improvement〔ɪm'pruvmənt〕*n.* 改善
transportation〔͵trænspɚ'teʃən〕*n.* 運輸
main〔men〕*adj.* 主要的　　growth〔groθ〕*n.* 成長；發展

49. (**B**) 洛杉磯何時開始成為太平洋沿岸最繁忙的港口？
　　　(A) 在一八九〇年代。　　　　(B) 在一九一四年。
　　　(C) 在一八八五年。　　　　(D) 在一九二〇年。

50. (**C**) 選出適合本文的標題。
　　　(A) 洛杉磯的過去　　　　(B) 洛杉磯的未來
　　　(C) 洛杉磯的發展　　　　(D) 洛杉磯的工業
　　　appropriate〔ə'proprɪɪt〕*adj.* 適合的

51. (**B**) 殖民之後的那幾年間，洛杉磯的主要商業活動是 ＿＿＿＿＿＿。
　　　(A) 漁業　　　　　　　　(B) 貿易
　　　(C) 拍電影　　　　　　　(D) 鑽井探勘石油
　　　directly〔də'rɛktlɪ〕*adv.* 立即
　　　following〔'fɑləwɪŋ〕*prep.* 在～之後
　　　commercial〔kə'mɝʃəl〕*adj.* 商業的　　drill〔drɪl〕*v.* 鑽孔

52. (**D**) 本文中提到舊金山，是因為下列哪一個原因？
　　　(A) 舊金山離洛杉磯很近。
　　　(B) 舊金山和芝加哥相連接。
　　　(C) 在一八九〇年代，舊金山發現石油。
　　　(D) 舊金山連接洛杉磯和美國的其他地區。

<u>第 53 至 56 題為題組</u>

Until I met Mrs. Bench, nursing wasn't quite what I had expected. Mrs. Bench, a tiny, ancient lady, was my first patient. That morning, I bustled in with my equipment and said cheerily, "Good morning, Mrs. Bench. I'm your nurse today. I'm here to give you a bath, and make your bed."

直到我遇到本齊太太，我才發現護理工作和我所想像的不太一樣。本齊太太是一位矮小的老太太，她是我的第一個病人。那天早上，我匆匆忙忙拿著設備到病房內，快樂地說道：「早安，本齊太太。我是妳今天的護士。我現在要幫妳洗澡及舖床。」

> nursing ('nɜsɪŋ) *n.* (職業性的) 看護；護理
> tiny ('taɪnɪ) *adj.* 極小的　　ancient ('enʃənt) *adj.* 年老的
> bustle ('bʌsl̩) *v.* 匆忙 (來去)　　cheerily ('tʃɪrəlɪ) *adv.* 高興地
> ***make one's bed*** 舖床

"March yourself right out of here. I don't intend to have a bath today." Squaring my shoulders, I looked her right in the eye. "Mrs. Bench, my job is to give you a bath. Now, let's get started." To my alarm, big tears formed in her eyes.

"I'm dying, and nobody cares, just as long as I'm clean."

"Don't be silly," I said briskly. "Nobody is going to die." I ignored her protests and bulldozed ahead with the bath.

「妳馬上出去。我今天不打算洗澡。」

我挺起胸膛，直視她的眼睛。「本齊太太，我的工作是幫妳洗澡。現在，我們就開始吧！」令我嚇一跳的是，她的眼睛開始流出大滴大滴的眼淚。

「我快要死了，沒有人在乎我，妳們只在乎我身體乾不乾淨。」

「別傻了！」我用活潑的口吻說著。「沒有人會死。」我不理會她的抗議，強行要她進入浴缸。

> march (martʃ) *v.* 行進　　square (skwɛr) *v.* 使挺直
> ***square one's shoulders*** 挺直肩膀；挺胸
> ***to one's alarm*** 令某人驚慌的是
> briskly ('brɪsklɪ) *adv.* 輕快地；活潑地
> protest ('protɛst) *n.* 抗議　　bulldoze ('bul,doz) *v.* 強行；脅迫

The next day, <u>Mrs. Bench anticipated my coming and had her ammunition ready.</u> "Before you do anything," she said, "define 'nursing.'"

I eyed her doubtfully. "Well, nursing is hard to define," I hedged. "It has to do with taking care of sick people."

At that Mrs. Bench whisked out a dictionary. "Just as I suspected. You don't even know what you're supposed to do." She flipped to a page and read slowly: "'To nurse: to tend the sick or aged; to take care of, nourish, foster, develop or cherish.'" She closed the book with a bang. "I'm ready to be cherished."

隔天，<u>本齊太太料到我會來，而且已經準備好要反擊我的砲彈。</u>「在妳做任何事之前，」她說，「先替『護理』下個定義。」

我用懷疑的眼神看著她。「這個嘛，護理很難下定義，」我避免正面回答。「護理跟照顧病人有關。」

一聽到我那樣說，本齊太太突然拿出一本字典。「就跟我猜的一樣，妳根本連自己應該做什麼都一無所知。」她很快翻到一頁，慢慢地唸出：『護理：照料病人或老人；照料、鼓勵、照顧、使成長，或加以疼愛。』她砰的一聲闔上字典。「我準備好要被疼愛。」

anticipate〔æn'tɪsə,pet〕v. 期待；預料

ammunition〔,æmjə'nɪʃən〕n. 彈藥；抨擊別人的材料、手段或依據

define〔dɪ'faɪn〕v. 下定義　　eye〔aɪ〕v. 注視

doubtfully〔'dautfəlɪ〕adv. 懷疑地　　hedge〔hɛdʒ〕v. 避免直接回答

have to do with 與～有關　　whisk〔hwɪsk〕v. 急速移動

suspect〔sə'spɛkt〕v. 懷疑；猜想　　flip〔flɪp〕v. 快速翻動（書頁等）

tend〔tɛnd〕v. 照料　　***the aged*** 老人

nourish〔'nɝɪʃ〕v. 滋養；鼓勵　　foster〔'fɔstɚ〕v. 照顧

cherish〔'tʃɛrɪʃ〕v. 愛護　　bang〔bæŋ〕n. 突然的一聲巨響

"Good heavens, Mrs. Bench," I said, "what are you talking about?"

Grinning broadly, she patted a chair next to the bed. "Just sit down. Cherishing is easy to learn. You start by listening."

Listen I did. She told me about Mr. Bench. "He was a tall, raw-boned farmer. When he came courting, he tracked mud into the parlor. Of course, I thought I was meant for finer things, but I married him anyway.

「天啊！本齊太太，」我說，「妳在講什麼啊？」

她咧嘴而笑，輕拍床邊的椅子。「坐下來。愛護這回事很好學。妳先從傾聽開始。」

我照辦了。她告訴我關於本齊先生的事情。「他是個個子很高，骨瘦如柴的農夫。當他來追求我時，他走進客廳，鞋子上還沾著泥巴。當然，我本來以為自己註定要嫁給富家子弟，但反正我還是嫁給了他。」

Good heavens 天啊！　　　grin〔grɪn〕*v.* 露齒而笑
broadly〔'brɔdlɪ〕*adv.* 寬廣地　　　pat〔pæt〕*v.* 輕拍
raw-boned〔'rɔ,bond〕*adj.* 削瘦的　　　court〔kort〕*v.* 求愛
track〔træk〕*v.* 鞋子沾（雪、泥等）帶進來
parlor〔'pɑrlɚ〕*n.* 客廳
be meant for 註定要屬於　　　finer〔'faɪnɚ〕*adj.* 較高貴的

"For our first anniversary, I wanted a love token, coins of silver or gold hung on a fine chain." She smiled and fingered the silver chain she always wore. "The anniversary day came, and Ben hitched the wagon to drive into town. In a fever of anticipation, I waited on a slope, looking for the dust in the distance that would mark his coming." Her eyes clouded. "He never came. Riders found the wagon the next morning. They came out with the news, and this." Reverently, she drew it out. It was faded now from rubbing against her skin, but one side was wreathed with tiny hearts and the reverse said simply, "Ben and Alma. Love eternal."

「結婚一週年的時候，我想要一個象徵愛情的紀念品，一條細的鍊子，上面掛有銀幣或金幣。」她微笑著，用手指撥弄她一直戴著的銀鍊。「週年紀念日那天，班駕著馬車進城。我急切盼望他的歸來，所以站在斜坡上等待，看著遠方的塵土，因為那能夠表示他回來了。」她的眼神黯淡許多。「他並沒有回來。隔天早上，馬夫找到馬車。他們把消息告訴了我，還有這個。」她心懷虔誠地把鍊子拉起來。因為和肌膚摩擦的關係，鍊子現在已經失去光澤了，但是有一面纏繞著一個小小的愛心，愛心的背面簡短地寫著：「班和艾瑪。永恆的愛。」

anniversary (ˌænəˈvɜsərɪ) *n.* 週年紀念日

token (ˈtokən) *n.* 紀念物　　chain (tʃen) *n.* 鍊子

finger (ˈfɪŋɚ) *v.* 用手指觸摸　　hitch (hɪtʃ) *v.* 拴住；套住

wagon (ˈwægən) *n.* 四輪馬車　　fever (ˈfivɚ) *n.* 狂熱

anticipation (ænˌtɪsəˈpeʃən) *n.* 期待　　slope (slop) *n.* 山坡

in the distance 在遠方　　mark (mɑrk) *v.* 表示

cloud (klaʊd) *v.* 變陰沉　　rider (ˈraɪdɚ) *n.* 騎馬者

come out with 告訴　　reverently (ˈrɛvərəntlɪ) *adv.* 虔誠地

fade (fed) *v.* 失去光澤　　rub (rʌb) *v.* 摩擦 < *against* >

wreathe (rið) *v.* 包圍；纏繞　　reverse (rɪˈvɜs) *n.* 背面

eternal (ɪˈtɜnḷ) *adj.* 永恆的

"But it's a penny," I said. "Didn't you say they were silver or gold?"

Tears rimmed her eyes. "It's sad to admit, but if he'd come home that day, I'd have seen only the penny. As it was, I saw only the love."

Mrs. Bench died that night. I could never forget how she faced me with a piercing look and said, "Young lady, as a nurse, you only see the penny. Don't be fooled by the penny. Look for the love."

「但那是一分錢銅幣，」我說。「妳不是說是銀幣或金幣嗎？」

淚水在她的眼眶中打轉。「要承認是很令人難過的，但是如果那一天他有回來，我就只能看到一分錢銅幣。事實上，我只看到愛。」

本齊太太那晚去世了。我永遠不會忘掉她用深刻的目光對我說：「年輕人，你身為護士，只看到一分錢銅幣。不要被一分錢銅幣欺騙了。要尋找愛。」

penny (ˈpɛnɪ) *n.* 一分錢硬幣　　rim (rɪm) *v.* 把…圍起

as it is 事實上　　piercing (ˈpɪrsɪŋ) *adj.* 深刻的

fool (ful) *v.* 愚弄；欺騙

53. (**D**) 在本文中，本齊太太 ＿＿＿＿＿＿ 。

(A) 拒絕洗澡，因為她認為自己夠乾淨了

(B) 很滿意護士為她所做的事情

(C) 認為自己嫁錯人，而且並不愛他

(D) 給護士一個很好的教訓，告訴她護理的真諦為何

lesson (ˈlɛsṇ) *n.* 教訓

54. (**D**) 在「本齊太太料到我會來，而且已經準備好反擊我的砲彈」這句
話中，"ammunition" 指的是 ＿＿＿＿＿＿＿。
(A) 疼愛的行為
(B) 強調傾聽
(C) 子彈或砲彈
(D) <u>給護士的考驗</u>
act ﹝ækt﹞ *n.* 行為　　emphasis ﹝'ɛmfəsɪs﹞ *n.* 強調 <*on*>
bullet ﹝'bʊlɪt﹞ *n.* 子彈　　shell ﹝ʃɛl﹞ *n.* 砲彈

55. (**C**) 從本文中，可以推論出本齊先生 ＿＿＿＿＿＿＿。
(A) 很懂得社交技巧，知道在追求女性時該怎麼做
(B) 送本齊太太一條上面掛有銀幣的鍊子
(C) <u>留給本齊太太一枚上面刻有他們名字的一分錢硬幣</u>
(D) 在結婚一週年紀念日當天，拋棄了本齊太太
infer ﹝ɪn'fɝ﹞ *v.* 推論　　socially ﹝'soʃəlɪ﹞ *adv.* 在社交上
desert ﹝dɪ'zɝt﹞ *v.* 拋棄

56. (**B**) 本文最好的標題為何？
(A) 查字典。　　　　　　　(B) <u>一分錢硬幣。</u>
(C) 本齊太太的愛情故事。　(D) 我當護士的經驗。
consult ﹝kən'sʌlt﹞ *v.* 查閱

第貳部分：非選擇題

一、英文翻譯：

1. 擁有手機的優點之一，就是無論你去哪裡，都很容易聯絡得上。
   One advantage of owning a cell phone is that you can be easily
   reached wherever you go.

2. 此外，如果有緊急的情況，你可以立刻打電話。
   In addition, you are able to make a phone call at once in case of
   emergency.

二、英文作文：(作文範例)

A New Place

Going to a new and unfamiliar place can be exciting, but also frightening. It is exciting because we know we will experience many new things and perhaps meet interesting people. It can be frightening because we do not know exactly what to expect. We worry that we will not be able to adjust, will meet some trouble or will feel lonely away from our familiar surroundings and friends. This is much the way I felt when my family moved to Taipei from the country.

When we made the move, I was in junior high school. I felt worried because I would have to adjust to a new neighborhood and school environment without the support of my friends. But I also felt excited to be moving to the big city and to have an opportunity to experience a different way of life. My adjustment was surprisingly easy because my new school offered many activities through which I could get to know my new classmates. Once I had made a few friends, all the rest was easy. They helped me to understand the school rules and to find interesting and fun things to do in the city. From this experience I learned that new experiences are nothing to be afraid of.

> unfamiliar〔͵ʌnfəˋmɪljɚ〕*adj.* 不熟悉的
> frightening〔ˋfraɪtn̩ɪŋ〕*adj.* 可怕的
> experience〔ɪkˋspɪrɪəns〕*v.* 經歷
> exactly〔ɪgˋzæktlɪ〕*adv.* 精確地；正確地
> expect〔ɪkˋspɛkt〕*v.* 預期；期待
> adjust〔əˋdʒʌst〕*v.* 適應
> lonely〔ˋlonlɪ〕*adj.* 孤單的　　move〔muv〕*v.* 搬家
> neighborhood〔ˋnebɚ͵hud〕*n.* 鄰近地區
> ***school rules*** 校規

大學入學指定科目考試英文模擬試題 ⑥

第壹部份：選擇題（佔 72 分）

一、詞彙與慣用語（15％）

說明：　第 1 至 15 題，每題選出一個最適當的選項，標示在答案卡之「選擇題答案區」。每題答對得 1 分，答錯或劃記多於一個選項者倒扣 1/3 分，倒扣到本大題之實得分數為零為止，未作答者，不給分亦不扣分。

1. Rochelle and Jessica have a ＿＿＿＿＿＿＿＿ dislike; they both don't like chocolate milk.
　(A) general　　(B) common　　(C) inferior　　(D) superior

2. It is reported that a ＿＿＿＿＿＿＿＿ to the victims is likely to replace the World Trade Center.
　(A) memory　　(B) memorial　　(C) memoir　　(D) memorandum

3. The boss ＿＿＿＿＿＿＿＿ with anger when he saw the sales drop.
　(A) collided　　(B) covered　　(C) corrupted　　(D) exploded

4. The ＿＿＿＿＿＿＿＿ spring weather was a great relief to all of us who had struggled through the long, harsh winter.
　(A) temperate　(B) temporary　(C) impulsive　(D) severe

5. No one wanted to play poker with Jim, because he was a ＿＿＿＿＿＿＿ cheater.
　(A) celebrated　(B) famous　　(C) notorious　　(D) noble

6. Ms. Haynes ＿＿＿＿＿＿＿＿ her son after she learned that he had got a ticket for speeding.
　(A) elevated　(B) admonished　(C) persuaded　(D) acknowledged

7. Charles ＿＿＿＿＿＿＿＿ his girlfriend's voice to the sound of a cat howling in the night; that is, he said his girlfriend sounded like a cat howling.
　(A) mimicked　(B) equalized　　(C) compared　　(D) complimented

8. Sam hoped that the value of his collection would _____ rapidly; instead, the collection has slowly become worthless.
   (A) appreciate   (B) qualify   (C) awaken   (D) approach

9. Last year in Italy, an active volcano _____, sending a slow-moving river of hot lava through the town.
   (A) explored   (B) exposed   (C) erupted   (D) distributed

10. A man is known by the _____ he keeps, so we should be careful in choosing friends.
    (A) companies   (B) competitors
    (C) proponents   (D) companions

11. The football team _____ eleven players on offense and eleven players on defense.
    (A) comprises of   (B) consists of
    (C) makes up   (D) composes of

12. Many young people like to _____ with friends in nightclubs or Internet cafes.
    (A) hang out   (B) live up
    (C) play out   (D) get off the ground

13. Burglars _____ Miss Chen's house last night, and she was seized with panic.
    (A) broke down   (B) broke out   (C) broke off   (D) broke into

14. We try to get as much knowledge as possible for fear that we might not _____ the times.
    (A) catch up on   (B) put up with
    (C) keep up with   (D) get away with

15. It is not fair to _____ kids with disabilities just because they are different.
    (A) pick on   (B) split up with
    (C) get acquainted with   (D) pick out

二、綜合測驗（15％）

說明：　第 16 至 30 題，每題一個空格。請依文意選出一個最適當的選項，標示
　　　　在答案卡之「選擇題答案區」。每題答對得 1 分，答錯或劃記多於一
　　　　個選項者倒扣 1/3 分，倒扣到本大題之實得分數爲零爲止。未作答者，
　　　　不給分亦不扣分。

第 16 至 25 題爲題組

An otherwise healthy man died last week as a consequence of
doing the good deed of donating part of his liver for transplant. This
incident has ___16___ questions about the issue of living donations.
The increasingly common use of living organ donors ___17___ kidney
transplants more than a decade ago. ___18___, at many transplant
centers the majority of kidney transplants are now from living donors.
Most of the living donors are so-called related donors, ___19___ have
a blood, family, or emotional relationship to the organ recipient. This
relationship creates ___20___ the impetus to donate and ethical worries
about the donation, since related donors may be willing to or feel
compelled to ___21___ the risks of organ donation when their loved one
stands to receive ___22___ benefit. The problem is that ___23___ the
medical benefit to the recipient is great, all the risk of the donation
falls to the donor. So we must ask ___24___ the benefit to the donor of
seeing a loved one's life ___25___ is sufficient to balance the risk he is
asked to undergo.

16. (A) raised　　　　(B) aroused　　　　(C) risen　　　　(D) reared
17. (A) put into practice　　　　　　　(B) was taking place
　　　(C) occurred　　　　　　　　　　(D) began with
18. (A) In fact　　　　(B) Above all　　　　(C) At best　　　　(D) In addition
19. (A) whom　　　　(B) whose　　　　(C) who　　　　(D) which

20. (A) either   (B) among   (C) between   (D) both
21. (A) compromise   (B) ignore   (C) observe   (D) demonstrate
22. (A) very great a   (B) such great a   (C) so great a   (D) how a great
23. (A) however   (B) therefore   (C) while   (D) instead
24. (A) what   (B) whether   (C) that   (D) how much
25. (A) saved   (B) saving   (C) save   (D) to save

第 26 至 30 題為題組

The 28-year-old had spent six years working nights while she gained her university degree during the day. When she finally graduated, she had her eye on a teaching ___26___ at a nearby primary school. With the help of her friends, she had an interview with the Head.

"I noticed a tiny hole in one of my stockings earlier," she ___27___. "I thought about changing them, but I knew I'd be late if I did. And by the time I got to the interview, it was enormous. I walked in apologizing for not ___28___." The would-be teacher didn't get the job. In fact, one of her friends told her that the Head's only comment was: "If someone doesn't take the time to present her best image at an interview, what kind of teacher is she going to be?"

First impressions are ___29___ ones. In other words, if you're viewed positively within the critical first four minutes, the person you've met will probably assume everything you do is positive. Give the interviewer a bad impression, and often he will assume you have a lot of other unsatisfactory characteristics. ___30___, he or she may not take the time to give you a second chance. Most employers believe that those who look as if they care about themselves will care more about their jobs.

26. (A) profession   (B) position   (C) career   (D) occupation
27. (A) repeats   (B) reminds   (C) recalls   (D) responds
28. (A) looking at all   (B) looking at him
    (C) looking round   (D) looking my best
29. (A) lasting   (B) remaining   (C) continuing   (D) persisting
30. (A) Except   (B) More   (C) Worse   (D) However

三、文意選填（10％）

說明： 第31至40題，每題一個空格。請依文意在文章後所提供的 (A) 到 (J)
選項中分別選出最適當者，並將其字母代號標示在答案卡之「選擇題
答案區」。每題答對得1分，答錯或劃記多於一個選項者倒扣 1/9 分，
倒扣到本大題之實得分數為零為止。未作答者，不給分亦不扣分。

第31至40題為題組

　　For many Americans, Ann Mary Robertson was a noted folk artist
as well as a great woman, who never yielded to her age.

　　Ann Mary Robertson, ___31___ as "Grandma" Moses, was born in
1860. She began to paint at the age of 78, after giving up needlework
due to a health problem. Two years later her ___32___ exhibition was
held and this 80-year-old self-taught artist experienced a sudden
success. Moses had spent her life first as a hired girl and ___33___ as
the wife of a farmer. Her ___34___ reflected the peaceful, simple
country life. Different ___35___, such as harvesting, country fairs, and
landscapes in all seasons from snow-covered villages to ___36___ fields,
were pleasant subjects she chose for her work.

　　People were attracted to Moses' appealing subjects. However, they
were just as moved by the story of this gifted old lady who, ___37___ no
formal training, became world-famous in a handful of years and who opened
up for them a world of peace and ___38___ pleasure they wished to enjoy.

By the time of her death in 1961, Moses had created more than 1500 works of art. Moses once said, "I have written my life in small sketches, a little today, a little yesterday...I look back on my life as a good day's work. It was done and I feel satisfied. I __39__ the best out of what life offered." Her enthusiasm __40__ painting has won her the fondness of the public, who view her as a legend of senior citizen wizardry.

(A) with   (B) then   (C) simple   (D) for   (E) paintings

(F) known   (G) first   (H) made   (I) scenes   (J) summer

四、篇章結構 (10 %)

說明： 第 41 至 45 題，每題一個空格。請依文意在文章後所提供的 (A) 到 (E) 選項中分別選出最適當者，填入空格中，使篇章結構清晰有條理，並將其英文字母代號標示在答案卡之「選擇題答案區」。每題答對得 2 分，答錯或劃記多於一個選項者倒扣 1/2 分，倒扣到本大題之實得分數爲零爲止。未作答者，不給分亦不扣分。

第 41 至 45 題爲題組

Mount Rainier, the heart of Mt. Rainier National Park, is the highest mountain in the state of Washington and in the Cascade Range. __41__ It is 14,410 feet above sea level and has an area of about one square mile.

__42__ However, the volcano has been sleeping for centuries.

Mount Rainier has a permanent ice cap and extensive snow fields, which give rise to more than forty glaciers. These feed swift streams and tumbling waterfalls that race through the glacial valleys. __43__ There are alpine meadows between the glaciers and the forests, which contain beautiful wild flowers. __44__ Paradise Valley, where hotel accommodations are available, perches on the mountain's slope at 5,400 feet. __45__ Its 90-mile length can be covered in about a week's time.

(A) Forests extend to 4,500 feet.

(B) The Wonderland Trail encircles the mountain.

(C) Numerous steam and gas jets occur around the crater.

(D) The mountain's summit is broad and rounded.

(E) The Nisqually Glacier is probably the ice region that is most often explored by visitors.

五、閱讀測驗（22 %）

說明： 第 46 至 56 題，每題請分別根據各篇文章的文意選出一個最適當的選項，標示在答案卡之「選擇題答案區」。每題答對得 2 分，答錯或劃記多於一個選項者倒扣 2/3 分，倒扣到本大題之實得分數爲零爲止。未作答者，不給分亦不扣分。

第 46 至 48 題爲題組

Sweets, cereals, hamburgers and French fries, snack foods, toys, clothing......These products are the focus of a phenomenal amount of TV advertising that is directed toward children. A typical youngster may see more than 50 commercials a day! As early as 3 years of age, children distinguish commercials from programs. However, preschool children often believe that commercials are simply a different form of entertainment—one designed to inform viewers. Not until 8 or 9 years of age do most children understand the persuasive intent of commercials. At the same time that children grasp the aim of commercials, they begin to realize that commercials are not always truthful.

Commercials are effective sales tools with children. Children grow to like many of the products advertised on TV. They may urge parents to buy products that they have seen on television. In one study, more than 75% of the children reported that they had asked their parents to buy a product they had seen advertised on TV. More often than not, parents had purchased the product for them!

The selling power of TV commercials has long concerned advocates for children, because so many ads focus on children's foods that have little nutritional value and that are associated with problems such as obesity and tooth decay. The U.S. government once regulated the amount and type of advertising on children's TV programs, but today the responsibility falls to parents.

46. The main idea of the article is _____.
    (A) children can learn useful social skills from watching television commercials
    (B) television commercials have great influence on the consumer behaviors of the young
    (C) television's view of the world is sometimes distorted
    (D) no beneficial behavior results from television viewing

47. According to the article, television commercials frequently focus on _____.
    (A) children's toys for different ages
    (B) characteristics of children in different stages of life
    (C) the tools that convey factual information
    (D) children's foods that contain little nutrition and probably result in certain health problems

48. Which of the following statements is **TRUE** based on the passage?
    (A) Commercials, for children of 3 years of age, are simply a different form of entertainment.
    (B) Preschool children, when viewing TV, can grasp the aim of commercials and begin to realize that they are not always truthful.
    (C) Parents never buy products children have seen on TV.
    (D) Parents bear a responsibility for tolerance of the increased aggression in children's behavior.

第 49 至 52 題為題組

　　Meetings can waste a great deal of time. But you can make your meeting run more smoothly by following a few simple rules. First, have an agenda. This will help keep you focused on what is important. Next, decide who needs to be involved. More people mean less efficient discussion. Finally, keep the discussion moving. Thank each speaker as he or she finishes and move on to the next speaker. This encourages people to make their remarks brief.

　　The problem with meetings, of course, is that no one likes them, no one wants them, and no one needs them. Yet, everyone has them. Meetings are the corporate world's response to primitive socializing behaviors. People feel more comfortable in making decisions in groups. They can then share blame if a decision turns out to be the wrong decision. Sharing credit for a correct decision is not often found in groups. Then individuals tend to remind people of how persuasive they were in the meeting when the "right" decision was made.

　　What happens after a meeting is more important than what happens during the meeting. The skills used then are more professional and less procedural. So no matter how well you run a meeting, it is the work that gets done after the meeting that is important.

49. What is one way to run a meeting well?
　　(A) Watch how your manager runs meetings.
　　(B) Minimize the number of participants.
　　(C) Let the group make decisions.
　　(D) Let everyone speak.

50. What is the purpose of the meeting agenda?
    (A) To keep the speakers organized.
    (B) To allow free discussion.
    (C) To thank the speakers.
    (D) To keep focused on important items.

51. How should you receive other people's comments at a meeting?
    (A) Try to keep others from talking.
    (B) Thank them and move on.
    (C) Give them as much time as they want.
    (D) Criticize them in public.

52. In conclusion the author feels
    (A) the real work is left to the professionals.
    (B) all meetings should be in the morning.
    (C) no one should receive credit for their work.
    (D) meetings should be held more frequently.

第 53 至 56 題為題組

People used to be born at home and die at home. In the old days, children were familiar with birth and death as part of life. Nowadays when people grow old, we often send them to nursing homes. When they get sick, we transfer them to a hospital, where children are usually unwelcome and are forbidden to visit terminally ill patients—even when those patients are their parents. This deprives the dying patient of important family members during the last few days of his life and it deprives the children of an experience of death, which is an important learning experience.

At the University of Chicago's Billings Hospital, some of my colleagues and I interviewed and followed approximately 500 terminally ill patients in order to find out what they could teach us and how we could be of more benefit, not just to them but to the members of their families as well. We were most impressed by the fact that even those patients who were not told of their serious illness were quite aware of its potential outcome. They were not only able to say that they were close to dying, but many were able to predict the approximate time of their death.

It is important for next of kin and members of the helping professions to understand these patients' communications in order to truly understand their needs, fears and fantasies. Most of our patients welcomed another human being with whom they could talk openly, honestly, and frankly about their predicament. Many of them shared with us their tremendous need to be informed, to be kept up-do-date on their medical condition, and to be told when the end was near. We found out that patients who had been dealt with openly and frankly were better able to cope with the imminence of death and finally to reach a true stage of acceptance prior to death.

53. According to the passage, the writer regards the experience of death as _____.
    (A) terrible
    (B) unnecessary
    (C) heart-breaking
    (D) important

54. Based on the passage, those terminally ill patients who were not told of their serious illness _____.
    (A) knew nothing about their outcome
    (B) were quite conscious of the potential outcome
    (C) were resistant to impending death
    (D) were usually ignorant of their outcome

55. The purpose of the writer's research at Billings Hospital was to
    _____.
    (A) find out what dying patients could teach about death and how
        medical professionals could be of more benefit to them and
        their families
    (B) determine in detail the stages through which the dying pass
    (C) analyze the difference in the concepts of death held by the old
        and the young
    (D) suggest where people should die

56. What could most likely be inferred from the passage about the
    writer's attitude toward death and dying?
    (A) No man is indispensable.   (B) Dead men tell no tales
    (C) All that lives must die.   (D) Live and learn.

第貳部份：非選擇題（佔 28 分）

一、英文翻譯（8 %）

說明： 1. 將下列兩句中文翻譯成適當之英文，並將答案寫在「答案卷」上。

　　　 2. 未按題意翻譯者，不予計分。

1. 我們都同意，「戰爭與和平」這本名著，值得一讀再讀。

2. 我們所必須做的，就是讀完這一整本書，然後寫一份報告。

二、英文作文（20 %）

說明： 1. 依提示在「答案卷」上寫一篇英文作文。

　　　 2. 文長至少 120 個單詞。

提示： 台北市發行彩券（Lottery）引發許多社會現象與社會問題。你是否贊
　　　 成停止彩券發行？請以 Should the Lottery Be Abolished?（彩券應
　　　 該廢止嗎？）為題，說明你贊成的原因或反對的理由。

大學入學指定科目考試英文模擬試題⑥詳解

第壹部分：單一選擇題

一、詞彙與慣用語：

1. (**B**) Rochelle and Jessica have a <u>common</u> dislike; they both don't like chocolate milk.
   羅歇爾和潔西卡有<u>共同</u>討厭的東西；他們都不喜歡巧克力牛奶。
   (A) general〔'dʒɛnərəl〕*adj.* 一般的
   (B) ***common***〔'kɑmən〕*adj.* 共同的
   (C) inferior〔ɪn'fɪrɪə〕*adj.* 較劣的
   (D) superior〔sə'pɪrɪə〕*adj.* 較優的
   dislike〔dɪs'laɪk〕*n.* 不喜歡；厭惡

2. (**B**) It is reported that a <u>memorial</u> to the victims is likely to replace the World Trade Center.
   根據報導，罹難者的<u>紀念館</u>可能會取代世界貿易中心。
   (A) memory〔'mɛmərɪ〕*n.* 記憶
   (B) ***memorial***〔mə'morɪəl〕*n.* 紀念碑；紀念館
   (C) memoir〔'mɛmwɑr〕*n.* 研究報告；(*pl.*) 回憶錄
   (D) memorandum〔‚mɛmə'rændəm〕*n.* 備忘錄
   victim〔'vɪktɪm〕*n.* 受害者　　replace〔rɪ'ples〕*v.* 取代

3. (**D**) The boss <u>exploded</u> with anger when he saw the sales drop.
   當老闆看到銷售量下跌時，他<u>勃然大怒</u>。
   (A) collide〔kə'laɪd〕*v.* 相撞
   (B) cover〔'kʌvə〕*v.* 覆蓋
   (C) corrupt〔kə'rʌpt〕*v.* 腐化；腐爛
   (D) ***explode***〔ɪk'splod〕*v.* (感情) 激發；發作
   　　explode with anger 勃然大怒
   sales〔selz〕*n. pl.* 銷售量　　drop〔drɑp〕*v.* 下降

4. (**A**) The <u>temperate</u> spring weather was a great relief to all of us who had struggled through the long, harsh winter.

對我們這些辛苦經歷過漫長嚴冬的人而言，春天<u>溫和</u>的天氣眞是令人舒暢多了。

    (A) ***temperate*** (ˋtɛmprɪt) *adj.* 溫和的

    (B) temporary (ˋtɛmpəˏrɛrɪ) *adj.* 暫時的

    (C) impulsive (ɪmˋpʌlsɪv) *adj.* 衝動的

    (D) severe (səˋvɪr) *adj.* 嚴厲的

    relief (rɪˋlif) *n.* 使人欣慰之物；輕鬆

    struggle (ˋstrʌgḷ) *v.* 努力

    harsh (harʃ) *adj.* 嚴酷的

5. (**C**) No one wanted to play poker with Jim, because he was a <u>notorious</u> cheater.

沒有人想和吉姆玩撲克牌，因爲他是個<u>惡名昭彰的</u>騙子。

    (A) celebrated (ˋsɛləˏbretɪd) *adj.* 著名的

    (B) famous (ˋfeməs) *adj.* 有名的

    (C) ***notorious*** (noˋtorɪəs) *adj.* 惡名昭彰的

    (D) noble (ˋnobḷ) *adj.* 高貴的

    poker (ˋpokə) *n.* 撲克牌

    cheater (ˋtʃitə) *n.* 騙子

6. (**B**) Ms. Haynes <u>admonished</u> her son after she learned that he had got a ticket for speeding.

海尼斯太太在知道她兒子超速被開罰單後，<u>訓</u>了他一頓。

    (A) elevate (ˋɛləˏvet) *v.* 提高

    (B) ***admonish*** (ədˋmanɪʃ) *v.* 訓誡；告誡

    (C) persuade (pəˋswed) *v.* 說服

    (D) acknowledge (əkˋnalɪdʒ) *v.* 承認

    learn (lɝn) *v.* 知道   ticket (ˋtɪkɪt) *n.* 罰單

    speeding (ˋspidɪŋ) *n.* 超速

7. (**C**) Charles <u>compared</u> his girlfriend's voice to the sound of a cat howling in the night; that is, he said his girlfriend sounded like a cat howling.

查爾斯把他女朋友的聲音<u>比喻</u>爲晚上的貓叫聲；也就是說，他說他女朋友的聲音聽起來像貓在叫。

(A) mimic ('mɪmɪk) *v.* 模仿
(B) equalize ('ikwəl,aɪz) *v.* 使相等
(C) ***compare*** (kəm'pɛr) 比喻 < *to* >
(D) compliment ('kɑmplə,mɛnt) *v.* 稱讚

howl (haʊl) *v.* (動物) 長嗥；咆哮

8. (**A**) Sam hoped that the value of his collection would <u>appreciate</u> rapidly; instead, the collection has slowly become worthless.

山姆希望他的收藏能夠很快地<u>升值</u>；但相反地，這些收藏卻漸漸地變成毫無價值。

(A) ***appreciate*** (ə'priʃɪ,et) *v.* 增值
(B) qualify ('kwɑlə,faɪ) *v.* 使合格
(C) awaken (ə'wekən) *v.* 喚醒
(D) approach (ə'protʃ) *v.* 接近

collection (kə'lɛkʃən) *n.* 收藏
worthless ('wɝθlɪs) *adj.* 無價值的

9. (**C**) Last year in Italy, an active volcano <u>erupted</u>, sending a slow-moving river of hot lava through the town.

去年在義大利，有一座活火山<u>爆發</u>，噴出大量的熾熱熔岩，緩慢地流過整個小鎮。

(A) explore (ɪk'splor) *v.* 探險
(B) expose (ɪk'spoz) *v.* 暴露
(C) ***erupt*** (ɪ'rʌpt) *v.* 爆發
(D) distribute (dɪ'strɪbjut) *v.* 分配

volcano (vɑl'keno) *n.* 火山　　***active volcano*** 活火山
river ('rɪvɚ) *n.* 大量的湧流　　lava ('lɑvə) *n.* 熔岩；岩漿

10. (**D**) A man is known by the <u>companions</u> he keeps, so we should be careful in choosing friends.

觀其<u>友</u>，知其人，所以我們應該慎選朋友。

(A) companies（'kʌmpənɪz）*n. pl.* 公司【須改為 company（同伴）】

(B) competitor（kəm'pɛtətə）*n.* 競爭者

(C) proponent（prə'ponənt）*n.* 提議者；擁護者

(D) *companion*（kəm'pænjən）*n.* 同伴；朋友

11. (**B**) The football team <u>consists of</u> eleven players on offense and eleven players on defense.

橄欖球隊是<u>由</u>攻守兩方各十一位球員所<u>組成</u>。

(A) 須改為 comprise（kəm'praɪz）*v.* 包括；由～組成

(B) *consist of* 由～組成

(C) 須改為 be made up of 由～組成

(D) 須改為 be composed of 由～組成

offense（ə'fɛns）*n.* 攻擊；攻方

defense（dɪ'fɛns）*n.* 防禦；守方

12. (**A**) Many young people like to <u>hang out</u> with friends in the nightclubs or Internet cafes. 許多年輕人喜歡和朋友在夜總會或網咖<u>逗留</u>。

(A) *hang out* 逗留

(B) live up to 依（某種標準）生活

(C) play out 演完；做完

(D) get off the ground 順利開始；有進展

nightclub（'naɪt,klʌb）*n.* 夜總會　　*Internet cafe* 網咖

13. (**D**) Burglars <u>broke into</u> Miss Chen's house last night, and she was seized with panic.

昨晚有竊賊<u>闖入</u>陳小姐的家，使她感到非常恐慌。

(A) break down 故障　　　　(B) break out 爆發

(C) break off 突然停止　　　(D) *break into* 闖入

burglar（'bɝglə）*n.* 夜賊　　seize（siz）*v.*（疾病、恐懼等）侵襲

panic（'pænɪk）*n.* 恐慌

14. (**C**) We try to get as much knowledge as possible for fear that we
might not <u>keep up with</u> the times.
我們儘可能地吸收知識，以免<u>跟不上</u>時代。

(A) catch up on　趕完；彌補　　　(B) put up with　忍耐
(C) *keep up with*　跟上；不落後於
(D) get away with　逃避懲罰

for fear that　以免　　　times〔taɪmz〕*n. pl.*　時代

15. (**A**) It is not fair to <u>pick on</u> kids with disabilities just because they are
different.
只因為殘障的孩子和別人不一樣就<u>欺負</u>他們，這樣是不公平的。

(A) *pick on*　欺負；罵　　　(B) split up with　和～分開
(C) get acquainted with　熟悉；認識
(D) pick out　挑選

fair〔fɛr〕*adj.*　公平的　　　disability〔͵dɪsə'bɪlətɪ〕*n.*　身體殘障

二、綜合測驗：

<u>第 16 至 25 題為題組</u>

　　An otherwise healthy man died last week as a consequence of doing
the good deed of donating part of his liver for transplant. This incident has
<u>raised</u> questions about the issue of living donations. The increasingly
16
common use of living organ donors <u>began with</u> kidney transplants more
17
than a decade ago. <u>In fact</u>, at many transplant centers the majority of kidney
18
transplants are now from living donors. Most of the living donors are
so-called related donors, <u>who</u> have a blood, family, or emotional relationship
19
to the organ recipient.

　　上星期有一個原本很健康的人，因為做好事，捐贈自己部分肝臟作移植，
而死亡。這件事引發了關於活體捐贈這個議題的問題。利用活體器官捐贈者，
現已日漸普遍，這個方式開始於十多年前的腎臟移植。事實上，在許多移植中
心，大多數的腎臟移植都來自活體捐贈者。大部分的活體捐贈者，都是所謂有
關係的捐贈者，他們和器官接受者有血緣上、家庭上，或感情上的關係。

otherwise〔'ʌðə‚waɪz〕*adv.* 在其他方面
consequence〔'kɑnsə‚kwɛns〕*n.* 結果
as a consequence of 由於；因為（= *as a result of*）
deed〔did〕*n.* 行為　　donate〔'donet〕*v.* 捐贈
liver〔'lɪvə〕*n.* 肝臟　　transplant〔'træns‚plænt〕*n.* 移植
incident〔'ɪnsədənt〕*n.* 事件　　issue〔'ɪʃjʊ〕*n.* 問題；議題
donation〔do'neʃən〕*n.* 捐贈　　organ〔'ɔrgən〕*n.* 器官
donor〔'donə〕*n.* 捐贈者　　kidney〔'kɪdnɪ〕*n.* 腎臟
majority〔mə'dʒɔrətɪ〕*n.* 大多數　　related〔rɪ'letɪd〕*adj.* 有關係的
recipient〔rɪ'sɪpɪənt〕*n.* 接受者

16.（**A**）(A) ***raise***〔rez〕*v.* 提高；養育；引起；提出
　　　　(B) arouse〔ə'raʊz〕*v.* 喚起（某種情緒）
　　　　(C) rise〔raɪz〕*v.* 上升；升起
　　　　(D) rear〔rɪr〕*v.* 養育（= *raise*）

17.（**D**）(A) put into practice　付諸實行　　(B) take place　發生（不用被動）
　　　　(C) occur〔ə'kɝ〕*v.* 發生（不及物動詞，不加受詞）
　　　　(D) ***begin with***　由～開始

18.（**A**）(A) ***in fact***　事實上　　　　　　(B) above all　尤其；最重要的是
　　　　(C) at best　充其量　　　　　　　(D) in addition　此外

19.（**C**）關係代名詞引導形容詞子句，修飾先行詞 related donors，先行詞為
　　　　「人」，故關代應用 ***who***，選 (C)。

This relationship creates both the impetus to donate and ethical worries
　　　　　　　　　　　　　　20
about the donation, since related donors may be willing to or feel
compelled to ignore the risks of organ donation when their loved one
　　　　　　　　21
stands to receive so great a benefit. The problem is that while the medical
　　　　　　　　22　　　　　　　　　　　　　　　　23
benefit to the recipient is great, all the risk of the donation falls to the donor.
So we must ask whether the benefit to the donor of seeing a loved one's
　　　　　　　　　24
life saved is sufficient to balance the risk he is asked to undergo.
　　25

　　這種關係會產生捐贈的動機，以及有關捐贈的道德憂慮，因爲有關係的捐贈者可能是自願的、或是覺得有責任，而在當所愛的人可以得到這麼大的好處時，忽視器官捐贈的風險。問題在於，雖然受贈者能在醫療上得到很大的好處，但所有的風險都落在捐贈者身上。所以我們必須問清楚，捐贈者所得到的好處，也就是看心愛的人獲救，是否足以平衡他們被要求經歷的風險。

> impetus（'ɪmpətəs）*n.* 刺激；動機
> ethical（'ɛθɪkl）*adj.* 倫理的；道德的
> willing（'wɪlɪŋ）*adj.* 願意的
> compel（kəm'pɛl）*v.* 強迫
> ***feel compelled*** 覺得有責任
> risk（rɪsk）*n.* 風險　　***stand to*** + *V.* 作好準備（= *be ready to*）
> benefit（'bɛnəfɪt）*n.* 好處；利益
> sufficient（sə'fɪʃənt）*adj.* 充足的；足夠的
> balance（'bæləns）*v.* 平衡；使均衡
> undergo（ˌʌndɚ'go）*v.* 經歷（= *go through*）

20.（**D**）依句意，動機和憂慮均會產生，應用 ***both*** A and B，故選 (D)。

21.（**B**）(A) compromise（'kɑmprəˌmaɪz）*v.* 妥協；讓步
　　　　　(B) ***ignore***（ɪg'nor）*v.* 忽視
　　　　　(C) observe（əb'zɝv）*v.* 觀察；遵守
　　　　　(D) demonstrate（'dɛmənˌstret）*v.* 示威；示範

22.（**C**）***so great a benefit*** 如此大的好處（= *such a great benefit*）

23.（**C**）依句意，「雖然」受贈者得到很大的好處，但捐贈者的風險更大，選 (C) ***while***，表「雖然」之意，相當於 although。而 (A) 然而，(B) 因此，(D) 相反地，均不合句意。

24.（**B**）依句意，我們要問清楚，受贈者所得的好處「是否」能平衡捐贈者所經歷的風險，選 (B) ***whether***。

25.（**A**）依句意，捐贈者或許可以看到，自己所愛的人「獲救」，爲被動語態，故選 (A) ***saved***。

第 26 至 30 題爲題組

The 28-year-old had spent six years working nights while she gained her university degree during the day. When she finally graduated, she had her eye on a teaching <u>position</u> at a nearby primary school. With the help of
26
her friends, she had an interview with the Head.

一位二十八歲的小姐花了六年的時間，晚上工作，白天唸大學。當她終於畢業時，她注意到附近有一所小學，有一個敎書的職位。經由朋友的幫助，她得到和校長面談的機會。

> degree (dɪ'gri) *n.* 學位   *have one's eye on* 注意
> *primary school* 小學 (= *elementary school*)
> interview ('ɪntə,vju) *n.* 面談

26. (**B**) (A) profession (prə'fɛʃən) *n.* 職業，(C) career (kə'rɪr) *n.* 職業；生涯，
　　　　(D) occupation (,ɑkjə'peʃən) *n.* 職業，均不能在其前面加 teaching，
　　　　故選 (B) *position* (pə'zɪʃən) *n.* 職位。

"I noticed a tiny hole in one of my stockings earlier," she <u>recalls</u>.
27
"I thought about changing them, but I knew I'd be late if I did. And by the time I got to the interview, it was enormous. I walked in apologizing for not <u>looking my best</u>." The would-be teacher didn't get the job. In fact,
28
one of her friends told her that the Head's only comment was: "If someone doesn't take the time to present her best image at an interview, what kind of teacher is she going to be?"

「我稍早時注意到，我的絲襪上有個小洞，」她回想著。「我想過把絲襪換下來，但我知道，如果我去換，我就會遲到。而等我到達面試地點時，那個小洞變得好大。我走進去，爲了自己沒能以最佳狀態出現而道歉。」這位想成爲老師的小姐沒有得到這份工作。事實上，她的一位朋友告訴她，校長唯一的評論是：「如果一個人無法在面試時，花點時間展現自己最好的一面，那她將會成爲怎樣的老師呢？」

tiny〔'taɪnɪ〕*adj.* 微小的　　stockings〔'stakɪŋz〕*n. pl.* 長襪

enormous〔ɪ'nɔrməs〕*adj.* 巨大的

apologize〔ə'palə,dʒaɪz〕*v.* 道歉

would-be〔'wʊd,bi〕*adj.* 想成爲～的

comment〔'kamɛnt〕*n.* 評論

present〔prɪ'zɛnt〕*v.* 呈現　　image〔'ɪmɪdʒ〕*n.* 形象

27. (**C**) (A) repeat〔rɪ'pit〕*v.* 重複　　(B) remind〔rɪ'maɪnd〕*v.* 提醒

　　　　(C) *recall*〔rɪ'kɔl〕*v.* 回想　　(D) respond〔rɪ'spand〕*v.* 回應

28. (**D**) 依句意，她爲了自己沒能「以最佳狀態出現」而道歉，選 (D) *looking my best*。而 (A) 完全不看，(B) 不看他，(C) 環顧四周，均不合。

First impressions are <u>lasting</u> ones.　In other words, if you're viewed
　　　　　　　　　　　29
positively within the critical first four minutes, the person you've met will probably assume everything you do is positive.　Give the interviewer a bad impression, and often he will assume you have a lot of other unsatisfactory characteristics.　<u>Worse</u>, he or she may not take the time to give you a second
　　　　　　　　　　　30
chance.　Most employers believe that those who look as if they care about themselves will care more about their jobs.

　　第一印象最持久。換句話說，若你在非常重要的前四分鐘之內，給人的評價是正面的，你遇見的這個人，可能就會認爲，你所做的一切都是好的。如果給面試官一個壞印象，他通常就會認爲，你有其他許多令人不滿意的特質。更糟的是，他或她可能也不會花時間給你第二次機會。許多雇主都相信，那些看起來很在乎自己的人，會更加在乎自己的工作。

impression〔ɪm'prɛʃən〕*n.* 印象　　*in other words* 換句話說

view〔vju〕*v.* 認爲；評價

positively〔'pazətɪvlɪ〕*adv.* 正面地；肯定地

critical〔'krɪtɪkḷ〕*adj.* 非常重要的

unsatisfactory〔,ʌnsætɪs'fæktərɪ〕*adj.* 令人不滿意的

characteristic〔,kærəktə'rɪstɪk〕*n.* 特性

29.（**A**）(A) *lasting*〔'læstɪŋ〕*adj.* 持久的

(B) remaining〔rɪ'menɪŋ〕*adj.* 殘留的

(C) continue〔kən'tɪnju〕*v.* 繼續（形容詞不用 continuing，而是 continuous 或 continual）

(D) persist〔pɚ'sɪst〕*v.* 堅持；持久（形容詞不用 persisting，而是 persistent）

30.（**C**）依句意，「更糟的是」，雇主不會給你第二次機會，選 (C) *Worse*。

(A) 除了～之外，(B) 此外（用於正面意義），(D) 然而，均不合。

三、文意選填：

第 31 至 40 題為題組

For many Americans, Ann Mary Robertson was a noted folk artist as well as a great woman, who never yielded to her age.

對許多美國人而言，安·瑪麗·羅伯森是著名的民俗藝術家，也是一位偉大的女性，她從不向自己的年紀屈服。

noted〔'notɪd〕*adj.* 著名的　　folk〔fok〕*adj.* 民俗的
as well as 以及　　　　**yield to** 向…屈服

Ann Mary Robertson, [31]**(F) known** as "Grandma" Moses, was born in 1860. She began to paint at the age of 78, after giving up needlework due to a health problem. Two years later her [32]**(G) first** exhibition was held and this 80-year-old self-taught artist experienced a sudden success. Moses had spent her life first as a hired girl and [33]**(B) then** as the wife of a farmer. Her [34]**(E) paintings** reflected the peaceful, simple country life. Different [35]**(I) scenes**, such as harvesting, country fairs, and landscapes in all seasons from snow-covered villages to [36]**(J) summer** fields, were pleasant subjects she chose for her work.

安·瑪麗·羅伯森，即著名的摩斯「嬤嬤」，出生於一八六〇年。她因為健康問題放棄女紅之後，在七十八歲時開始畫畫。兩年之後，她舉辦第一次畫展，這位八十歲無師自通的藝術家，一砲而紅。摩斯的一生，先是受雇於人，而後嫁作農人婦。她的畫作反映寧靜、簡樸的鄉村生活。不同的景緻，如收割、鄉間市集，和從白雪覆蓋的村落到夏日田野，諸多的四季風景，都被她選爲作品裏賞心悅目的主題。

> **give up** 放棄　　needlework (ˈnidḷˌwɝk) n. 女紅；縫紉
> **due to** 由於　　exhibition (ˌɛksəˈbɪʃən) n. 展覽
> hold (hold) v. 舉行
> self-taught (ˈsɛlfˈtɔt) adj. 自學的；無師自通的
> sudden (ˈsʌdn̩) adj. 突然的　　hire (haɪr) v. 雇用
> reflect (rɪˈflɛkt) v. 反映　　peaceful (ˈpisfəl) adj. 平靜的
> simple (ˈsɪmpḷ) adj. 簡樸的　　scene (sin) n. 景色
> harvesting (ˈhɑrvɪstɪŋ) n. 收割　　fair (fɛr) n. 市集
> landscape (ˈlændskep) n. 風景　　village (ˈvɪlɪdʒ) n. 村莊
> field (fild) n. 田野　　pleasant (ˈplɛznt) adj. 令人愉快的
> subject (ˈsʌbdʒɪkt) n. 主題　　work (wɝk) n. 作品

People were attracted to Moses' appealing subjects. However, they were just as moved by the story of this gifted old lady who, [37](A) with no formal training, became world-famous in a handful of years and who opened up for them a world of peace and [38](C) simple pleasure they wished to enjoy.

　人們深受摩斯迷人的主題所吸引。然而，這位天才老婦人自身的故事，也使人們深受感動，她從未受過正規的訓練，卻在少數幾年間就聞名於世，並爲世人開啓他們渴望享有的，一個擁有寧靜、簡樸樂趣的世界。

> **be attracted to** 被…所吸引　　appealing (əˈpilɪŋ) adj. 迷人的
> moved (muvd) adj. 感動的　　gifted (ˈɡɪftɪd) adj. 有天賦的
> formal (ˈfɔrmḷ) adj. 正式的；正規的
> **a handful of** 少數的；不多的　　**wish to** 想要 (= want to)

By the time of her death in 1961, Moses had created more than 1500 works of art. Moses once said, "I have written my life in small sketches, a little today, a little yesterday…I look back on my life as a good day's work. It was done and I feel satisfied. I [39](H) made the best out of what life offered." Her enthusiasm [40](D) for painting has won her the fondness of the public, who view her as a legend of senior citizen wizardry.

當摩斯在一九六一年去世時，她已經創作了一千五百多幅的畫作。她曾說過：「我用小幅的畫作來記錄我的人生，畫一點今天，畫一點昨天…回顧我的一生，它就像是要做一整天才做得完的事。我做完了，而且覺得很滿足。我充分利用了生命所賜予的一切。」她對作畫的熱誠，贏得大眾的喜愛，並視她為年長者展露奇才的傳奇人物。

> sketch〔skɛtʃ〕*n.* 畫作；寫生　　***look back on***　回顧
> ***a good day's work*** 一整天才做得完的事
> ***make the best*** (*out*) *of* 善用；充分利用
> enthusiasm〔ɪn'θjuzɪˌæzəm〕*n.* 熱誠　　　fondness〔'fɑndnɪs〕*n.* 喜愛
> ***view ~ as*** 視 ~ 為…　　legend〔'lɛdʒənd〕*n.* 傳奇人物
> ***senior citizen*** 長者；老人　　wizardry〔'wɪzədrɪ〕*n.* 奇才；絕技

四、篇章結構：

第 41 至 45 題為題組

Mount Rainier, the heart of Mt. Rainier National Park, is the highest mountain in the state of Washington and in the Cascade Range. **41(D) The mountain's summit is broad and rounded.** It is 14,410 feet above sea level and has an area of about one square mile.

來尼爾峰國家公園的中心——來尼爾峰，是華盛頓州和喀斯開山脈的最高峰。山峰的頂端又寬又圓。它位於海拔一萬四千四百一十英呎的位置，面積大約一平方英哩。

> range〔rendʒ〕*n.* 山脈　　summit〔'sʌmɪt〕*n.* 山頂
> broad〔brɔd〕*adj.* 寬的　　rounded〔'raʊndɪd〕*adj.* 圓的

42(C) Numerous steam and gas jets occur around the crater. However, the volcano has been sleeping for centuries.

在火山口四周有許多蒸氣和煤氣火焰。然而，火山已經沉睡了好幾個世紀。

> numerous〔'njumərəs〕*adj.* 許多的　　steam〔stim〕*n.* 蒸氣
> ***gas jet*** 煤氣的火焰　　occur〔ə'kɝ〕*v.* 出現
> crater〔'kretə〕*n.* 火山口　　volcano〔vɑl'keno〕*n.* 火山
> century〔'sɛntʃərɪ〕*n.* 世紀

Mount Rainier has a permanent ice cap and extensive snow fields, which give rise to more than forty glaciers. These feed swift streams and tumbling waterfalls that race through the glacial valleys. [43](A) Forests extend to 4,500 feet. There are alpine meadows between the glaciers and the forests, which contain beautiful wild flowers. [44](E) The Nisqually Glacier is probably the ice region that is most often explored by visitors. Paradise Valley, where hotel accommodations are available, perches on the mountain's slope at 5,400 feet. [45](B) The Wonderland Trail encircles the mountain. Its 90-mile length can be covered in about a week's time.

來尼爾峰有常年不化的冰帽,和廣大的雪地,因而造成了四十多條冰河。這些冰河注入了通過冰河谷的急流,和傾盆而下的瀑布。森林綿延四千五百英呎遠。冰河和森林之間有高山草原,上面有漂亮的野花。尼斯高利冰河可能是觀光客最常探險的冰河地帶。天堂谷有飯店住宿,座落於五千四百英呎高的斜坡上。仙境小路環山而行。它九十英哩的長度大約要一個星期的時間才能走完。

permanent (ˈpɜmənənt) adj. 永久的　　***ice cap*** 冰帽

extensive (ɪkˈstɛnsɪv) adj. 廣大的　　***give rise to*** 造成

glacier (ˈgleʃɚ) n. 冰河　　feed (fid) v. 注入

swift (swɪft) adj. 急促的　　stream (strim) n. 水流

tumbling (ˈtʌmblɪŋ) adj. 傾下的

waterfall (ˈwɔtɚ͵fɔl) n. 瀑布

race (res) v. 疾速前進　　glacial (ˈgleʃəl) adj. 冰河的

valley (ˈvælɪ) n. 山谷　　extend (ɪkˈstɛnd) v. 綿延

alpine (ˈælpaɪn) adj. 高山的　　meadow (ˈmɛdo) n. 草地

region (ˈridʒən) n. 地帶　　explore (ɪkˈsplor) v. 探險

accommodation (ə͵kɑməˈdeʃən) n. 住宿

available (əˈveləbl) adj. 可獲得的

perch (pɜtʃ) v. (在較高或較險處) 座落

slope (slop) n. 斜坡　　trail (trel) n. 小道

encircle (ɪnˈsɜkl) v. 環繞

cover (ˈkʌvɚ) v. 走完 (一段路程)

五、閱讀測驗：

第 46 至 48 題為題組

Sweets, cereals, hamburgers and French fries, snack foods, toys, clothing......These products are the focus of a phenomenal amount of TV advertising that is directed toward children. A typical youngster may see more than 50 commercials a day! As early as 3 years of age, children distinguish commercials from programs. However, preschool children often believe that commercials are simply a different form of entertainment— one designed to inform viewers. Not until 8 or 9 years of age do most children understand the persuasive intent of commercials. At the same time that children grasp the aim of commercials, they begin to realize that commercials are not always truthful.

甜食、穀類加工食品、漢堡、薯條、點心、玩具、衣服…這些產品是針對兒童為訴求的大量廣告中的主角。一般小孩一天可能會看到五十多支廣告。兒童最早在三歲的時候，就會區分廣告和節目的不同。然而，學齡前的兒童經常以為，廣告只是另一種不同形式的娛樂——目的在於告知觀眾訊息。大部分的兒童直到八、九歲的時候，才知道廣告的意圖是要說服觀眾。同時，當兒童了解廣告的目的為何後，他們就開始意識到廣告未必是真實的。

sweet〔swit〕*n.* 甜食　　cereal〔'sɪrɪəl〕*n.* 穀類加工食品

focus〔'fokəs〕*n.* 焦點；重點

phenomenal〔fə'nɑmənḷ〕*adj.* 驚人的

advertising〔'ædvɚˌtaɪzɪŋ〕*n.* 廣告　　direct〔də'rɛkt〕*v.* 針對

commercial〔kə'mɝʃəl〕*n.*（電視、電台的）廣告

distinguish〔dɪ'stɪŋgwɪʃ〕*v.* 區別 < *from* >

preschool〔pri'skul〕*adj.* 學齡前的

entertainment〔ˌɛntɚ'tenmənt〕*n.* 娛樂

design〔dɪ'zaɪn〕*v.* 設計　　***be designed to*** 目的是為了

inform〔ɪn'fɔrm〕*v.* 告知　　viewer〔'vjuɚ〕*n.* 觀眾

persuasive〔pɚ'swesɪv〕*adj.* 有說服力的　　intent〔ɪn'tɛnt〕*n.* 意圖

grasp〔græsp〕*v.* 理解　　aim〔em〕*n.* 目的

not always 不一定（= *not necessarily*）

truthful〔'truθfəl〕*adj.* 真實的

Commercials are effective sales tools with children. Children grow to like many of the products advertised on TV. They may urge parents to buy products that they have seen on television. In one study, more than 75% of the children reported that they had asked their parents to buy a product they had seen advertised on TV. More often than not, parents had purchased the product for them!

廣告對小孩而言，是很有效的推銷工具。兒童會逐漸喜歡上電視廣告中的許多產品。他們會吵著要爸媽買在電視上看到的產品。有一項研究指出，超過百分之七十五的兒童表示，曾經要求父母購買電視廣告的某個產品。父母多半都會買給他們！

　　effective〔ɪ'fɛktɪv〕*adj.* 有效的　　grow〔gro〕*v.* 逐漸變成
　　advertise〔'ædvɚ,taɪz〕*v.* 廣告　　urge〔ɝdʒ〕*v.* 催促；力勸
　　more often than not 通常（*= often*）　　purchase〔'pɝtʃəs〕*v.* 購買

The selling power of TV commercials has long concerned advocates for children, because so many ads focus on children's foods that have little nutritional value and that are associated with problems such as obesity and tooth decay. The U.S. government once regulated the amount and type of advertising on children's TV programs, but today the responsibility falls to parents.

長久以來，電視廣告的推銷力，一直讓兒童保護者感到擔憂，因為許多廣告的焦點都集中在兒童食品上，那些食品的營養價值很低，而且都和像是肥胖和蛀牙這些問題有關。美國政府曾經管制兒童電視節目的廣告量及類型，但現在責任則是落在父母身上。

　　concern〔kən'sɝn〕*v.* 使擔心
　　advocate〔'ædvəkɪt〕*n.* 擁護者；提倡者
　　focus on （注意力）集中於（*= concentrate on*）
　　nutritional〔nju'trɪʃənl〕*adj.* 營養的
　　associate〔ə'soʃɪ,et〕*v.* 聯想；有關聯　　obesity〔o'bisəti〕*n.* 肥胖
　　tooth decay 蛀牙　　regulate〔'rɛgjə,let〕*v.* 控制；管理
　　fall to （責任）落在…的身上

46.(**B**) 本文的主旨是 ＿＿＿＿＿＿ 。

　(A) 兒童藉由看電視廣告，可以學到有用的社交技巧

　(B) 電視廣告對年幼消費者的行為有很大的影響

　(C) 電視看世界的角度有時候是扭曲的

　(D) 看電視不會導致有益的行為

social（＇soʃəl）*adj.* 社交的

consumer（kənˊsjumɚ）*n.* 消費者

behavior（bɪˊhevjɚ）*n.* 行為　　view（vju）*n.* 看法

distorted（dɪsˊtɔrtɪd）*adj.* 扭曲的

beneficial（ˌbɛnəˊfɪʃəl）*adj.* 有益的　　***result from*** 造成…的結果

47.(**D**) 根據本文，電視廣告的焦點經常集中於 ＿＿＿＿＿＿ 。

　(A) 不同年紀的小孩的玩具

　(B) 不同階段的小孩的特質

　(C) 傳達事實的工具

　(D) 營養價值低的兒童食物，而且可能導致某些健康問題

characteristic（ˌkærɪktəˊrɪstɪk）*n.* 特性

stage（stedʒ）*n.* 階段；時期

convey（kənˊve）*v.* 傳達

factual（ˊfæktʃuəl）*adj.* 基於事實的

nutrition（njuˊtrɪʃən）*n.* 營養　　***result in*** 導致

48.(**A**) 根據本文，下列敘述何者正確？

　(A) 廣告對三歲的兒童而言，只是一種不同的娛樂形式。

　(B) 學齡前的兒童看電視時，能夠了解廣告的目的為何，並且開始
意識到廣告未必是真實的。

　(C) 父母從不購買小孩在電視上看到的產品。

　(D) 父母對於容忍小孩的行為變得愈來愈具侵略性，要負起責任。

bear（bɛr）*v.* 承擔　　tolerance（ˊtɑlərəns）*n.* 寬容

aggression（əˊgrɛʃən）*n.* 侵略性

<u>第 49 至 52 題為題組</u>

　　Meetings can waste a great deal of time. But you can make your
meeting run more smoothly by following a few simple rules. First, have
an agenda. This will help keep you focused on what is important. Next,
decide who needs to be involved. More people mean less efficient
discussion. Finally, keep the discussion moving. Thank each speaker as
he or she finishes and move on to the next speaker. This encourages
people to make their remarks brief.

　　會議可能會浪費很多時間。但是你可以藉由遵循一些簡單的規則，讓你的
會議進行得更順利。首先，要有一個議程。這會有助於你集中注意力在重要的
事上面。其次，決定需要參加會議的人。越多人參加，表示討論會越沒有效率。
最後，讓討論持續進行。當說話者結束時，要謝謝他們，然後讓下一位接著說。
這會鼓勵大家把話說得精簡一點。

> ***a great deal of*** 很多的　　run〔rʌn〕v. 進行
> smoothly〔'smuðlɪ〕adv. 順利地
> agenda〔ə'dʒɛndə〕n. 議程　　***focus on*** 專心於
> involve〔ɪn'vɑlv〕v. 使參與　　efficient〔ɪ'fɪʃənt〕adj. 有效率的
> move〔muv〕v. 進行　　remarks〔rɪ'mɑrks〕n. pl. 話
> brief〔brif〕adj. 簡短的

　　The problem with meetings, of course, is that no one likes them, no
one wants them, and no one needs them. Yet, everyone has them.
Meetings are the corporate world's response to primitive socializing
behaviors. People feel more comfortable in making decisions in groups.
They can then share blame if a decision turns out to be the wrong
decision. Sharing credit for a correct decision is not often found in groups.
Then individuals tend to remind people of how persuasive they were in
the meeting when the "right" decision was made.

　　當然，會議的問題在於沒有人喜歡、沒有人想要，而且也沒有人需要它們。
但是，每個人都要開會。會議是整個世界對原始的社會化行為所做出的回應。
人們在團體中做決定，會覺得比較舒服。如果一個決定結果是錯的，大家可以

分擔責備。在團體中分享正確決定的榮耀則不常見。當做出「正確的」決定時，人們又喜歡提醒別人，自己在做那個決定的會議中是多麼努力說服大家。

corporate（'kɔrprɪt）*adj.* 全體的　　response（rɪ'spɑns）*n.* 回應

primitive（'prɪmətɪv）*adj.* 原始的　　socialize（'soʃə͵laɪz）*v.* 社會化

behavior（bɪ'hevjɚ）*n.* 行為　　blame（blem）*n.* 責備

turn out 結果　　credit（'krɛdɪt）*n.* 榮耀

individual（͵ɪndə'vɪdʒʊəl）*n.* 個人　　***tend to*** 傾向於

remind sb. ***of*** sth. 提醒某人某事

persuasive（pɚ'swesɪv）*adj.* 勸說的；口才好的

What happens after a meeting is more important than what happens during the meeting. The skills used then are more professional and less procedural. So no matter how well you run a meeting, it is the work that gets done after the meeting that is important.

會議之後所發生的事，比在會議中發生的要來得重要。到時候要使用的技巧比較專業，但比較不按程序。所以無論你的會議進行得有多順利，會議結束後所完成的事，才是最重要的。

professional（prə'fɛʃənḷ）*adj.* 專業的

procedural（pro'sidʒərəl）*adj.* 程序的

49.（**B**）哪一個是讓會議能順利進行的方法？

(A) 看你的主管怎麼主持會議。　　(B) 把參加的成員減到最少。

(C) 讓團體做決定。　　(D) 讓每個人發言。

manager（'mænɪdʒɚ）*n.* 主管

minimize（'mɪnə͵maɪz）*v.* 使減到最小

participant（par'tɪsəpənt）*n.* 參加者

50.（**D**）會議議程的目的是什麼？

(A) 讓說話者更有組織。　　(B) 允許自由討論。

(C) 要感謝說話者。　　(D) 要一直專注於重要項目。

organized（'ɔrgən͵aɪzd）*adj.* 有組織的

item（'aɪtəm）*n.* 項目

51. (**B**) 會議中，你應該如何接受別人的意見？
   (A) 試著阻止別人說話。
   (B) 謝謝他們，並且繼續進行會議。
   (C) 儘量多給他們時間。
   (D) 公開批評他們。

   comment〔'kɑmɛnt〕 n. 意見；評論
   keep sb. from + V-ing 阻止某人～
   criticize〔'krɪtə,saɪz〕 v. 批評　　*in public* 公開地

52. (**A**) 在結論中，作者覺得
   (A) 眞正的工作要留給專業人士。
   (B) 所有的會議應在早上進行。
   (C) 沒有人應該獲得工作上的榮耀。
   (D) 應該要更常召開會議。

   conclusion〔kən'kluʒən〕 n. 結論　　hold〔hold〕 v. 舉行

第 53 至 56 題爲題組

People used to be born at home and die at home. In the old days, children were familiar with birth and death as part of life. Nowadays when people grow old, we often send them to nursing homes. When they get sick, we transfer them to a hospital, where children are usually unwelcome and are forbidden to visit terminally ill patients—even when those patients are their parents. This deprives the dying patient of important family members during the last few days of his life and it deprives the children of an experience of death, which is an important learning experience.

以往人們都是在家裏出生，在家裏死亡。昔日，孩子們非常熟悉生與死是生活的一部分。現今，人們年紀一大，我們就送他們進養老院。他們一生病，就把他們轉入醫院，醫院通常不歡迎小孩，而且也禁止他們去探視末期病患，就算病患是父母親也一樣。這種做法，等於在垂死病患生命的最後幾天，剝奪他們會見家中重要成員的權利，也剝奪孩子經歷死亡的機會，而經歷死亡是一種重要的學習經驗。

used to ~ 以前（都）~   ***be familiar with*** 熟悉

nowadays〔'nauə,dez〕*adv.* 現今   ***nursing home*** 養老院

transfer〔træns'fɝ〕*v.* 轉移；調動

unwelcome〔ʌn'wɛlkəm〕*adj.* 不受歡迎的

forbid〔fɚ'bɪd〕*v.* 禁止

terminally〔'tɝmənlɪ〕*adv.* 末期地

patient〔'peʃənt〕*n.* 病人

deprive A ***of*** B 剝奪 A 的 B 權利

At the University of Chicago's Billings Hospital, some of my colleagues and I interviewed and followed approximately 500 terminally ill patients in order to find out what they could teach us and how we could be of more benefit, not just to them but to the members of their families as well. We were most impressed by the fact that even those patients who were not told of their serious illness were quite aware of its potential outcome. They were not only able to say that they were close to dying, but many were able to predict the approximate time of their death.

在芝加哥大學附屬的比林斯醫院，同僚與我訪談並追蹤大約五百名末期病患，以便瞭解他們能教導我們什麼，以及我們要如何提供他們更多幫助，不僅是針對病患，也針對病患的家中成員。我們印象最深刻的是，就算未被告知嚴重病情的患者，都相當明瞭可能的結果。他們不僅會說自己離死期不遠，許多人甚至能預測大概的死亡時刻。

colleague〔'kɑlig〕*n.* 同僚；同事

interview〔'ɪntɚ,vju〕*v.* 訪談   follow〔'falo〕*v.* 追蹤

approximately〔ə'prɑksəmɪtlɪ〕*adv.* 大概

in order to 為了   ***find out*** 找出；查出

be of benefit 有助益   impress〔ɪm'prɛs〕*v.* 使印象深刻

be aware of 明瞭；知道

potential〔pə'tɛnʃəl〕*adj.* 可能的

outcome〔'aut,kʌm〕*n.* 結果   ***be close to*** 即將

predict〔prɪ'dɪkt〕*v.* 預測

It is important for next of kin and members of the helping professions to understand these patients' communications in order to truly understand their needs, fears and fantasies.　Most of our patients welcomed another human being with whom they could talk openly, honestly, and frankly about their predicament.　Many of them shared with us their tremendous need to be informed, to be kept up-to-date on their medical condition, and to be told when the end was near.　We found out that patients who had been dealt with openly and frankly were better able to cope with the imminence of death and finally to reach a true stage of acceptance prior to death.

很重要的一點是，讓近親和從旁協助的專業人員，了解病人要傳達的訊息，以便真正懂得他們的需求、恐懼與幻想。大部份的病患都歡迎有人與他們公開、誠懇、坦白地談論他們的困境。許多患者告訴我們，他們很需要有人告訴他們最新的治療狀況，以及生命何時即將終止。我們發現被以公開、坦白的態度對待的患者，更能應付死期將近的事實，並在死前達到真正接受事實的階段。

> ***next of kin*** 近親　　profession (prə'fɛʃən) *n.* 專業；職業
> communication (kə͵mjunə'keʃən) *n.* 訊息
> fantasy ('fæntəsɪ) *n.* 幻想　　***human being*** 人
> frankly ('fræŋklɪ) *adv.* 坦白地
> predicament (prɪ'dɪkəmənt) *n.* 困境
> tremendous (trɪ'mɛndəs) *adj.* 巨大的
> up-to-date ('ʌptə'det) *adj.* 最新的；最近的　　***deal with*** 對待
> ***cope with*** 對付　　imminence ('ɪmənəns) *n.* 迫近
> stage (stedʒ) *n.* 階段；程度　　***prior to~*** 在~之前

53. (**D**) 根據本文，作者視死亡的經驗為
   (A) 恐怖的。
   (B) 不必要的。
   (C) 傷心的。
   (D) 重要的。

54.(**B**) 根據本文，未被告知嚴重病情的末期病患

 (A) 完全不知道結果。

 (B) 相當了解可能的結果。

 (C) 抗拒迫近的死亡。

 (D) 通常忽略自己的結果。

 be conscious of 察覺；知道 resistant〔rɪˈzɪstənt〕*adj.* 抗拒的

 impending〔ɪmˈpɛndɪŋ〕*adj.* 迫近的 *be ignorant of* 忽略

55.(**A**) 作者在比林斯醫院研究的目的是

 (A) 瞭解垂死患者能教他們關於死亡的哪些事，以及醫療專業人士，如何提供病患以及其家人更多幫助。

 (B) 仔細地決定死亡得經過那些階段。

 (C) 分析老人與年輕人對死亡看法的差異。

 (D) 建議人們該死於何處。

 in detail 仔細地 analyze〔ˈænḷˌaɪz〕*v.* 分析

 concept〔ˈkɑnsɛpt〕*n.* 看法；觀念

56.(**C**) 我們最有可能從本文推論出作者對死亡和垂死的態度是

 (A) 沒有不可或缺的人。 (B) 死人不會洩密。

 (C) 凡人皆得死。   (D) 活到老，學到老。

 indispensable〔ˌɪndɪsˈpɛnsəḷ〕*adj.* 不可或缺的 *tell tales* 洩漏祕密

第貳部分：非選擇題

一、英文翻譯：

1. 我們都同意，「戰爭與和平」這本名著，值得一讀再讀。

 We all agree the masterpiece "War and Peace" is worth reading over and over again.

2. 我們所必須做的，就是讀完這一整本書，然後寫一份報告。

 All we have to do is read the whole book and write a paper about it.

二、英文作文：（作文範例）

Should the Lottery Be Abolished?

Since the implementation of the lottery in Taiwan, the public has been in a lotto frenzy. Many people condemn the lottery and argue that it has become a social problem and should be abolished. Others think that the lottery is their only hope to become a millionaire overnight. While the lottery can provide people with instant wealth, it can also cause people to drift away from reality. Some people spend their entire month's salary in hopes of winning the jackpot even though the chance of hitting it is slim to none.

Why do people decide to risk so much? It has a lot to do with the economic recession. Many people have had to settle for less than what they are used to. When the lottery started, people began to daydream and created false hopes for themselves. Will they ever hit the jackpot? Perhaps one day they will. *However*, until that day comes, it will do the society no good if people continue to daydream about the lottery. If the lottery craze continues, it would be best to abolish the lottery because it has become a cancer eating away the core values of our society.

implementation (ˌɪmpləmɛn'teʃən) *n.* 實施
frenzy ('frɛnzɪ) *n.* 狂熱　　condemn (kən'dɛm) *v.* 譴責
provide sb. with sth. 提供某物給某人
drift (drɪft) *v.* 脫離　　reality (rɪ'ælətɪ) *n.* 現實
salary ('sælərɪ) *n.* 薪水
jackpot ('dʒæk,pɑt) *n.* 頭彩　　*slim to none* 幾乎沒有
recession (rɪ'sɛʃən) *n.* 不景氣
settle for less 安於不滿的事物　　craze (krez) *n.* 狂熱
core value 重要的價值觀

近年指考與學測英文科出題來源

1	*Against All Odds*, Newbury House, pp. 46-47
2	Jack C. Richards, et al. (2003). *Strategic Reading 2: Building Effective Reading Skills*, p. 110 New York: Cambridge University Press
3	Langille, J. & Kalman, B. (1998). *The Space Shuttle*. Crabtree
4	Lucas, S.E. (1998). The art of public speaking (6th ed.). New York: McGraw-Hill.
5	*Steps to Writing Well*, 7th ed.
6	*Time Express*, Oct & Nov 2005, p. 32.
7	Wener, P.K. (2002) *Mosaic I: Grammar (4th ed.)*, p. 100. New York: McGraw Hill
8	Zukowski/Faust Jean, Susan S. Johnston, and Clak S. Atkinson (1997) *Between the Lines* (2nd ed.), p.108. New York: Harcourt Brace & Company.
9	http://fcis.oise.utoronto.ca/~daniel_schugurensky/assignment1/1936piaget.html
10	http://www.asia-planet.net/taiwan/penghu.htm
11	http://www.cnn.com/2005/TECH/01/03/cnn25.top25.innovations/
12	http://www.mikadosoc.ie/forum/viewtopic.php?t=24206
13	http://www.mwsc.edu/psychology/research/psy302/fall95/lowery.htm
14	http://www.persiangulfonline.org/takeaction/news0409-2.htm
15	http://www.starlinktraining.org
16	http://www.terry.uga.edu/~rgrover/chapter32.html
17	http://www.time.com/time/asia/travel/magazine/0,9754,127305,00.html

劉毅英文「*97年學科能力測驗*」15級分名單

姓 名	學校班級	姓 名	學校班級	姓 名	學校班級	姓 名	學校班級	姓 名	學校班級
徐曼寧	永春 307	王瑜瑄	北一三誠	譚喆	附中1131	謝松育	成功 321	藍昕	成功 312
彭盈熒	延平 311	王美評	北一三義	陳思樺	市大同 312	張偉志	建中 324	林士淳	成功 324
邱建嘉	大同 301	張奕詞	北一三公	蔡明臻	大同 304	田智瞻	建中 324	蕭鴻昇	成功 322
張巍庭	北一三樂	蔡孟璇	北一三禮	賴奕陵	中山三博	柯婷軒	板中 304	鄭嘉酉	北一三莊
韓瑋倫	和平 304	陶巧妤	中山三廉	陳建安	建中 320	羅喬陽	附中1152	江佳蓉	中正 302
郭彤	景美三義	余婉琤	中山三公	張紫鈺	市大同 303	鄭鴻	附中1148	孫仕霖	北一三莊
盧冠豪	和平 304	王婷韻	大直 302	張耕豪	市大同 303	汪鼎傑	成功 318	王婷婷	北一三愛
劉羽庭	永平 608	李孟穎	內湖 309	周紫馨	中山三平	邱唯倫	成功 304	董于萍	北一三愛
蔡毅昕	建中 311	陳昱銓	松山 311	林婉晴	衛理三慧	吳采蓁	北一三良	蘇薇穎	北一三愛
陳彥廷	政附 305	張天陽	松山 311	杜文潔	中山 3平	柯惠瑄	北一三善	王爾萱	景美三善
易亞琪	北一三義	郭芙瑄	景美三眞	黃庭翊	市大同 305	林家蓉	北一三良	李佩蓉	北一三射
黃思偉	延平 311	蔡明驊	成功 321	方皓	成功 301	李欣頻	北一三禮	陳昱陵	景美三善
陳思樺	延平 311	李昕珉	進修生	吳泰儀	市大同 306	曾仲楷	成功 303	王薇榕	景美三善
陳瑩	景美三愛	王楷鈞	北一三和	朱怡甄	北一 3樂	黃敬傑	附中1151	曹文萱	北一三樂
賴怡安	中正 322	翁梓華	建中 328	陳紹筑	景美 3讓	林元甫	建中 305	楊子瑩	北一三莊
黃舒鈺	延平 305	洪子涵	中山三廉	許思涵	中山三孝	謝志鴻	建中 305	高楷婷	北一三愛
孟鉦棋	松山 315	張子禕	市大同 313	李姵穎	北一三仁	陳稚翔	建中 305	周婷瑄	北一三信
張哲維	市大同 315	徐瑋宏	成功 308	黃馨霈	北一三義	王景權	建中 305	謝卿儀	北一三和
蔡宇婷	北一三義	陳又瑜	板中 305	許佳卉	板中 304	陳以健	建中 305	曾介平	建中 301
林沛馨	松山 301	王臣康	板中 316	陳映竹	延平 311	王暐涵	附中1142	梁晨	中山三博
吳昱潔	北一三仁	王思匀	北一三信	彭郁婷	光仁三信	黃淳廷	附中1142	李承勳	建中 327
林怡廷	北一三仁	林恆安	北一三和	葉平萱	北一三恭	賴政榕	附中1142	林健安	市大同 307
吳子新	北一三仁	莊詠筑	北一三和	鄭哲偉	松山 316	盧建行	建中 305	劉嘉華	中山三廉
莊郁暐	建中 322	張懃云	中山三勤	周敬凱	建中 317	王顥婷	中山三博	柯亭宇	建中 322
薛雅文	松山 306	李宜頻	北一三眞	吳承蓁	北一三仁	王睦仁	中正 302	吳則霖	建中 325
洪巧柔	北一三射	簡湘庭	北一三信	簡廷容	北一 3和	趙聿婷	北一三信	康倫殷	中山三智
林煒強	建中 308	許爾婷	北一三讓	林敬薇	北一 3和	林玉晴	北一三孝	翁珮華	中山三信
席祖詒	中山三孝	黃彥騰	附中1140	鄭瑜萱	附中1132	曾書庭	建中 305	鍾欣芸	中山三忠
呂柏緯	成功 310	張婷雅	北一三眞	林俊杰	成功 302	李若怡	北一三和	林承翰	建中 323
蕭子健	和平 309	嚴啓峰	建中 317	陳怡萍	北一 3書	林英佐	建中 304	溫振華	成功 304
陳思樺	中山三敏	張瑜芳	景美三恭	曾馨如	市大同 305	李宛臻	北一三仁	陳思函	北一三俊
林怡萱	中山三孝	盧思樺	附中1129	黃郁絜	北一 3恭	鍾徹	建中 318	凌子祐	延平 302
陳怡如	延平 311	王斌銓	中正 312	張詔程	建中 320	劉彥澤	成功 317	黃雯絜	景美三美
孫詩淳	中山三業	戴愷廷	建中 328	陳明宜	內湖 320	游茹茵	中山三樂	林怡慈	北一三良
林聖雄	建中 322	陳國維	建中 311	吳以恩	市大同 305	林修安	松山 313	林育男	延平 310
高瑀珮	內湖 318	王思佳	衛理三愛	朱驤凡	建中 315	何東明	建中 322	陳姿陵	延平 312
陳玟誼	內湖 318	黃郁喬	北一三讓	陳昱臻	松山 302	劉亭君	北一三良	陳怡穎	中崙 310
李岱貞	中山三禮	陳皓佑	東山三義	洪睿英	內湖 314	張閔淳	明倫 302	林延舟	建中 309
孫佑嘉	建中 330	鄭富元	成功 310	葉芷瑄	內湖 313	魏志庭	建中 324	曾緯	成功 306
羅文婕	景美三俊	朱嬿婷	板中 320	張幼萱	內湖 313	簡郁潔	中山三忠	龐暄	延平 309
吳妮諺	中山三禮	徐淳輔	板中 308	王亭皓	附中1141	劉彥德	成功 322	陳南蓁	北一三勤
陳和揚	建中 330	趙人蓀	成功 324	劉彥均	附中1141	周宜澄	板中 318	江志文	延平 309
梁立明	建中 311	王子芮	板中 308	李岳勳	成功 303	陳重任	成功 301	李葦諭	北一三勤
梁中明	建中 304	莊崝竹	附中1131	詹景東	附中1137	楊翔斌	成功 308	郭德蕙	北一三義
王將瑀	北一三數	陳知婕	中山三博	邱友辰	成功 314	王彥智	成功 322	蕭彤芸	中山三捷
陳靜宜	景美三眞	葉靜儒	中山三博	江佳穎	北一三俊	黃子誠	成功 301	陳佳敬	延平 310
陳昱璇	附中1138	梁曦	附中1135	向芷萱	北一三書	鄭旭高	成功 301	林政嘉	建中 302

姓名	學校班級	姓名	學校班級	姓名	學校班級	姓名	學校班級	姓名	學校班級
陳芷萱	北一三義	溫珩如	北一三毅	張惠雯	北一三孝	黃繼農	建中302	游珮樺	景美三愛
李峻逸	成功303	林宛萱	北一三良	周沁嫻	北一三眞	陳迦樂	建中302	林宛爛	國三重309
周繼暉	附中1150	張芮瑜	景美三良	張貝如	中山三廉	王振翔	清水602	張宇昕	松山304
陳彥安	成功323	王安妮	北一三樂	石芳慈	北一三誠	張富傑	建中325	施雲天	建中323
彭上軒	和平313	鄭閔文	中山三智	王士誠	松山309	吳善加	建中306	周伯威	建中303
張浚仰	成功319	陳佑貞	中山304	鄭宇恩	基女301	鄭博元	建中301	吳逸然	成功319
黃柔慈	北一三眞	李佳勳	景美三讓	邱子豪	成功310	邱郁筑	中山三仁	黃筠涵	錦和603
許智瑄	北一三仁	楊雅筑	中山303	謝玫伶	北一三禮	林昱豪	新莊312	謝蕙宇	中和318
林耀煒	成功322	黃胤銘	建中320	翁煜修	附中1147	李孟儒	建中327	許偉恆	建中318
何宇泱	成功322	鄭雅双	中正321	陳儀庭	市大同308	張寧芮	景美三恭	李育珊	延平313
陳宣辰	成功303	顏好庭	北一三誠	賴柏勳	進修生	蘇鈺婷	附中1139	林逸平	建中330
徐正綸	建中320	楊智涵	北一三孝	黃柏曄	成功302	李啟賓	附中1142	陳皎萍	新莊308
林禹伸	成功301	林婉婷	北一三孝	許智鈞	附中1151	施彖兆	建中314	張文嘉	永春308
林群晧	建中305	林欣潔	北一三平	洪舜奕	進修生	余常均	成功301	廖庭祥	延平311
許純彬	成功301	彭珮玟	北一三平	金佳霖	市大同306	徐崇婉	松山305	劉一淨	市大同305
蔡子平	建中320	陳齊賢	北一三平	劉晉嘉	建中328	周孫丞	附中1148	張俊麒	建中324
張洺偉	建中305	徐巧容	北一三信	吳光彘	中正311	黃建文	東山三忠	曾立中	板中305
董晉宏	成功311	吳宜璇	北一三信	張凱翔	成功303	黃偉博	永春314	陳鴻宇	成功324
林彥均	成功322	胡郁璞	北一三愛	蕭亦翔	成功326	唐百博	成功309	洪慈敏	中山三孝
林楷軒	成功315	陳儀珊	北一三愛	何郁賢	西松三忠	李怡蓉	北一三溫	徐曼薰	景美三樂
黃翊柔	北一三御	吳健揚	建中306	謝怡萱	大直301	馮挺瑄	大同307	費麟翔	建中322
陳家敏	附中1131	林家榮	內湖302	任柏融	市大同305	郭若琦	市大同307	林歐昇	建中323
江佳樺	中山三禮	李穆先	北一三儉	高瑄	育成308	楊于萱	北一三毅	王楚渝	建中311
吳秉原	成功318	吳佩蓉	新莊309	洪睿臨	內湖307	陳彥安	附中1139	陳亭蓁	北一三公
白君彥	成功318	洪心柔	中山三敬	許雅婷	中山三和	陳冠華	附中1152	陳映均	二信三愛
陳家豪	建中323	季節	附中1136	吳珮慈	中山三和	董牧喬	南山三忠	陳郁琦	內湖314
簡佑佳	附中1146	陳英學	市大同303	李秉哲	成功303	李宜	松山304	蘇品仔	景美三樂
蔡仁傑	成功308	陳昶宏	成功318	劉庭豪	成功307	宋偉藩	進修生	張維方	中崙603
劉泓緯	成功307	劉純卉	市大同314	阮筠婷	延平312	司徒彤恩	和平306	蔡亞眞	大同305
鄭凱陽	建中324	王嬿雯	北一三數	劉九榕	延平311	蕭宇翔	內湖301	林博源	建中323
馬運鼎	建中307	洪紫涵	北一三良	許博智	成功314	童皓	附中1137	陳陽	成功323
林昱辰	建中320	謝怡君	中山三敬	楊尚儒	建中312	柯明佑	建中329	方正華	進修生
許鈺晟	海山607	王柏隆	成功317	劉得祺	建中312	余士元	南山358	詹迪翔	進修生
毛武揚	建中323	林郁蓉	南湖306	李佳翰	建中313	邱子容	北一三和	王明慧	海山602
鄭皓方	北一三恭	程映瑋	附中1153	張喬鈜	市大同314	陳煥文	建中319	王文潔	麗山307
王曦涵	景美三良	蔡秉勳	進修生	周欣慧	景美三誠	王泓凱	建中328	陳禹涵	景美三誠
謝沛柏	延平302	陳育修	附中1142	曾宇帆	延平310	郭育昕	建中329	鍾丞凱	附中1143
周子庭	建中328	李金翰	建中320	蘇墊力	永春313	陳世涓	北一三書	林威辰	南湖312
陳彥亨	建中328	余昇翰	中正314	楊婕	中山三誠	劉紘睿	光仁三仁	楊佳恬	北一三數
張庭嘉	建中328	張雅筑	中山三孝	陳曌之	成功316	潘亭樺	延平305	李思穎	中山三樂
陳冠杰	建中328	吳彥成	附中1137	蔡秉杰	建中323	李宜倩	北一三愛	徐子勛	進修生
方思閎	附中1127	柳冠碩	東山三忠	江卓衡	建中320	洪靖雅	武陵318	楊潔姿	景美三恭
羅映詠	景美三禮	謝承祐	進修生	吳函諭	建中323	王君翃	松山307		
沈孟暎	建中328	姜毅	延平311	戴佑珈	板中306	廖璇好	中和315		
黃奕中	建中328	謝志辰	建中315	楊傑全	建中302	歐怡均	松山319		
楊適豪	建中328	翁明靖	建中315	蔡凱任	建中302	余晏芳	北一三和		

※ 凡是未報「劉毅英文」高三下的同學，均不計算在內。

全國高三109萬元英文單字大賽得獎同學名單

名次	姓名	學校	班級	獎學金	名次	姓名	學校	班級	獎學金
1	林嬙	師大附中	1165	10萬元	51	林述亨	建國中學	107	1萬元
2	關采瓦	仁愛國中	809	1萬元	52	王柏琇	中山女中	一敏	1萬元
3	江姵璇	北一女中	二書	1萬元	53	蘇哲毅	建國中學	219	1萬元
4	金寧煊	建國中學	214	1萬元	54	何宜謙	北一女中	一和	1萬元
5	謝欣容	松山高中	203	1萬元	55	許承郁	建國中學	226	1萬元
6	張峰亮	延平高中	214	1萬元	56	鍾秉軒	建國中學	212	1萬元
7	顏齊慧	師大附中	1154	1萬元	57	蔡巧寧	北一女中	二莊	1萬元
8	蔡佳珉	北一女中	二真	1萬元	58	黃允升	政大附中	114	1萬元
9	顏齊賢	建國中學	226	1萬元	59	王羿富	萬芳高中	205	1萬元
10	吳和諭	建國中學	214	1萬元	60	林偉誠	大同高中	109	1萬元
11	鄭維	建國中學	214	1萬元	61	賴眉潔	弘文高中	103	1萬元
12	張宇任	建國中學	106	1萬元	62	劉大維	台南一中	219	1萬元
13	林瑞怡	大直高中	203	1萬元	63	王郁仁	五權國中	223	1萬元
14	陳威廷	建國中學	202	1萬元	64	呂佳能	中正高中	124	1萬元
15	吳珈維	台中一中	204	1萬元	65	殷偉珊	景美女中	二真	1萬元
16	黃翊傑	百齡高中	207	1萬元	66	陳泰安	建國中學	214	1萬元
17	白旻樺	大同高中	205	1萬元	67	胡錚宜	清水高中	401	1萬元
18	王相宗	台中一中	206	1萬元	68	朱駸軒	師大附中	1161	1萬元
19	林貝瑄	北一女中	二誠	1萬元	69	賴昱凱	建國中學	122	1萬元
20	何維傑	建國中學	104	1萬元	70	吳映慧	華盛頓中學	201	1萬元
21	張博雄	板橋高中	219	1萬元	71	蔡易儒	台中一中	222	1萬元
22	沈英琪	永和國中	913	1萬元	72	林宣幼	衛道國中	114	1萬元
23	鄭景謙	建國中學	222	1萬元	73	李佳昂	建國中學	229	1萬元
24	許書瑋	西松高中	二忠	1萬元	74	張品御	台中一中	213	1萬元
25	李思葭	大同高中	202	1萬元	75	蔣依融	興雅國中	915	1萬元
26	徐忠義	建國中學	112	1萬元	76	蔡佩岑	成功高中	109	1萬元
27	張雅婷	北一女中	二平	1萬元	77	周姿吟	北一女中	二書	1萬元
28	汪玟儀	北一女中	一溫	1萬元	78	陳柏諺	政大附中	206	1萬元
29	洪一軒	板橋高中	207	1萬元	79	鄭羽嫣	大直高中	204	1萬元
30	林羿辰	北一女中	二勤	1萬元	80	洪銘駿	建國中學	119	1萬元
31	林佑蒼	建國中學	226	1萬元	81	劉桐	崇光女中	一義	1萬元
32	陳麒中	建國中學	109	1萬元	82	張雅甄	北一女中	二勤	1萬元
33	龔國安	師大附中	1173	1萬元	83	林欣儒	中山女中	二業	1萬元
34	盧廷羲	中和高中	107	1萬元	84	邱于真	中山女中	二誠	1萬元
35	林芸安	北一女中	一儉	1萬元	85	黃羽婕	永平高中	509	1萬元
36	李宛霖	中山女中	一簡	1萬元	86	陳奕廷	建國中學	219	1萬元
37	李泓毅	中和高中	214	1萬元	87	黃雨萱	台中家商	外語2	1萬元
38	朱得誠	新莊高中	203	1萬元	88	傅筠	台中女中	212	1萬元
39	林芳瑜	北一女中	二恭	1萬元	89	劉育豪	成功高中	219	1萬元
40	簡翔澐	北一女中	二誠	1萬元	90	李苡萱	北一女中	二恭	1萬元
41	郭哲妤	北一女中	二毅	1萬元	91	林之嵐	師大附中	1165	1萬元
42	陳慕天	建國中學	230	1萬元	92	楊子昀	曉明女中	二丁	1萬元
43	林詩涵	海山高中	502	1萬元	93	吳芳育	建國中學	222	1萬元
44	劉珮伶	北一女中	二數	1萬元	94	陳韋華	政大附中	103	1萬元
45	林佳慧	中正高中	103	1萬元	95	吳全勳	建國中學	216	1萬元
46	陳彧安	台中一中	219	1萬元	96	黃韻儒	北一女中	二忠	1萬元
47	王奕云	大同高中	215	1萬元	97	谷宜臻	北一女中	一仁	1萬元
48	何冠廷	建國中學	229	1萬元	98	徐楷穎	景美女中	二美	1萬元
49	林彥儒	建國中學	101	1萬元	99	陳駿彥	建國中學	226	1萬元
50	黃立揚	成功高中	216	1萬元	100	王振宇	中崙高中	102	1萬元

劉毅英文家教班

台中總部：台中市三民路三段125號7F　　TEL：(04) 2221-8861
台北高中部：台北市許昌街17號6F　　　TEL：(02) 2389-5212
台北國中部：台北市重慶南路一段10號7F　TEL：(02) 2381-3148

指考英文模擬試題

主　　　編 / 劉　毅

發　行　所 / 學習出版有限公司　　　☎ (02) 2704-5525

郵 撥 帳 號 / 0512727-2 學習出版社帳戶

登　記　證 / 局版台業 2179 號

印　刷　所 / 裕強彩色印刷有限公司

台 北 門 市 / 台北市許昌街 10 號 2 F　　☎ (02) 2331-4060・2331-9209

台灣總經銷 / 紅螞蟻圖書有限公司　　　☎ (02) 2795-3656

美國總經銷 / Evergreen Book Store　　☎ (818) 2813622

本公司網址 / www.learnbook.com.tw

電 子 郵 件 / learnbook@learnbook.com.tw

售價：新台幣一百八十元正

2008 年 9 月 1 日新修訂

ISBN 978-957-519-879-4